To

Aunt Hel

and Uncl

Some of my fondest childhood memories involve you two, Cory and hanging out in your house. Thanks for your never-ending support, kind words and thoughtfulness. You are my second set of parents and I love you both dearly!♡

P. McDougall

2014.

CAPTURED DEVOTION

Patricia McDougall

For my Bill, the rare gem whose unconditional love captures my daily devotion.

First Edition – March 2014

ISBN
978-1-4602-1981-2 (Hardcover)
978-1-4602-1982-9 (Paperback)
978-1-4602-1983-6 (eBook)

Produced by:

FriesenPress
Suite 300 – 852 Fort Street
Victoria, BC, Canada V8W 1H8

www.friesenpress.com

Distributed to the trade by The Ingram Book Company

Table of Contents

THE KIDNAPPING

"Look princess, let's get one thing straight. I'm the boss here, not my brother. So if you think being nice to him is buying your ticket out of here, you can forget it." He took his sneering face out of mine and I began to breathe again. He turned and walked out of the dingy space. He slammed the door behind him, leaving me in near darkness. I shivered even though my skin felt warm.

How did I get myself into this situation? I couldn't help but let the blame fall upon my father. That stupid car.

Trying to study, a note thrust itself under my nose. Irritated I swatted it away and kept studying.

"Suit yourself. But it's something that might interest even you. It's out front of our building. I know the whole campus is a buzz about it." I only saw the back of my roommate as she left our room. Her comments did leave me curious and I unfolded the note she had thrown in front of me.

Hope you enjoy it. Happy Graduation. Love Dad.

I looked at the front of the note, puzzled. It read **Jady Donner.** It was addressed to me but I hadn't been in contact with my dad for four years. What was this all about? I reluctantly walked outside our building. Staring at me, bigger than a cockroach amongst ants, a huge black Cadillac sat gleaming in the summer sun. It left me speechless for a moment.

I sat down on the curb in front of the beast. Why now? What did he want from me?

My last name was even on the license plate. *His* last name. Our family name. Donner Drugstores were a chain of pharmacy's that stretched across the country. If someone didn't make the connection before they would now. All efforts I had made to keep a low profile were gone. Typical of my dad to want to scream his wealth to everyone. It was not me though.

Back in my dorm, I flopped on my bed, my head going round and round jumbled with thoughts. What the hell did I want with this car? I could give it away to charity. That would be a good idea, but somehow it didn't satisfy me. He would think I had kept it. I hated him even more just then. Always a cruel and thoughtless man, this just didn't make any sense. Was he feeling a sense of guilt over mom? Had he had a turning point in his life? Was he dying? I realized then there was only one way to find out. I would bring the car back to him.

That night I lay in bed thinking of all the things I wanted to say to him. Recalling all the horrible memories that I had worked so hard to block out.

I was very young when I picked up on the feeling that my father was disappointed in me. Being so little, I tried hard to figure out what I had done to displease him and badly wanted to reverse his feelings. I learned the truth by accident, overhearing a conversation between my father and mom. If you want to call it that. I listened to him yelling at her. It was all one sided with no response from my mom the entire time. I think her silence hurt me even more in that moment. His words had stuck in my brain like bubble gum under a table.

"You can't get anything right can you? First it took you forever to get pregnant and then you give me a girl. A stupid, useless girl. I can't let a girl take over a company that I took so long to build. I wanted a son! And then to make yourself even more useless to me, you fix it so you can't have anymore." I stood around the corner in shock and sadness. The tears rolled down my face and I couldn't believe my mom was not sticking up for herself or for me. For the first time I felt anger towards her. Redirecting it, I turned to face the monster spewing the horrible words. I came around the corner full of hatred.

"You leave her alone!" My mom looked up but her beaten eyes said it all. I didn't really know it then but a person doesn't need to be physically beaten to have those eyes. My father directed his words at me now rather than at the lump of a person I called mom.

"You watch your mouth or you'll both be out on the street." I stood behind my mom, but I shut up. No older than five or six, the thought of living on the street sounded terrifying. He left us then and I crawled into my mom's lifeless arms. I had to hang on tight around her neck so that I didn't fall off her lap. He left us in his wake of destruction.

"Mom, why doesn't he like me? Is being a girl so bad?" It took my mom a while to reply, but when she did she sounded so tired.

"You're a beautiful girl Jady. Don't you ever forget that. It's not your fault, it's mine. You're too young to understand now. but when I had you something went wrong and I had to have surgery. You will be my only child, honey, and that's what make you so special." I didn't feel very special right then, but her arms came back to life and wrapped around me. Comfort came and I let her body surround me. I knew I wouldn't forget the words of my father, but I tried to bury them very deep.

I pulled the covers up tight around me, wishing I had my mom's arms still. I had to settle for my blanket for now. Why did he have to go and do this? Why couldn't he have left things alone? Now, trying to think of all the things I wanted to say to him, I remembered how hurtful his words were. How they kept me from having normal relationships with anyone. Here I was twenty-two years old, without a best friend or boyfriend. I was so scared to let anyone get close. I had been working on my teaching degree for the last four years and now it was time to look for a job. I was terrified to go out into the world and have to interact with people. That's why I chose to work with kids. I could handle a room full of children, but the thought of having to speak in front of adults scared me more than spiders scared others.

I thought back to another conversation I had overheard. This time between my roommate and her friend. Being older and much thicker-skinned, the words didn't hurt as they did when I was a child.

"How do you put up with her?"

"She's not that bad. She's just quiet."

"She's a moody bitch that never smiles."

"I think she just needs time to warm up to people."

"It's been three years! The stupid thing is I'd kill for her looks! She's got that shiny black hair that is wasted in her ponytails, her skin is perfect and always looks tanned even in the winter and those green eyes! If she would smile she's actually be pretty. And she's always wearing those ratty jeans and t-shirts. I just don't get it. How does she expect to get hired as a teacher looking like that?" My roommate had then steered the conversation to an upcoming party and I walked away, my face burning. I didn't want to be sociable and pretty girls couldn't blend into the crowd unnoticed.

I would return the car, see a bit of the countryside and give myself time to think about the next step in my life.

***

Exams were long over and school was shutting down for the summer. As I packed up my things, I felt sad and nervous leaving the only place that really felt like home. Never being big on material things or collecting clothes, everything I owned fit into one suitcase. The plan was to drive the car to my father, do some job searching and hop on a bus to my next destination, wherever that may be.

As I loaded my lonely suitcase into the beast, my roommate told me to drop her a line sometime. We both knew this was probably never going to happen. I wish I was a different person. I knew I could be if I just made the effort, but it was so much safer this way. If I didn't get close, I could never get hurt.

I climbed in the big car and felt smaller. I had to adjust the seat all the way up just to touch the pedals. I drove off and felt a sadness wash over me as the big brick building that had housed me for the last four years loomed behind me.

I wanted to drive until the evening and find a motel to check into for the night. I would be able to get there by tomorrow night if I put in another ten to twelve hours of driving the following day. I enjoyed driving, and had had my share of beaters over the last few years. The last one, a Datsun B210 died on me a couple of months ago. Working at odd jobs to pay my way through university, I always had enough to get by. I looked down at the gas gauge and saw he had even filled up the tank. This thing must be a hog on gas. I wondered how he had it delivered to me? I knew it wouldn't have been himself. He probably had one of his many gophers bring it. How anyone would want to work for him was beyond me. But then again maybe its just women he liked to pick on.

As I turned on to the highway, I felt better. I reclined the seat a bit and put it into cruise control. This car had its perks, but I still hated it. I turned on the radio and scanned for a good station to listen to. I finally found one that had classic rock and could handle that. I was humming along to RESPECT by Aretha, feeling better than I had in a long time. Maybe this trip was just what I needed. Maybe this talk with my father was the therapy I should have sought out long ago. Deep down I hoped if I got everything off my chest, it would start a new chapter for me. If I could let go some of this anger, maybe I could live a normal life. Maybe I could actually interact with people. Too many maybes, I wasn't one to count on anything. Only time would tell what fate would dictate. For now I needed to run through my head what I planned to say.

Why did you wreck my life? How was that for starters? On second thought, I might want to start off a bit subtler.

After that first altercation with my father, many years ago, I wanted to hate him but I couldn't. I so wanted him to love me. I became quite a tomboy to show him how tough I was, that I could be as good as any boy. He usually ignored me or shooed me away like a seagull after his lunch. It didn't stop me from trying. I dressed and acted so much like a boy that people who had never met me just assumed I was. Teased relentlessly at school about my odd behaviour, I got into many fights, which suited me just fine. I could not only prove my toughness, but it got my father's attention momentarily since he had to come down to the school each time to deal with it. Even being yelled at seemed better than being ignored. At least he knew I existed. Eventually, he just sent me away to a private school where, surrounded by girls and forced to wear a uniform, I could no longer hide my femininity. The school, never involving the parents, handled punishment in house. So that ended my fighting days.

My new scheme entailed applying myself to my studies. I thought if I showed my father how smart I could be, then maybe he would see my potential, not only as his daughter, but also as someone who could take over his business someday.

This time, I immersed myself so much in school, I left no time for friends or for any social interacting. All the way through to graduation I was on the honour roll. Each term, the school had a big assembly to hand out awards for our accomplishments and every time I was alone. No one came to see my achievements or to congratulate me. My mom around this time was starting to get very sick and couldn't leave the house and my father didn't give an excuse. He just wasn't there. I still didn't give up hope. I made up a special invitation for him to my grad. I went home during spring break especially to give it to him. It was the first time I had gone home in a long time. They weren't expecting me and it was obvious.

My first clue that something was amiss, was when the cab dropped me off and I stepped into the front lobby. I couldn't explain it, but it was too quiet. I put down my suitcase and went up to my mom's room. It was so dark in there that at first I couldn't see her. When I turned on the lights I drew my breath in with horror. She looked like a deer I had seen once. Someone had hit it in the winter and when all the snow had melted all that was left was the carcass. It was like nothing but bones were lying in my mom's bed. I rushed to her side to make sure she was still breathing.

"Mom, what's going on?" For a brief moment her eyes fluttered open and a small smile played on her lips.

"Jady, you're home. I've been wondering where you were."

"Mom, I've been at school. What's wrong? Why didn't you call me?" She faded out without answering. Outraged, I went to find my father. All thoughts of inviting him to my grad were gone. Now I just wanted answers.

Here I was again looking for answers and my anger resurfaced. No matter what his reasons, could I ever forgive him? I knew the answer to that question. My mission was not to forgive him, but just to let myself be heard. I rubbed my eyes.

On the road now for five hours, I needed to stretch my legs and get some fresh coffee. The next green sign indicated a gas station just five minutes ahead.

Hungry, I munched on a sandwich as I walked around the tiny park surrounding the store. Being the end of June, the crisp air was uncommon but welcoming. Winter had gone on for a long time this year and spring was still hanging on. The grass was a new bright green as nature washed away the remnants of winter with its showers. Things were looking alive and bright. It was at times like this, when I had something to appreciate, that I wished I had someone to share it with. A person I loved and who loved me without conditions. The dream to have children and raise them in a loving healthy atmosphere just didn't seem attainable. I released a big sigh, finished my sandwich and walked back to the car. I read somewhere that women sigh so they don't scream. I tend to sigh a lot.

I wanted to travel at least another five hours before I found a motel to crash for the night. I wasn't sick of driving yet but I was getting tired of all the thoughts swimming around in my brain and all the memories these thoughts dredged up.

I called for an ambulance, and as it turned out, she had advanced lung cancer. She had had it for some time. The hospital made her as comfortable as they could, but they didn't need to tell me, she didn't have much time. I knew my father to be a horrible man, but capable of this kind of cruelty? How could he just leave her there to die? With all his money, how could he not have made sure she got the care she needed? He never did come to the hospital, so I went to him for some answers.

My anger choked me when I found him in one of his many offices. I sat down in a chair across from him. Browsing over papers, he didn't even look up.

"I realize all you care about is money, so I will talk to you in terms you might be able to understand. I think I know why you did what you did. You couldn't divorce her because that would cost you, so when she began to get sick, you saw it as your way out. You wanted her to die and rot in that bed and that would solve your problems without costing you a dime. Am I close?" Still no reaction or even an acknowledgement that I existed in his space.

"But what you didn't factor in, is that I would come home early and find her. You're lucky on one account, I am too late to save her, but I will make this little plan of yours cost you a lot of money." He finally looked up and his dreadful smirk made my entire body tense with hatred.

"You go ahead and try. There isn't a prosecutor, judge or officer of the law that would touch anything to do with me. So go ahead and try your best."

If I had a gun with me, I would be doing life for a crime I would not regret. Armed with only a smirk in return, I stood up to go,

"We'll see about that." As soon as my back was turned, my smirk disappeared. I knew he was right and that I didn't stand a chance. I didn't have to look back at him to know that his smile was still firmly planted on his horrible face.

***

I had passed a small hotel about fifteen minutes back and was beginning to regret not stopping. I hadn't felt tired when I had passed it and yet now, exhaustion overwhelmed me. I looked down at the gas gauge, regretting it even more. The little arrow flicked into the red zone. How could I not have noticed that? I swore this thing ate gas faster than someone wolfing down hot dogs at an eating contest. I came upon another green sign that announced a gas station just a short way up the road. Too tired to push through the next four hours, I hoped there would be a hotel as well.

I tried to occupy my mind to keep awake. I dug through my snacks and found some jujubes. They'd do the trick for now. I smiled as I remembered my mom. She and I had always fought over the black ones. I tried to hide them all, but she always seemed to get to them first. We would make a game of trying to find each other's secret hiding spots. She hid hers in a bowl she kept by the microwave. I hid mine in my nightstand, in a heart shaped box that once contained chocolates. I chewed on this memory and missed her.

She had died not long after I had discovered her. There was nothing I could do for her other than give her the medicine prescribed to lessen the pain. As I watched her leave this world, my anger and hatred for my father grew. I vowed to hurt him someday like he was hurting her.

I finished my year and very soon after, I moved out. I found a university as far from him as I could, immersing myself in studies again. I really thought I had let go of a lot of that anger, but from the way I gripped the steering wheel every time I thought of him, that didn't seem to be the case. Through my own soul searching, I realized revenge wasn't the answer. Making sure I didn't let him weaken me or stamp out my spirit like he had done to my mother, seemed the only solution. But this gift was like a slap in the face that I couldn't ignore. I needed closure and I wanted to let him know I didn't need his help, his money or this car. He needed to know he had missed out on an opportunity to know a really great daughter and I wanted nothing to do with him, not now, not ever.

I saw the gas station then, and much to my dismay I realized that's all it was. A gas station. No other building in sight. Oh well, I'll get another coffee and continue on with my original plan.

Being late when I pulled up to the pumps, only one person worked the till, no one manned the gas pumps. It took forever to fill that beast and as I stood there, two motorcycles pulled up. They removed their helmets and started to fill their bikes. The pumps blocked my view of one of them, but the other one looked much older than me and a bit disheveled. Dusty from the ride, he looked up as thunder boomed in the background. He had a slight beard and when he glanced up from the pumps to talk to his friend, his eyes appeared older still. In those eyes held a look of a long hard life. He didn't seem very warm and when he looked my way, I examined the horizon, the bad vibe increasing. Not that I wanted to make friends. I smiled to myself, why start now?

The ding of the pump told me the car was full. I put the gas cap back on and walked towards the store to pay. I noticed the hard looking guy was gone and as I went past the pumps I saw that his friend was still there. He looked up at me, this time I didn't look away. I couldn't. His eyes, those eyes, were amazing. They were almost black, yet not sinister or without kindness. Those eyes smiled at me and his mouth followed. I couldn't help myself and I smiled back and then suddenly found my feet very interesting, dropping my gaze. Drawn back in for another look, I noticed he was dusty as well, having dark hair that matched his eyes. He had a slim build and looked great in jeans. Still looking at me, he smiled. Blushing I finally looked away and walked into the store.

What's wrong with me? I never noticed anyone, never mind a complete stranger in the middle of nowhere. Give your head a shake, you have a job to do here and you have a long way to go. That settled, I paid my bill and determined, I did not look again when I left the store. I headed straight to the car and got in. But as I drove away I couldn't help but give one last glance. Sitting on his bike, just about to put on his helmet, he looked my way tipping his finger to his brow. Like a silly teenage girl, I waved back and then feeling foolish I drove away.

At least it gave me something to think about as I continued on my way. It was easy to daydream about those eyes. I caught the two bikes in my rear view mirror. They passed me as the rain began to fall. This steady downpour did nothing to help me stay awake.

A good half hour later, despite the rain hampering my visibility, I noticed a blinking red light ahead. I turned up the speed on my wipers and saw one bike standing on the side of the road. Black eyes, waving a flag of sorts and obviously signaling me to pull over. It looked like the other bike was lying on its side with the wheel off. The other guy nowhere to be seen. I could feel the knot in the pit of my stomach telling me it wasn't a good idea to pull over. Those black eyes clouded my judgment and I pulled to the side.

It all happened so fast. I got out of the car, pulling my hood up to shield myself from the rain. I started walking towards him to ask him if he needed help. The look on his face should have warned me. He didn't look kind anymore. He looked scared and concerned. I shrugged it off to the accident I thought had taken place. He mouthed the words "Run" and confused I turned and was hit with a vicious blow. Hard enough that I smelled the gravel shoulder. My head spun as I was grabbed and dragged back towards the car. I tried to make sense of what was happening. Thrown back behind the wheel, someone was talking to me.

"Drive." came the command. The world swam back into focus and I looked into the cold eyes of the other guy.

"What?" I stammered, still confused as to what just happened. Revealing the weapon that struck me down, a gun looked me in the eyes. The voice holding it repeated the order.

"Drive. Follow him." His head beckoned towards the red light, now on the road again ahead of me. My hand trembled as I started the car again and shifted it into drive. I felt like I was in no condition to drive, almost as dizzy as if I had too much to drink, but, I followed the light and chastised myself over and over for not listening to my gut instinct. I should have pulled over at the last hotel. I should not have pulled over for black eyes. I was scared as to what lay ahead of me. No one knew where to find me. Nobody even knew whom I was and I was afraid no one was ever going to get the chance.

***

We drove for quite some time through the pouring rain. I wasn't tired anymore instead my heart was racing. Just when I thought we were going to drive long enough to greet the morning, my captor demanded I pull over. I did as I was told without hesitation.

He opened his door and slid out, the whole time the gun pointed in my direction.

"Move over to the passenger side." After I did, he pulled a bandana out of his pocket and tied it around my eyes. I could hear his footsteps crunching on the gravel and before I could even think of escaping, I heard the driver's door slam shut. We were moving again.

I had so many questions I wanted to ask, but I didn't dare. I wanted to know where they were taking me. What were their plans? Why me? I had seen so many movies of women being taken and always thought I wouldn't be so stupid. If I ever was, I would know exactly what to do. I didn't have a clue. I would just have to bide my time and take opportunities as they arose. I could hear this guy's breathing and I wished I could turn up the radio. I didn't want to be reminded of this complete harsh stranger sitting beside me, taking me to God knows where and planning to do God knows what. The bile in my throat rose as I lingered on this thought. I swallowed hard, not wanting to throw up right now. I leaned my head back on the headrest and tried to let sleep take me, just to ease my stress and uneasy stomach. As I did this, I noticed I could see just a sliver from under the bandana. It was so dark and the rain did nothing to help decipher my surroundings. The chances of me seeing any landmarks in these conditions were pretty slim. I closed my eyes and tried to think of something else besides my present condition.

Nothing came to me. I had already rehashed the bad father scenario and my mom's horrible death. Sadly, my life had only comprised of university since then. I had immersed myself in books and had made no effort to socialize or meet anyone.

I felt the car take a turn and by looking through my sliver of the world I could see forest surrounding me. Where the hell were we going? The headlights focused on the rain and a gravel road. I closed my eyes yet again and sleep took me for a while because the next time I opened my eyes we were stopped in front of a cabin. From what I could see, although it looked old and run down, it was a log cabin that I could picture holding some charm in its infancy. It was dawn and the rain had subsided.

It wasn't until I saw both men come out of the cabin that I realized I had been alone. I kicked myself furiously for falling asleep. I had missed a valuable opportunity to escape. I looked to my left through my tiny window of vision, my neck becoming sore from craning it back. The keys were gone from the ignition. In some twisted way this consoled me. All my years of university, had not taught me how to hot wire vehicles. I could hear the voices getting louder and I sat up straighter. Now what? My door opened and my blindfold was abruptly pulled off. Yanked from the car by Mr. Harsh, a horrible thought popped into my head. I may not know their names, but I knew what they looked like. Anytime captives knew their captors' faces in movies, they never survived. They, meaning I at this moment, could identify them with ease.

I dug in my heels and fought harder in my panic. I screamed as loud as I could. Maybe there were neighbours. The man holding me only laughed and kept dragging me towards the cabin.

"It's pointless, princess. There's no one around to hear you." Calling his bluff, I didn't stop. His slap across my face echoed in the forest. The pain also echoed in my face, right down to my cold feet.

"Just because I said there was no one around to hear you, doesn't mean I don't. Now shut up." Then we were inside and it was grey and bleak with a musty, not lived in smell. He pushed me through what looked like a kitchen and down a small hall into a back room, containing only a dingy mattress on the floor. I panicked again and started to back up, only to be blocked by a human brick wall.

"Just get in there." I took maybe two steps into the room and the solid, log door closed behind me. Alone, I surveyed my surroundings. A small room with no windows. maybe a storage space at one time. The only furniture being the mattress, with huge rust colored stains that I convinced my brain was water stains. Forest transformed into walls and grey linoleum that might have been another colour in a previous life, completed the dreary room.

Their loud voices came through the crack under the door. I strained to listen to what sounded like an argument.

"I don't care what you say, this is a very stupid idea!"

"I'm telling you we scored when we crossed that little princess's path. There's money to be had. Look at the car she's driving. The license plate is the same name as all those fancy drugstores all over the place. Rich people always love to ram everyone else's nose in the fact that they have money."

"I couldn't care less if she herself was made of gold, this is a dangerous game we're playing and we're sure to be caught. You should have stuck to the original plan and just taken the car, not her with it! This is big..." The voice was cut off and the tiny cabin shook as if a huge plane had flown too close overhead.

"You just shut your mouth! What do you know about anything? You're nothing without me, you hear me nothing! I've done everything for you. I've always taken care of us and I will now! Just shut your trap and do what I tell you to do. You hear me?" I didn't hear the answer, but I'm pretty sure Black Eyes had. By first impressions alone, it was obvious Mr. Harsh ran the show and Black Eyes did the bidding. Well at least he had enough sense to realize this was a stupid idea. I had no money and I really doubted my father would give them any for me either. The panic set in again. What would happen to me then, once they found that out? They couldn't. I needed to play along. I needed to go along with the whole idea that my father would pay big for me to come out of this alive. I had to play this game long enough to give me time to figure out how to escape. I knew if I relied on my father to get me out of here safely, I would end up buried beside my mother.

***

It wasn't too much longer before I heard a vehicle outside. It didn't sound like either the motorcycle or the caddy but the sound soon faded away. I wondered if they both were gone. I went to the door and tried it, but found it locked. As I contemplated how sturdy it might be, it opened. I stepped away from it, afraid and uncertain. I felt an instant wave of relief wash over me when I saw Black Eyes. I cursed myself for the feeling since I had no idea who he was and he was as guilty as the other for the position I was in.

In his hands he held some bedding, a bottle of water and what looked like a sandwich. He didn't make eye contact as he put the things down on the mattress.

"I thought you might be hungry or thirsty. Sorry about the shape of the mattress, hopefully these sheets will help." He said all this to my feet.

"My name is Riley and my brother's name is Byron." He paused as if waiting for me to say something. When I didn't he reached into his back pocket and took a piece of paper and pen.

"Byron wants you to write down some of your information. Your name, your father's name and a phone number we can reach him at." My mind spun with how I could stall these two.

"I don't know how to reach him. I was on my way to find him. I…I ran away a long time ago and I've lost contact." My voice seemed to startle him and he looked up for an instant.

"Well, just write down both yours and his name then and we'll see what we can find out." He handed me the paper and pen and I wrote it down, using the wall as support.

"Jady, that's a nice name." If he expected a thank you, it was not coming. I wanted to be nice to him since I thought I would need him to keep his brother in line, but inside I was seething with anger. I felt trapped and helpless and it frustrated me that I might have to rely on this stranger to help me. Black Eyes shifted from side to side and when he realized I wasn't going to say more, he backed out of the room and silently closed the door, locking it again. I couldn't help thinking he looked like a beaten puppy.

I once again surveyed my prison. Because there were no windows, I wouldn't be able to tell if it was day or night. I looked at the food and water. I wasn't hungry but the water looked appealing. I checked it to make sure the seal wasn't cracked. I was afraid of being drugged. I downed half of it and then looked at the bedding Black Eyes had brought in. I was suddenly exhausted. Even though I had slept for a bit during my capture, I was still very tired and just wanted to lie down. I wrinkled my nose at the mattress again but when I looked around the room at the cold, hard floor, my options looked pretty bleak. I made up the bed and crawled under the blanket. I thought I'd have a hard time falling asleep but I crashed as soon as my head hit that rusty, old mattress.

A loud bang woke me with a start and it took me awhile to figure out where I was. It was the smell of the mattress and the glaring light bulb above my head that reminded me and I bit my lip so as not to cry. I don't remember what I had been dreaming about, but I was sure it was better then this nightmare. I heard Byron's voice then and I realized the loud bang must've been the door slamming on his return. I heard their muffled voices then and slowly rose from the mattress, moving towards the door to see if I could hear them better. The only thing I could figure out from their conversation was that he had gone to pick up the other motorcycle and something about selling the caddy. I heard footsteps approaching, backed away, and sat down on the edge of the mattress. The door opened with such force that it banged against the wall. Byron stood before me looking fierce and angry.

"What do you take us for? Fools?" I shook my head, not understanding.

"Do you really think we believe you don't know where your own father lives and how to get a hold of him?"

"I…I was telling the truth. I ran away and he's moved since then. I don't know where he's living now."

"So how do we even know your daddy cares what happens to you? We didn't pick you up just to have a pet y'know?" He looked proud of himself for this witty statement and looked toward Riley who was standing behind him, still in the doorway, and smiled. I was speechless for a moment so scared that he had come to the truth without even realizing it.

"What's to say we shouldn't just get what we can for your fancy car and be done with you?" I looked then at Black Eyes and there was no hiding the reaction on his face. He was startled with his brother's comment and briefly looked my way again, his eyes apologetic. The words *be done with you* stuck in my brain and I had a hard time sounding calm when I did speak.

"I told him," I nodded toward Black Eyes, "I ran away. My father's obviously been looking for me all this time because when he found me he sent me that car. I assumed it was a peace offering and I was driving it to him to make amends. I was just going to go to one of his stores and find out where to find him." The lies made my stomach turn, not because of whom I was telling them to, but because the thought of making amends with my father made me want to throw up.

"Why did you run away?" This came from Black Eyes and I think both Byron and myself were surprised. Black Eyes seemed to regret he had spoken and examined his shoes again.

"Just teenager stuff. I was pretty spoiled and wanted things my way. When I didn't get them, I took off." This seemed to not only satisfy Byron but he was also nodding, as if to say he had known that's what it was all along.

"This had better be the truth. I want some good pay off for all this hassle. In the meantime I hope your little castle will be good enough for the princess." His sneer made my blood boil again and I was glad when he turned and left. I heard the door lock. My hatred for him was mixed with a disgust for myself because I didn't seem to feel that way about Black Eyes. It was like staying angry at a puppy that bit you and couldn't help itself. It just didn't seem to know any better.

***

Ironically, it was my father who ended up buying me the time I needed. Byron did track him down. I knew it wouldn't be hard, he was a well-known man. Fortunately for me, he was away on vacation overseas and had left no contact information. At least that's what his receptionist was saying. From what I could hear through the door, Byron found this unlikely, but didn't want to push the issue. He only wanted to deal with my father. He figured the less people involved the better. Everything was working out better than I had anticipated. This gave me the time I needed to come up with a plan for escape.

Sitting in this fortified prison, I felt claustrophobic and a sudden need to breathe into a paper bag. Why couldn't this be one of those old cabins built of walls that could easily have holes punched into it during a bad temper tantrum? Why did it need to be built from logs that looked they had been previously hugged by Greenpeace?

I needed to find a way to get Black Eyes on my side. I hadn't thought of any specific details yet, but I knew one thing for sure, I needed him. This was hard for me for two reasons. I had never depended on or needed anyone else in my whole life and I had no real social skills for dealing with other people. I had no idea where to begin, and I knew I would find it extremely difficult to be nice to someone who had put me in this predicament.

As if on cue, there was a light knock on the door and I heard the lock rattle. The door opened and in walked Black Eyes with a tray of food, balanced on one hand. I tried not to glare at him, remembering I had to make an effort to make friends. He put the tray down on the floor and walked out, returning shortly with a small TV tray and two chairs. He moved the tray onto the little table and plunked himself in one of the chairs. He smiled bashfully.

"I hope you don't mind, but I'll join you for a bit. It's getting a bit boring here, especially when Byron's gone." His face turned red then as he realized what he said.

"Sorry, I guess I don't need to tell you that, you're probably bored out of your skull. Do you like to read? I can get you some books or magazines." I was about to shake my head when I realized again I needed to be nice.

"Anything would be great. The hours drag on in here." My words sounded unnatural to my own ears, I hoped they didn't sound like that to him. I hoisted myself off the bed and sat in the other chair. I started to eat what he brought me and realized how hungry I was. While I ate, he talked and I found his voice easy to listen to.

"He wasn't always like this." I assumed he was referring to Byron. "We all started out okay, but…" he paused then unsure of himself. Something deep within me realized he needed to talk. To almost justify himself and his brother's behaviour. As much as I really didn't want to hear his excuses, I was not eager to spend the day alone in my dim surroundings. I looked at him,

"But what happened?" Seeming relieved, Black Eyes continued,

"As we got a bit older, my mom passed and my father lost his job. He took out his frustrations on Byron. I always felt guilty for that, it was never me. Our father sent us out at an early age to steal things for him. We were expert shoplifters and eventually got really good at picking people's wallets too. We brought everything back to my father initially, but then we realized he was drinking all the profits and we still had an empty fridge. So we started hoarding food and keeping back some of the money to buy things we needed." Black Eyes had been playing with his hands in his lap the whole time, not looking at me, but then he paused and looked up. It was my turn to look down at my food as I continued to eat. Those eyes were so full of childhood innocence and there was not even a speckle of malice.

"I don't know why I'm telling you this, nothing can justify what we've done to you. It's just how things started. We knew only one way to survive, by stealing anything and everything we could get our hands on. When we got old enough to get jobs I could keep one no problem and I actually liked earning a living the proper way, but Byron couldn't hold down a job. He's a roller coaster you see, that's what my mom used to call him. When he was down, he sleeps for days on end, won't shower or eat and you can't do anything to get him out of his funk. Then he's up and barely sleeping at all, eating everything in sight and full of wild ideas. So when he was down, he'd miss work because he slept in and then when he was up he seemed happy, but just beneath the surface he was so angry he told his bosses where to go. I know something is really wrong with him, but don't know what to do about it. There's no way I could get him to see a doctor. I tried working to make enough money to support us, but the more time I spent away the worse he got. When he was down I was scared he'd off himself and when he was up he would plan crazy stunts like bank robberies and jewelry heists. He sees things on TV and thinks he can pull them off. So I stay with him and try to keep him in line the best I can. Obviously, he's up right now and this," he nodded his head towards me, "this was his new idea. At first I tried to talk him out of it, but then I thought if we can get some real money from it, maybe I can sit on him awhile or maybe I can get him some help. The doctor might be free, but it's not like we have a health plan or anything. I know it must sound crazy to you and I'm sorry you're caught in the middle of it, but I'm really hoping this works out. I promise you, you won't get hurt and we'll let you go as soon as we get the money." He took a deep breath then and I could see he had been wanting to talk about this to someone for a very long time. I smiled at him, spontaneously, it felt foreign on my mouth. I realized then that I had him all wrong. He was not the beaten down puppy, but he was a kind person who was trying his best to take care of someone he loved. This was unknown territory for me. I felt the invisible turn of the tide as I lifted my eyes to look into his, this time I let them linger before I finally looked away.

***

Our days started to fall into a routine of their own. I would wake up on the ratty old mattress and heave a huge sigh as once again I realized it wasn't a bad dream. I really was living out a bad movie. I would lie there and listen to the voices on the other side of the wall. Most of the time it was a discussion about where they were going to get their money for the day. It wasn't always something criminal. Sometimes Black Eyes won and the plan consisted of selling or pawning something. On a rare day, Black Eyes would convince Byron to actually work a job like paint someone's house or by the sound of it they owned a steam cleaner or something. Byron would go clean someone's carpet for some extra cash. No matter what the day brought the consistent factor was that Byron always left with a grumble about how the princess was supposed to make them money not cost them more since they had to feed me. Black Eyes always consoled him by saying they just had to be patient, the pay off was coming. I would hear Byron's truck or motorcycle leave and then Black Eyes would come and feed me breakfast. He always kept me company now while I ate. He had dug up some magazines, which he had swiped from some waiting rooms somewhere. All the labels were ripped off, I assumed it was so I couldn't see addresses. He talked while I ate or flipped through the magazines and pointed out interesting articles. Riley made it easy for me to be sociable. I really didn't have to talk a lot, he did most of it and I just sat back and listened. Once in a while, he asked me a question but nothing too personal. He seemed to sense that I wasn't going to share anything too close and he never tried to pry. Time would just fly when Black Eyes hung out with me. Before we knew it, it was lunchtime and he would go and make us something and come back once more and we'd eat lunch together. After lunch we would usually play cards unless he had errands to run. When he wasn't keeping me company I would sleep away the afternoon or read some of the magazines or books Black Eyes had brought me.

After a week of our little world, I could hear Byron complaining one morning.

"Why do I always have to be the one to scrounge up money? Why can't you go out and I stay here and baby sit?"

"Sure, you can stay cooped up here all day bored out of your mind and then put up with all the whining and complaining from the spoiled princess." Initially, I was stinging from his words but as I heard the rest of the conversation I realized how smart Black Eyes was and how good he was at manipulating Byron.

"Forget it! Is that what she does?" I could almost hear the snicker in his voice. "Man, I don't need that shit. No thanks, you can deal with her." I couldn't help but feel relieved, I didn't want Byron to be the one looking after me and as much as I hated to admit it I looked forward to my days with Black Eyes.

The door rattling startled me out of my thoughts and I realized I was sitting on the edge of the mattress smiling to myself as Black Eyes walked in with my breakfast.

"Sorry, I didn't mean to scare you."

"No, I'm fine. I was just daydreaming." He just nodded, once again not asking questions. He sat in silence while I ate, he seemed lost in his own thoughts too this morning. I broke his thoughts with a question that surprised both of us.

"You don't really think I'm a princess do you?" I was shocked when the words came out and wished I could take them back. What did I care if he did feel that way? When I looked at him, he was smiling and I blushed and felt even more stupid. I felt like a high school girl who values what other people think. What was going on? I had never cared what other people thought about me.

"You are as far away from being a princess as I am from being a door mat for Byron." I couldn't help but smile at him.

"Most people that meet the two of us assume that's what I am. The quiet ones usually are." I smiled this time.

"Quiet one?" It was Black Eyes's turn to blush.

"I usually am, you make it easy to talk. Maybe it's because I'm used to being around Byron who monopolizes the conversation, both in quantity and volume. You, on the other hand are the quiet one and for the first time in a long time, I get to talk and I think you actually hear me, or at least you're an awesome pretender." He smiled his wonderful smile and I wanted to tell him I wasn't pretending, I was really listening. In fact, I loved listening to him, even if it was just chitchat about nothing. I wanted to tell him I never had a friend and didn't know how to talk to someone, even just to chitchat. I finally broke the silence by asking another question.

"Did anyone ever tell you how long my father would be on vacation?" I regretted the question even more then the other one. Black Eyes's smile faded and it was like I burst the bubble of illusion that he had created for himself.

"No, they didn't. They thought at least two weeks. I should go and do some things around here. I'll be back at lunch." He smiled again but it was weak and then he was gone and the door was closed. I wondered if I had wrecked any progress

I had made. Oddly I couldn't help but be happy that I had another week. I tried to convince myself that I was feeling that way because I needed more time to plan my escape but deep down I knew the real reason and it was for this one that I vowed not to bring up my father and this situation again.

***

The next morning Black Eyes brought my breakfast but this time he did not stay to chat as he usually did. Even worse, I got no smiles and no words at all. I spent the rest of the morning beating myself up for putting my foot in my mouth yesterday and tried to think of a way to turn things around again.

When he came to deliver my lunch, I shocked us both by blurting out,

"I'm sorry." He stopped on his way out without turning around. I continued,

"I'm really a sort of a loner. I don't make friends easily and I really don't know how to talk to people. If I said anything to make you mad, I really am sorry. I didn't mean to. I'm just socially stupid." He turned around then to speak to me,

"You didn't make me mad, it just brought me back to reality. I need to remember why you're here."

"I realize that, but while I am here we might as well make the best of it."

"I know, but I really got lost in it all and it was easy to pretend you were just a friend visiting. You are not my friend and I am not yours. In another time, our paths would not even cross and even if they did, you wouldn't have given me a second glance." His face became serious and once again he went to go.

"But our paths *did* cross and I *did* give you a second glance. At the gas station I couldn't help but notice you and believe me when I say I don't usually pay attention to anyone around me.

But you…well, you caught my eye." I couldn't believe this was coming out of my mouth. I just wanted him to stay. I wanted him to talk to me again. This time when he looked at me, that wonderful smile was back. I was so happy to see him sit down in the chair across from me.

"Seriously, you must have a lot of friends."

"No, really. I'm not good at things like that."

"Why?" Black Eyes had finally started asking questions and I found myself answering them. I listened to myself pour out my life, about my father, my mom and why I was the way I was. I realized I was jeopardizing the story I had already given Black Eyes and his brother. He didn't seem to blink an eye at what he now knew had been a lie. It was like he had always known and he wasn't surprised at all. At the time, I told myself I was telling him all this to win his trust and to keep him coming back, but it also felt good to finally talk to someone about it all. He just sat back and listened, asking questions when I left gaps. Before we knew it, we heard Byron's truck pull in and Black Eyes sat up with a start.

"Sorry to leave you so abruptly, but well, I don't think I need to explain it to you." I nodded my head, suddenly feeling exhausted from pouring my guts out. As he closed the door, I lay back on the mattress and fell asleep.

When I woke sometime later, I had a pit digging in my stomach. Did I do the right thing? Would he tell Byron everything? I guess this was the point of truth. This was when I would find out whether I could count on him to help me out of this situation. Even if my father did pay their ransom demands, I really didn't think Byron would let me go alive, no matter what Black Eyes had to say. I was a huge liability and Byron didn't trust me. I closed my eyes again and wondered what my next move would be. In the morning I would know more. If Black Eyes told Byron the truth then things would change.

Byron would doubt like I do whether he'd get any money out of my father and my time might be done. If Black Eyes keeps our confidences then I'd have the rest of the week to work on convincing Black Eyes to let me go. The morning felt a long way off.

***

When I heard the door rattle, I woke with a start and felt a sense of panic. Everything came back to me and I wondered who was coming through the door and what fate had in store for me. When I saw Black Eyes come through with my breakfast and a smile I could have hugged him. My smile must have been huge.

"Wow, someone's either very happy or hungry this morning."

"I'm just happy. I...felt sort of like a heel for talking so much yesterday. The last thing you needed was me boo hooing to you."

"Are you kidding me? It was nice to know I wasn't the only one with a crappy childhood, no offence." He added quickly.

"None taken." I ate my breakfast and we sat in comfortable silence until I was done. After he took my tray away he came back,

"I have a surprise for you today." He handed me a jacket and much to my amazement he beckoned me to follow him outside of my four walls. I had only been outside of my prison to go to the bathroom and sometimes Black Eyes gave me more time for a sponge bath. I put on the jacket he handed me and followed him outside. I hadn't realized how long it had been since I had seen the sun. My eyes burned and watered.

"Oh, I'm so sorry." He handed me his sunglasses and I put them on relieved. I took in a deep breath of fresh air and promised if I lived through this I would never take the smell of freedom for granted again. I couldn't believe I was outside. This was what I had hoped for but never thought it would actually happen. I could survey my surroundings and see if there was any possible way to escape. Black Eyes started walking down a path and beckoned for me to follow. It was quite a hike and I had to stop many times to rest. Not only was I out of shape from spending more time studying than exercising, I was also a bit stiff from being cooped up. Black Eyes kept apologizing but told me the reward was worth it. I pushed myself forward, intrigued as to what he meant by "reward." When we reached what I assumed to be the top, my breath was taken away and it was not by the beautiful view that I'm assuming was Black Eyes idea of a reward.

It *was* amazing. It was also like a punch in the stomach. Devastated, I sat down trying hard not to cry. Black Eyes came to my side, thinking I was hurt.

"What's wrong?" How could I answer him? How could I tell him that what he thought of as an amazing sight was my dead end. There was nothing but forest for as far as the eyes could see. We were far from civilization and all thoughts of escape were lost amongst those miles and miles of trees.

I held up my hand and managed to speak.

"I'm okay, just a bit winded." I needed time to absorb what my eyes were telling me. I wanted to scream my frustration into the vastness. My anger was focused at the wilderness that stood before me. What was I going to do now? How was I ever going to escape? There was nowhere to go. Black Eyes was standing with his back to me staring out into the forest. I didn't need to see his face to know he was smiling. It was obvious he loved his surroundings and looked around him with adoration, feeling comfortable and at home. Yet for me, those same trees filled me with dread and only thickened the walls of my prison. It only reinforced my need for him. He knew this land and I needed a guide out of it. I stood up and brushed the dirt from my pants.

I walked towards him to try and see the view through his eyes. I needed to get closer to him, to become a friend he could trust.

"It's absolutely amazing. I can see why you wanted to bring me here."

"C'mon over here." He motioned for me to follow. In a small little clearing there was a rustic bench with a well-used fire pit. He sat down on the bench and starting pulling things out of his backpack. He set up something he called a spotting scope, adjusted it a few times while looking through it. He beckoned me to come closer.

"Look." I nestled up to the eyepiece and gasped, pulling away. There was a group of at least ten deer and they appeared to be right in front of us. I tried to see them without the scope, but with the naked eye not even a spot could be detected. I brought myself up again and watched them, fascinated. They were munching away on the grass, not a care in the world, clueless that they were being spied upon.

"How did you know they were there?" I spoke without taking my eyes off of them.

"I come up here a lot. It's my favorite place to be, to get away." He stopped and I pulled away from the deer to look at him. He shook his head as if to shake away lingering thoughts.

"Anyways, if an animal is in this area, I know where they are. Here let me show you something else." He readjusted the scope to a different location and motioned for me to look again. This time it was a massive moose and her calf. I watched them for a long time and this time when I looked away, Black Eyes had a wonderful lunch all spread out. If it weren't for the circumstances, this would've been an ideal date. The sun, the view, the food and the company. This is the nicest thing anyone had ever done for me. I needed to stay focused.

"This is really great." I ate and enjoyed the view, casually, like this kind of thing happened all the time. We ate, taking turns looking through the scope. Black Eyes kept moving it and by the time we finished eating, we had seen more deer, a family of raccoons, an eagle's nest and a large herd of elk. I had never seen so many animals outside of a zoo and was thrilled. Black Eyes was patient with all my questions and I was surprised at how much he knew. As if reading my thoughts he told me he had read whatever he could get his hands on about all the animals in the area. I couldn't help but be impressed. We sat for a while longer and then almost regretfully Black Eyes looked at his watch.

"We'd better go." I couldn't help but shiver. I was already sensing the damp coolness of my little room and as much as I didn't want to admit it, I was going to miss Black Eyes' company. I wanted to feel some resentment towards him for instilling something in me I had never experienced before. I had never felt loneliness before. I was always happier alone, until now. I felt a glimmer of satisfaction, hoping he felt the same, which meant my plan was working. If I was feeling closer to him, maybe he felt the same and would want to help me out. We walked back down towards the cabin in silence. I took in deep breaths of the sweet air, wishing I could save it and take it with me into the little room.

***

After a long, lonely and restless night, I became excited when I heard Byron's truck leave in the morning. It was less than two minutes later when smiling Black Eyes burst through my door. He had his backpack with him again and a set of keys I had never seen before. I wondered what he was up to today.

Again we went outside and he didn't say much as he walked though the bush on a different path. We came to a shed and he pulled open the double doors that looked as if they were about to fall off their hinges. Inside was a quad that he started and backed up. After pulling the doors shut again, he beckoned for me to get on.

"I've never been on one of these before."

"I'm not asking you to drive it, just hang on." I hesitated only briefly before hopping on the back. He looked so excited and it was contagious.

Initially, as we drove I was self-conscious of our closeness. I tried to keep some distance and hang on to the back, but after hitting some rather big bumps and being thrown closer, I finally gave in and hung on to Black Eyes instead.

The sun was shining on us and there was not a cloud to be seen. Everything around us was in full bloom and the smells of summer were intoxicating. We went down winding paths that led us to every mud hole imaginable. At first he slowed down when going through them but after awhile, maybe when he could feel me ease up on my grip, he would go full speed through the deepest, muddiest pits. I would tuck my feet up high and laugh so hard. We rode all morning, covering quite a distance through the thick forest. The area was just starting to look familiar when we topped a high hill and there we were back at the fire pit we had been at yesterday. This time I wasn't upset with the view, I wanted to be there, with Black Eyes. When we got off the back of the bike, I instantly missed his closeness, but as I looked at him I burst into laughter. He had taken off his sunglasses and it was only those two round circles that were without mud, the rest of him was covered from head to toe.

"You shouldn't laugh so hard princess, you don't look much better." I looked at myself to see he was right. I smiled. When he referred to me as a princess it didn't sound like the insult it did when his brother said it, it just sounded sweet.

He built up a fire and from his bag he took out hotdogs, marshmallows and a of couple cans of coke. He tossed me one and I finished half of it, thirsty from the sun and the ride.

"That was fun, thanks."

"No problem, it was fun to be with someone. It was different. I haven't done that for a very long time, not since Becka... " His voice trailed off, a look of sadness shadowing his face and then he turned to the fire and played around with it. I so wanted to ask who Becka was, but I also didn't want this moment to go away. By the look on his face just then, Becka did not bring back happy memories.

Once he got the fire the way he wanted it, he hunted around the bush for a couple of good sticks and took out a knife. He whittled the ends to sharp points and placed a hot dog on each one. He handed one to me.

"Tell me you at least know how to roast a hot dog?"

"I've seen it done once or twice in the movies." Black Eyes laughed and shook his head. I had told the truth, I had always wanted to do these kind of things but really had no one to do them with, my own fault of course. I had spent my entire life studying inside concrete walls, building up walls of my own to keep people out. People like Black Eyes.

We roasted our hot dogs, eating a couple each. The outdoors made me pretty hungry. We then roasted a few marshmallows, mine a lovely black and his a golden brown. I finally gave up and asked him to roast me a few good ones. The difference in taste was astounding. We finally packed up, stamped out the fire and got back on the quad. As soon as I was behind Black Eyes again, I had to resist hugging his back. To feel him close to me again gave me tingles that were foreign to me. I rested my head in between his strong shoulder blades and took in the scenery as it whizzed past us.

After we rode again for a while, Black Eyes brought the bike to a stop. Disappointed and thinking we were back already, we got off. We weren't back, we had stopped beside a small lake. He dug around in a box that he had strapped to the front and pulled out a blanket. He handed it to me,

"Here, you really need to wash those clothes. Byron will wonder what's up if he sees you all coated in mud when you're supposed to be in a room all day." I hadn't even thought of that. I walked off into the bush until I thought he could no longer see me. I stripped off my clothes and wrapped myself in the blanket. I was about to bring them down to the lake and wash them myself when Black Eyes came and took them from me.

"It's okay, I'll do it, you might find it a bit awkward." I smiled with appreciation. I was wondering how I was going to keep myself covered in the blanket *and* wash my clothes. I sat down on the bank and watched him very gently wash my clothing in the lake. The mud came off and clouded the clear, blue water. He hung them from a nearby branch in the sun.

"They shouldn't take too long to dry." He stretched out on the bank beside me and pulled his baseball hat down over his eyes. I so wanted to take off my blanket and have him closer. I wanted him beside me, in the sun with only the trees as witnesses. I stuffed my urges, curled up the best I could, without revealing too much, and soon fell asleep listening to the water, lapping at the shore.

It was the cold that made me wake up and I sat up wondering where I was. Disorientated, I thought the coldness was from my dark room. As I looked around and remembered where I was, I saw it was only a cloud covering the sun that made me shiver. I also realized that the blanket was all around me but not covering me anymore and I was sitting in just my underwear. I quickly looked around to see where Black Eyes was. He had his back to me and was taking my clothes from the branch. Embarrassed, I clutched the blanket around me again, but I could see from the grin, as he handed me my clothes that it was too late for modesty.

"So you are a true princess after all." He grinned again, turning away so that I could get dressed. I had almost forgotten. All over my pink underwear were silly little gold crowns. I had bought them not because I had thought they were cute but they had been in the bargain bin and now my face was three shades darker than it had been a few minutes ago.

"You just never mind! You probably have boxers with little moose running all over them." He turned around with a mock surprised expression.

"How did you know?" I laughed as I pulled my clean, dry shirt over my head. I looked at him to see him staring at me, still smiling.

"You really are beautiful." Stunned into silence, I walked past him and got back on the quad. No one had ever said that to me before and I never would have used that word to describe myself. Wanting to say something but also needing to change the subject I said jokingly,

"So that's why you dragged me through every mud puddle known to man. It was just a ploy to see my underwear." He hung his head as he trudged back to the bike.

"You have uncovered my secret." Black Eyes started the bike, turning around to look at me. With a sexy grin, I could barely make out the words,

"Princess," and we drove back through the woods, avoiding all mud holes on the return trip.

***

I couldn't sleep all night. What was I doing? I knew I need to get close to him to help me escape but I was supposed to be using him and *pretending* to like him. I was not only no longer pretending, I was falling for him. I needed to stay focused. This was not reality, we were living a fantasy. He was a criminal and I was his victim. I needed to go back to the real world. This thought saddened me. The real world, where I had no friends, where no one loved me and I loved no one. I had no job yet to speak of, no home and no family. Why did it have to be this way? Why couldn't Riley and I have met under different circumstances? Riley's words came back to haunt me. Because you wouldn't have given him a second thought. He was right, my walls were built up so solidly, and I would have brushed him off like anyone else who tried to get close. It took these circumstances to allow someone to get close. I laughed to myself. Someone only has to kidnap me, hold me against my will in order for me to get to know them. Now what? My brain told me to stick with the plan. Stay close, get him to help you escape. My heart said, wait. You still have two days at least, why rush it? Spend more time with him, make sure he's really hooked and then ask him. Yes, that's it. I ignored the thoughts my brain was trying to push forward. *But in the meantime you're getting hooked too*. Yeah, yeah, whatever. That's the plan and it will work out fine. I tossed and turned for quite some time that night before I could fall asleep.

***

"Good morning princess." I opened my eyes to see Riley standing over me.

"How long have you been standing there?" I stretched and yawned, still tired but eager to spend another day with Riley.

"Long enough to know you snore."

"I do not!" I actually didn't know if I did or not, no one had ever spent the night with me before. Riley smiled,

"No, actually you don't, but you sure look darn cute when you're sleeping." I pretended to scowl at him and then motioned for him to turn around so I could get dressed. I was getting tired of the same outfit day after day, but at least now they smelled a bit cleaner. I drew back my hair and tried to stick it into a ponytail. There were stubborn stray hairs poking out in every direction.

"You look great, now come on." Riley also seemed eager to start the day and I was curious to see what he had planned this time.

"I hope you're up for a long walk." I wanted to tell him I was up for anything as long as I could spend time with him, but I was beginning to feel like a needy, clingy woman rather than a self-sufficient, independent one. Instead I said,

"Bring it on." He handed me my own backpack and we headed out. We started on the same path as the initial day, crested the now familiar hill with the fire pit, but this time we headed back down the hill in a different direction. We walked in silence, lost in thoughts that only nature could inspire. I was fantasizing that I had met Riley in the same way, but without the Byron factor and of course minus the kidnapping. Then this would be a real date rather than a day pass from my prison cell. I wondered what Riley was thinking about and I was just about to ask him when he stopped abruptly ahead of me. He put his finger to his lips and crouched down low, pulling me down with him. He was pointing towards the clearing to the left of us. There was a doe deer with a calf that was just getting up on its feet. It was pretty wobbly and its mother was nudging it from behind to help it out. We were both lying on our stomachs watching. Once the calf was more solid it went to feed from its mother. Riley and I turned to each other, grinning and happy to have witnessed such an event.

"This is very late in the year for a deer to have a calf." Riley whispered and he was so close I could feel his breath on my face.

"That was amazing." I whispered back.

Riley rested his forehead on mine and sighed. We stayed that way for a while and finally we got up and backed our way out. Back on the path, we walked side by side this time and started talking about the past. It was Riley that opened the door this time.

"When Byron talked to your father's receptionist she said your father was on holidays, but we could talk to his sons if we liked, they were in charge while he was away. Do you have brothers?"

"Nope. Well I guess so, they would be stepbrothers. After I was born, my dad began having an affair, actually countless affairs and one of his mistresses had the two sons he had always wanted. After my mom died, he married this woman. I have never met them and I don't even know their names. I guess they're helping him out in his business." I was quiet then.

"I'm sorry, I didn't mean to bring up old crap."

"No, it's not that. I just wonder if he had any other children with anyone else. If he had any other daughters that he chose to ignore or pretended they didn't exist." Riley reached over and squeezed my hand,

"I would never ignore you." I smiled at him and let my hand stay in his. It felt good there.

"How did you know he was having affairs?"

"He really made no effort to hide his infidelities. His mistresses came and went from the house as often as the suitcases he took with him on his many vacations. I think this was when I really started to lose respect for my mom. Even as young as I was, I couldn't understand why she never said anything, why she put up with it. Now when I look back I can see she loved the money more than the man and had grown accustomed to the life of luxury he provided for her. I guess in some ways she had the upper hand. She knew he wouldn't divorce her, it would cost him too much, and so she took advantage of everything she could. Unfortunately for her, all the money in the world didn't help her in the end. Once she lost her strength and voice, he had the power to do what he wanted and he wasn't about to spend another dime on someone he had wanted to be rid of years before. He saw his chance and took it." Riley stopped walking then and turned to face me. Without another word he pulled me into his arms and held me close. Instinctively I wanted to pull away, but the feeling of protection within those arms was stronger and I gave in. I let him hold me and I leaned into him. We held each other that way for a few minutes before we both pulled away. Without another word Riley took my hand and we continued walking, quiet again.

Just when I thought I'd have to cry uncle because I couldn't take another step, we came upon a lake, a rather large lake. I took off my shoes and soaked my sore and tired feet in the brilliant clear, blue and cold water. I sat back on my elbows and closed my eyes. The sun felt warm and made me feel sleepy.

"I haven't hiked that far...ever." I confessed. Riley laughed and plunked down beside me. He never seemed to tire.

"I hike these trails a lot, or whenever I get a chance anyways. I even tracked down a set of used cross-country skis and ski down these trails all winter long. It's amazing and every season brings something different. Colours, animals, sounds and smells, it's never the same." As I had on quite a few occasions since meeting him, I wondered exactly who this man was.

"How is it that someone who seems so gentle and kind is still...still,"

"Still committing crimes and hanging out with a brother that's trouble?"

"Yeah, something like that. I understand the crime part, you explained that. Maybe I don't understand because I don't have any siblings, but if he doesn't want help why not just... just walk away." My words sounded so cold and heartless, but I just couldn't relate.

"The way you walked away from your father?" Riley said the words softly and when I looked at him I could see he didn't say it to be mean.

"Yeah, I guess."

"Before you left your father, you gave him plenty of chances didn't you? You always hung on to the hope he would change and suddenly become a better person, one who would love you for who you are and not what you weren't?" I could see what he was getting at, but why did he think his brother didn't love him? I was about to ask him when he got up and walked towards some bushes beside the shore. I could see him rustling around looking for something. He came out with a fishing rod in his hand.

"We're catching lunch today."

"Seriously?" Riley dug around his backpack and fished out a container of worms. He strung one on and handed me the rod. He might as well have handed me a car engine and told me to fix it, both were equally foreign. Riley could see my awkwardness as I handled the fishing rod.

"Here, let me show you." Riley showed me how to cast and to reel in the line. While I sat with the line in the water he gathered up wood to make the fire.

"Aren't you counting your chickens before they hatch? Maybe you should take over if you really plan to eat." My laughter was cut off as a sudden tugging at my line caught my attention.

"Now what do I do?"

"Reel it in." I looked at the bent line a bit before I followed his advice. It just seemed too simple. Then there it was, a fish wriggling around at the end of my line. Riley helped me plop it on shore. I looked away as he thumped it and then he put another worm on my hook and handed it back to me grinning.

"What was that you were saying?"

"Yeah, yeah, never mind." I waved him away with my hand. "Just go finish the fire, I'm an expert now."

Before long we had enough fish for a wonderful lunch. Riley had brought some foil and he wrapped each one up and put them on the hot coals.

He pulled out a blanket and we stretched out in the sun. It felt so good to be outside and not in that room. I felt so tired. I really didn't sleep all that well in that musty room. That, combined with the hike, made me feel as if I hadn't slept in a long time.

I woke up before Riley and sat up on my elbow looking at him. The warmth that washed over me this time was not brought on by the sun. I resisted snuggling up close to him. I wanted to rest my head on his chest and breath him in. I wanted his arm around me holding me close. But it was not just the closeness I desired. I liked hearing his voice, it was kind and calming. I liked spending time with him, sharing in the things that he enjoyed. Was this what being in love was all about? Was that what I was feeling? Was it just the circumstance we were in? Did he revive feelings I had buried. If I was back in the real world, would I be aware of the men around me and find this feeling with someone else? Somehow I didn't think so. It was him, it was Riley that I wanted. Before I could think about this dilemma any further, one of Riley's eyes opened. He shaded his hand over his eyes.

"I'm glad you're still here. I thought I was only dreaming."

"Something smells good." I changed the subject, hoping he couldn't see on my face what I had been thinking.

The fish was delicious and it just fell away from the bones. He had brought some bread and cheese to go with our meal and it was better than anything I could have had in a fancy restaurant. The ambiance definitely could not be matched.

After our meal, we packed everything up and started to make the long hike back. I didn't dread it like I thought it would. I wanted time to slow down. I wanted to soak up every minute I could with Riley before I had to go back to my dungeon.

***

Sitting in my room that night listening to their murmured conversation made me think what life was like for them after I went back to my prison every evening. Usually Riley would make sure we were back by suppertime and Byron would come home shortly after. They would eat together out there on the other side of the door and Riley would bring me a meal to be eaten by myself, within my four suffocating walls. The more time I spent on the outside the tinier this room became. Tonight, Riley seemed to linger even longer at my door after bringing my food. I could tell he didn't want to leave, but staying any longer would arouse suspicions. I nodded and smiled and waved my hand, indicating I was fine, but when the door closed and he disappeared I was anything but okay.

I wondered what Riley thought about as he sat having dinner with his brother. Did he think about me? Did he feel guilty that I was in here by myself, no windows, nothing to do other than read the magazines or books he brought me. I opened one trying to make the time go faster. I wasn't tired and it seemed like forever until morning. I tried to lose myself in the book but my mind was constantly drifting back to Riley. I replayed our days together in my mind, wishing as always that things were different. I slammed the book shut suddenly angry with myself. What was wrong with me? I wasn't like this. I didn't pine after a man and I certainly wouldn't let one take advantage of me. It was time to start thinking of an escape plan. I needed to get out of here and Riley was going to help me do it.

Outside my room, the murmured conversation turned louder and broke my train of thoughts. It was Bryon's voice that was getting loud and I could hear things being smashed and thrown around.

"Who do they think they are that they can keep me waiting like that? Do they think I have nothing better to do? They told me nine o'clock and that's when I was there. I waited two fuckin' hours before someone showed up and then they acted like it was nothing." I couldn't hear Riley's murmured reply and I imagined he was trying to calm Bryon down. It didn't seem to be working.

"They had also promised to pay cash at the end of the job and they didn't do that either. They told me I'd have to come back tomorrow for it. For Christ's sake, do they think I don't have other jobs? These fuckin' people with money think they have control over the rest of us. They say something and we just sit and wait. They're just like that fuckin' princess in there and her useless family." I cringed as I heard another crash. I was terrified he was going to come barging in the room and vent his frustration on me.

"Enough of this waiting. I'm going in tomorrow and I'm going to find out if his highness has returned yet. I'm going to pick up that cash too and spend the night in town. I need a night off from this bullshit." Riley's murmured response told me nothing. Was he trying to talk him out of it? Was he agreeing with him in order to buy us some more time together. I had a mixture of feelings that made me feel nauseous. Either way it was not a good ending for me. If my father was back, Byron would realize I wasn't worth a dime to my father, and then what would he do to me? Even if by some miracle my father did pay the ransom my time here was done. Whatever world

Riley and I had created was over. Our fantasy was about to end and it depressed me to think about returning to my life. My past demons pushed a thought into my head that I had wanted to ignore. What if Riley didn't feel like I was feeling. Was I just part of this game? Would I be instantly forgotten as soon as this thing was over? Did he care what happened to me? Would he prevent his brother from hurting me or worse yet, killing me if he didn't get what he wanted? I knew I shouldn't rely on him to protect me, I've never relied on anyone other than myself and I shouldn't start now. It wasn't a matter of asking Riley to help me, I needed to play on his empathic nature and *tell* him he was going to get me out of the mess he put me in.

I was restless all night trying to think of a way to bring up an escape plan with Riley. I grappled with these strange new feelings of compassion. I had never hesitated to say what I felt before and now I was hesitating because I was afraid of the reaction. I was scared he was going to be adamant and refuse, siding with his brother. Or he would choose to help me and then hurt himself as his brother might turn against him. I knew one thing for sure, I would not bring up my thoughts until the end of our time together. The last thing I wanted was to wreck what might be my last day with Riley.

***

When Riley walked into the room in the morning, I knew it was going to take a lot more than determination to muster up the courage to ask for his help. All my nighttime plans dissipated like smoke as soon as those black eyes met mine. I gave my head a shake as if to clean the fog and willed myself to stay strong. This was my life we were talking about.

I was mildly disappointed not to see a backpack in his hands, but soon enough we were outdoors again and walking up the path towards the shed where the quad was stored. My heart raced at the thought of being so close to him again. Riley had a large bin attached to the back of the bike and I felt like a kid at Christmas, excited about the anticipation of the morning and the surprises that came with it. What did he have in store for us today?

Riley started up the bike and backed out. This time I got on with ease and confidence as if I had done this all my life. Riley smiled my way and I knew he was amused. He looked tired today as if he had had a restless night too. What did he think about at night? Did this whole thing bother him too? Was the fight with his brother weighing on his mind? Was he worried about this coming to an end? I so wanted to ask him all these things, but I wanted to enjoy this time with him even more.

This path we took was more overgrown with little mud or water holes. There were a few times we had to stop to move trees blocking our trail. The last time we went out I had looked around me at nature's beauty as a newborn surveys the surroundings, now I felt like I was looking at everything through eyes of regret. Everything appeared to me as I'm sure it would appear to a convict on death's row. I wished I had seen all these things before and appreciated them then instead of just now. I wanted more days like this, I wanted more time. Even if I survived this and Byron let me go, I could not see myself doing this by myself or with anyone else without thinking of this time with Riley. I tried to brush off these lingering thoughts as one would brush off a spider's web, but like the web's sticky substance, the thoughts seemed to want to stay.

As we drove along, the air we passed through would be cool and then a warm pocket would envelop us. It was like being in a lake, finding those warm patches as you swam along. I snuggled into Riley's back with the pretense of hanging on and I met no resistance. We drove for quite some time, much further than on the last time out. We stopped around midday, pulling into a clearing that was not man made. Knowing what I had learned from Riley, many animals had bedded down in this spot where we were about to eat lunch.

With the stillness around us, I finally did ask a question,

"What was all that yelling about last night?"

"Byron's just in a mood. It's been building for some time. He's getting restless and needs to move on. He wants this..." He paused then, looking uncomfortable as he searched for the words. "this scheme of his completed." A shiver passed over me and Riley misinterpreted it as he handed me his jacket. I took it anyways and wrapped it around me, resisting the urge to breath in deeply and cement his smell in my brain. I wasn't cold, I was scared at what 'completed' meant to someone like Byron. I wondered if Riley could really be so naive as to think his brother would not hurt me or did he think he had more control over this situation than I gave him credit for. Again, as if reading my thoughts, Riley spoke quietly,

"I won't let him hurt you." I didn't know what to say. I wanted to have faith in him, but I really couldn't see how a person like Byron could let me go. For some reason the name Becka popped back into my head and I so wanted to ask Riley about her. Was she an old girlfriend? How did she factor into their lives and where was she now? I didn't ask though, deep down I really didn't want to know. Instead, I changed the subject.

"Do you actually live out here all the time or do you have a place in the city?"

"No, we still have our father's house and if it were up to Byron we would spend all our time there. I try to coax him out here when I can, it keeps him out of trouble." I nodded silently, and in between bites I voiced my thoughts.

"You know you're spoiling me." I motioned to the spread of food before us.

“What do you mean? Spoiling you with a dry sandwich and a few cookies? Man, we’ll have to come up with a new nickname if this is enough to make you happy.” Riley was smiling as I explained.

“Well, I’ve never let anyone do anything for me before. I’ve been fending for myself for so long, I can’t remember the last time someone made me a meal, even if it is just a sandwich. It’s nice.” I suddenly felt very foolish. He’s making you a meal because you’re his prisoner and he needs to keep you alive. But, my heart protested, he didn’t need to be so nice to me or to take me out and actually make it enjoyable. My heart so wanted to win out over my bitter, angry soul and right now, it was winning the battle. I was enjoying myself. Here, in the woods with Riley there was no stress, no thoughts about bills or school, or where I was going to work. I didn’t think about my father or the rat race we were a part of. Surrounded by nature and it’s alluring beauty, and having Riley by my side made me want to freeze time.

“I’m glad I can do something for you, considering...the circumstances. Well we should get going, we still have a ways to go before our destination.” The twinkle in his eyes told me he had special plans. Maybe he saw this as our last time out together too. I didn’t know how to feel about that, so I pushed it away.

When I went to get back on, Riley stopped me.

“You drive.”

“Me? I don’t know how.”

“It’s easy. I’ll help you. C’mon princess, you can do it.” His cocky attitude brought out the competitiveness in me and I took on the challenge. He showed me how to change gears, how to increase our speed and where the brakes were. It took a bit of muscle to maneuver the handlebars but before long we were cruising and I was loving it. After I had felt like I had got the hang of it, I relaxed and it was then I felt his presence behind me. He too had leaned back initially hanging on to the steel bars behind him. But now his body was resting against mine and his arms were comfortably around my waist. Anytime we came to a cross roads, he would point to which road to follow. The scenery was changing again and we were back to wet boggy ground. The puddles were reappearing and I stopped, motioning for him to take over, not sure if I could handle the mud. He yelled above the motor,

"You can do it, just take it easy."

The very first hole was pretty shallow and we went through it easily enough. The second one appeared just as deep and feeling pretty confident I revved up the throttle and gunned it. As soon as we hit it, I realized it was way deeper than it looked and it swallowed us up. More out of surprise than skill I kept the throttle pinned and we sailed out of the pit, mud up to our eyeballs, laughing like lunatics. I had to pull over I was laughing so hard.

"What the hell was that?" Riley finally got the words out when he got a breath. "I thought I said to take it easy?"

"That *was* taking it easy!" We were still chuckling as we continued. As the path got boggy and the mud puddles got bigger and more frequent, I convinced Riley to take over. I was scared of getting us completely stuck.

He maneuvered us through as if we were on an ordinary highway. Yet it was the furthest thing from it. The trail was diminishing and we had to duck and weave like boxers in the ring so as not to get hit by oncoming branches. Where the heck was he taking me today? Just when I thought we were going to have to get off the bike and push it through this jungle we broke through and came across a huge lake. How I didn't catch even a glimpse of it as we drove along was beyond me. I remember once watching a special on TV about African animals, and was amazed when a skyscraper high giraffe miraculously disappeared within seconds into the bush, a *green* bush. That was this lake. How did this huge blue lake remain invisible this whole time we drove along beside it?

We got off the bike and unstrapped the bin from the front, heaving it down to the ground. While in neutral, he pushed the quad so the trees swallowed it. We walked along the shore for a bit, both of us carrying the bin, which turned out to have some weight to it arousing my curiosity even more. Then, like another giraffe, he pulled a canoe from another hiding spot. He had another plastic bin stored beside the canoe and out of it he pulled two life jackets. Again the name Becka came to mind and I wondered if he had brought her there too. I pushed the thought from my mind, determined to enjoy every second.

"Go on, get in." I was a bit nervous. I looked out at the vastness of the lake and then to the small canoe. I put on my lifejacket, took a deep breath and hanging on to the sides walked to the front of the canoe as it tipped and swayed. I sat down with relief and Riley gave a big push and jumped in.

"You're actually going to have to help. I'm not going to do this all by myself." I felt him prodding my back with the paddle, I grabbed it and started paddling. I really didn't know what I was doing but, like the bike, I figured it out pretty quickly. We stayed close to the shore at first, likely for my benefit and by the time we headed out more into the open water I felt more at ease. We could hear the loons calling and dragonflies buzzed past us eating up mosquitoes. When we were by the shore the water was so clear I could not only see every rock, but I could also see what colour they were. But now, as we ventured further out, the water went from clear to black and I knew it was very deep. I could also tell from Riley's steering that he was not just paddling along, he seemed to have a destination in mind.

We passed by two or three islands and we then veered towards the next one. He steered us towards the shore and in one final burst, the canoe scraped the rocky bottom and we had landed. I got out and pulled us up further, assuming he wanted to take a break here before heading back. It was already late afternoon and we had a long way back. I stretched and surveyed our surroundings. You could not see where we had come from with the quad. We were a long ways from there. We were a long way from anywhere.

"C'mon we're almost to where I want to be." I picked up the other end of the bin yet again and followed him as we took a tiny footpath on an island that was a lot bigger then I expected. We broke through on the other side staring out onto another part of the lake.

"There, that's what I wanted to show you." I was looking across to another island and there was a small cabin in the middle of it.

***

"What is that?" It was a silly question, of course I knew what it *was*, I was just surprised to see another sign of life this far out here.

"I mean, who does it belong to?" Riley was already stretched out on his belly with a pair of binoculars held up to his eyes.

"I don't know their names. They're an old couple that come out every summer. They canoe across just like we did and stay there the whole time. This is the only year since I found the cabin that they came just for a little while and left." He was scanning the other island as if to test his theory.

"Nope, no sign that they've been back." I stretched out beside him and he passed me the glasses. I looked for myself. It was a cute, old wooden building. It had a small porch attached to the front. There was a rustic looking table and chairs that appeared hand made and about to fall apart any second. An outhouse and a shed near the back were painted a lighter shade of green. The house itself might have been a dark green once and it had a peeling, black-shingled roof. The windows were trimmed with a rusty red but it was so faded that it was hard to tell. If it had been a vibrant red once, it would have looked like Christmas, especially surrounded by snow.

"They never came out here in the winter time?"

"It always looks like they're packing everything up and locking down in the fall but I don't have a snowmobile to get back here so I can't say for sure. There's no road so you can only get here by quad and canoe or boat." I smiled to myself as I pictured this old couple on a quad nestled in nice and close like Riley and I had been. It made me sad that they weren't here now, wondering if something had happened to one of them or both and that's why they weren't there.

"I always wished they were my parents and I imagined what life would have been like if I grew up with them instead. I would have loved to spend my summers out here with a real family." He sounded so full of sorrow that I wanted to console him, but instead I squeezed his forearm and handed him back the binoculars.

"I could go for a life like that too. They must have had to lug a lot of food up there to get through the summer."

"They had a trailer on the back of their quad and they needed to make a few trips in the canoe to get everything up there." I imagined what life would be like for them. The old man would be chopping wood in the front and his wife would be baking fresh bread in an old stove. I could almost see the smoke coming from the chimney. Watching sunsets on the porch or hearing the thunder coming across the lake as storms passed over. Listening to the loons every day and catching fresh fish for supper. Riley disrupted my daydreams as he got up from the ground and brushed himself off.

"Well, we should get started if we want to be ready by night time." He picked up the bin again and waited. I picked up the other end and we were off again in a different direction.

"What exactly are we doing?"

"You'll see soon enough." We didn't walk much further and we were on the other side of this small island overlooking another part of the lake. There was a clear section in the woods and it was here that Riley rested the bin. He started to pull things out of it. When I saw what they were my heart started pounding so hard I was afraid he was going to hear it. He had taken a tent and sleeping bags from the magical tickle trunk. I didn't know what to feel. I was so excited at the thought of sleeping close to Riley all night and yet terrified.

"What about Byron? Won't he be wondering where we are?"

"I know you heard us fighting. He went into town and won't be back until tomorrow. Once he picks up that cash, he'll be drinking his face off and then sleeping it off somewhere."

"Aren't you worried he'll get himself into some kind of trouble if he's alone?" I don't know why I cared. I think I was more worried how it would effect Riley somehow.

"He's done this many times before and I never go with him. I don't like to drink and I don't like to be around others when they've been drinking. Guess I've been around enough drunks in my day." He left it at that and I thought if he's not worried why should I be? The fear left me and only the excitement remained. I must have been standing there for awhile, lost in my thoughts because Riley was now waving his hand in front of my face.

"Hello? I know you're a princess, but hey, you don't get off easy around me. Help me with this tent." I laughed,

"Me? Help with a tent? Do I look like a boy scout?"

"No, but I think you'd make a pretty cute girl guide. I'd buy your cookies." I blushed and tried to make myself useful. He showed me what to do step by step and left me to it while he gathered firewood before it got too dark to see.

In the time it took me to snap all the pieces together and feed them through the tiniest of flaps, Riley had a roaring fire going. He came to help me finish putting the tent up and when he handed me the sleeping bags to lay out it dawned on me how close the quarters were. Again the thought of being so close to him made me both nervous and filled with anticipation. I crawled back out of the tent and Riley was already pulling something else out of the bin, seemingly oblivious to our sleeping arrangements. He had dragged out two small fold out chairs and he set them up by the fire, which was now starting to die down to glowing embers. He plunked himself down and poked around at the fire.

"Pull up a seat and enjoy the entertainment." I sat and looked to see what he meant. There was a glorious sunset in front of us reflecting in the lake. Whatever wave or ripple had been in the water up to now was stilled. The lake was a mirror filled with the brightest pinks, oranges and reds I had ever seen. There was a few clouds left in the sky, which only added to the amazing sight as the glowing sun peeked from behind them and cast a ray of light skyward.

"Wow." I couldn't think of anything else to say. I wasn't even in my seat yet and I almost fell on the ground as I groped around behind me, not wanting to take my eyes off the sight. It was changing by the second and I didn't want to miss any of it.

I could then hear Riley clunking around in the bin again and he pulled out a grill and some groceries. He set up the grill on the fire and put two thick steaks on it. They sizzled as they touched the heat, and my stomach responded in turn, grumbling. I hadn't realized I was hungry until then and now those steaks couldn't cook fast enough. The smell made my mouth water. Riley wrapped two potatoes and a few cobs of corn in foil and threw those right in the coals. I thought it was going to be torture to watch these things cook, but the sun was sinking rapidly behind the horizon and the show caught my attention once again. Fish jumped in the lake right in front of us and you could see the ripples from their jumps go forever. As soon as the sun disappeared, the air chilled and I moved closer to the fire. Riley handed me a sweatshirt and I pulled it over me, once again drawing in his smell. Before I could stop it, my eyes misted over when I thought, if this was it and our time was over I was hanging on to this sweatshirt and hoped his smell would stay on there as long as possible. The thought of never being able to smell him again saddened me.

"Don't. Stay here with me. Right here in the now. Don't go there, not tonight." I could only see his face in the firelight now and he was not looking at me, but I could see from the slump of his shoulders that he was trying not to think about it too. He turned over the steak and spoke quietly.

"We are just two normal people out camping and enjoying each other's company. There is no tomorrow." Then he did look at me and his hand reached out to brush my hair out of my eyes.

I wanted to reach out and grab his hand. I wanted to lean into his touch. I wanted to yell at him and ask to never leave here. I wanted to say there *is* a tomorrow and with it comes the end, the end to all of this, maybe the end of me for all I knew. There were so many unsaid things that were left hanging in the air between us. We both looked back at the fire and were silent as we stood staring at the flames, lost in our own thoughts. Finally I broke the silence and tried changing the heavy air that weighed us down like an x-ray vest at the dentist.

"Is it ready yet?" Riley laughed and got a fork and poked the potatoes and corn. He brought me a flashlight and I held it while he sliced into the steak. The fire blazed up where the drippings fell, lighting up his handsome, chiseled face.

"Looks like it." I helped Riley unwrap the foil and he placed it all on paper plates and smothered everything in butter and salt. I sat back in my chair and waited for my plate, but Riley surprised me yet again.

"We've got to move somewhere else for our dinner show." He motioned for me to stand and handed me both plates. "Wait here." He took our two chairs and disappeared into the woods, which were now only lighted by the full moon. He was back seconds later and took one plate from my hands.

"You're lucky you came back when you did, I was about to eat both servings."

"If you did, guess who would be cooking *me* dinner?" I laughed and followed him through the bush. We broke through on the other side. He had set up the two chairs near the lake overlooking the shore on the other side of yet another island. On that shore was a huge pile of branches and cut down trees. It was a beaver's lodge. Just then a loud cracking sound echoed across the lake and I almost dropped my dinner.

***

"It's okay." Riley whispered. "Have a seat and watch." I finally sat down, but forgot about the dinner on my lap for the time being. The sound came again and when my eyes adjusted to the moonlight, I could see the big splash and the ripples emanating from it. Then a small brown head popped up, holding a large branch in its mouth. It was swimming towards the lodge.

"It's their tails, against the water." The heat on my lap reminded me of my food and I finally dug in and watched in awe. I was torn between which was better, the meal I was eating or the view before me. For what seemed like half the night we watched as the beaver family worked and played. We could actually see them cutting down trees and then bring them to add to their home. They loved slapping their tails against the water and I couldn't believe how loud it was. A funny thought entered my head and I voiced it before thinking,

"How do the other animals sleep through this noise?" Riley just about choked on the water he just drank.

"You know I've never thought of that before. I suppose it's like any other noise that's around all the time, you just get used to it."

We watched for a little longer and then the chill of the air enveloped us fully and we moved back to the warmth of the fire. My mind kept wandering to the small tent and where I would be sleeping tonight. I snuggled down deeper into the chair and his sweatshirt and stared up at the stars.

Riley roasted some marshmallows for dessert and we gobbled them up. Everything seemed to taste better by campfire and by the light of the moon. The fire started to die down and Riley made no motion to fire it back up. My eyes were getting heavier and I knew it must have been very late. I really wanted this night to last and didn't want to resign yet, but with all this outdoor air, my body was exhausted and fading fast.

"Well, we should call it a night." I could tell by Riley's voice that he was also avoiding it. Was he nervous too or did he want to stretch this time out as well?

I followed him into the tent and as I settled on one sleeping bag, I could hear the zipper close behind us. I shivered and pulled the sleeping bag up around me. I could feel him beside me and then his breath was hot on my face. His hand touched my face.

"Just wanted to see where you were."

"I'm right here." I could almost sense his smile. He let his hand come down and settle on the outside of my sleeping bag, on the curve of my side. I could feel the warmth generating from his hand.

If there was any a time to discuss an escape, it would be now. The darkness gave me confidence that seemed invisible in the daylight. But I couldn't. I realized I wanted to use this feeling of security in a different way. I reached out and touched his face. I loved the way that his skin was soft when my hand went down his face and then so rough as I came back up. I let my hand rest on the back of his neck. He scooted his sleeping bag closer like a caterpillar in a cocoon. Our noses were almost touching. I was sure he could hear my heart now and that it was as loud as the beaver's tails against the water. If he did, he didn't say anything. Maybe his heartbeat was drowning out mine.

"I just want this night to go on forever." His whispered words blew right in my mouth.

"I've never felt this way before. I had such a lovely wall built up around me and then your darn eyes come along and brick by precious brick you broke down all my defenses in a few days."

"It doesn't feel like a few days, it feels like so much longer. You shouldn't ever be behind a wall, you are not meant to be hidden, you're meant to be showcased for all to see. But I have to admit it's kind of nice to be the first one behind the wall." I was no longer cold. "Jady, I can't even begin to tell you how sorry I am about all of this...well not *this* but the whole kidnapping plan. But the selfish part of me can't help but be thankful you were brought into my life. You've awakened something in me, a hope, for something better. I *want* something better. I want to *be* someone better."

"I like you just the way you are."

"You know what I mean. I don't want to be doing what I'm doing anymore. I want a real life and I know this sounds crazy but somehow, someday I want you in it." My eyes misted over in the dark. He said it, he wanted me in his life. In real life, not just this fantasy life we had created. And I wanted him, I had never wanted anyone in my life, not since my father's betrayal and my mother's death.

"You never need to be sorry. You've shown me a world I never knew existed and I feel alive now too. I see everything differently. I was so full of bitterness and anger and you've dissolved all that. Everything always looked so gray to me and now it's like someone came along with a paintbrush and coloured everything anew. No matter what tomorrow brings I want to thank you for these last few days. They have been the best days of my life."

"Remember there is no tomorrow." His warm lips then met mine and our arms pulled each other in.

After what seemed like an eternity, we pulled back to catch our breath. Without further discussion we crawled out of our individual sleeping bags and unzipped both of them. We lay one down underneath us and used the other one as our cover. There was not a single barrier between us now. Our bodies entwined again as if they were meant to be that way. I was touching his face as if I wanted to memorize every curve, line and crevice. His soft voice broke the silence of the night.

"I don't want to go any further, not right now." As if knowing what he was about to say I didn't let him finish.

"I don't feel any pressure or feel forced if that's what you're thinking."

"No, I know that. I just want...I *don't* want it to be under these circumstances." I understood what he was saying but I was too scared to voice my thoughts as if voicing them would bring them to pass. I was so terrified that this was it for us.

This was our last and only chance. I never knew I wanted this, I never knew what I was missing and now that I knew, now that I felt this way I didn't want to waste another moment. But deep down I wanted it to be right too. I wanted it to be right for both of us. I pressed my head into his chest and nodded, fighting back tears. As close as I was to him right now I wanted to be even closer. It felt so good to rest my head against him and hear his heart beat. Riley stroked my hair and I lifted my head and inched my way back up until our lips were touching again.

"Is it okay if we just do this?" I whispered in between kisses. I kissed his lips, cheeks, eyelids and forehead and ended again where we began.

"Oh yes, this is just fine." The loons serenaded our passion and the night welcomed us home.

***

We awoke sometime in the early morning to rain gently falling on the tent. Our bodies were so close it was hard to tell we were two. I took a deep breath of him in and was so thankful it was not a dream. Here he was, still there, still beside me. Riley kissed the top of my head and I could tell he felt the same. We listened to the rain, our hearts beating against each other and the waves lapping up on the shore. It wasn't much longer and all the sounds of nature lulled us back to sleep.

It was the sun this time that woke us and it was suddenly hot and humid in our little space. Riley got up and unzipped the tent door and peeled it back to reveal the most beautiful morning. The sun hadn't been up very long and there was a mist hanging over the lake, all the nocturnal animals now silent. The only sound was the last remnants of the rain dripping from leaves. I was afraid to speak, not wanting to disturb this tranquility. We lay there for a while and let nature wake up first. The birds began their morning song and the odd squirrel would chatter with their neighbor. A few splashes coming from the lake told us the fish were jumping again.

As much as we didn't want to, we knew we needed to get up and get the day started. We had a long way back and we both knew without it being said that we had to beat Byron to the cabin. I shook out the tent and packed it up. Then I rolled up our sleeping bags with the same remorse a child feels watching the Christmas tree come down. I wanted to hang onto the hope that Riley seemed to have. There will be more of this, someday. I wanted to believe that but the heavy dread I felt made it impossible. Watching Riley pack up the rest of our camp very slowly told me he had a hard time hanging on to his hope this morning too.

Suddenly, all the feelings overtook me and I disappeared into the woods with the pretense of going to the washroom. I found a large rock by the shore and curled up on it. I cried silently, feeling so empty. I cursed myself for letting him in, for letting my wall down. This was why it was safer not to feel. I felt like I was tearing up inside. I wanted this, what we had, to go on forever. I didn't want it to end. I wanted to stay in that tent with Riley like two people in a bubble. No one could hurt us or come near. The tears slowly drying up, a saying entered my head, better to have loved and lost than never to have loved at all. Is that true? Or would it have been better not to have even known this existed and I could have gone through life never knowing what I missed? I think I agreed with the saying. Even if I could never have it again, I have the memory of this night. This memory will always be with me and when I'm down and struggling, it will be this time I will think about and smile, not cry. With this in mind, I got up, brushed myself off and returned to Riley.

The wood all around us was too wet to have a fire this morning so we both munched on granola bars and an apple. I already missed our closeness of the previous night but before I could give it any more thought, Riley came up and put both arms around me. I deflated against him and held him tight. He kissed me again and looked into my eyes,

"It's going to be okay. I promise." I didn't know if he was saying this to reassure himself or me but it did help a little. I smiled and gave him one more squeeze. We loaded up the canoe and took off across lake, almost feeling guilty to disturb its perfection. The smells of this morning were completely different, as if the rain had brought to life all the pine and woody scents. When we made it to the other side, I helped Riley pull the canoe back into its hiding spot and we carried the bin to the quad.

Going back was very slow. More rain had fallen than we thought and what was boggy the day before was now a swamp. We had to find a path to go around many times and that also meant bush whacking and cutting new trails. It was exhausting work, but it kept our minds off the destination, which was not as exciting as the one on the way there. We finally made it through the wettest areas and were back on more solid ground, the trail getting more noticeable.

We could both feel a time crunch and as much as we wanted to hang onto every minute, we ate a quick lunch, never leaving the back of the quad. When I finished eating I hugged Riley's back and he turned and held me close. He never made me feel like the closeness we had shared was gone, he made sure I knew he was there, right there. I think I was so scared that we would be so distant once the security of the dark was no longer there, but I could see by his eyes in the daylight that all the feelings of the previous night still existed.

We made it back to the shed by late afternoon and I could tell from the tenseness of Riley's muscles that he was more nervous than he let on. He was just as scared as I was that

Byron had made it back to the cabin before us. As we rounded the corner, I think we both breathed a sigh of relief when we saw Byron's truck was not there. With the nerves settled, a new feeling took over, sadness. This wonderful time we had just spent together was now over and I was about to return to my little room and then what? What was in our future?

We quietly walked back and down the decrepit hallway to the windowless cell. He lay down on the small mattress and patted the spot beside him. I lay down and nestled my head into the curve of his arm.

"What now Riley?"

"I'll figure it out, don't worry. After all these years you've decided to put your faith in somebody and I don't take it lightly that that somebody is me. I won't let you down." His words comforted me but I couldn't still the flutter of worry that lingered in my stomach. We lay like that, holding each other close until we could hear the faint rumble of the truck approaching. As it got closer my heartbeat quickened. Riley got up on his elbow to look at me. He brushed the hair out of my eyes and kissed my forehead and then gently, my lips.

"It will be okay." He got up then and I so wanted to hang on to him and beg for us to run, run now. But where? Where would we run? Riley gave one last glance before he closed my door and gave a light-hearted wink and then he was gone. I curled up on the mattress and wished I could just disappear.

***

I could hear the truck door slam, and by now I could tell by the harsh slamming that Byron was in a foul mood. The flutter in my stomach grew. His leaden boots trudged up the stairs and the door crashed behind him. Then his pacing as he talked in a loud booming voice.

"Jesus fucking Christ, can't something go right around here? First, as I drive in, the truck is making a racket that sounds like a mutt growling at me. Then I get in and make a phone call and of course that fuckin' chic's *daddy* won't be back until tonight so he won't be back in the office until tomorrow morning. I phoned Joe's and told them about the truck and they think it's the water pump bearing which is the best news of the day. That we can fix ourselves and they have the part there. So tomorrow morning I'll go in and make the phone call and you can go to Joe's and get the part. We'll take the bikes. Hopefully we can finally offload the bitch and get some money for babysitting her."

"I think we should let her go." The pacing stopped abruptly.

"What?" Byron's voice reached a level I hadn't heard yet.

"This is not worth it. This job is not like stealing a car or a wallet here and there. This is serious shit that could get us major time."

"You've got to be fuckin' kidding me!!! Of course this is serious shit! I want serious dough! I'm tired of this bullshit chump change. What the fuck has gotten' into you?" There was a long pause and Riley tried answering.

"I just think..."

"Wait a fuckin' minute! You've gone and fallen for this stupid bitch haven't you? Oh my god, I knew it! I knew I should've been the one watching her! You are such a stupid fuckin' softie. She's not a stray puppy you can keep and take care of! Do you really think she gives a shit for you? Did it ever cross your dumb ass mind that she's using you to get away? She's a spoiled rotten rich bitch that just manipulates idiots like us to be at her beck and call. Guys like us are her servants. The idiots who fix her vehicle, who serve her at the convenience store or fix her toilets! The ones she wouldn't give the time of day unless they want something. You are so stupid!" My heart was pounding but it was more out of anger than fear at the moment. I hoped Riley wasn't believing this stuff and hopefully knew me well enough by now to know I wasn't like that.

"Don't call her a bitch. She's not like that at all." Riley's voice sounded angry too and I couldn't help but smile. The smile vanished as I felt the walls shake as something or someone was thrown against them.

"You're not listening!! She doesn't care about you and she never will." There was a pause again and I could hear a chair being moved. I could picture Riley slowly using it to get up off the floor and I winced for him.

"You haven't told her have you." I anxiously waited for Riley's answer. Told me what?

"You haven't told her about Becka have you?" My heart skipped a beat as the name came up again. The maliciousness in Byron's voice was undeniable.

"So she doesn't know you are a killer." My heart stopped then and unknown to me the tears fell as I hear Byron's vicious laughter fill the house.

"Go ahead, tell her now. Go and tell her how you killed Becka and see if she still loves you." I waited in desperation for a response. Anything to dispel this statement. Please Riley tell him it's not true. Stand up to him and defend yourself against these lies. There was nothing. Instead I heard slow footsteps and then a door close.

"That's what I thought." Bryon had spoken these words to himself and now his heavy footsteps echoed in a different direction and another door closed.

My tears turned to sobbing. How could this be? I had finally let someone in and I was betrayed yet again. No, there had to be something to this. There had to be an explanation. I so wished I could talk to Riley. I needed to hear it from his own mouth. I needed for him to tell me it was not true. All that we had, these last few days could not be for nothing. Could he be a killer? Was it Riley all this time that was manipulating me? No, he wouldn't have asked Byron to let me go if this was the case. Why didn't he tell me himself? I stared up at the ceiling kicking myself now for not following through on my plan. I should have asked Riley to help me escape when I had the chance. I stared up at the ceiling, my feelings battling amongst themselves within me. How could I have feelings for someone who killed someone else? The wonderful glow from the last few days was fading fast and now all I felt was anger, sorrow and fear. What had happened to Becka? What was going to happen to me?

Even though I didn't know what time it was, I could tell from the grumbling in my stomach that suppertime had come and gone. My hopes that Riley would come and we could talk were diminishing by the minute. He wasn't going to come. He wasn't going to help me escape. Whatever power Byron had over him, Becka was the magic chain that kept Riley bound to him all these years. As the hours passed, I was surprised that it was not my anger that grew but my determination. Somehow I knew that after all this time, fate could not be so cruel as to let my heart fall to a ruthless killer. There had to be more to this story. I needed to talk to him. But how? In the morning they would both be gone. I had no way of knowing who would leave first or if they would leave at the same time. I was just going to have to wait until the morning and see what happened. I lay back on the mattress, wide-awake. There would be no sleep tonight.

***

I was disappointed to hear both bikes start up in the morning. As I resigned myself to try to sleep to let the time pass, footsteps approached my door. I didn't know whether to be scared or excited. A note slipped under the door then he was gone and I could hear both bikes leave. I was almost too nervous to get the note. I forced myself to get up and retrieve it.

I need to do a few things. I will be back to get you out. I will get you back to your life.

I should have been happy, Riley was coming back for me. He was going to help me escape despite his brother, but I detected anger and defeat in the note. He had given up on his hope for a better life. He had given up on me. He believed his brother's words and he didn't think I would want to be with him once I learned the truth. This terrified me even more. Whatever he had done to Becka was so bad he didn't think I would want a life with him anymore. What could he have done that was so terrible? I could not picture this kind and gentle man I had come to know hurt anyone. I didn't want to think about it anymore, but unfortunately, I had nothing else to do while I waited to see what events would come to pass.

In a deep sleep, I didn't hear the bike return. I didn't know someone was back until I could feel a presence in the room. By then it was too late. Byron stood over me with a gun in his hand.

"Get up." I was still groggy and prayed I was dreaming. The pain in my rib as he kicked me woke me fully and told me I was definitely not dreaming. I got up slowly and he shoved me out the door and down the hall. This is it, I thought, did he get the money from my father? Is he done with me? What happened to Riley?

Byron escorted me at gunpoint down the same path I had walked not too long ago with Riley. When I thought of the mood I had been in then it seemed so distant and foreign in this moment. I walked in a daze, almost wishing he would just get it over with already. All I kept thinking was, please don't hurt me, just make it quick.

We headed up to Riley's lookout spot and Byron scanned it with distain. His eyes were filled with rage and I was now wondering if my father had snubbed him and that's why I was being taken out of the picture. I was shaking like it was minus thirty at the same time as my heart beat in every muscle of my body. He walked me right to the edge, that same edge I had looked out over with dismay when those miles of trees spelled disaster. Here they were again telling me the same thing. I turned to face Byron and waited to see what my fate was. I was scared, but I was angry too. Angry that he was about to take away my life just when I thought I might enjoy it. I almost laughed at my next thought. Take my life just as I finally had something to live for. The gun was staring right at me and I had to resist the urge to scream at him and vent my anger. I think part of me still hung on to the hope that he was there just to scare me, maybe to get more information from me about my father. When Byron spoke, his words were unexpected.

"You thought you could turn him on me, didn't you? Your pretty face and wicked sweet nothings. You thought you could get him to take your side and let you free? I know about women like you. Women who, with a snap of the fingers, think they can get anything they please. Well, *princess,*" I cringed when this nickname came out of his polluted mouth. " You might be able to fool my stupid brother but you can't fool me. I can't be manipulated with lies."

"You mean the way you manipulate Riley with yours?" I spit out my words in anger without thinking and was rewarded with a flash of pain across the face. He had hit me with his free hand and I felt the blood dripping from my nose.

"You just shut the fuck up. You don't know anything. He's my brother. I know him inside and out. You've known him for a few days and you think you're the expert. You don't know shit about him. He's not what you think he is. He's just playing you to get laid. Once we got the money for you he would kill you just as soon as I would."

"You're a liar!" I was fuming now and didn't care what he did. "Riley would never hurt me! And you'll never get your money you stupid son of a bitch! My father won't give you a cent and so all of this was for nothing! You're the one that's an idiot! You're the one I played and told the lies to! You'll continue to live your life like the miserable loser you are!" I heard the click as he pulled back the hammer. I was aghast as his angry scowl turned to a menacing smile.

"Riley wouldn't think twice about hurting you. You see he's done it before." My breath caught in my throat and my anger swung back again to fear. His ugly smile grew.

"We had a sister. Her name was Becka and Riley killed her. He didn't just kill her, he fed her to a pack of wild dogs."

"You're lying!" I was screaming. I wanted him to stop talking.

"Why do you think he's not here rescuing you at this very minute? How do you think I got him to go along with me all these years? 'Cuz I rescued his ass back then, I covered for him and helped him run away and we've been running ever since. You think he can run away with you and live happily ever after? Is that what he told you? He can't go anywhere, he'll be arrested the minute they figure out who he is. You are in love with a cold blooded killer." His harsh laughter filled the valley beneath us and it literally pushed me over the edge. I was so shocked by his words, I took a step back forgetting where I was. I was suddenly falling backwards with my arms flailing. There was nothing to hold on to and I tumbled into the abyss. Unfortunately, I hit the first boulder at full speed and was fully aware of the pain I was in. My fall didn't stop there, there was still a long way down and gravity was winning the war. The pain was excruciating and I was hoping for death to take me to end this suffering. I tried to curl up in a ball to protect myself but every part of me was too heavy and like they were separate entities, my arms and legs just splayed out again like a starfish. Finally, after so many razor filled boulders, spear- like branches and anvil stumps I left my body at the bottom, in a mess no one would have recognized for a human being.

***

I could hear someone calling my name.

"Jady, can you hear me?" I wanted to answer, but found I couldn't. I couldn't even open my eyes or move.

"Oh god please, please be okay. I'm going to get a board and move you onto it. I'm sorry it's the only way right now." I could hear the snapping of branches and I knew he was walking away. I wanted to scream, 'Don't leave me!' but of course nothing came out. The more I became aware of my surroundings the greater my pain became. It was like my whole body was slowly waking up and I really wished it would stay sleeping. When I heard the branches again I panicked and thought Byron had returned to finish the job. Riley's voice calmed me instantly and my heartbeat slowed again.

"Okay, I'm going to try to move you as gently as I can. Oh God, I hope I'm not doing more damage but I have no choice, I need to get you out of here." The desperation and panic in his own voice quickened my heartbeat again. Was he afraid of my condition or was he more afraid of Byron?

Thank God I couldn't scream otherwise I would've when he moved me. Not only would it have terrified Riley, it would have brought Byron down upon us for sure, if my instincts were right and he was still out there. Riley tried the best he could to move me slowly, but it just made the pain last longer. Imagine the feeling you have when you stub your toe, now imagine that pain in every inch of your body. I felt the tears fall down the sides of my face and I gritted my teeth not even realizing I was biting my tongue as well until the taste of blood dripped down my throat. It was easier to focus on one painful part of my body than to visualize what the rest of me must look like if it was in this much agony. Finally, I was on the board and then I could hear Riley fiddling around in the bushes beside me.

"I attached logs on either side of the board and tied ropes around the ends so that I can drag you to the quad. I'm just going to strap you to the board with these tie downs so you don't move too much and hopefully this will cut down on the pain." I think just then he noticed the tears because his voice cracked and I could feel his lips touch my forehead, cheeks and eyelids.

"Oh Jady, I'm so sorry, I'm so sorry." I could feel his tears then falling on my face. "I shouldn't have left you, I should have just grabbed you and then we would be long gone right now and none of this would have happened." He touched his forehead to mine then and cried freely. "I can't stand to see you like this." I wanted to console him, but even if I could find my voice I didn't know what I would've said. I didn't know what to believe anymore. Where did he go? Why was he back now? If he had killed Becka, why didn't he just leave me here to die? I could feel him leave my side and then the pain was back as he tightened the belts around me.

"I'm going to move you now. It's going to be rough going, but the quad is not far and then it will get a bit better." Talking me through his movements helped. I wanted to feel my eyes, wondering why I couldn't open them, but now my arms were pinned by my sides. I tried to take deep breaths and calm myself. The straps around me lessened the pain as we hit bumps and made our way through the woods. Then we were stopped again. Riley's laboured breathing told me it had been hard work for him to drag my dead weight all that way.

"We're at the quad. I'm going to lift your head up first and then slide the rest of you on. I'm putting you on the back rack. I'll strap you down again so that you won't move too much." My tears fell even faster now, not just because of the pain from my injuries but from the memories still fresh, when I was riding behind him on the same quad, holding him close. Now I was being strapped to the rack like one of his bins. What kind of condition was I in? Would I ever be the same again? Would I be able to walk? To talk? To see? I tried to push these thoughts away as panic rose up my throat and threatened to cut off my breathing.

Now I was at an angle with my head in the air, the board resting against the quad. Then the sound of the board sliding across the rack and my body moving, suddenly the same level as my head. I winced as the straps were again applied this time holding me to the bike. I could sense that although his movements were gentle, his breathing was quick and I sensed an urgency that scared me.

The quad's motor echoed in the forest and we were moving. Riley had done a great job fastening me to the bike and the pain was almost tolerable. I wondered where he was taking me. He couldn't ride all the way into town on the quad, as much as I was somewhat comfortable now, I knew it wasn't going to last and I wouldn't make a trip like this into town, knowing it had to be quite a ways.

I faded in and out of consciousness and when we stopped again, Riley was propping up my head and trying to get me to swallow some water. My mouth felt caked together and Riley gently wiped it. I choked on the first gulp and then tried to sip instead, the coolness of the water felt good down my throat. I tried again to speak, but only a groan escaped.

"Don't try talking yet Jady. Just rest and try to drink a little more." I took a few more sips before I clamped my mouth shut, feeling queasy and not wanting to throw it all up.

"I'm going to move you now into the canoe. I know this all sounds crazy to you right now, but I will explain it all later." Riley's voice sounded concerned still, but not rushed. Was it because we were out of Byron's reach? He must be taking me to the island, but the thought of sleeping on a hard floor made me want to break into fresh tears. I didn't think I could do it. This board was already too much. Even the smelly, dirty mattress of that small room was more appealing to me right now. I just wanted to curl up on something soft and go to sleep.

Riley's groans as he moved me made me grasp the awkwardness of what he was trying to do. Move a big, unwieldy board with a one hundred and twenty pound weight on it. Not to mention doing it gently so as not to harm the weight. As much as he tried, I came down hard in that canoe and I could feel Riley's head fall into my chest and this time a scratchy scream escaped my mouth.

"Jady, I'm so sorry." Riley's breathless voice was near my face. I could feel his hands on my head as he stroked my hair. His touch felt so comforting, so full of care and concern. Half of me wanted to pull away, suddenly unsure of everything, yet the other half of me wanted him to take me in his arms and tell me it wasn't as bad as it felt, that I was going to be okay. Instead his hands left me and I felt the canoe being pushed into the water and then we were afloat. The last thing I heard before I blacked out again was the splash of the paddle as it hit the water, moving us across the lake.

THE CABIN

I had no concept of how much time was passing. It could have been seconds, minutes or days. It was all the same to me. I was in and out of consciousness and I preferred it when I was out. There were only two constants the entire time. One being Riley, who was always by my side with comforting words whenever I did manage to open my eyes. The other was pain. There was not a single part of my body that did not feel it. Even the effort it took to talk was too painful. I also didn't know what to say yet. I wanted to ask him. I wanted to know the truth and yet I didn't. I was so afraid it would change everything I had come to believe about him and us. I wasn't afraid of him, though maybe I should be. I already doubted a lot of Byron's words. If Riley had played me and was planning to hurt me, why would he have me here trying to take care of me. Was he making sure I stayed alive so that they could get their money for me? I needed more time to sort all this out in my mind.

During this time, Riley was trying very hard to make me comfortable and take some of the pain away. I noticed we were in a building of some kind and I assumed we were in the cabin that belonged to that elderly couple. It was cozy in here and it felt safe. I was wearing clothes that didn't belong to me and I had white strips of cloth covering most of my wounds. Riley washed the wounds frequently and it seemed every time I came to I had clean bandages on. For the first bit, I couldn't move at all so he fed me and made sure I had plenty of water to drink. For the first while he just brought me broth, but then as my strength slowly returned and I could sit up, he brought me more solid food. It was all canned stuff and I didn't know whether he had brought it along or if these people had a stash of things they kept here all year round.

I wanted to feel anger. I wanted to hate him. Once again it was because of him that I was in the mess I was in. I couldn't hate him or be angry towards him at all. The look in his eyes and the gentle feel of his hands told me he cared, told me that he felt the same way towards me as he had the night in the tent. Regardless of the pain I was in, I was happy to be alive. Happy to be by his side. I thought I was done and that I would never see him again. We were back in our own little world and it's this fantasy again that stopped me from asking what needed to be asked.

At first it seemed that Riley was almost afraid to talk to me, as if his words would also increase my pain. That silence would heal me faster, but after awhile he started talking to fill in the time and sometimes he would be mid-conversation when I would wake up from my state.

"Miraculously, I don't think you have any broken bones. I have felt along all of them and none seem to be out of place or sticking out anywhere. I was so scared because there was so much blood, but once I cleaned you off I could see that it was all from cuts and scrapes. It was quite a fall." He would shake his head in disbelief and repeat this sentence frequently as if the fact I survived it was unheard of. I couldn't believe it myself. I shuddered when I thought of how far I had fallen and all the obstacles I had hit. Right now it was hard to see because Riley had all my wounds covered, but when he did peel them away to clean them, the sight of myself turned my stomach. I was the colour of a very ripe plum, all over. No wonder it hurt so much to move.

“I should have rode into town and got help but I was so afraid to leave you. I was afraid once I came back with help you would be gone from me. I should never have left you alone in the first place. I can’t believe I did that.” He choked up when he talked like that and usually busied himself with something else at that moment. “I took you to the only spot I have ever felt safe. A spot no one else knows about. Not even Byron.” He murmured his brother’s name under his breath and I was unsure if it was anger or fear behind that.

“I know you’re not supposed to move someone with a head or spine injury, I know that much. But I didn’t know what else to do. Byron is still out there and I was terrified to leave you, even now.” He hung his head in shame and I wanted to reach out and touch his head to tell him it was okay, but at the mention of his brother and the fact he was still alive and maybe searching for us made me stop. How did Riley get away? How did he manage to rescue me? Would Byron find us? Does Riley feel a loyalty to him still and would he leave me if he had to choose? But he did choose. Somehow, I don’t know how yet, but he made a choice to come to my side rather than stay with Byron. There were so many unanswered questions swimming in my head that I had to shut them down. My head was pounding. I couldn’t ask them yet. It was all too painful, both physically and emotionally.

As my awareness increased, I could tell when a day would pass by, followed by a night. It had been at least a few days that we had been here. Riley, during this time, unconsciously answered some of the questions that had been running through my mind.

“I know this isn’t the best arrangement, and if the couple decides to all of a sudden pop out here, we’ll deal with that as it comes. I want to give Byron enough time to think we're long gone. By then you will be stronger and able to get around more without so much pain. I want to make our way back to the cabin and we can take my bike and I can get you back. What you do then is up to you. What we did was wrong. The kidnapping crossed the line and what my brother was about to do is unforgivable." Riley shook his head and turned away to busy himself with something but I could see he was torn between anger and sadness.

I couldn't take it any longer,

"Riley what happened? Where did you go? What happened to Byron?" At first Riley looked so happy to hear my voice that he ignored the questions. His hands went to my face.

"Thank God, I thought you had lost your voice. I was so scared. When I saw you there, in that heap, I thought I had lost you forever." He covered his face with his hands and lay on my chest. "I'm so sorry. I'm so sorry for everything. I should've never gone along with the whole thing right from the beginning."

"Riley please, just tell me what happened?" His head came up then he looked at me, lost for a second.

"What?" I was just about to repeat the questions when he took a deep breath and began.

"I left that morning with the intention of coming back as soon as Byron was gone. I was going to take you into town, where you would be safe. But something didn't feel right. So I rode my bike for a bit and then pulled over hiding the bike and waiting. Byron rode past me and I waited for a while. Just when I was about to give up and come back to get you he came back. He whipped right past me. In a panic to get the bike started again I flooded it and had to wait to get it started. I got here as fast as I could and looked first in the cabin and then I ran up to the lookout. All I saw was Byron standing at the edge of the cliff with a gun in his hand. I thought I was too late. I was so angry I charged him and knocked him to the ground before he had time to think about aiming that thing at me. I knocked him senseless and took his gun." Riley stopped then and hung his head. I had a hard time hearing him then,

"Jady, I so wanted to kill him. I thought he had killed you. I aimed that gun for the longest time at his face, so angry. But I couldn't do it. He's my brother, no matter what's he done, I can't forget what he's done for me." I didn't stop him to ask him to clarify this, I just let him talk.

"I then crawled to the cliff and saw you...in that pile at the bottom." Riley choked up again and patiently I waited. I didn't console or reach out to him, although every fibre of my being wanted to. He was hurting and I could see that, but I was hurting far worse. My body was paying for his mistakes and I was still so unsure about everything and doubting whether I could trust him or not. I had a temporary wall of protection back up and I was barely peeking over the top to listen to him.

"I scrambled down to the bottom, sure you were dead. But I felt a pulse. I couldn't believe it. Then I had to decide what to do. That was when I thought of the cabin and I didn't know how much time I had before Byron came to again. I was so scared the whole time here that you wouldn't make it, but look at you! Not only did you make it, but also you're getting stronger every day. There's definitely a strong spirit watching out over you."

I wanted to ask more but my head was starting to pound. I remember having migraines a long time ago and needing to be in the dark and to lie still. I couldn't talk and even the sound of others talking hurt. That was what it was like now. I closed my eyes, my temples throbbing so hard I was sure you could see them pulsating if you looked. Riley, somehow understanding, brought me a cold cloth and placed it on my forehead. I slept.

***

Just when I thought I was getting better, a fever took hold and the next few days went by in a blur. I woke up screaming on quite a few occasions from nightmares that left me as soon as I awoke. I was having delusional thoughts during the day. A few times in terror I thought Byron was there and almost believed it until I saw my father and mother appear. Riley would carry me to the cool lake and hold me immersed until I cooled down and then he would carry me back to bed.

Eventually the fever broke and I felt better than I had since arriving at the cabin. I could actually get up and go to the outhouse on my own steam. I could feed and clean myself. I could walk down to the water and wade around in the shallows, not feeling quite strong enough to go for a swim. My bruises slowly faded from the black and purple to a dark green. I looked like the gobstopper candies I loved as a kid. They were like giant gumballs and would change colours the longer you had one in your mouth. I was intrigued to see what color I would turn next.

As my strength returned, Riley began talking about making our way back to the other cabin soon. I knew I wasn't ready yet to go, not because I wasn't capable of it physically, but I needed more questions answered first. Questions I kept putting off from asking. But it was the responses to these questions that would decide if I would go to the police or not once we re-entered civilization. There was also a large part of me that still didn't want to leave. As much as doubt lingered in the foreground, I still cared about Riley and loved being near him.

Even though I was feeling better and better, I hid this from Riley. I wanted some time with him before I discovered the truth about Becka. As much as I wanted to be close to him I found myself keeping a safe distance. He sensed this, didn't question it and gave me my space. I think he assumed I was angry at him for what happened with Byron. I think he felt extremely guilty for not being by my side sooner and preventing the fall. I was angry at him, but not for this. Once he had told me his side I felt only compassion for him and my feelings for him grew stronger. I believed him when he said he was coming back for me. I could tell by the way he cared for me and the constant look of concern on his face that he would have never hurt me like Byron said. Did that mean the other things Byron had said were also lies? The way Byron used Becka as his manipulative tool left me doubtful.

As we tiptoed around each other we explored the cabin. The owners had stockpiled a lot of food. We figured maybe it was from the days when they spent the winter out here as well. Or maybe they did have plans on coming that summer and something happened. They had shelves and shelves of canned food, some store bought but many of it came in jars that I'm sure they canned themselves. We found a fenced off area in the back, now overgrown with weeds. The small white signs marked the graves of vegetables long gone. There were big bags of flour and sugar in plastic containers. We assumed it was to keep the mice out of them. Rice and oats were in similar bins.

There was one small bedroom filled by the bed it contained. The only other piece of furniture was a dresser that looked even older than the couple Riley had described. The kitchen and living room shared the same space with one little step separating the two rooms. The kitchen had a old wood stove with two doors. One you could fill with wood and the other one for baking. It was where I pictured them baking their fresh bread. There were many black cast-iron pots, pans and loaf pans that supported my daydreaming. There was no fridge as there was no electricity, but there was a small icebox, just outside the door, that they must have stored their supplies in the winter. A small sink with no taps and just a drain told me they brought their water in from the lake. A considerably large walk-in pantry filled with shelves of food took up a big portion of the kitchen. In this pantry were also big plastic bins containing winter clothing. There was a wonderful massive counter that had pieces of multi colored marble put together on it like a puzzle. I thought of how many trips they would have to make to lug each piece up there. The cupboards contained many different colours of dishes and bowls, nothing matching and yet every piece unique and beautiful. Some were made from pottery, others bright blue, orange or green tin. The utensils were just as mismatched and no two sizes alike. Lastly, there was a wooden kitchen table that, although small, had a lot of weight to it. Considering it's weight and the rustic look to it, I could see them constructing it right here, using the woods around them. The chairs were the same. Because of this, nothing was level and everything wobbled when you sat or put anything down on it. I could imagine them giggling about it each and every time.

The living room had a wooden floor with one throw rug on it. This one rug looked well worn where it sat under a small hand carved table. This table looked like an ongoing experiment. There were large rocks on the tabletop but it was hard to tell what their color was since they were buried in layers and layers of lacquer. The winter months had cracked it time and time again and it appeared that just as many times they had been filled, trying in vain to heal the wounds of winter. It gave it the look of a dried up river bed and, although I'm sure it was not the look they were going for, it looked beautiful despite it's cracks and lacerations. There was also a cot that by the indentations in it, had been used as their couch. A fireplace took up one whole wall, made with large stones and this one seemed to be more for cozying up to rather than heat. Given the small space of the cabin, once you had the one in the kitchen fired up that would be more than enough warmth. There were pictures up on the walls, but nothing revealing them or their family. It was all handmade work. Cross-stitching, needlepoint and amateur paintings were abundant and revealed how they filled their time. There was also quite a few little shelves filled with books. Most of the content was of wildlife, gardening, and picture books of rivers, lakes and mountains. Then every once in a while a tiny fiction book would peek forth disclosing an intermission from their factual side.

I loved every inch of their space and when I pictured them going about their daily lives it made me miss what Riley and I had. Would we get it back? Would the secret he was holding change everything?

We cooked our meals side by side, but the lighthearted flirtatious behaviour was gone. We were suddenly just two people sharing the same space. I wanted to reach out and touch him. I wanted to feel his lips on mine again. He seemed so far away at night on the cot while I had immense space in the double bed. Was he missing me as he lay in the small cold cot? Did he think what we had was gone? Had he given up hope on a better life for himself? I'm thinking the conversation he had with Byron about Becka squashed all hope he had been building.

***

My questions were answered before I was ready. I had never asked them, it was Riley that ventured first and broke the silence between us. We were sitting on the porch enjoying the sun but the scene we portrayed was not the loving one I had envisioned of the cabin couple.

"I need to tell you something. Something I've never told a soul or talked about with anyone. Byron knows about it, but we don't talk about it. First I need you to understand. I'm sorry I got you involved in all this. I should have kept my distance and never got close to you. It hurts me to say it, but I can't picture life without you. I know that's being selfish. I'm not meant to be with anyone. I'm not meant to be loved or to love anyone. I hurt everyone who comes close to me. I'm not worthy of being a part of your life and I can't express enough how sorry I am to lead you to believe we could have something together in real life. I can't have anything with anyone. Once I return to the real world I will have to pay for what I've done. I've been running for too long, it's time to stop." Riley took a deep breath, but was unable to meet my eyes. It looked like it pained him to talk. It looked like it had been him that fell off that cliff and was unable to speak because of the agony it gave him.

"Becka was my sister. She was the sweetest, most loving girl. Despite her environment, despite the lack of mother, she was still just a happy little girl. She died when she was eight and it was me..." I held my breath, unable to believe what he was saying. Riley had a sister. Riley closed his eyes then as if picturing Becka.

"We protected her. We kept her away from our dad's wicked tongue and hand. We tried to be both her father and mother. We bought her girly things and always made sure she was fed first. We never forgot a birthday, going without just to make sure she had a cake and presents. Byron had been different back then. He really loved her and was so tender and caring. She was my partner in adventure. On weekends we would come out to the cabin, I think dad saw it more as an opportunity to dump us off more then anything. It was in better shape back then. Byron and I saw to it. That room, that room you were in was Becka's room. Because it had no windows we colored windows on large sheets of paper and would make the scenes outside bright and colorful. We always changed them up, creating seasonal scenes of rainy days and rainbows. Our dad was drinking himself into the grave in the city and left us to fend for ourselves. We learned to ride the quad at an early age and that's what we used to explore the nature around us. Byron preferred to be left at a lake and spend the day fishing, but Becka and I would go find and watch animals. We built tree forts and created our own fantasy world of pretend campfires and a home in our forts with a whole family present. We used smoke mushrooms under our pile of sticks to cook by and we tied ropes in the trees from which to swing. We uncovered baby bunnies and birds and never disturbed them. Then Byron would find us and being a little older, he would build us a real fire and he would cook the fish he caught. We would have us a feast. We almost preferred these weekends even though the food would be scarce. We didn't have to worry about avoiding the wrath of dad and we could immerse ourselves in nature forgetting the city life that was so bleak and empty. We weren't criminals on the weekends and we enjoyed the break even though it meant slimmer pickings of food.

Becka loved books. Especially the books about animals. She loved being read to and Charlotte's Web was her favourite. She cried every time. She enjoyed school more than we did. I loved to learn too, but I was already aware of the differences between us and the other students. They had nice clothes and neatly packed lunches. We were the kids the teacher always had to scrounge to find winter stuff for or have go to the staff room to see what she could find us to eat. Becka was oblivious to all this. Oblivious or she really didn't care. She always wore a smile and no one seemed to notice as much that she had holes in her pants or mismatched socks. We tried even harder for her sake to make sure she had nicer things, but she was still burdened with the fact of her relations. Though she was never ashamed. Byron was different and hated school and if I noticed the differences, Byron not only noticed but would accentuate them. He would wear the filthiest of clothes just to see if anyone would dare say anything. As tender as he was towards Becka, he took his anger out on any kids that coughed when he would walk by. All that pent up anger and frustration from our home life had to come out somewhere.

Becka was small for her age and that made her even more fragile and in need of care in our eyes. We even got her a small puppy once, but it ran away. We looked for days for that little thing not being able to stand that heartbroken face. We never found it and we felt like we failed her. We didn't do that again. We couldn't blame the dog for running away, if it wasn't for Becka we would've too. But Becka was too little and we couldn't stand the thought of dragging her from shelter to shelter or putting her in danger and hitching rides." Riley paused then catching his breath. He was enjoying this part, enjoying reminiscing about Becka, but he was also procrastinating. His face grew more troubled and I could tell he was struggling to continue, but he was trying hard to push himself forward.

"I just want you to know the truth. I want you to know everything. I want you to understand why we can't be together. I didn't just want to dump you off in town and not explain why I wouldn't be staying. It's time for me to face the music." It made me sad to hear him say these words. To voice out loud we had no future. As much as I didn't want to hear what he had to say, I did need to hear what was preventing us from having the life together we both wanted so badly.

"We always walked to school together. Our house was just on the outskirts of town and we went to a rural school. It was about a twenty-minute walk on nice days and a little longer in the winter. We used to ride the school bus, but Byron was forever getting kicked off, talking back to the bus driver, or starting fights with other kids. So we walked with him.

On this one day after school, Byron had ripped off some kid's bike and was riding it home. I was asked by some kids at school to stay behind to play on the playground, something they never did so I was excited, although I remember trying to act cool about it. I told Becka to stay with me and play, but she was pumped about some new project her teacher had assigned and wanted to get home and get started. I remember hesitating. I didn't like the idea of her walking alone but I wanted to have friends. I told myself that she had walked that road many times before and she was eight and not a baby. I let her go. That decision, that stupid selfish decision, cost us our sister and changed everything for us." Again Riley paused and he was trying very hard to keep his composure.

"It was so long ago now and yet I can see everything like it was yesterday. I was ten then and Byron was thirteen. It was nice outside, being June. We had less than a month of school to go. The playground was an old one, something that would be torn down now for safety reasons. There was no gravel underneath anything and the paint was peeling from all the metal structures. Most of the swings were gone so we just hung ropes over the bars to hang on to and climb. The seesaws were made from wood and you never left them without a splinter or two. I remember playing for a while and then the guilt of letting my sister walk alone overcame my wish for friends. I told them I needed to get going and they were still yelling for me to stay for a while as I ran down the road. There was a horrible feeling in my stomach and it wouldn't go away. I was probably ten minutes down the road when I could hear a bunch of dogs barking and snarling. They sounded like they were fighting. As I came closer, I could see it was the pack of wild dogs that roamed our area and had been growing in numbers the last few years. Every once in a while a farmer shot one if it got too close to their cattle, but there were always more puppies to fill the void. They were not friendly, but usually kept a wide berth from people.

They were fighting over something. It looked like a piece of cloth. A piece of pink cloth. The cloth was oddly familiar and once I figured out it looked just like Becka's skirt I ran. I had no fear as I came upon those dogs though I should have. They were in frenzy, but I paid no heed. I ran into the ditch they were gathered in and yelled and screamed at them. They scattered, and as they did I saw her." Riley stopped and started to cry. This time I went to him. I put my arms around him. He was no killer. It was not his fault. How long he had been carrying this guilt around him like a lead weight. Anger surfaced in my throat momentarily as I thought of how Byron had taken advantage of this guilt. I held him and just let him cry. I didn't say a word. I cried with him, feeling his hurt and pain. His broken words were spoken into my chest.

"There was so much blood. I knew just by looking at her that she was dead. I was filled with so much anger then. I wanted to kill those dogs; I wanted to kill Byron for taking off on that bike. I wanted to kill my dad for being a useless drunk. But most of all I wanted to kill myself because I shouldn't have left her alone. I lay in that ditch right beside her until it got dark and then I debated running away, but I needed Byron. Only he would be able to understand the grief I was feeling. I didn't want to leave her there for the dogs to come back to. I lifted her up and carried her the rest of the way home. I still kept waiting for her to wake up, to lift her head and smile at me and tell me she was fine, put her down and let her walk. But she didn't.

Byron met us five minutes from the house, coming out to look for us. When he saw what I was carrying he dropped the bike and came running. He grabbed her from my arms and asked me what happened. When I told him, I can still remember the hatred in his eyes and this time it was directed towards me. He was so angry with me for letting her walk alone. I never said a thing. I knew he was right. There isn't a day goes by that I don't wish I had never stayed to play, that I had walked with her home." I could see the deep regret etched in his face and I couldn't hold back my words any longer.

"Riley, you were only ten. You were just a kid yourself. You can't hold yourself responsible for what happened. If that's the case, Byron's just as much to blame for getting kicked off the school bus or stealing the bike and leaving the two of you. Can't you see that? It's nobody's fault." Riley got up with a look of shock on his face.

"No, Byron's not to blame. If it were reversed he would have never stayed at that playground and played, he would have walked her home." Riley's voice was defensive and almost angry. I replied, quietly, knowing I was pushing it now, but unable to stop.

"You don't know that. He was just as eager to make friends as you were. He was the older one and left you two to walk alone. If you had been with her, those dogs probably would have attacked both of you." He was struggling with this statement. He had been blaming himself for so long and Byron had been using it to manipulate him that he was stuck. Byron's years of brainwashing won over.

"No, I would have fought them off. I would have made sure they didn't hurt her." I felt like I was talking to a child. He had reverted back to that time and the pain in him was fresh and sore.

"Listen to me, it's not your fault. No one is to blame. Do you understand me? You did not kill Becka, those dogs did."

"I'm just as guilty for what happened to Becka as what happened to you." His words stopped me. I had to think for a minute before I responded, focusing solely on the fall from the cliff not the kidnapping.

"You can't be responsible for the things your brother chooses to do." I was tiptoeing around the fact that Byron used Riley's guilt against him, thinking he was a bit too vulnerable and defensive right now. I gently prodded him along in his retelling, steering him away from arguing with me.

"What happened after you met Byron?"

"We talked about it and decided not to tell our dad. We weren't afraid of the beating, we just wanted to bury her ourselves, and we didn't want him touching her in any way. Byron convinced me not to go to the police. He told me they would put me away for what I had done and that they would put him in foster care." Riley saw me want to interrupt and show him the irrational logic of this, but he stopped me.

"I know enough now that I didn't break any laws, but at the time I did believe his words and I think in some way Byron believed it too." I bit my tongue, not quite agreeing with this. "Look, I know you want to be angry at Byron for this because of what he did to you and I can't blame you, but you need to understand that from then on he looked out for me and was not only my big brother, but also my parents.

Byron stole dad's truck and we drove out to the cabin, burying Becka out there." My mind raced, trying to think if I saw anything around the cabin that resembled a burial plot. Nothing came to mind.

"That was when we started running. There was nothing keeping us there now. Without Becka there was no reason to stay. We hitchhiked as far away as we could. We stole from everyone along the way and fed ourselves when we could. That's how we lived, that's how we still live. Over the years Byron's become worse. I think it was what happened to Becka that triggered his illness. It wasn't until about five years ago that we made our way back to this area and rediscovered our old cabin. We found out that father had drunk himself into the grave shortly after we had run away. Now it's time."

"Time for what?"

"Time to tell people what really happened to Becka. Time to take responsibility."

"Who? Who are you going to tell?"

"The police. They need to know there was a death that wasn't reported. There must be a law against that." I couldn't believe that one person who could be so smart in some areas really could be so utterly stuck in a child-like ignorance in others. Riley wanted to be punished. He felt an obligation to set the record straight plus he was carrying the guilt of both his sister's death and the onset of his brother's illness. Regardless, I wasn't afraid of him anymore and I cared for him even more. He needed serious help to try and undo the years of brain-washing his brother had subjected him to. Help that I couldn't give him. But it was help he wasn't going to receive in prison either or if he returned as his brother's partner in crime. If Riley went to the police and told his story they wouldn't take him away for what had happened to Becka, but they would take him for all the crimes he had committed since then and to Riley's guilt ridden mind this would be justice served. I needed to keep him here for a while to figure out what to do. Now that I knew he wasn't a killer I wanted a life with him and I wasn't about to let him go easily.

***

After Riley's confession, things between us changed, for the better. We went about our days like a couple and not like the roommates we had been up to that point. We cooked our meals together and shared them on the porch. We tidied up our little "home" and read to each other by candlelight in the evenings. One thing stayed the same though, Riley slept on the cot. He didn't say it, but he still felt unworthy of getting close again. The guilt he carried over Becka had doubled with the guilt he felt over what had happened to me and he was scared. I gave him his space and didn't push it or bring it up again until he brought up leaving.

"We really should be going soon."

"Going where?"

"I need to get you back to continue on with your life and I need to find closure."

"What exactly do you plan to do? Stroll into the police station and tell them your sister died 15 years ago and you feel responsible?" I felt bad that I said it so bluntly, but I needed him to wake up.

"No, I understand now that probably there's no one out there who really cares what happened to my sister besides me and Byron. But I feel I should come forward and admit to all the crimes I've committed since then. Its time to come clean, do time and then start a new life."

"Riley, I think what you're trying to do is noble. I respect you for that. I think just admitting it and knowing you won't do it anymore is enough of a fresh start." I knew I was being selfish but I couldn't stop myself.

"Riley, I love you. I love you more than I've ever loved anyone and you've made me love myself. I want to spend my life with you *now*, not ten years from now when you're finished your time." There I said it and he was so quiet that just when I was about to regret it, he leaned in and kissed me for so long and so hard I was taken aback. I had missed his touch so much.

"Jady, I've loved you from the moment I kidnapped you." We both laughed and then we finished what we had started in the tent a lifetime ago. The cot remained empty from that moment on.

"So, now what?" The question came from me, surprisingly. We were lying in bed listening to the night sounds from our window. It was so nice to hear them with Riley by my side. Before, the calling of the loon had sounded so lonely, now it sounded mysterious and romantic.

"Now, I want a snack of canned…hmmmm..let's see, maybe peas this time." I punched him in the arm playfully.

"You know what I mean. What are we going to do? I don't want to lose you Riley. Can't we just stay here forever?" He smiled.

"I wish. I will do what you want and I won't go to the police, I can't expect you to wait for me while I do my time." I quickly interrupted him.

"I would wait forever for you Riley I just don't *want* to. I really don't think you are the kind of person who deserves to sit in jail. You are rehabilitated. You are a good person. You want to turn your life around."

"That means a lot to me Jady. I'm really worried about Byron out there. I don't want to spend our life running scared he will find us. But I can't turn him into the police without implicating myself."

"Why can't we just stay here for awhile until we figure out what to do?" I really didn't want to leave and the thought of having to be looking over our shoulder everywhere scared me.

"Well, we do have more then enough food to last us for quite some time. We can replace it all later. Aren't you going to get sick of me in this small space?"

"I could ask you the same question."

"Oh, I'm already sick of you. Can't you tell?" He started covering me with kisses, and, giggling, I closed my eyes and enjoyed his affections.

***

Once we had made up our mind to stay awhile we took a serious look at our food situation. We were just entering August and we had more then enough for quite a few months. Riley would catch fish to supplement our canned goods and then we set about exploring our island to see what else it had to offer.

We found plenty of raspberry bushes and we even found a few patches of blueberries. Mushrooms were everywhere and Riley said the 'Cabin Couple' (which we had decided now was their permanent name) had a book describing ones to pick and ones that were not good. We would study it later and see if we had anything we could eat. There was wild rhubarb and tons of tiny strawberries that were just ripening now. We were going to come back with bowls later and collect them. They would taste great on our pancakes or oatmeal. We could haul all our water from the lake and use it to cook and clean with. If I were by myself, I wouldn't even be considering staying, but with Riley by my side and his knowledge of our surroundings I knew we were going to be just fine.

We fell into a routine that if anyone would have been looking in on us, would seem we had been doing it forever. We lay in bed until the heat of the morning chased us out. We made our breakfast of either oatmeal or pancakes and we ate on the porch watching nature wake up around us. The birds were becoming accustomed to our presence and knew if they waited long enough they would get tossed a few pieces of our pancake. The blue jays were the least shy of the bunch and the greediest. They would always chase away the other birds to get their hand outs first. We shared a cup of coffee, as it was in limited supply. Then we would take a walk around our island to see what had ripened or bloomed overnight. We'd harvest what was ready and pick a few mushrooms to compare with the pictures in our book. Our island wasn't that little as it turned out, and it did take us a few hours to make the tour. By the time we were done we usually had a bowl full of something for a following meal and we were ready for lunch. We would usually have canned meat of some kind with a can of veggies.

The heat of the day would hit by then and we would find a shady spot near the lake to lie around with the mushroom book trying to see if the ones we had picked in the morning were safe or not. We would take refreshing swims; fish for our supper and on many occasions fall asleep on a blanket on shore. We never went minutes without reaching out and touching each other. I would hold Riley's hand or caress his broad shoulders. Riley helped wash my hair in the lake and then tenderly combed it out with his fingers. If we did take a nap we were never far apart, if at all. I was always so terrified I would fall asleep and wake up and it would all be a dream. But there he would be, still sleeping or staring at me and smiling.

Once the hottest part of the day was over we would head back to the cabin to make supper. The small space was more bearable as the sun passed its peak. Luckily for us, it really cooled off at night and made sleeping possible. We would start a fire outside in a stone pit we almost tripped over one day on our walk out. It was overgrown with weeds and we had cleaned it up. We would cook up our catch of fish and make some rice or pasta and another can of veggies. Our dessert was usually some of the berries we had picked that morning. We would sit by our fire, eating our wonderful meal and watch, as nature got ready for bed. We always moved to the porch, which had the best view of the sunset, and once the show was over we would break out a candle or two and either read or play some cards. The day spent in the outside air would eventually catch up with us and, exhausted, we would retire into the cabin, our little bed and each other's arms.

***

I was craving bread. I figured it couldn't be too hard. We had flour, water, and the 'Cabin Couple' even had many packages of yeast. I had found a few of their cookbooks and there were some recipes for bread. The only problem was that most of the recipes called for either oil, butter or shortening. Of which we had none. I remember vaguely a cooking show that focused on low fat recipes. They added applesauce to everything. That we had. I stuck that in. The whole thing turned out to be quite a process and took me a good portion of a day. Once I had everything mixed, I had to knead and let it rise for an hour. While it was doing this I took our dirty laundry down to the lake. This pile consisted of one set of clothing we had and then a couple of t-shirts and shorts we found in a cupboard. They weren't an exact fit, but they did the trick and they weren't too huge. I washed the clothes with a bar of soap, which we did have plenty of, rinsed them off really well and then hung them over branches to dry in the heat. By this time the hour was up and I went back to knead the dough. This was harder than I thought and my arms and shoulders were starting to hurt the second time round.

Riley kept checking in on me. He had found an axe in the shed and was having fun cutting wood. He came into the tiny kitchen and he held me from behind, resting his chin on my shoulder, inspecting my work.

"I'm doing just fine. You'll see, it will be the best bread you ever had"

"I'm sure it will be. Now plant me a kiss and I'll leave you to it." I turned to kiss him and saw that he was dripping in sweat.

"Ewww. Get lost." He tried to move closer and he had his eyes closed and his lips puckered in fun.

"Don't you want a big wet kiss." I playfully pushed him away,

"Get back to work, I'm busy here." I smiled as I went back to my kneading. So this is what it felt like to be in love. I couldn't stop smiling and I got a kick out of everything he did. When you spent the amount of time together as we had been, with no TV, no telephone or computer, there were no distractions. We were each other's entertainment. I loved listening to him read to me at night. He had the calmest, deepest voice. When we played cards, I would watch him count the symbols on the cards or he would try and hide his fingers as he used them as his manipulatives. Apparently his math skills weren't as good as his wood cutting skills. Listening to him at night when he slept, was better than any guard dog. I always knew I was safe if I woke in the middle of the night and heard his deep breathing.

I was finally done kneading and now it had to rise another hour. I made us some lunch and went to bring Riley his by the woodpile he was gradually accumulating.

"Wow, you really have been busy." I handed him his lunch of canned ham and pickled beets.

"Where's my bread?"

"Ha Ha You're *so* funny. Patience, my darlin', patience. The best things come to those who wait."

"You mean like you?" He gave me a peck on the nose and this time I kissed him back, sweat and all.

"Right back at ya'." We sat then and ate our lunch, listening to the dragonflies whirring around us, doing their job and eating mosquitoes. Those darn mosquitoes were probably the only thing not pleasurable about this place. They always found their way into our room and we would spend many a night fumbling to light a candle, trying to find the little bugger that disturbed our sleep with it's highly annoying whine. We had bites all over us and we tried to keep the scratching down to a minimum by soaking them in vinegar every night, a trick Riley had learned which really worked. We always laughed at how we smelled like pickles for a while afterwards.

Lunch finished, I asked Riley to start a fire to cook my bread with. I had wanted to make it in the wood stove but that would heat up the cabin too much, so I would try it on the fire outside instead. With the heat from the day the bread had risen nicely and now I just had to wait until the fire had died down to perfect coals.

I checked on our clothes. The sun and the breeze had dried them quickly. I folded up our small fashion line and headed back to check on the fire. It looked good so I got my pan of bread. We put it on the grill and I went to wash up the dishes from lunch while it cooked. I didn't know how long it would take over the fire in comparison to an actual oven so I was just going to keep checking it. Finally, when I stuck a long stick in it, the stick came out clean and I removed it with a pair of old work gloves the Cabin Couple had kicking around. I didn't think I could wait for supper and as I was about to call Riley to come try a piece, he appeared grinning.

"Could smell it all the way over there. That would taste good with some of the strawberry jam."

"You read my mind." The instant I turned it upside down to get it out of the pan and it fell with a hard thud on the counter, I knew it wasn't going to be as I had imagined. As I cut into it and had to actually saw it like you would a piece of cardboard, I felt like crying. Not only was I disappointed, but also I felt like an idiot in the kitchen. I wanted to make something nice for us and besides it was a lot of damn work. Riley took a piece slathered it in jam and gobbled it down like it was the best thing ever. With his mouth full he mumbled,

"Best bread I ever had." I bit into mine and it was drier than the Sahara and heavy like a stone. I kissed him.

"I do love you, you big liar."

"Seriously, it's not that bad. Try it with lots of jam." I laughed and the tears disappeared. I wasn't giving up. I would try again and again until I got what I wanted.

We did end up finishing that whole loaf, but we used up a lot of jam. That's when I got my next idea. I would try my hand at jam. Between the raspberries, blueberries and the small strawberries I should be able to come up with at least a few jars. Once again I referred to the recipe book. Since the Cabin Couple seemed to do a lot of canning they had everything I needed. I pictured what their garden must have looked like when it was producing. I wished we would have got here sooner in the year to plant a crop of our own, now it was too late in the season to produce anything.

I gathered up everything I would need and got to work. Then I got Riley to make a fire again and I boiled all my fruit in a big pot adding the sugar as directed. I went back inside and got my jars ready and hauled another pot with water to the fire. Once the berries started to thicken, I ladled them into the jars and sealed them. I put them in the big pot of water and let them boil. This time my experiment worked and our jam was really good. It made up for the bread incident.

Riley was creating quite a big pile of wood, but the first few nights he had blisters on his hands and his shoulders were pretty sore. We took turns massaging our sore shoulders. He made fun of mine since they were only from kneading bread.

The heat didn't seem to be letting up and the cabin at night was no longer cooling off. We decided to pack up the tent and sleeping bags and head to our original little island. It was nice to be back there and to look at the cabin from a different perspective. I didn't look at it anymore as something belonging to someone else. I thought of it as our home. I also didn't picture the Cabin Couple going about their daily routines, I pictured us.

We set up the tent and this time I had a little better idea of what I was doing. Riley built a fire and we sat by the shore with our fishing lines in the water trying to catch our dinner. This time I was the lucky one and I was overjoyed that it was a nice sized fish. It seemed to taste even better.

We watched our beaver family and this night they seemed to be all caught up in their work because they were more intent on playing. They swam and splashed and just seemed to be having a great time. The full moon had come around again and we decided to take a midnight swim. It felt so cool and refreshing after the long hot day. We dried off and lay outside on top of our sleeping bags, enjoying the night air on our skin.

"I never thought we would be here again. I thought that trip here was our last day together." I voiced my thoughts out loud.

"Really? Why?" Now I was regretting speaking out loud because my answer would include his brother whom we seemed to avoid bringing up. But I couldn't' t think of any other response.

"I honestly thought once Byron got the money for me or if he didn't get the money for me he would get rid of me." There was a long pause and I was so sorry for speaking.

"Did you really think I would let him do that?" It was my turn to pause. I didn't know how to answer that.

"I really didn't know how much control you had over him. It seemed he ran the show and made most of the decisions."

"Regardless if I had fallen in love with you or not, I would not let him hurt anyone." After he spoke, he realized what he said and rolled over to face me.

"But I did, didn't I? I did let him hurt you? You had every reason to doubt me. He would have killed you if you hadn't fallen. I would have showed up too late. My god, I came so close to losing you. How could I have let it get that far?" I felt him wanting to pull away out of guilt, but I didn't let him. I drew him near.

"You tried. You did come back for me. You did save me. Here I am, completely healed and alive. You only went along with the kidnapping in order to help your brother, your heart was in the right place. You had no intention of ever hurting me. Everything is meant to happen for a reason and if you hadn't kidnapped me, our paths would never have crossed again and we wouldn't be here today. We just have to do everything the hard way." I could almost feel his smile in the dark.

"I can't believe how much I love you."

"Let me show you how much I love you." We dragged our sleeping bags back inside and our cool tent became steamy.

***

On one of our tours around the cabin, we ventured through the garden and to our surprise what we thought was a vegetable cemetery was actually completely utterly alive and growing like crazy. We tried to think of how this could have happened. We figured when the 'Cabin Couple' came out at the beginning of the summer they planted their garden. This made it even stranger that they'd left and hadn't been back. It could only mean one of two things, that something happened that meant they had to leave in haste and wouldn't be back. Or they planned to leave and would be back. The latter one would be difficult to explain as to why we were there and eating all their food.

We had thought of that before, but we still didn't feel guilty or that we needed to rush off. For some reason everything felt right for the first time in our lives and we decided if they came we would cross that bridge when we came to it.

In the meantime, we had struck gold in the garden. There were beans growing and small green tomatoes everywhere.

This was just the taller plants that we could see. We needed to do a lot of weeding to see what was all in there. We tried to do it early in the morning before it got too hot. It was much more difficult than we thought. It was hard on the knees and the back. We started with a couple of hours in the morning and then went back to it after supper. It took us two days at this pace to untangle the good growth from the bad. I'm sure along the way we pulled some good as well. Neither one of us really had a clue as to what the difference was. Some had blossoms on them so it was easier to tell. Also the planted stuff seemed to have some row design to it, while the weeds were everywhere. We had some beets already growing and small cucumbers. There was carrots, peppers, dill and onions. There were tons of lettuce, but our most exciting find was potatoes. They would be a great addition to our meals.

For the next few nights after our discovery, I read and reread the canning books and recipes. Every morning I would take a tour of the garden and report the progress back to Riley. He was amused with my excitement. I couldn't wait for things to grow and in a large enough amount to create things.

We were eating fresh lettuce and beans with supper. We cut off the tops of the onions and some dill and wrapped them with our fish. Every night we felt we were at a fine restaurant. We were having so much fun coming up with new combinations. I had finally mastered the bread making and had even ventured out to make buns. I figured out just the right amount of time over an open fire so as not to have concrete. There wasn't a night that Riley didn't catch a fish. We were pretty proud of ourselves.

Riley and I would pick beans side by side and then take them by the lake to clean and cut them up. I would look over at him and just smile. I loved watching him in peace in that garden or by the quiet of the lake. I wanted him to be happy and to feel loved and safe all the time. Every once in a while he would get me to stop what I was doing and he would just take me in his arms to just sit. I would lean my head back on his strong chest and feel his breath on the top of my head. We didn't say a lot during these times. He would give me a kiss now and then and we would just enjoy the moment. I could feel his love for me coming through in waves and it was hard to believe we were there, together.

"Sometimes, I still can't believe you're here with me." Riley professed during one of these moments.

"You kidnapped me remember?" This had become an ongoing joke that eased the tension and guilt of the circumstances involved in our meeting. It always brought a laugh.

"I mean, I look over at you. You're an educated, beautiful woman and I can't believe you haven't been ever seriously involved with someone. You shouldn't be here. You should be living with some guy who goes to medical or law school."

"I wasn't meant for anyone but you. I had been waiting for just the right one, I just didn't know it. I was never interested in all the bullshit that went along with dating. I was too busy studying. You guys are all about drinking and partying and getting laid. Besides I could say the same to you. You could have picked up a Bonnie to go along with you as Clyde somewhere along the way."

"Hmmm...I could say the same thing. All the Bonnies out there just wanted to drink, party and get laid. As if you haven't noticed I'm a bit different. I'm happy in the bush. My one and only love until you was nature."

"Well, I feel pretty honoured to be in such good company."

"You should be." He took my face in his hands and whispered, "You could take the most gorgeous sunset, the haunting call of the loon, the iridescence of the dragonfly, the bright wings of a butterfly and the gentleness of a baby fawn and put them all in a bottle and they would still pale in comparison to you."

"I didn't realize you were such a poet. That was beautiful, *you* are beautiful. Thank you." I kissed him and went to get a snack of bread and jam. Sometimes I was overwhelmed by his attention and compliments. I was not used to them, but I was smiling and feeling like a princess as I walked away.

***

As we sat on our porch every night admiring the view, there was one lone mountain that centered itself in our scenery.

"It looks just massive." I commented one night.

"That's Shas Mountain and, actually not as big as it looks. I mean it is big, but we could walk up there no problem."

"You're joking! We would never make it up there. Okay, let me rephrase that, *I* would never make it up there. Besides there is still snow at the top!"

"I betcha you could. We would just have to take our time, but I think we could still do it in a day. Wouldn't that snow feel good right about now?" That I could picture, and it was very appealing.

" I'd love to try. That would be an amazing view from up there."

"Are you feeling up to it?"

"I've never felt better." I knew what he meant. Ever since the fall, he was always checking in with me to make sure I didn't have any injuries that either weren't healing or some new pain that was a reaction to an unhealed wound. I reassured him I was fine.

"Let's go tomorrow." I was eager to try, but a bit nervous about not succeeding. Riley hugged me,

"We'll give it a try and see how we feel as we go up. If it's too much, we can always try again." He always knew the right thing to say to make me feel better.

Early the next morning, the weather was in our favour and didn't feel as hot as it had been the previous few mornings. We packed a lunch and settled on some thermoses to bring water. Riley carried the backpack and we set off in the canoe. We would have to paddle across the lake and look for a trail-head. Riley had never been up the mountain before, but when we paddled the lake, he saw what might have been the start of the trail. We headed that way. Sure enough as we pulled the canoe up, we could see a distinct path that led up the mountain. We hid our canoe in the bushes and headed down the brushy route.

"Let's hope this is it and not just an animal trail." In reality it was an animal trail, it was not one that had been carved out by people, but it would lead us up.

At first the trail was pretty flat but soon enough it started to incline drastically. It switch backed constantly and we had to stop many times, we were so winded. We couldn't stop for long as there was one thing we didn't account for. The mosquitoes. They were horrendous here and they followed us all the way. We had brought hoodies just in case it was cool at the top and we put them on even though we were far from cold. We tightened the hoods as tight as they would go to keep the bugs out of our ears.

This alone should have made us give up, but there were a few things Riley and I had in common. We were both stubborn, competitive and determined to finish what we started. We weren't going to let these pests bully us into quitting. We kept pushing forward.

We were surrounded by trees and forest and could not get a real sense of how far up we were. Not that we wanted to stop for long to see anyways. After about two hours of a steep incline I had to take a break. I ignored the mosquitoes and took a long cold drink of water. It felt good on my dry, scratchy throat. My calves and quads were burning. Riley came and sat beside me. I couldn't help but laugh. He looked hilarious with his hood cinched so tight around his face.

"You shouldn't laugh, it's a mirror image there princess." He laughed with me and we sat for a few minutes longer before the bugs chased us away.

I let my mind wander to distract it from the pain. How long would we stay at the cabin? I knew we needed to leave before it started to get too cold, but I was not looking forward to going. How would we survive financially? I knew I could find a job and could probably make enough money to support us, but I knew this wouldn't sit well with Riley. He would want to contribute. But in order for him to work he needed to resurface in the world on paper. What would happen then? Would Byron find us? Did he have a record or a warrant out for any of his past crimes? I couldn't imagine going back and then losing him. I loved what we had here. Could we stay here longer? Long enough for Byron to give up on us?

Just then a view peeked through the trees. It was glorious and all bugs were momentarily forgotten.

"Wow! That's amazing." We could see even further than from his lookout. The landscape was filled with trees and dotted with many lakes. There were also more mountains that we couldn't see from our little porch below. But we weren't at the top yet, and by looking up we still had quite a ways to go.

"Still up for it?" My legs were letting up a bit. It was my lungs that were on fire now, but I felt alive and exhilarated. That view was just a tease. I wanted to see more.

"Yup, race you to the top!" Riley laughed and we walked hand in hand for a bit until the path was so narrow it became impossible. Single file, we continued on.

The view disappeared again, but we could now see where the tree line ended and a rocky path began. There were a lot of small rocks so we had to watch our footing. It was like mini avalanches, set off by each step. A few times I slid quite a ways before I either caught a root growing out of the ground or Riley reached out a hand. We could see the top now and it looked like one big mammoth rock. I could barely breathe once we reached it, but I was so elated to be there.

"I can't believe we just did that! Incredible! Look at the view, now that was worth every ache." We could see snow in patches all around us. Now we could also not only see what we had gotten a glimpse of about an hour and a half ago, but we got to see everything at 360 degrees. It was so beautiful to see in every direction. You wouldn't think there could be so many different shades of green and blue. Some of the lakes were that gorgeous aqua colour that almost doesn't look real in nature and then there were lakes that were so dark, you can only imagine their depth.

We got out our lunch and even though we were now above the tree line and the temperature had dropped quite a bit, it didn't take long for the mosquitoes to find us. I looked over at Riley eating his sandwich and could see his back was covered. He looked like he had fur, but it was moving. We still took our time. We were in no rush to hike all the way back down. It had taken us about four hours to get up there. There was a mossy area just below the rock and we lay down there to rest. We took off our hoodies and then our t-shirts. We put our hoodies back on, cinched them up and used our shirts to cover our faces as we lay down in the soft moss. We tried to ignore the incessant whining.

The cool air had a different scent than down below. More like what an ice cube tray would smell like if it was infused with a touch of pine. It was refreshing. Despite the mosquitoes, we both dozed off for a bit, which I'm sure we would pay for later in baths of vinegar.

"Going down always seems to be easier and faster." Riley encouraged me. I had my doubts, but I was still feeling high from our achievement.

He was right though and we could almost keep ahead of the swarm following us. Man, they didn't give up either. When we saw the bottom, it was almost a relief. We hadn't made many stops on the way down, we just wanted to get away from the bugs now. My feet barely reached the bottom and I was stripping down and jumping in the lake. The bug bites were driving me crazy and I was drenched in sweat. The water felt glorious and Riley quickly joined me.

"That feels so good! Thank you for convincing me to try. I can't believe I did that." He swam closer so that our bodies were touching.

"I can. I believe you can do anything. I'm pretty proud of you Miss Jady." He kissed my lips, probably the only part of me without a bite.

"Thanks, I'm pretty proud of me too." I smiled and kissed him back. We wound our arms around each other, treading like mad to keep our heads above water. We stayed that way for a bit, until the exhaustion of our day's feat caught up to us and we headed back to our little cabin to make supper. We would sleep well tonight.

***

The next day I thought I was sore, but it was the day after that really made me cry uncle. It hurt to walk, I had huge blisters on the heels of my feet. It especially hurt to sit down, my quads were screaming. I took it easy and Riley babied me for two days. While I sat on the porch, Riley brought us our coffee. He made our breakfast and then we went down to the lake and I spent the morning relaxing, my feet soaking in the water. Riley kept checking in on me as he went about cutting more wood and doing our berry walk to see if we had any more fruit on our island. He brought me a bowl of what he had picked and one of the fluff fiction books I hadn't read yet. He joined me for a swim. The cool water felt good on my sore and aching body. Of course he felt minimal pain, he was in much better shape than I was.

As I lay there enjoying being pampered, I couldn't help but think how lucky I was in an ironic sort of way. I had found my soul mate and now we were marooned on our own little island of paradise because of a few very traumatic and tragic events. How do things work that way? Why was I meant to have such a crappy childhood? Was it my bitter, mistrustful character which left me alone for my life up to now, that made me appreciate what I found all that much more? How was it in such a short period of time that I was able to trust and fall in love with this man? I didn't have all the answers, but I knew that I loved and trusted Riley more than anyone or anything. I was certain of it.

The sound of snapping sticks broke my thoughts and I shaded my eyes to see my handsome knight bringing me lunch.

"I was just thinking about you." I smiled and pulled him down for a kiss.

"Hmmm...I'm always thinking of you." Riley sat down beside me and we ate our lunch together.

"I have a surprise for you. Close your eyes and open your hand." I closed my eyes but was reluctant to open my hand.

"You're not going to put some slimy, crawly thing in my hand are you?" I might've trusted him, but I had also come to know him as quite a prankster.

"Nope, just open your hand."

"Okay, but I'm warning you, if it is a bug I'm throwing it at you." I felt a couple of hard things drop in my hand.

"I think they're a bit old, but they will probably taste good anyways. Okay, open your eyes." When I did I was looking at two black jujubes and my eyes teared up. I curled my fingers over them and the tears fell harder. Riley was quickly by my side, sensing a feeling stronger than happiness at the sight of candy.

"Hey, what is it?" I held up my other hand, signaling for him to give me a minute. I rested my head on his shoulder and just let the tears fall. Where the grief came from, I didn't know. I didn't know if I had ever let myself really feel anything after my mom had died. I was too busy feeling anger. Now that I was experiencing love, it seemed to have opened the gates to other emotions as well. After awhile, I had myself composed enough to talk.

"My mom and I had a thing about black jujubes. We both loved them and would make a game of fighting over them." I uncurled my fingers and looked at the candy now. They did seem very old and hard. I felt like I couldn't eat them, that they were the last jujubes on earth and I would need them to be my last one reminder of my mom. Feeling silly, I popped one in my mouth. It took forever to even get it going.

"Tell me about her." I leaned back and rested my head on Riley's chest and closed my eyes, letting the licorice taste call up my mom's face.

"She was beautiful. I could see what my father saw in her and why he married her, although he denies this. She grew up in a really small town and was raised on a farm. But being the only child and a girl at that, her father saw no use for having her take over the family homestead. So they raised all the money they could, which took a lot of work for them, and sent her off to college. She was going to be a teacher and come back and work in their town, but she met my father and he whisked her away marrying her before she finished. Now that I say it out loud, I wonder if that was intentional. He didn't want her to be too smart and he needed her to be dependent on him for money." I pushed away the anger that was rising and thought again of my mom.

"That was about as much as she shared with me about her past. She didn't share a lot of things with me, but I pieced many things together over the years by overhearing her conversations with friends. It seems, their honeymoon didn't last very long. After he whisked her away from the farm and to his house in the city, she learned very quickly that he was never home and that she was expected to keep the house and work in the one drugstore he had running back then. The ironic thing was she never saw him there either. It was at this time he had his brainstorm to open up stores all across the country and he was busy running around making the arrangements. I think my mom would have been okay with this if when he came home, he was nice to her. But he was only nice long enough to get her in bed hoping to make a baby and then each time they didn't succeed he would be cold and indifferent until the next attempt. Mom told me she so badly wanted to go back home, but her parents had poured all their life savings into her schooling and she had just thrown it away for my father. She was ashamed to go back.

Finally, after over a year of trying, she became pregnant and he tried to be nice at first, but when even that was too much for him, he just bought her things and hired more servants to look after the house and her. His business was taking off and he was starting to do really well with his chain of drugstores. I think my mom got hooked on this new life and saw it as her pay off for sticking with him. Then it all came to a crashing halt when I was born and I wasn't the boy he so badly wanted. He still paid for her to continue living her life, but he had given up trying to have a baby with my mom and turned his attentions elsewhere." I sighed as I thought of how much this must have pained my mom. Now knowing what it felt to love someone, I can't imagine what it would feel like to be hurt by that same person. Riley wrapped his arms around me tighter and gave me a squeeze.

"She really tried not to let what was going on with father effect me and my life. She made every birthday party special. She would always make my cake and not let the staff make it. My favourite was a white cake with strawberry Jell-O and whipped cream for filling and icing. Whenever she made it there would always be leftover topping and she would save it for me in a bowl that I would eat all on it's own. It's funny, even then I wasn't that great at making friends, but every year as my birthday approached I would have many of them. My mom threw the best parties and everyone wanted an invite.

She bought me anything I wanted, but I enjoyed the time she spent with me more. She took me to movies and we would go shopping and out to eat. She didn't have a lot of friends either, she really didn't fit into the high society country clubs my father started going to and she didn't fit into the suburbia stay-at-home mom groups. I was her friend and she talked to me like a friend and not a daughter, but I was happy to be there for her. I faked being sick quite often especially when she looked like she was feeling blue. I don't know when it happened, but somewhere along the line we switched roles and I started taking care of her. The parties became less extravagant and the user friends died off. We didn't spend time together out, but it became more watching TV, ordering out and sitting on the couch. She loved Chinese food and old movies. Her favourite was East of Eden with James Dean. I've watched that movie more times than I care to count. I started to read books on the couch beside her, not wanting to see the movie again, but wanting to be close to her. Then I was sent away to school when I was twelve and while I was immersed in my studies, she slowly gave up, gave in, and cancer found a home." I took a deep breath and looked silently at the single old jujube. I curled my fingers back around it protectively and decided I wasn't going to eat it.

***

There wasn't a current calendar in the cabin, but we did find a pocket one that had the five-year at a glance page. We were able to mark off the days and try to keep track of our time that way. Although we were in paradise and it felt like one long vacation where days, minutes, and seconds hardly mattered, we felt we needed to keep one foot in real time.

We had been on our little island a little more than seven weeks and it was nearing the end of August. We had been so busy the last couple of weeks that the days were not only flying, but we were falling into bed early and exhausted. The garden was growing so fast that between the daily picking, cleaning, cooking and canning that was almost enough in itself to take up our days. Then, as if in competition with the vegetables, the berries were so ripe, they fell off the stem if you just brushed up against them. Raspberries, strawberries and blueberries galore. It was more then we could eat daily and it seemed a shame to put them to waste so we canned them too.

When I had first seen all the canning supplies the Cabin Couple had, I assumed they had gone a bit overboard on the quantity of things. I had assumed incorrectly. I was using it all and it made me feel good to replenish what we had eaten.

Riley continued to cut wood since we were going through quite a bit cooking our harvests. He was getting a very good stockpile built up and it just became part of his daily routine to cut wood for a few hours while I canned. When he was done, he always came and helped me. We had our own little assembly line going and it felt good to be working side by side.

Riley also stumbled upon some unopened, very new looking paint cans in the shed. When we pried them open we could see they were the colour the cabin would have been in its infancy. We put the lids back on and mulled over the idea for a few days. They obviously had planned to paint and then didn't. So it came up again that something happened to prevent them from coming back to finish the plans they had begun. We didn't want to intrude any further than we already had, but we also thought it would be a nice gesture to paint it for them. Would they appreciate this?

We finally decided, who wouldn't want help painting their place? It's a lot of work for anyone never mind people who were older. So we took advantage of the awesome summer we were having and started a project that became much bigger than we anticipated. First we looked at the amount of sandpaper they had, which wasn't all that much, so we decided just to sand the really rough spots out and this alone took quite a few days and used up all the sandpaper we had.

Now I had never painted before, but Riley had painted many a house and gave me lessons. We cut in all the window and doorframes. Even with the rollers that the cabin people had obviously bought for this reason, it was a hard job and we really wanted to take our time and make sure it was done right. I really got into it and enjoyed it initially, but after a few days and super sore shoulders from having to hold the roller above my head for so long I was not as enthusiastic. Then just when I thought I couldn't do it another day, my back and shoulders got used to what I was asking of them and it became easier. The difficult part was that it was all-wooden siding, which meant you could not just roll straight everywhere, you had to do each and every panel individually. We also did the shed and the outhouse. When we had finished one coat of green on the main parts, we stood back and admired our work. It looked amazing and then we couldn't wait for it to dry so we could paint the red trim.

When that was done a few days later, we were proud of our accomplishments and thought that even if the 'Cabin Couple' were furious over our "summer rental", they couldn't possibly be angry at our paint job. It was incredibly satisfying to look at a cupboard full of food that you yourself put there, to see the stack of wood that was also self-created and to now see the cabin newly dressed and looking so fine by our own hands.

I could imagine what it must have looked like when they first built it or bought it. I was even more in love with it than when I had seen it initially. I also felt even more possessive over our temporary home and found myself sad at the thought that we would need to leave it. I knew all along that this would be the case at some point but I always tried to ignore these thoughts. Again I wanted to pretend this was our life, our home and we didn't need to go anywhere. But as we crossed off the days and felt summer coming to a close, we knew without having to speak it aloud that we had some decisions to make and we needed to make them before it started to get cold. Each night as I snuggled up to a very warm Riley, the frosty nights that would soon be on our doorstep were the furthest thing from our minds.

***

As we made our daily tour of our island, we could see nature's signals that summer was ending. The berries were dwindling too less than a quarter pail every few days. The leaves up high were still very green but the growth near the ground was already glowing red and orange. The mornings and nights were getting cooler and the garden was slowly closing shop. The cucumbers and beets were done and tomatoes, dwindled to about one a day to eat fresh with our meals. Beans and carrots were oblivious to the colder temperatures and we were still harvesting buckets of these daily, eating as much as we could, since the canning supplies were done. The potatoes were also cold weather crops and we were still finding plenty.

The smells in the air were also changing. It was getting cleaner and crisper. It was not only what you could smell, like the leaves slowly turning, but it was the smells that were missing that were more evident. The sweet smell of the clover and the almost medicinal one of yarrow were gone. It's funny how a few weeks ago I would never had known what smells I was missing out on and now they were completely familiar to me.

We had been reading a book that the Cabin Couple had on herbs and natural remedies. Red clover and yarrow tea were good for many things so we cut plants and dried them. There were also rose hips everywhere, which were packed with vitamin C but these, according to the book, could not be harvested until after the first frost.

It was the rose hips that made me open the conversation. As much as I wanted to put it off, I wanted to know what our plans were. We were sitting by the lake cleaning the endless beans and carrots. I looked around at the supply of natural vitamin C and suddenly wanted to be there for first frost, to see all the leaves turn colours and to watch the geese fly overhead. I had stopped cleaning and was staring at the rose hips when Riley spoke,

"What do you think about staying a little longer?" I smiled and hugged him close, spilling the beans and carrots that were in a bowl on his lap.

"Okay! Does that mean you agree?" I laughed and nodded.

"We have plenty of food again and you have cut enough wood to get us through a few cold nights." It was his turn to laugh. He knew I was teasing him; he had cut a mountain of the stuff.

"Let's give it at least until mid-October and talk about it again." I hugged him again and got excited about seeing fall on our island.

"Let's take a break, Miss Gardener and go for a canoe ride."

"Sounds good to me." I put down the bowl and the paring knife and shook off all the ends of beans and carrots that had collected in my lap. I went back to the cabin and grabbed a jacket. The hot summer days were gone and the air on the lake was cool.

Once we were out on the water though, the sun warmed us up and it was calm and clear. We canoed around for a while, always finding new shores tucked behind hidden islands that you couldn't tell were islands until you got close and saw the water surrounding it. The water was getting lower this time of year and we couldn't go as close to shore as we had done on previous canoe trips. We stopped to watch a family of otters play. They were so busy splashing around that initially they didn't notice us and then suddenly they turned and looked our way and disappeared. One brave little one poked his head up one more time to give us a last glance before he was gone too.

We paddled to another spot and Riley threw over his make-shift anchor, which was a rope tied tightly to a large rock. We both fished for awhile and then after I caught one I laid back in the canoe and let the warm sun and the sound of the waves lapping up against the canoe lull me into an afternoon nap.

When I opened my eyes again it wasn't that much later, but it was a large black cloud that had moved over the sun that caused me to wake up and feel cold. Riley had caught our supper and was just pulling up our anchor.

"I think we're going to get a nasty storm tonight." I looked around me at the black clouds rolling in. The distant sound of thunder backed up his theory and we paddled back home, hoping to get there before the rain fell.

The first drops hit just as we pulled up the canoe and by the time we closed the door behind us, the wind was howling and the rain was pelting our skin. We dried off and actually built our first fire in the stove. We made our supper there that night and even made two mugs of hot chocolate to get rid of the chills that the rain had brought.

When we were done, we cozied up on the couch with a homemade blanket and watched the show. The lightning flashed right overhead and the thunder shook the small cabin. It was scary and exhilarating at the same time. The rain poured down and we discovered a few leaks in the old roof that we didn't find in previous rains. This one was coming down hard. We placed pails or bowls under the leaks, but they were slow and nothing that concerned us too much. It was dry in our room, which was comforting.

It was nice to be inside, warm and safe, cuddled up with Riley and enjoying one of the last storms of the summer. The wind howled all around us and every once in a while you could hear some crashing and cracking and we hoped we would not see a tree poking through our roof any time soon.

Luckily enough, the wind died down when we went to bed and the lightning could no longer be seen out the window. The thunder was getting farther and farther, only the rain remained and it accompanied us into our dreams.

***

I was getting pretty good at the bread making thing. I was now adding dried berries to it and it made it even better. We had been busy all day with our usual routines, cleaning and preparing our harvests and Riley obsessively cutting wood for an hour. I had made bread to go with supper and we were just sitting down to eat when we heard a rattle by the kitchen window. It was followed by a loud crash as something on the porch got knocked over. Moving fast, Riley went and pulled something from under the cot. It was a rifle that I hadn't seen before. I don't know what shocked me more, the sounds coming from outside or the fact that Riley had a gun hidden in the cabin all this time and I had been completely unaware.

Riley put his finger to his lips and crept towards the kitchen window. He hopped up on the counter and slowly peered over. I backed away and went to look out our bedroom window to see if I could see anything out there. As I was peeking around with my heart beating fast, two fat paws with long claws clamped themselves on the screen and there, doing a chin-up, was a bear. I screamed and backed away almost falling over my own feet in my rush.

"Riley!" The bear and the paws were already gone by the time Riley ran into the room. I would have thought I imagined it except for the long claw rips in the screen where he had been.

"What do we do?" I knew this was a silly question, but I had to ask anyways. A loud noise came again at the living room window and we ran over there. Once again, we looked out the window and the bear was just backing down.

"He's pacing the cabin, trying to find a way in."

"Our windows and doors are not that secure. He will find a way eventually." I was scared, but I also didn't necessarily want the bear dead.

"Can you just scare it away?" Riley smiled at my empathy and went to look out the window again. Nothing. We waited for five, ten minutes and could hear no more noises. It was getting dark out and it was harder to see.

"Maybe it's gone." I whispered.

"I doubt it." Riley whispered back.

"All we have is the screen door at the kitchen entrance right now. I didn't shut the wood door." It was now dark enough that we would need to light a candle in order to move around. Riley slowly felt around and found our candle and matches that were on the kitchen table. He lit the match and as the candle-light filled the room I screamed again. The bear was standing full length at the screen door looking in. I had no doubt in my mind now what to do.

"It's okay if you shoot it now." I was whispering again as if the bear would understand me and it would make him angry. But he just stood there for a bit and then it started to tear at the screen trying to get in. Just as Riley was taking aim to shoot it through the door it went back on all fours and ambled away. We could hear the porch furniture being moved around again.

"It's going back to the kitchen window. Cover your ears." Riley went back and crept up on the counter. He slowly unwound the crank on the kitchen window and pointed the gun down. I quickly covered my ears just in time to feel the floor tremble beneath me.

I was crouched with my hands over my ears and my eyes pinched shut when Riley's touch on my shoulder made me jump.

"It's okay now, I got him." Riley was grinning like a proud hunter at first but when we went outside to see the bear up close he looked a bit sad.

"He was a young one. I'm sorry little fellow."

"Was there anything else we could have done?"

"I could have fired a shot to scare it off, but now that it found us it would have come back again and again until it found a way in."

I looked at this bear, which didn't look young at all to me. He looked huge and scary.

I helped Riley drag him away from the porch and he got one of his sharp knives and skinned it. I couldn't get over the extremely large paws. They made me sad as I held them though. They were such teddy bear paws. They didn't seem real; it was like a storybook bear.

"Now what are we going to do with it?"

"Eat it." Riley replied nonchalantly. I didn't even think of that. Trying to hide my revulsion, I asked,

"You can eat bear?" I could see Riley was trying just as hard to hide a smile.

"Of course, they taste really good actually. We'll have to eat it tomorrow since we don't have a fridge to keep it cool. We'll put some meat in bags and put them in the water to keep them cool for now. I think it's time I built a smoke shack and then I can smoke the rest of the meat."

I wanted to be open to trying new things, but I wouldn't be able to eat this bear if I was around it much longer. I was over thinking the whole thing and pretty soon he would be Winnie or something.

"I don't think I can help you cut it up. Are you okay doing it on your own?" This time Riley didn't even try to hide his grin,

"No problem princess. C'mere." I leaned in and he gave me a kiss.

"What can I bring you?"

"A cup of coffee and all the candles we have." I gave the bear one last tender pat and in my head, apologized.

"I guess your bread smelled good enough to swim across the lake for." I smiled and gave Riley a quick kiss on the forehead and went to make him some coffee to help him with his task that would take him most of the night.

I heard him come to bed early in the morning and I think I said something, but I was pretty tired. I do remember he brought a cool breeze into the bed and I cuddled up close to share my warmth.

When I got up in the morning I tried to be quiet and leave him to sleep for a while. I went out and gathered some wood a bit more cautiously then I had previous to our bear visit. It was hard to believe it wasn't a dream, but the large bear fur hanging over the trees told me it was very real. Seeing the skin made me hurry, and combined with the morning chill, I had the shakes.

I gathered everything in the stove and within a few minutes had a nice fire going. I stood by the open door of the stove for a bit, rotating like a chicken on a spit, to get the warmth back into my body. Once I felt like my blood was flowing again I shut the door, grabbed our tin kettle and headed down to the lake. While getting water my mind drifted back again to the previous night. I was filled with mixed feelings. The experience was scary and yet I felt so proud to have Riley there to protect me. He never hesitated; he took command and knew exactly what to do. Yet the fact that he had a gun hidden in the cabin made me wonder. Then when I looked at the whole thing from a distance I wanted to laugh.

I brought the water back to the cabin and put it on the stove. I mixed up a batch of bannock and threw in some blueberries. The smell of it frying in the pan roused Riley from his slumber.

"What are you doing up? You've hardly slept." He looked so young and adorable with his hair all standing up and lines still all over his face. He came over and gave me a kiss almost leaning all his weight on me in his sleepiness.

"I'm up for the same reason the bear swam across the lake. The smell of your cooking. I'm going to go wash up."

"I'll make coffee and meet you on the porch." I flipped the bannock, a perfect golden disc dotted with blue. The water was boiling and I grabbed a blue speckled tin cup. It hadn't taken us long, we had learned to appreciate coffee black just to make our sugar last longer. When the bannock was done I cut it in half and put it on the tin plates that matched the cups. I brought the coffee out first and placed it on the wobbly table on the porch, Riley still not there. When I returned with warm bannock, he was sitting on the wobbly chair with his eyes closed smelling his coffee. Nothing was like the first cup of the day.

I waited until he had finished eating and then I asked him my burning question,

"What's up with the gun?" Riley looked surprised with the question, which actually surprised me in turn.

"What do you mean?"

"Why didn't you tell me there was a gun in the cabin?" His expression turned sheepish.

"Oh, well to be honest, initially I didn't tell you because I thought it would make you stress about Byron. But then I forgot all about it. I actually have it because I always have it. You need to remember that I'm not only a hunter, but I know animals and they're unpredictable and can be very dangerous. You should never be out in the woods without something to protect you. Last night was a perfect example." The answer was so logical it took me off guard. Why did I think it would be something more sinister than that? Why do I always think the worst of people? Even Riley whom I love and has made it very obvious he loves me and can be trusted? It reminded me that I couldn't expect to undo in a month what took years to do.

"Thank you. For being honest and for taking care of the bear last night. I really didn't even think a bear would do that. I was stupidly naive to think we were completely safe here on our island."

"No matter where you are in these woods, you are never safe from the creatures." He came over and scooped me up from my chair and started kissing my neck.

"You're especially not safe from this creature." I ran my fingers through his growing hair.

"This hairy creature I can deal with." Riley carried me back in the bedroom and we didn't get back up until lunch.

***

The next few days we were occupied with making the smoke shack. I had no idea what exactly a smoke shack was, but Riley explained it to me. He said they were used long ago when they had no fridges and they had to find a way to store their meat for the duration of the long winter. He told me there are still First Nations people that cure their meat this way.

We basically made a shack using the wood cut from the bush around us. The Cabin Couple did have a pail of nails, so that made the task easier. We made a fire pit in the middle and then Riley got to work making drying racks. This was the tedious and time-consuming task. When he was done it looked like a rustic place to hang clothes to dry. I was impressed, but I would be even more impressed when I had dried meat that tasted good. I didn't quite believe in this part of the process, but so far everything Riley told me turned out true so I had no real reason to doubt him.

Tonight we were going to try the fresh bear meat, done Riley style. He spent the entire morning cutting up most of the meat in long strips and these he put on the racks in the smoke shack. He built a big fire and then added wet wood. This made more smoke then fire and had a slow burn. Then he took the remaining meat and tossed it in the breadcrumbs I had made him from the ends of all our homemade bread. He put these pieces in a pan on the outside fire and cooked them until they were brown. Finally, he took it and wrapped it all in foil (we felt so privileged to have these luxuries, the Cabin Couple really did think of everything), put it in a pot, and again put it over the fire which had died down to small coals.

"Now, we just have to let it cook for a few hours." I was disappointed, I was dying to try it and a few hours felt like a lifetime. To distract me, Riley took me for our walk around the island. As I looked at the bushes stripped of their fruit and thought of the garden being emptied out, I wondered now what we were going to do with all our time. I loved the idea of staying here, but I had never thought of how we were going to spend our endless amount of time. I decided I was going to browse the Cabin Couple's collection of books tonight to see if I could come up with any ideas.

When we had done our rounds, I started my way down the path back to the cabin, but Riley stopped me.

"I have something in mind, but I need you to go down to the lake for awhile."

"Gee, I don't know. Hmmm, relax by the lake while you come up with a devious plot. I guess I can do that for you." I left him with a smile and made my way down to the lake. It was getting too cool out now for a swim, but it still felt good to walk close to the shore in bare feet. I loved the way the rocks and sand felt on my toes. Whenever I got tired of that, I went rock walking and tried to see how far I could make it around the island before I ran out of rocks that were above the water. A few weeks ago I couldn't make it very far, the water was so high, but now the water had dropped quite a bit and I found I could make it almost halfway around the island. I had to stop though, not because of submerged rocks, but there was a spot that didn't have any small rocks to choose from. It was one big massive rock that stuck out like a pictish standing stone in the middle of an ancient field of green.

When I made it back to where I had started, Riley was there waiting.

"You look like a little kid balancing and hopping along on those rocks."

"Are you done scheming?"

"Almost." He definitely had my curiosity. He sat down behind me on the shore and ran his fingers through my hair, which was also growing quite long. This was a wonderful habit of his and it kept all the tangles out.

"Well, I need to go check on supper. Stay here I'll be back." As he walked away I stared at his back, smiling. I caught myself and realized I had smiled more in the time I had known Riley than I had my whole lifetime. It was a great feeling. I went back to my rock hopping going the other way this time to see how far I could make it in that direction. I felt like a kid and it was also challenging. I could go further that way but this time I ran out of rocks. The water lapped up higher on this side. Hopping back I caught myself humming a tune, but couldn't place it.

This time when I got back Riley had a deck of cards and we played Crazy 8's. It seemed like summer camp for two sometimes. All the things I had missed out on as a kid I was enjoying now. Everything seemed backwards. I had so much responsibility and pressure growing up and needed to be more mature than anyone around me in order to cope with what life was dishing out. I didn't hang out with friends, go to summer camp, or have a first love or crush. Now I had no stress and I was hanging out with my first love, crush, and best friend all at the same time at the best summer camp ever. I shook my head at the craziness of it all.

Riley stood up and brushed off the sand and rocks from his clothes.

"Give me a few minutes and then come up." Even though there were no rocks for Riley, he practically hopped up the path in his excitement. It made me wonder all the more what he had planned.

I played a few rounds of solitaire, a game I knew really well, and then went up to the cabin trying not to run to see what was going on.

When I walked in the cabin, there were candles everywhere. He had them all lit and supper was laid out on the table. He had collected what flowers there were left and put them in a big container in the middle. Supper smelled fabulous. It tasted even better. I can't explain how bear meat tasted, but it melted in my mouth the way Riley cooked it. It was very rich and it was so tender. It wasn't like anything I had ever tasted. I knew it tasted like more. He had cooked up some of our potatoes with fresh dill from the garden and a big bowl of green beans and carrots. It was marvelous and I ate more than usual.

"Close your eyes."

"There's more?"

"Just close your eyes." I did and felt that now familiar smile creeping up. I heard him leave the room and then heard the outside door shut. Within seconds it opened and shut again.

"Okay open them." When I did I was more than surprised. In front of me was a large cake.

"Happy birthday." When I looked puzzled, Riley explained.

"I don't know when your birthday actually is, but I know I missed it. In fact I can bet it has been missed for many years and I wanted to make this one special. We can celebrate it now and when it's your actual one, which is...?"

"April...April 24th." I was so touched. Tears formed in my eyes at his thoughtfulness. I stood up, gave him a huge hug, and we just stood like that, neither one of us wanting to let go. I tucked my head into his chest and let the tears fall. He put his finger under my chin and lifted my head. He kissed my tears and then wiped them away with his thumbs.

"You don't need to cry. The cake won't taste that bad, I promise you. It's not like the favourite cake your mom used to make you but it *is* white and it *does* have strawberries in it." I kissed him and we enjoyed a big piece of cake.

"I won't even ask how you managed to pull this one off without eggs. It tastes amazing."

"That's not all. What's a birthday party without gifts." From under the table he pulled out a carving. It was rough looking, but it was more than obvious it was two swans and it was beautiful.

"You did this?" He nodded,

"I'll have to show you all the other practice ones. They don't even resemble swans, not even a chicken." I turned it over and over in my hands and was taken aback. It was really incredible that he had made this with his own hands. Well, Riley wouldn't be bored this fall, he had obviously found himself a hobby.

"I chose swans because they mate for life and I really wanted this gift to be special and to mean something. I don't want to just be a passing thing in your life. I don't know how we're going to pull it off, but I don't want to know life again without you in it." I put the gift down and crawled into his lap.

"I will do whatever it takes to always be with you. Thank you...for supper, for the cake and for the amazing gift. You can't possible know how much all of this means to me. You're right, I've missed a lot of birthdays and haven't really celebrated one since my mom stopped putting on her parties. This was better than any party she ever gave me." The tears beckoned again, but I didn't let them fall. I hugged Riley close and we went to the porch and enjoyed one more piece of cake watching the pink sun disappear on the horizon. I couldn't help but think all this was the icing on this day.

***

Seeing Riley's beautiful handiwork inspired me to try and find a hobby. I browsed through the cabin couple's library and came across a few possibilities. There were two books on how to crochet and how to knit. There was a trunk full of yarn and half finished scarves, sweaters and mittens. There was a very interesting book on how to tan hides and that one appealed to me greatly.

When Riley came in for lunch he found me sitting in the middle of the living room surrounded by these books. He came and sat beside me and began picking them up and browsing over them.

"So, what have you decided?"

"Basically, all of them."

"Okay."

"I'm going to start on the bear hide and try tanning that first. Then maybe I'll knit you a scarf."

"You make me smile."

We took our lunch out to the porch.

"Now that you're no longer a secret carver, what project are you going to try next?"

"I don't know, I like the idea of just looking at a piece of wood and see if it makes me think of anything. I think I saw an owl yesterday when I was chopping wood."

"I like owls. They're always portrayed in all stories as wise, but I think it's more than that." Riley waited while I took a bite and finished chewing.

"I think if people do become different things after they die, then an owl is an animal that has lived many different lives before. You know how as adults in the working world we have to start off as a rookie at a job and then work our way up. I see that in lives as well. The first time you die you might come back as a bug or insect, then maybe a small animal like a mouse and then it progresses from there. But I think an owl is higher up the ladder of things. It's a well respected job and position and you have to earn it."

"Whoa, that's pretty deep thinking for this early in the day." Riley's wry smile made me crack up.

"I know, its all this nature and having all this time to think. I've never had so much time to really be still with my thoughts. I like it."

"I've always loved nature for just that reason. I get the clearest thoughts when I'm out here."

"I thought it would be difficult to find things to pass the day with after we're done with the garden, but now I'm so excited to have all this time. I can't wait to start on all these projects. I've spent so much time in my life studying, that I have never taken the time for hobbies." Riley kissed me on the forehead and gathered up our dishes to take inside. I pulled my legs up to my chest and hugged my knees. My head was swimming with possibilities.

After a quick kiss planted on my lips, he rolled out of bed and got dressed. I did the same and started to make breakfast.

Riley had shown me how to render fat from the bear and I used the lard to make some piecrusts. There were still some berries hanging around, but they were overripe, pretty messy for munching on, but perfect for pies. When I told Riley my plans, he laughed,

"You're just becoming a regular Betty Crocker."

"Well, I wouldn't go that far, but I'm trying."

"You're doing a damn fine job." Another kiss and then a strong hug.

"Thanks." I squeezed him back and went to work on my piecrusts.

It took me a lot longer than I thought. I now understood why people bought ready made piecrusts. I laughed at my patchwork pies and then gathered all my dirty dishes and put them on the counter. I grabbed two pails and made my way down to the lake. After filling them, I lugged them back to the outside fire. I poured them into the large pot we always had on the grill. I needed to warm up the water to wash the dishes.

Hours passed without me even noticing, until Riley came in with my pot of water, which was only a quarter full now.

"Trying to humidify the air?" He poured the now very hot water in the sink and added a pail of cold with a squirt of dish soap. I went to get up and help him, but he stopped me.

"Don't stop what you're doing. I've got it, you're obviously deep in something over there."

"Thanks. I guess I lost track of time." I had been browsing the shelves when Riley came in. He went back out and returned carrying his catch of fish and had a basketful of carrots and beets.

"You just made my life easier."

"It's what I live for. I've got it. I'll make supper."

"I'll help you."

Riley cooked the fish over the fire outside and I sliced up the beets and carrots and threw them in their own pots of water to cook over the flames. The pies I had made earlier were cooked and I was looking forward to trying them after supper.

Full again from a fabulous supper and sitting in our favourite spot on the porch, Riley's question came out of the blue.

"Do you miss things from the real world?"

"What do you mean?"

"By the real world, or what sort of things?"

"Both."

"Well for starters I feel like we're on our own little fantasy island. It's like all the dreams and wishes I've ever had have come true at this place with you here with me." I was nodding as he spoke, sharing his feelings. "For the most part I don't miss a thing, I wouldn't trade anything in the real world for what we have here, but every once in a while something enters my head. Like tonight, I was thinking, 'man, that's good pie, it would taste awesome with ice cream.' Stuff like that just creeps in there. I was wondering if you had those moments."

"I do, but not as often as I would have thought. I really thought I'd be missing a lot more of civilization. Hot showers, steak, TV, or maybe music, I love music. But I'm not. I get those same thoughts as you that seem to drift in, but nothing monumental. I love not caring what time it is or when we get out of bed. I love having no structure and yet I love the little routines we've carved out for ourselves. It's you. You are more than enough and you leave me wanting for nothing."

Riley took my hand and brought me to my feet. The sky was very clear tonight and the air calm. He put his arms around me and we danced to music only we could hear.

***

I woke up sometime in the middle of the night and I couldn't go back to sleep. I got out of bed slowly and quietly so as not to wake Riley. I worked my way to the living room by feel alone, it was funny how quickly you came to know your space. I felt around the table for the candle and matches we kept there but it took me a while to strike the match in the right spot. Finally, with the flame glowing, I curled up on the couch with a home made afghan and pulled one of the fiction books close to the flame to see it.

Within minutes I was so absorbed, I felt Riley's weight on the couch beside me before I heard him.

"Holy crap, you scared me." Rubbing his eyes, he cuddled up closer to me and wrapped himself in the blanket.

"Sorry, the bed felt wrong." Riley barely mumbled. He lay down with his head on my lap and I had to readjust my book so as to keep reading. He didn't stay there long before he lifted his head back up.

"Now I'm awake." I put the book down. A question popped into my mind.

"How old were you when your mom died, Riley?"

"I was seven."

"You said before that life started out okay and then your mom passed. Do you remember a lot about life before your mom passed?"

"It's all I had to hang on to when life went to hell. But now when I look back, I wonder how much is real and how much I created to help me through those tough times." Riley put his head back on my lap and I played with his hair while he spoke.

"My mom was like two people in one. When she had sunny days she was stunning and her smile lit up the room. On her cloudy days her skin looked gray and she looked like she hadn't slept in days, yet she slept all the time.

Before we started school, she had way more sunny days. She loved Creedence and would crank the stereo while she cleaned or cooked and we would all sing and dance with her. She loved gardening and even though we didn't have much of a yard, she had a small area designated to her garden. She always gave us kids a couple of rows and I swear she went out at night and replanted our seeds because things always grew, but we were really bad at it and we would pick it before it did anything. She loved Lily of the Valley and she always had one little patch growing in the yard. My favourite was the year we tried growing our own pumpkins. They took over the entire little garden, but we each ended up with our own pumpkin to carve that Halloween and we were thrilled. The rest of our yard was horrible and my mom and dad couldn't even get the grass to grow, they eventually gave up. But her little garden and patch of flowers always flourished.

She loved to bake. She would always pull up chairs around a big bowl and we would take turns dumping in the ingredients. We probably drove her nuts. We were always spilling more flour on the floor and ourselves than in the bowl, and we ate whatever ingredients we could get away with. Our favourite part was licking the beaters. Those were the days when it was still okay and nobody thought about the raw eggs. The only problem was there was three of us and only two beaters, so we kept track each time who got them and took turns.

We didn't have a lot of money, even back then with dad working, but we always had a fridge full of food and she would try to make even ordinary things special. Our pancakes in the shapes of hearts for Valentines, or raisin smiley faces on our toast. She spent many hours with us playing, but her favourite thing to do with us by far was coloring. It wasn't ours, but it was Becka's and we would have done anything in order to spend more time with our mom.

Our dad was different then too. He was not a public affection kind of guy, but we could all tell how much he loved her. He actually smiled when he was around her and would touch her arm as he passed or talked to her. He would surprise her with small gifts or flowers. Because she liked Lily of the Valley so much, he would always buy her this perfume that smelled like it and even though he bought it for her every year on her birthday, she always acted surprised as if she would have never guessed. She was like that with everything. The smallest things we would bring her, be they rocks, bugs or even sticks she would look amazed and act like it was the most beautiful thing she had ever seen or that it was brand new to her too.

Then slowly, we all started school one by one and she gradually went downhill. It was like us being at home held her together. She had to smile and keep upbeat for us, but once Becka started school, she fell apart. I think even Becka sensed this and didn't want to go to school. She wanted to stay home with our mom. Her cloudy days took over and we barely saw the sun in her that last year. She would cry most of the time she wasn't in her room. She would stare vacantly out the window as she forever stirred a cup of coffee. When we talked to her, she would smile listlessly in our direction but we knew she really wasn't hearing a thing we said.

My dad tried even harder during those times. We knew he was spending money he didn't have on flowers, candy or dinners out, thinking maybe it was the chore of making dinner all the time that was pushing her over the edge. It was during that last year he somehow found the money to buy the little cabin and we actually all thought it would work for a while. She would come out on weekends and would lose herself in the raspberry patches for hours, humming some CCR tune. We all held our breath, hopeful. But she always came out of the bush with a small bowl of berries and still that sad look in her eyes.

We heard them arguing at night. Dad was trying to get her to see a doctor, but she was having none of it. She accused him of trying to put her away in a looney bin and she would yell at him that she was just going through a spell of empty nest and she's be fine, just to back off and try to be more understanding.

He tried, we all tried. We would do more chores around the house without having to be asked. Byron being almost ten would try to cook suppers to lighten her load. We would try to tell her funny jokes to make her smile. It was so hard not to find blame in ourselves. We really felt it was something we were doing that was making her so unhappy. But even though we were young, we knew more than my dad did that nothing we could do would change a thing. Eventually we hated coming home from school. We dreaded the feeling that hung in the air as we walked in the door. Our mom was gone and even young Becka knew it. None of us really talked about it, but at night we would all cuddle each other in comfort knowing something was wrong, terribly wrong."

Riley's voice was sounding tired at this point and my eyes were growing heavy from the mesmerizing tone of his soft voice. I wanted to hold him close and hear what he needed to say.

"A week before she died, she left for a few days. We figured she finally upped and ran away. She had left our father a note and whatever it said was the catalyst to our father's drinking. We were all very surprised when she came back home, my dad especially. Our happiness at her return was short lived though. Her depression had worsened and I know I wasn't the only one who wished, guiltily, that she had never returned.

So when the day came and we arrived home from school and couldn't find her, we weren't all that shocked. We didn't even make that much of an effort to find her, assuming she had run off and left us again. Thank goodness for that, because when my father came home from work he did just that, he looked for her. He didn't assume she had run off, he assumed something worse and he was right. He found her in the basement. We heard his tormented scream and howl of anguish, but we didn't run to him. We were terrified of what we would find. Instead we ran to our room and huddled together, crying." Riley took a deep breath and I rounded my body over his to hold him closer.

"That was it for my father. He took to the bottle something fierce, began taking out his anger on Byron, and soon after that, lost his job. So began our new path in life." Riley then yawned and I lifted his head and took his hand and led him back to bed. We cuddled close under the blankets.

"Did you ever find out what the note said?" His shoulders shrugged sleepily.

"Nope, I just thought it told my father she didn't love him anymore. To this day I have a hard time smelling those darn Lily of the Valley."

***

The next day I found it hard to leave Riley's side. Knowing this new piece of information about his life made me want to hold him closer. How could he be so kind and untarnished after a life like that? My life was nothing in comparison to his and I had been bitter and resentful until I met him.

Riley, oblivious to it all, went about his usual routines with a smile and a whistle. There was nothing about him that indicated he had poured forth a sad tale the previous night. I shook my head in amazement. I admired his strength.

We went out together in the canoe and tried to catch supper. It was definitely much cooler now when we went out on the lake and it wasn't until you could see the shores from this view that you realized fall was fast approaching. There would be patches of changing leaves random amongst the untouched ones, like someone had a paintbrush and splattered globs of yellow paint on a background of green. It was evident from the white lines on the larger rocks that the water level was dropping, reminiscent of the deeper summer lake. I was taking all this in as I held my fishing line and absently jigged my line. I was so inattentive that my pole was almost taken from me when I got a bite. At first I thought I was just snagged on the bottom, which happened to me quite frequently, but when it was an intermittent tug rather than a constant one I knew I had caught a fish. This still being new to me, I continued to be excited and was always thrilled. The fish played with me for a while and then I managed to get it close enough for Riley to net it. It was a fair size and I felt proud to be able to contribute to tonight's dinner.

We took our time paddling back, enjoying these last few summer evenings. Being the beginning of September, we were fortunate that it was still warm during the day, but it got pretty cool at night. We weren't lighting the fire at nighttime yet, but we found we did start a fire in the stove in the morning to get the chill out.

We had our usual dinner of fish, potatoes and fresh veggies. We didn't have to crack into any of our canned goods yet, the garden still giving us plenty for our daily meals. Usually by the time we spoiled ourselves with our new nightly routine of pie, it would be getting dark.

The stars came out to greet us, a few at a time like guests arriving. Wrapped in a few extra layers, we stayed on the porch to savour the clear night. We were rewarded on this night with spectacular northern lights. The sky danced with bright blues, purples and greens. A splash of pink would ripple through and then it would fade, teasing us to believe it was over, and then as if an encore had been called, it would begin again. I had never seen anything so beautiful. Just like any good show or book, I didn't want it to end and each time it reappeared I was elated. When it really was over, I knew it had left such an impression I would still see it in my dreams.

The good weather held for another week and then we had a week of rain and thunderstorms. Riley dug a deep hole in the ground, made a wooden box to fit in it with a lid. This we decided to use as cold storage for the veggies we picked and didn't can. The second week it got so cold at night I was afraid frost would wreck the rest of the tomatoes so we picked them green and put them in the cold box to ripen there instead.

Riley's smoked bear meat was ready and although it wasn't as tasty as the fresh roasted version it was still good and gave variety to our fish menu. When I cooked rice, I would throw in the dried meat and it would get tender along with the rice. It was a nice change. The berries were done, but the raspberries hung on the longest. We would still find a few on our daily tour even during the week of rains, but they were getting pretty soft and shriveled by this point.

For the most part, the rains kept us indoors. Riley took a break from his obsession with wood cutting and starting to read from the selection of non-fiction books.

I was tackling a knitting project and it wasn't going well. In fact this was the fifth time I had to take it apart. Frustrated I threw the attempted sweater across the room.

"I'm going for a walk." I muttered angrily.

"In the rain?"

"I need some air." As I walked in the cool rainy air, I took deep breaths. All this time I had forgotten about my temper and impatience when things don't go my way. It's interesting how our faults are invisible when there aren't the usual difficulties to bring them to light. All the things in the real world that usually caused me frustrations like phones, computers, anything electronic that didn't work like it was supposed to were absent here and with that came a stress-free life with no reason for anger. Now I found the feeling foreign. I didn't like it and I wanted to learn to handle it and try to keep my temper in check. I never cared before. I had no one to impress or anyone to worry about seeing me in a bad light, but now I was embarrassed for Riley to see that side of me.

The only fault I had seen in Riley so far was probably his overly trusting nature. He cared almost too much. I remembered how much he put up with from Byron because of the guilt he carried for so long regarding Becka. Because of his deep conscience, Byron easily manipulated him. Even this fault could be respected and loved.

My faults, on the other hand, were not so lovable. I had a bad temper, very little patience and sometimes my need for perfection made me somewhat of a control freak. Here, all these things were forgotten. I had been going with the flow and not even realizing it. I felt no need to control anything and with no care about passing of time, it was easier. What would happen when we eventually returned to the real world? Would I return to the old ways and then turn Riley off with this other side? But I also felt I needed him to see all aspects of me and love me anyways.

I felt his presence by my side as I walked back.

"Are you okay? I stopped, took both his hands in mine and looked at him.

"In the real world, I'm not the same person. I'm far from perfect. I have a temper when things don't go my way. I'm impatient and get frustrated easily. I like to control things. But for the first time in my life, because of you, I want to try to learn better coping skills. I really want you to love all of me, for who I am."

"Jady, I do love all of you. There isn't anything you could do that would make me stop." *Exactly*. But I kept my thoughts to myself. I would never use the love he had for me to manipulate him.

"Besides, you don't think this island and you have some magical effect on me as well? I'm a different person out there as well. I have a hard time trusting people and I tend to shut down around strangers. I turn inward and people assume this to either be ignorance or an extreme arrogance. You bring out the best in me. I've never been able to talk to anyone like I talk to you. I only hope your influence carries forward into the real world." I found this hard to believe. I just imagined he was always a friendly and outgoing person. I smiled and put my wet head on his shoulder.

"You constantly amaze and surprise me. Every time I think I can't possibly love you anymore, you do or say something and I do."

"You took the words right out of my mouth, princess." He lifted my head from his shoulder and held my face between his strong hands. Our lips met in the rain and although we were both soaked to the bone, we were far from cold.

***

The rain finally broke and feeling a bit claustrophobic, we decided to take a little trip. Riley had never been beyond this lake or Shas Mountain and we decided to go exploring. I packed food for a couple of days and Riley packed up the rest. We also packed up a bunch of the winter clothes since it was so cold at night.

We set out after breakfast and I found I needed the hat and mittens on the lake to begin with. We paddled across to the North, staying as close to shore as we could. The last week of rain and wind had created a lot more gold in the trees and there were many leaves already lining the ground and floating in the water. After a few hours of paddling, the larger lake turned into a narrow channel that we had to maneuver through. We had to watch for rocks jutting both out of the water and then the ones that were very dangerous were the ones barely beneath the surface. I had shed the hat and mittens already, as both the sun and the paddling workout, warmed me up. Another hour and we came up to the end. We pulled the canoe up to the bank and hauled all our gear out. I felt remotely bad that Riley had almost everything packed on his back but he looked more than capable of handling it. Besides I wasn't completely empty- handed. I had on a small backpack we had found with the winter gear and it had most of our food and another layer of clothes for me.

I helped carry the canoe across a piece of land. I was very thankful it wasn't far. We found another lake attached on the other end. We reloaded the canoe and headed back out on the water. This lake didn't seem as big and it didn't take long for us to come to another dead end. We did the same thing again, but this time the walk was farther and I had to take a break twice. On the second break we pulled up a big rock and ate our packed sandwiches of dried bear meat and cucumbers.

"Do you know what I do miss about the real world?" I asked in between bites.

"Enlighten me."

"Smart ass. It's a camera. There are so many beautiful things around us and I wish I could capture it to keep."

"I've thought of that myself too. But I've discovered over the years of watching wildlife that when I did have a camera with me, stolen ones mind you, I never saw half as much as I did when I didn't have one."

"Hmmm...I've heard that before. I've never been a picture taker. I've never had anything or seen anything worth taking a picture of."

"You will remember everything you think is worth remembering."

"I think you're very right." I looked around me in a new way as if my mind was a camera and I wanted to remember everything.

We kept up the paddling and carrying across land until dinnertime and then we found a place to set up our tent. I don't know how far we could've kept going. The land and water around here was endless. I had the hat and mittens on again and I was waiting for the fire to blaze up for some more heat. We had caught a fish on the last stretch and we had that on the fire along with a couple of small potatoes. It smelled just as wonderful as the first time we had this meal. All that paddling and walking had made me pretty hungry.

Sleepiness took over me instantly after we ate. I went and sat nearer to Riley and snuggled into him. He laughed.

"Y'know white fish makes you sleepy."

"Is this a proven fact? I think it was the millions of miles we put on today, myself."

"I remember a story a guy I worked with once told me. He was quite a partier in his younger days. He lived with his grand-mother and I think she was getting tired of his ways. Every Friday night she would make a supper of white fish and he would feel very drowsy and end up falling asleep and not going out with his friends. This went on for a few months before he finally caught on it was the fish." I was laughing.

"Can you imagine the commercial? Parents, do you want your teenagers to stop partying on the weekends? Feed them Captain Highlanders White Fish. It will solve all your wild teenager problems." It was Riley's turn to laugh.

"Wouldn't it be much better to eat fish every night rather than take a sleeping pill? It's not addictive or is it?"

"All right, now you're just silly from exhaustion. Let's go to bed." Riley poured water on the fire and we fumbled our way into the tent. It was very cold at first, but once we got close under the sleeping bags, we were shedding layers in no time.

Time in a tent with Riley always brought me back to our first night. That night felt so long ago now.

When morning came, even Riley's heat couldn't warm me up. I quickly put back on the layers I had shed the previous night and added more. It was freezing. The fact that I could see my breath proved this point beyond a doubt. Riley didn't seem fazed and didn't even stir as I squirmed my way into more clothes. When I donned as many clothes as I had brought, I nestled closer to Riley, not wanting to crawl out of the sleeping bag yet.

I must have fallen back to sleep because when I opened my eyes again, Riley was no longer beside me. I could hear the crackling of the fire. The smell of strong coffee brewing finally dragged me out of my warm cocoon.

I brought the sleeping bag with me and kept it around my shoulders as I sat close to the fire. As cold as it was, the day looked clear and bright. It would be another nice day.

"Good morning sunshine." Riley brought me a cup of steaming coffee and a bowl of cinnamon smelling oatmeal just as hot. I smiled up in tired appreciation. He sat down beside me and we ate our breakfast.

When the last drop of coffee was drained, I finally felt warm down to my toes and could part with the sleeping bag. I pin wheeled my shoulders. They felt a bit stiff from all the paddling but probably more from the carrying of the canoe.

We took our time packing up the camp and then left our gear in a pile and went to explore this new piece of land. The berry bushes looked picked through, but not by any humans or us. They had been stripped clean by some animal, Riley thought it was likely a bear. We followed the shoreline for quite some time, but it seemed we were on quite a large mass, not an island so we headed back the way we came. We ducked in and out, going further inland on the way back to see if there were any animal trails to follow. At one point we flushed out a doe deer and two of her calves. We just saw their white tails bouncing away. There was a lot of scraped bark on the trees higher up and Riley explained that this was from bucks rubbing their antlers. We could also see scratches in the bark even higher up that was evidence it was a bear without me having to ask. Those ones made me more nervous and I quickened my pace unconsciously until Riley told me to slow down.

"These are not fresh, so you can slow down, it's okay." I took a deep breath not realizing how nervous the bear's visit at our cabin had made me.

There were just as many tracks on the ground, many of them close to shore, animals coming to the water to drink. There were deeper, larger indents from moose and the smaller ones from the deer. There was an abundance of tracks I didn't recognize and Riley told me they were raccoons. We could hear them chattering occasionally on our island, but I had yet to see one. They were night hunters and way sneakier than beavers.

We made it back to where we had left our gear. Putting on our backpacks again, now lighter after eating some of our food, we made our way to the canoe. The wind had picked up a bit since yesterday and it took us a lot longer to make our way across to the first portage. We carried our stuff across and eyed up the next stretch of water. There were white caps on this stretch and we decided to stop for lunch and see if it picked up even more or died down.

After eating, the wind did neither. The water looked the same. This stretch wasn't a long one and we decided to chance it and then wait it out on the next piece of land. This part was a bit more sheltered and we stuck as close to the shore as we could. We just made it across when the wind picked up again and the rain came with it. It was falling heavy and hard and we tried to set up the tent as quickly as possible. Riley went out and made a lean-to from wood to give us even more shelter from the wind and rain. We quickly shed our wet clothes and huddled, shivering under our sleeping bags. We obviously couldn't make a fire and we weren't able to fish for our supper.

We chewed on our dried bear meat and soon the shivering subsided. It was only late afternoon, but it looked like we would be stuck in the tent for a while.

"When did you realize something was wrong with Byron?" The question came from nowhere, but it had been on my mind ever since he told me about his mom.

"After Becka died, we were both having a hard time. When a year had gone by, I was slowly healing and he was not even close. After watching my mom grapple with depression I knew the symptoms and was afraid of what I was seeing in Byron. But it was different with him. He was back and forth so frequently from way down to extreme highs that I knew I was dealing with something else, I just didn't know what back then. A few years ago I did some research at a library and found the bi-polar thing and that described him to a T. I tried showing the books to him, but he just ignored me and told me I was the crazy one. I guess I just hoped I could help him. I felt I had failed to help my mom, but maybe...just maybe I could help Byron."

I held Riley close feeling his pain and guilt.

"Hon, nothing you could have done would have changed a thing. I don't know a lot about the illness but I do know no one can help someone unless they want help themselves."

"I did read in one article that it is the hardest one to get diagnosed and to treat because the manic depressive doesn't see the manic side as a problem, they only feel the depression. But manic is just as dangerous. If it wasn't for the fact that I was terrified he would off himself, I almost preferred the depressed Byron to the manic one. At least the depressed Byron was subdued and didn't want to do a lot, but the manic one was angry and had the crazy, impulsive ideas." Riley suddenly sounded tired and I stopped talking and asking questions and just lay with him until I heard his breathing deepen and knew he was asleep.

My heart felt for him. To carry the burdens he carried; between the deaths of his sister and mom, his drunken father and living constantly on edge with his brother. He was always worried that Byron was either going to commit suicide like his mom or do something stupid like get himself or someone else killed. Riley had never been able to live life just for himself. This must feel like a vacation for him. As if to prove my point, Riley took a deep contented sigh and stirred, moving even closer to me and my warmth and comfort.

***

It was still dark out when we were awakened by the gusting wind. It threatened to carry our tent away with us in it. We clambered outside and, while Riley made a few more makeshift stakes, I pounded them in, trying to keep our tent from leaving the ground. I couldn't hear a word Riley was saying and I felt I had to hang on to branches nearby so as not to get blown away myself.

Finally when we felt the tent was secure enough, we crawled back in. The wind was whipping the tent around from the inside, but it seemed safer now. We were both breathing heavily from the sudden excitement. We had another piece of dried meat and bread, as we never did make it outside to eat. Making a fire now was out of the question. We drew in close together once again, but sleep was not about to come easily this time. Our hearts raced and I know I was wondering how long this wind was going to last. We had packed a lot of food, but not enough to keep us here for days.

"Bacon and eggs."

"What?"

"Bacon and eggs." I repeated, "I never really had cravings for things we didn't have on our island because food is so plentiful there. But now, thinking about it, I'm going over all the food that I could go for right about now."

"What, the dried meat and bread isn't good enough for you?" I could hear the sarcasm in his voice.

"Ha ha, you know what I mean. Isn't there any food you miss?"

"Hmmmm...cheese and peanut butter."

"Together?" It was my turn to be sarcastic.

"Very funny. Anything else. I could put in an order to the cook."

"Maybe a chocolate bar."

"This is probably not going to help us get back to sleep."

"Maybe not, but when we do, we'll have sweet dreams."

"Just don't eat my sleeping bag." I laughed and playfully hit him.

"Seriously now, do you want to go back?" I was surprised by the question. Without hesitation I answered,

"No. Not for all the chocolate bars in the world. Do you?"

"No." Riley held me closer and I felt his breath close on my neck. I spoke aloud what I had been thinking for a while.

"It scares me to think about it." His head moved and even in the dark I could tell he was looking right at me.

"Scared of what?"

"Scared of how things will change. We'll have to get jobs, deal with everyday stresses and I'm nervous that this peace we feel now will disappear." I did not mention the fact that there were repercussions to kidnapping which I wasn't sure we could escape. I didn't want to think about it. He obviously wasn't going to bring it up either.

"Regardless of what real life throws at us we have each other at the end of the day to look forward to. I will still have you next to me in bed every night and your face will still be the first thing I set eyes on every morning. It's you that brings me peace. If I have you, I can deal with everyday chaos."

"You always know the right thing to say to make me feel better."

"It's my job." I smiled, and feeling content, sleep came at last.

Nature is a funny thing. When we woke in the morning, if Riley had not been there the previous night to witness the wind, I would have sworn it was all a dream. It was deathly quiet outside the tent. Not a rustle or a ripple in our nylon home could be seen or heard. When we unzipped and peered outside, it was a different story. There were trees down everywhere. Our canoe had been thankfully only blown further inland, having done a couple of roll over's in the night. We had dragged all our gear into the tent with us so at least our stuff was safe.

It felt good to build a fire and have a big cup of coffee and the oatmeal with dried fruit tasted better than bacon and eggs on any day. I was very happy to see the sun shining, knowing that we would be back at our own cozy cabin by dinnertime.

The paddling that day was glorious with the water just like glass. It reflected all the trees on the shoreline and I was constantly taking pictures with my mind. There were a lot of broken trees down along the way and many branches floating. It had been quite a wind. For the first time I was worried about any damage it might have caused to the cabin.

When we rounded the final bend and the green and red sanctuary came into view I was relieved. It was the first time I thought,

"*It's good to be home*." I had never felt that way about any other place I had ever lived. It looked untouched by the wind. Those people knew what they were doing when they built their place. It was obviously solid and strong and could stand up to the forces of nature. I looked over at Riley and hoped over time that we could do the same.

***

We spent the next few days cleaning up the garden. The nights were getting pretty cold and it was only a matter of time before the frost came. We looked for covers for the cucumbers, peppers and beans that were still growing. The rest was already brown and withered and had finished producing. We pulled this all out and laid it on top of the soil. When it became wilted and soggy, Riley would mix it up with the soil that was there now, like compost. We weren't worried about the carrots and potatoes. Riley said they could survive a frost or two.

Taking a break from reading my book, I walked to find Riley and saw he was deep in concentration over his owl. What he had so far looked amazing.

"I can't believe what peace and tranquility can produce in two people." He looked a bit puzzled so I elaborated.

"I mean, in the real world, we get so caught up with our daily fast pace that we don't take the time to see what hidden talents we might have. Have you ever tried to paint, write or to carve before?"

"Nope."

"Exactly. Who knows what each of us is capable of? What if you're a brilliant writer, but have never given it a chance?"

"Well, considering I never finished school and can't spell worth a lick I might cross that talent from the list." I walked up and kissed him on the forehead,

"I'm sure lots of published, famous writers didn't finish school."

"The same thing can be applied to you. You could be a writer, poet or a painter."

"I know, that's what I'm saying. Anyone anywhere could have many skills they just have never tapped into because they're so busy with life itself."

"Wow, you're quite a thinker today."

"It just feels good to tap into my creative side. I've never done that before. It gets me excited thinking about other possibilities." He put down the owl and brushed off the wooden shavings.

"Say it again."

"What?" He was already walking towards me with his sultry bedroom eyes.

"Tell me again what gets you excited." I giggled all the way into our bed.

The X's were adding up on the calendar marking the days we spent at our cozy cabin. It was getting closer to mid-October and as the time approached, the chill dampened my mood. We had to have the stove going all the time now and it kept the small space quite cozy. I didn't seem to feel the warmth as the days went by and even Riley's sweet words and touches didn't help.

We had just gone to bed one night when a deep sigh escaped me.

"Okay, you've been moping around here for the past week. What's wrong princess?" I was almost afraid to voice my thoughts. I knew what I wanted was unrealistic. I didn't want to go, but how long could we actually stay here? It wasn't forever that was sure. Eventually we would have to go back, but it utterly depressed me to think about it. I took a deep breath.

"Look, I'm not saying this in order for it to be, I'm just sharing my feelings and what I *wish* we could do, okay?"

"Okay." Riley's voice sounded unsure.

"I wish we could stay...longer. I know, I know winter's coming and we can't, but I just feel so sad about going. I know we need to go at some point, but I just don't feel ready yet. It's absolutely tormenting me to return to, what you call, real life." I sighed again. Riley was quiet for so long I thought he had fallen asleep. I think I was almost drifting off myself when his voice made me stir.

"As much as I would love to grant that wish, it would be a tall order. I can't agree with you more and it makes me sad to think of leaving too, but forgive me if I sound like a hopeless romantic here. I am excited about the thought of living in the real world with you by my side. It makes me feel hopeful about my future for the first time in my life. To have a normal life. To have a girlfriend, a place to call home and to earn a living without committing a crime is more than I could ever ask for. Maybe it's being selfish, but I know there's an exciting future waiting for you too and I'm not going anywhere." This time it was my turn to pause for a while, holding back, not wanting to burst his bubble, but it needed to be said.

"But it's not that simple. Byron is still out there. And what about the kidnapping? Obviously I'm not going to say anything, but I'm so scared that Byron made a phone call or...I don't know what, but I just have a bad feeling about it." This time there was no hesitation when Riley replied.

"Well then, let my good feelings outweigh your bad ones. Trust me, Byron never made a phone call. He was going in that day that he...he hurt you to make the call and never did. How could he make the call after the fact? He doesn't know where we are. As far as we're concerned, he thinks we're back in the real world already. How can you ask for a ransom for someone that is already back? He doesn't know your family history. He doesn't know your father wouldn't know you're back even if you were. I'm telling you, the only one who knows about the kidnapping is you, and you already said, you're not turning me in." Riley kissed me then, but the seriousness was still evident in his voice.

"Although, by all rights, you should." I turned towards him and kissed him back.

"But then I wouldn't have you with me. How is that a good thing?" His positive words were working their magic. Maybe he was right, maybe everything would be okay in the real world.

"It's not. A world without you in it is not a world I want to be in." With his comforting arms around me I drifted off without any more worries troubling my sleep.

***

I never did really get the hang of knitting. I found crocheting easier, but I couldn't seem to make anything that required following a pattern. I could do straight lines like for scarves, blankets or tiny rectangles. I thought about the blanket it would become.I was trying to follow Riley's advice and get excited about our new life, but unlike Riley, I really had to work at it.

Our daily discussions about our future life and the plans we had for it helped immensely.

"I figure I can get a job painting or something to make ends meet. It will be hard to get anyone else to hire me without an education or a work history for that matter."

"But if you could pick any job in the world, what would it be?"

"I would love to work outdoors with nature. Maybe as a hunting guide or something like that."

"So why don't you try for that? Not to call it down or anything, but I don't think you need to be educated for that, meaning I don't think there's a course or anything is there?"

"I don't know, I don't think so. But it means being away from home for months at a time during hunting season and I can't bear that...not now. I will finally have a place to call home and someone to miss, I don't want to take off and leave already." I couldn't argue with that, I didn't want to be away from him either.

"Well, hopefully I can find a teaching job soon and between the two of us, after a few years we should be able to sock away enough that maybe we can afford to only work part time and then spend the rest of the time in the bush. I'll be your bush woman." I smiled and snuggled up close to him. We were talking while lying in bed, a habit we had settled into. The days were shorter now and we just went to bed earlier, talking for hours before sleeping.

"Now how about before we make any money? Where are we going to live?" This question came from Riley and being the optimistic one of the two of us, it surprised me. I could sense worry in his voice.

"You know I did have a life before you swept me away." I was interrupted by his laughter.

"Seriously now, I do have a bank account and I had been working to put myself through school. I don't have tons, but enough to get us a down payment on an apartment. Once we're both working we can look for something better." His body released its tension and I realized he had been worrying more than he let on. This time I was the reassurer.

"We will be fine. You have me convinced now and I'm sold. I'm excited now about the new chapter in our lives."

"So am I. I think we should pack up on Friday and head out. What do you think?" As excited as I was trying to be, the snowball that formed in my stomach as he said the words just became a snowman.

"Sounds good." I wrapped my arms around him and held him tight. The smell and warmth of him helped melt a bit of my chilled nerves.

We woke up to snow. It had fallen in the night and was still slowly settling on everything. I had never been one to notice the changing seasons, or anything changing around me for that matter, but this change was beautiful. The snow made everything look fresh and new. The smells around us had transformed overnight. The musty fragrance of dying leaves had been replaced with the scent of cold. Yet the chill was not an unwelcome one, it was refreshing. I felt like I wanted to do all the things I hadn't done since life was young and not yet tainted by bad memories.

This first snow was not ready to be played with yet. It was fluffy and just disintegrated when anything was attempted. Instead we bundled up and took a walk around our new white island. To see the snow sitting on the still colored leaves was an amazing sight.

As we were walking along, a noise like no other stopped us in our tracks. It was a crying sound, not like a baby, but a wounded animal. We ducked down low and tried to hear where the sounds were coming from. The sound came again, closer and just to the left of us. It didn't sound like a big animal, but we were still cautious.

We almost stepped right on her. It was a female raccoon and she was torn up pretty bad. She growled half-heartedly as we approached.

"What do you think did this to her?"

"Coyote, wolf even a bear." Sensing my worry, Riley added. "It might not have happened here. She might have been wounded across the lake and swam over."

"We need to do something for her."

"Oh, honey, she's in pretty bad shape." I looked at her sad, scared eyes and her heavy breathing and my heart went out to her.

"We just can't leave her." Riley smiled.

"You stay with her, I'll be right back." He disappeared back into the bush and I reached out my hand to gently touch this hurt creature. This time, she didn't even look up at me. She had her eyes closed now and only by her sides rising and falling could I tell she was still hanging on. She was covered in blood so it was hard to tell just where she was hurt. I rested my warm hand on her little head and talked to her in a soothing voice.

"We'll fix you up little one." Riley was back with a blanket in his hands. He wrapped the raccoon up in it with no protests. He handed the bundle to me and I carried this hairy baby back to the cabin.

Once we got back we heated a big pot of water on the stove. While it was warming, we laid her on the floor in front of the stove to keep her warm. We collected a few rags and with the warm water started washing her down to see what we were dealing with.

It looked like something had tried to bite her on her back, maybe to carry her away to eat. She had a few big, deep bite wounds on her back and we also found two more on her belly. How she managed to escape was beyond us. It was going to take her a while to heal from this.

Riley went and got an extra sheet and ripped it into long pieces. We wrapped her wounds and tied up the ends, hoping she wouldn't chew it off. Her breathing was a bit steadier and we left her beside the stove to rest.

We made a cup of coffee to warm up and settled on the couch, watching our new roommate.

"She's not that fat."

"Well that's a nice thing to say." Riley laughed.

"No, I mean shouldn't she be fatter at this time of year to get ready to hibernate?" I didn't even bring up the fact that she was motherless knowing full well what probably happened and not wanting to think about it.

"How is she going to do that in her condition? It's going to take a while for her to heal up and by that time everything around us will be covered in snow. She's not going to be ready to hibernate." I'm not a mother, never had any real maternal instincts or the ticking clock thing, but I suddenly felt very protective over this small, vulnerable life. Riley remained quiet and I let him be with his thoughts, knowing him enough at this point to understand he needed time to think things through.

"She needs time, and some TLC." I went over to where Riley was sitting on the couch and climbed onto his lap. I wrapped my arms around his neck.

"We can give her TLC." After another long pause Riley finally spoke,

"We can just stay long enough to make sure she's all right and fatten her up to get her ready to hibernate. If we get out of here before the ice forms on the lake, we should be good. We have more than enough food and warm clothes."

"Thank you, thank you, thank you." I was like a kid on Christmas who has just received the exact thing she had asked for. I covered Riley's face with kisses. He laughed.

"I'm just as happy as you are. I didn't realize how anxious I was about leaving until I just spoke those words aloud and the knot in my stomach disappeared. I want to stay here as long as we can too." He kissed the tip of my nose before his tone became serious. "But honestly Jady, we do need to go at some time and we really need to leave before the lake ices over."

"I know. I know." I got up off the couch and went to check on our baby. She was still fast asleep.

"Grace."

"What?"

"That's what I'm going to name her. Grace. She's my saving grace."

***

For the next few days, while I floated on air, happy to be able to stay for a while longer, Grace slept on and off. When she was awake, she was groggy and weak and seemed oblivious to her new surroundings. While she was in this state, we were able to check and change her wounds. They were still looking pretty rough.

This all changed on day four. We woke up in the middle of the night to crashing and scampering. We scrambled to find a candle and sleepily lit it. It got quiet again and when we didn't find Grace in her usual spot, we had to wait for another noise to know in which direction to look. Finally, another crash coming from the cupboards led us over there. We found ourselves surrounded by pots, pans and all our tin dishes. All the cupboard doors were open so we had to shine the candle into each one to see which one she might be in. Her growl and hiss gave her away before we saw her glowing eyes.

"Shhh, it's okay baby. Come on out. It's okay." The growls continued. Riley walked away with the candle and came back with a piece of fish he had dried in the smokehouse. He crouched down in front of Grace and showed her the food.

"C'mon Grace. Look what I have." She eyed him suspiciously, but her nose twitched and she pawed the air reaching. Riley moved back a little bit. She moved closer, curiosity and hunger getting the better of her. Her growls diminished. When she was all the way out of the cupboard, Riley rewarded her with the fish, which she devoured, constantly taking in her new company.

Riley managed to get her back in front of the stove and in the meantime I had put down a small blanket for her. She completely bypassed the blanket and both of us and crawled under the river rock table. She peered at us warily, but was no longer growling.

We shut all the cupboards. Sitting down on the couch, we contemplated some plans. We would have to raccoon- proof this place.

"There were twist ties in one of the cupboards. We could use them around the handles of the cupboards." We put that plan into effect immediately, not wanting to be woken again that night.

Grace let us sleep the rest of the night and she slept away the rest of that day under the table. But the next night, in an encore performance, she woke us again.

"So this is what it's like to have a baby." Riley sleepily grumbled.

"Not even close." I mumbled back, although I really had no idea either.

This time she had found her way into the pantry and had managed to break two jars and there were flour paw prints all over. They led us back to her spot under the table where she was happily munching on some pickled beans.

After a candlelight clean up, we had to devise a way to block her from the pantry now. We slid over one of the heavier bookshelves, deciding that in the morning we would come up with a better plan. It would be a big pain to have to move the heavy shelf every time we needed something from the pantry. We gave her a bit more to eat and went back to bed.

The next day she slept for the morning, but actually came out in the afternoon to see what we were up to. Since I had more time again, I was working on small crocheted squares with hopeful sights set on it becoming a future quilt. I put my crochet hook down for a minute to look for a different color of yarn. Grace was so quick. She would run up, snatch my hook and then run quickly back to her table growling. I watched her turn it around and around in her delicate paws, sniffing it, trying to decipher whether it was something edible or not. When she realized it wasn't, she would come back for another look to see if there was anything else to snatch. She was an amazing creature. Her wounds didn't seem to hinder her at all, but she was a pretty scrawny raccoon.

Riley tied a washer to the end of some yarn and would drag it along in front of her hiding spot. All you could see was a little paw shoot out and try to pull it in. It became a tug of war game and Grace always won. Initially she would pull the whole yarn under the table and the game would be over until she came out to eat and Riley would fish it out again. But after a few times, Riley would actually find the yarn placed in different locations where he was known to sit. Grace obviously enjoyed the game too.

After a few nights of interrupted sleep, we finally had the cabin Grace proofed. She slept under the table most of the day and we'd become used to hearing her playing for half of the night. She loved things that made noises so Riley constructed a few toys for her. The noisy ones were entertaining during the day, but we packed them away at night. She stole everything. If I was missing something, I could usually find it later in her water dish. She took everything there to wash and inspect it.

She was starting to get used to us. Every day she got a little closer and only growled in play. She loved to wrestle around with Riley, but he had to watch because she easily got over stimulated and then her play got pretty rough. She loved shiny things and I had to remove my earrings in fear she'll do it for me and not as gently as I would've liked.

We made an interesting discovery though. Riley was playing with her and this was one of the times when she started to get really rough. Riley picked her up by the scruff of her neck like you would a cat and she instantly became calm and docile. As soon as he let go and placed her on the floor she ran under her table. She came out a mere minute later, walked up to Riley and nudged his hand and then went and lay down. We guessed she was sorry.

I loved her paws; they were the neatest things I'd ever seen. They were like baby's feet, long and narrow, and so soft. She could do anything with them that we do with our hands. Everything she touched she had to examine thoroughly. She was so much fun to watch.

We felt like new parents, trying to get things done while Grace slept. I worked on my quilt; Riley cut wood and got water for the day. We didn't want her to get outside. She seemed to be feeling better and we even took the bandages off and let her clean her wounds herself, but she was still very thin. She would not have enough time on her own to eat all that she needed to in order to be in shape for hibernation.

We decided another month should give us enough time to fatten her up and the ice should not be on the lake yet. I was happy to have it.

There was enough snow on the ground that we could play with the snowshoes and the cross-country skis. Riley broke us a trail around our island and we would venture out when Grace was sleeping. We were trying to make the most of every minute we had left. We made every meal as if it were our last and we never got tired of sitting out on the porch and watching the sun go down. Although now it went down very early and we had to bundle up to watch the view.

The squirrels, chipmunks and the blue jays would come out and munch on what was left of the sunflowers in the garden. The blue jays especially, would stand out with their brilliant colour against the white. They were my favourite until the Pine Grosbeaks graced us with their presence. First came the yellow ones, but the pink ones were brilliant. I couldn't believe a wild bird could have such outstanding colours. It only added to my list of times I wistfully wished for a camera.

In the morning we would have our coffee on the porch, as well. Watching the day slowly wake up was a joy I never appreciated before. I used to hate mornings and would sleep as long as I could. Now I loved the way the sun coloured everything as it rose. After we'd had breakfast, Grace was usually sleeping, so we used this time to do our daily chores. We stoked the fire and Riley brought water up from the lake. I put a big pot on the stove to use periodically during the day to wash dishes or our hands.

Now that we couldn't swim and wash in the lake, we would fill a big metal basin with the warm water and sponge bathe. The time I looked forward to the most, was our once a week hair washing. Riley had started the routine one night and we'd made it into a habit. He filled up the sink with the warm water and I sat in a chair as I would at a hair salon. He wet my hair and then took his time massaging and shampooing my scalp. It was absolutely heavenly. After he rinsed and wrapped my hair in a towel, he gently combed it all out. My hair had become quite long and he really took his time. After he was all done, I returned the favour, although it only took half the time. His hair had also lengthened and he had an adorable beard growing. I wasn't sure about it at first, but now I loved running my fingers through it and I would shampoo and massage his chin when I did his hair. He would close his eyes and moan in contentment. I knew it got itchy on him, but we had looked everywhere and had never turned up a razor. This routine of ours was like fore play and it always ended up in the bedroom.

After one of these hair-washing nights, we lay in bed having our end of day discussion.

"Y'know, sometimes I compare this time we have to the end of the world."

"What do you mean?" I could tell from Riley's voice that he was on the verge of laughing.

"No, seriously, I remember a mantra I heard once and scoffed at, but now I think it's very true."

"What's the mantra?"

"Love like you've never been hurt, dance like no one is watching and live every day like it's your last. It's some Irish proverb or something."

"I like that."

"I just think this time we have is something we're never going to get back or replicate. I know we have an exciting new chapter to look forward to, but you have to admit, it will never be like this again."

"I know. But if we hang on to that mantra we can make every day special no matter where we are."

"Do you really think we can hang on to this...this feeling."

"I *know* we can." We held it each other close and listened to Grace barreling around the living room. I didn't have to see Riley to know he was smiling.

***

Grace spent every waking hour eating. Riley had to catch a few fish now to sustain her newfound appetite and us. We would put pieces of her fish on a plate and then hide it around the room, under rocks or logs we brought in from outside. It became such a fun game of hide and sniff. We would put her in our room while we hid the food, and then release her. She would instantly sniff her way around and overturn everything she found on the floor, inspecting every inch. It didn't take her long to find her treats and after playing this a few times she now went to the treats instantly.

As much as we would have loved to treat her like a pet, we both knew we couldn't. She needed to be returned and the more we could keep her in her usual routines the better. Of course this was hard to do in a cabin, but the hide and sniff game was at least one feeble attempt.

It didn't take long for her to get plump and get a nice waddle going when she walked. It made us laugh to see her run across the room. Just by her own cleaning, her wounds were healing very nicely.

We knew she was getting closer and ready to hibernate when we sat on the cot one night and found it lopsided. Upon closer inspection we found she had stuffed torn pages from magazines, pillowcases, and my yarn, making herself a nice nest under the cot. We figured one more week, she would be fat enough, the ground would not be too frozen and we could release her.

It was going to be difficult though. Despite the fact that we were trying to remain neutral and think of Grace as a wild animal, we couldn't help, but get attached to the furry critter. She was so similar to human children. She was curious, loved to play and even had temper tantrums when she didn't get her way. She also loved to mimic. Riley was sitting on the cot one-night reading a book. She hoisted herself up and sat back with her paws resting on her belly. She looked so funny that we broke into laughter many times that night as we imagined the sight again.

As the week flew by, I once again became anxious, knowing that once Grace left we would soon be going too. It was amazing what a ticking clock can do for your senses. I thought of every delicious meal as my last. Every sunset and sunrise I tried to imprint on my brain. Every animal call I imagined closing my ears to keep the sounds from escaping my memory. I found myself sighing frequently and near tears. Finally I could take it no longer. Now knowing that Riley shared my feelings of doubt about leaving I summoned the courage and spoke my mind.

"I think we deserve to give it a full year."

"Give what a full year?"

"Our stay here. I think after everything we have been through, we deserve a full year to appreciate all the seasons first before we go anywhere."

"You mean stay the winter?" Riley didn't sound like he thought my idea was idiotic, he just sounded surprised.

"Yup. We can do it."

"I have no doubt that I can do it, but do you really want to?"

"Listen mister, I've already dispelled the princess myth, what more proof do you need that I can handle the wilds of nature."

"I don't doubt that you have the strength and the courage, but winter can do funny things to people. It sometimes can feel suffocating when you can't go anywhere or do anything when the temperatures trap you indoors for a long period of time. Not to mention the short days and an abundance of darkness."

"I feel like I've spent my life running and not really enjoying anything. I want time to stand still. I want to take the time and appreciate everything. The last few days I've felt like someone has told me I only have a week to live. I've been trying to soak everything in and retain it. Every single time we push back the date of departure I feel okay again until the day approaches. I think after a year I will be ready to move forward. I'm not ready and I don't want to go. I want until the beginning of next summer to stay."

"Well, okay then."

"That's it? Okay then?"

"Well, I'm assuming you've thought this through and you seem pretty determined. I love this life, always have. I really thought you'd want to get back to the luxuries of city life by now. I am surprised, but pleasantly." He pulled me into his arms. "I would never argue anything that had to do with hogging you all to myself for an extended period of time. I think the idea is marvelous." The happiness I felt then was overwhelming. I felt like a kid at the beginning of summer vacation. The time always felt like it was forever. Of course I knew better. It would still go by faster than I would like, but I was going to do my best to soak up every second.

Now that we decided to spend the winter, there were a few things we needed to do in order to be ready before the cold weather set in. We had to look at our food supplies and ration it out properly so that it lasted our whole stay. I felt bad that we were now going to use up all the canned goods that we worked so hard to replenish for the Cabin Couple. I consoled myself with the fact that I had saved a lot of seeds and that, come spring, I would make sure to start a new garden for them to pluck and pick from.

We had plenty of wood to last and Riley kept up his wood cutting routine so we would never run short. We had the bin of winter clothes plus the Cabin Couple's snowshoes and cross-country skis.

Our only concern was the lack of protein. We would still be able to ice fish, but it would not be as plentiful as we had been used to. The dried bear meat would not last all winter. The only other solution was that Riley would plan a hunting trip and go get a deer to keep us going. With the smoke shack we would be able to dry it and not worry about it going bad.

"You could come with if you want."

"Look Riley, I love you and want to share in your interests, but I draw the line on hunting. I could handle the killing of the bear because I felt it was for protection and I can even eat the meat you bring home, but I can't be there when you actually pull the trigger. As much as I can't stand the idea of time away from you, I'm not at all scared about being here alone for a day or two either."

"Okay, that brings us to the next topic." Riley motioned towards the big hairy bump, now sleeping in her nest under the cot.

"I know, I know."

"She's ready. She's healed, healthy and well...pretty fat."

"Hey, hey, that's not nice. Its just baby fat." Riley smiled.

"Well, whatever the case might be, she needs to find a place to nestle down before we get any more snow or it gets any colder."

"All right."

"We'll start off slow and just let her out when she pleases and see what she does on her own. Once she figures it out, I'll go hunting."

"Okay." I knew we would have to let her go, but it was still going to be hard. I had never had a pet as a kid and although Grace was far from a cuddly lap dog she was the closest thing I ever had.

"Y'know, once we are settled in the real world, I would like a cat."

"For you, princess, anything. Why a cat and not a dog?"

"Well, I don't think it's fair to have a dog when we'll be working all day long. A cat is more than content to be by itself for a while. At least that's what I've seen from watching other people and their pets. Dogs seem so much more in need of affection and time."

"You can have whatever you want." Riley wrestled me to the ground and pinned my hands above me. "Are you sure you don't want a hippo or a tiger?"

"Ha ha." I was squirming and giggling, trying to free my hands. He repositioned himself and held my two hands in his one strong one and tickled me with the other. I was laughing so hard I couldn't breathe.

"Please...stop." I tried bucking him off, but he stayed put. He finally let go of my hands and I reversed our positions. Now I was on top and I tickled his face with my hair.

"I sure love you." He parted my hair and lifted his head so our foreheads touched.

"I sure love you too, even if you are demanding." This time I pinned his hands and dug my bony chin into his chest. It was his turn to squirm, but I didn't have his strength and it didn't take long for him to free himself. I got up and ran away before he had a chance to get me again.

"Don't worry, I'll get you later." Riley gave me a wry smile and sat down with a book.

"I'm counting on it." I returned his smile.

***

At first, Grace was puzzled and a bit scared when we left the door open for her. She sniffed at the air, but stood her ground. We left it open for a few minutes and then about an hour later we opened it again. This time she got a bit closer and stuck her paw out to investigate. She touched the snow and then licked her paw. She waddled out a little further, but snow falling off a branch made her scramble back under the safety of her table.

Another hour went by and we tried again. This time we lured her out with some fish and played her hiding game outside. Hiding fish under some rock and logs outside, she quickly found them and munched away, ever wary of her surroundings. She stayed outside for quite some time, exploring her new environment always aware of our presence and making sure we were within her sight. She waddled back to the closed door as she neared her normal sleeping time.

We let her sleep in her nest and did the same routine for the next few days. Each day she stayed out longer and longer. The first day we stayed with her and then on the next couple of days we went about our normal routines of cutting wood and hauling water and sometimes she would amble along with us and other times she went her own way, her curiosity getting the best of her. She would come back to where we were though and was always at the door come naptime.

On the fourth day, she immediately took off on her own adventure and was not at the door at her usual time. I couldn't help but be worried. I was concerned about her getting hurt again before she got a chance to find someplace to sleep for the winter.

"She will be fine. I don't think she's gone for good just yet."

She was gone all that night and most of the next day but around dinnertime there was a loud banging on the door. We opened it, and there came our Grace all nonchalant as if raccoons always knocked on doors to be let in. She started to look for her food in her regular hiding spots and when she found them empty she came and chattered at us, as if giving us a hard time. We laughed and fed her some fish and veggies. After eating, she went to sleep.

She kept up this new routine over the next week, each time staying away longer. Finally five days passed and the weather turned colder and she didn't return. I imagined I heard her knock from time to time and it was bittersweet that she was gone. It was sad to have her gone, her presence and the silence in the cabin was very noticeable. Yet the fact that she didn't return, meant she had probably found some hollow log or hole in a tree and was nestled in, safe from the cold.

In an attempt to cheer me up, Riley suggested we take a trip over to our first island and go fishing. We wanted to stock up a bit before he went hunting, then I would have a few days worth of dried fish just in case it took him a bit to get something. We also wanted to go for a canoe ride before the lake froze over.

We bundled up and packed a lunch. Once again the scenery from the lake was completely changed. The leaves were all gone and only the pines were standing firm and green. There was a thin layer of snow wrapped around everything like packages waiting for spring to open. You could not tell what surprise was under each bump and lump. It could be a log, rock a mossy hill.

We paddled over to our original little place. It was hard to imagine that we had looked upon the little cabin about four months ago and had never fathomed we would be spending our winter there.

We didn't bring a tent. As much as our body heat kept us warm, the cold ground would do a number on our bones. We built a big fire and found a spot along the shore to throw in our lines.

"Here I'll bait yours. Can you get me a couple of carrots from our lunch?"

"For bait?"

"No," Riley laughed, "For me, I'm hungry." I laughed too and went back to the fire to grab our bag of goodies.

My line was already in the water when I returned and he handed it to me with a smirk.

"What are you up to?" I handed him the carrots suspiciously.

"What do you mean?"

"That smirk means you're up to no good."

"I don't know what you're talking about." But the smirk remained and I stayed alert waiting for some prank to take place.

After Riley had caught three fish and I had nothing I decided to check my line to make sure some fish hadn't stolen my bait. As I pulled my line out of the water I noticed I still had something at the end of my line but it wasn't bait. It looked like a wooden ring.

"What the..." I turned to ask Riley and saw he was down on one knee. He unhooked the ring from my line and held on to my hand.

"If I had to be stranded on an island anywhere in the world I would pick you to be with me. I've never been so close to anyone in my life. I have never felt so open, so confident to be myself and to be loved unconditionally. Sometimes I feel unworthy of you, but when I think of you with someone else, it not only drives me crazy, I can't possibly think of anyone else worthy enough of you or your love. You're it princess, you're the love of my life and I want to grow old with you by my side. I want to wake up in the middle of the night and hear your deep breathing. I want to feel your cold feet on mine. I want to see you build things with just the tip of your tongue sticking out when you're in deep concentration. I want to see the frown on your forehead when you're frustrated with something. I not only love everything about you, I want the time to love you even more. Jady, will you marry me?" He stopped and took a deep breath. I could feel tears streaming, they felt warm against my cold cheeks. I was almost too choked for words.

"Yes. I can't think of anyone else in the world that I'd rather spend the rest of my days with." Riley slipped the ring on my finger and stood up to hold me close. I kissed his face and ran my fingers under his toque to wrap them in his long hair. I pulled him in for a long sweet kiss.

"You're amazing." I whispered in his ear.

"It's you that makes me feel amazing." I stepped back then to see what was on my finger. I slipped it off to examine it closer.

"You carved this?" Riley nodded. It was incredible. It was intricate knot work that swirled around delicate hearts.

"How?"

"He has some small chisels amongst the tools. I used them, then burnt it and shaded it down to make the knot work darker."

"It's the most beautiful thing I've ever seen."

"You're the most beautiful thing I've even seen."

I was the happiest woman alive.

***

I watched him pack up his gear for his hunt, wishing I could think of an alternative. We needed the food for the winter, yet I felt guilty because it was my badgering to stay that created the need. Would it be better just to leave the island rather than be parted from Riley for a few days? If we left the island, I would be parted from him daily as we worked our separate jobs. No, I could handle a few days on my own. I handled most of my life alone, what were a few days? A few days felt like an eternity now that I had tasted real companionship.

I helped Riley load everything in the canoe. We lingered beside the boat, fingers entwined, our breath hanging in the cold air. I don't think Riley wanted to go any more than I wanted him too.

"All right, the sooner I go, the sooner I'll be back." I leaned my body into his and his arms enveloped me. Our kiss was long and warm.

"Be safe and come back soon." Riley kissed me again.

"I will, I have a fiancé now."

"Mmmmm...say that again."

"I love you, my fiancé."

"I love you too." We finally let each other go and I pushed Riley and his canoe into the calm, cold water. The air was still and fog hung over the lake. It didn't take long until I couldn't see him anymore. I could just hear his paddle cutting the water.

It had only been a few minutes and I felt so lonely. I sat on the rocks, shivering until I couldn't hear the paddling anymore.

I spent the day trying to keep myself busy so that I couldn't feel the silence in the house. I kept the fire going in the stove, brought in enough firewood for a few days, hauled water from the lake and baked a fresh loaf of bread. This took me to lunchtime.

After I ate I curled up on the couch with a fluff fiction book in which I didn't need to think too much. I got lost in the world of romance and make believe for a while, but then I found my mind drifting. I reread the same sentence a few times before I finally put down the book, lay back and closed my eyes.

How did I get from being solely independent to being dependent on a man for company and entertainment? I needed to see this as a holiday and enjoy this time to myself. When we left here I would be sharing my space with someone other than my mother and forced roommate. Yet that's what we'd been doing all this time on our little island and I hadn't felt suffocated or uncomfortable at all. I went from working very hard to keep to myself and letting no one in, to allowing someone to share the sink while we brushed our teeth. I now had someone sleep next to me in a small double bed and not feel claustrophobic. We cleaned our dishes side by side and I let Riley wash and comb my hair. Our intimacy was brought on by circumstance and we were thrown together. There were no baby steps with our relationship and yet the whole thing felt completely and utterly natural. I smiled to myself, missing him, but feeling completely happy. I took a deep breath, sighed and pulled the blanket over my body. I let myself drift off for a luxurious afternoon nap.

When I woke up it was nearly dark and the air in the cabin felt chilly. Damn, I had let the fire go out. Grudgingly, I crawled out from under the warm blanket and went to find a warm sweater.

I went to the stove and piled up some kindling. Once it was burning I stacked up some logs and shut the oven door. I made myself a cup of coffee and warmed my hands around the cup.

When the shivering stopped, I made supper. After I had cleaned up I got busy reading another book from the slim collection we had. After a while I leaned back and stretched. My back and eyes were sore from leaning forward trying to read by the dim light of the candle. It was time to call it a night.

I stoked up the fire, hoping it would last most of the night. I carried my candle into our room and crawled into the cold bed. I missed Riley terribly. He usually went to bed first, warmed up my side and then moved over. He always curled up beside me and warmed me up before we drifted off.

That night I had to get up and put on another layer of clothes and a warmer pair of socks. I shivered for quite some time before I felt warm enough to sleep. My night was filled with dreams of Riley and each time, I woke disappointed to find the spot beside me empty. Suddenly a couple days was feeling like an eternity.

***

I opened my eyes in the morning to find the cabin cold and dark. I pulled the blankets close around me and went back to sleep. When I opened my eyes again, it was still cold, but at least the sun was up which made greeting the day a bit more cheerful. I felt stiff and tired as if I hadn't slept at all. I made my way over to the stove and with cold and awkward fingers; I managed to make a fire. I sat in front of the warm glow for a bit, warming myself until my hands felt limber enough to curl up into a fist.

I wasn't really hungry, but I thought warm oatmeal would hit the spot. Washing it down with a cup of coffee, I was starting to feel better and thought I'd venture outside.

It was actually warmer outside than in. The sun was shining and made the snow glisten and sparkle. The clear blue sky was enough to bring a smile to even the most depressed soul. I grabbed the metal pot and went down to the lake to get some more water. The fog was all gone this morning and the lake was filled with the reflections of shore. It looked absolutely amazing and I wished Riley were there to see it too.

As I walked back to the cabin, a bitter feeling snuck in. Before I had met Riley I was perfectly happy with my lone existence. Nothing bothered me and I never knew loneliness. I was absorbed in whatever I was studying at the time and left no room for forlorn thought. But now that I had a taste of what it was like to have a friend, to have company, to be in love I knew I could never go back. I can't live without him ever again. Not in the sense of co-dependency, in which I couldn't ever be without him for a minute, but I knew I would never want to be without him in my life.

To be honest I was wondering what this time apart would do. I wondered if I had the time to look at the whole picture without him in it, if I would feel differently, if the old feelings would return. The feelings of wanting to be alone, to live independently, of wanting my own space. There was none of that, I just wanted him back. I wanted to see his smile, to hear his voice and to feel his touch.

I placed the pot of water on the stove and, seeing as it was still cold in the cabin, decided to take our usual walk around the island, alone. I couldn't decide whether to ski or snowshoe. Finally deciding on skis, I filled up the too large ski boots with extra socks rolled into the toes and ventured out.

I couldn't help but take a multitude of deep breaths, the cold air feeling good as it filled my lungs. It still stunned me that I had missed out on all this for so many years. I was beginning to feel good about being on my own. I really listened to all the sounds around me and took in the pristine look of the snow-covered forest. For the first time I took notice of what wasn't around me. There was no grey or brown snow that covered the city streets. There was no honking of vehicles in their mad rush to get to somewhere. No people yelling at each other or sirens of emergencies in the distance. The vibrations of the bass as people's car stereos drove by. The radios forecasting the horrible things taking place around the world. We had no idea of what was going on around us and we didn't care. If there was a war and we were about to die, I was more than happy to be exactly where we were. It was a place millions of people wished they could spend their last moments on earth. I was filled with appreciation and gratitude for this time.

I looked around me and saw I was halfway around. I stopped and pulled out a snack of dried bear meat and berries. That was the other thing I noticed that neither my body nor myself missed. I had never felt so healthy and full of energy. There were no chocolate bars, bags of potato chips or the other junk food I had polluted myself with for so long. Not being one to cook and always-grabbing things on the run, it was all foods of convenience and therefore packaged to survive a bombing. Eating the way Riley and I had been eating these last months was like a cleanse and I couldn't imagine what a tub of popcorn smothered in butter would do to my stomach right now.

Continuing on, I had gone a little farther when I noticed the surroundings with a bit more clarity. This spot looked familiar, but not from our walk arounds. I unclipped my skis and walked on duck feet to the edge of the island. I was standing on that huge rock that hung over the lake. It was the one that had stopped me in my rock hopping efforts. From up top it appeared even larger and I took a few more steps to peer over to see how far the water had dropped now. It looked like I could walk on the rocks all the way around now, the rock heads were all above water. I wouldn't be able to do it with these rigid boots on. When I looked down at my funky shoe wear I noticed my lace had come undone. I bent over to tie it and as I stood back up the world spun around me. I held out my hands to steady myself but it was too late.

LOVE ON TRAIL

I heard the sounds of water sloshing and felt nauseous with the swaying motion. I opened my eyes to see the sky above me. The dusky sky looked blurry and added to my sickness so I closed my eyes again. I tried to move and felt my body scream in protest. I could hear laboured breathing not belonging to me. The sound of a paddle slicing through water and occasionally bumping the sides was familiar. Was the whole island time a dream? Was I just on my way there in the canoe now? What happened? I wanted to ask questions, but lost consciousness again before I could voice them.

The smell brought me around again. It was oil and grease covered in rust. I came around in a strange environment. I could feel I was on the move again, but this time not on water. It was too dark to see my surroundings and I could hear nothing except for the sounds of wheels on the road. It hurt too much to stay awake.

This time when I opened my eyes I knew exactly where I was and I was alone. The hospital smells and sounds assaulted my senses. From pine trees to medicinal pine cleaner. From the call of the loon to the sound of trolley wheels, footsteps in an echoing hallway, a distant phone ringing and voices...so many voices. I wanted to shut everything out. I didn't want to be there. I tried to sit up, but the pain in my head was intense and I immediately lay back down. Again I wondered what had happened. I knew the island time was not a dream, it couldn't have been. The last thing I remembered, Riley had gone hunting and I had been on my own. I had gone for a ski. Then that rocky ledge and the world started spinning. That's all I remembered. What happened? Where was Riley?

I saw a nurse walk down the hall and quickly glance in.

"Oh, you're awake." She came in and checked on me. She was an older woman. Definitely a grandmother to someone. She was short and strong looking. She handled herself around me like someone who has done this for along time.

"I'll send the doctor in shortly to do a further check. You're pretty lucky, only a broken arm." Then she lowered her voice, "Although I guess there's a lot of pain that is not visible on the outside, you poor girl."

"What? Where's..." But I didn't get a chance to finish. The doctor walked in then and lowered his glasses to his nose to look at my chart.

"Can you tell me your name?"

"Jady Donner." I couldn't help but notice a raised eyebrow.

"Can you tell me what happened?"

"I...I went for a ski" the eyebrow rose again and a quick glance passed between nurse and doctor. "I went too close to this large rocky outcrop and I bent over to tie my laces. When I stood up, I got really dizzy. That's all I remember. How did I get here? Did Riley bring me here? Where is he?" I was holding back tears of panic. Why wasn't he here?

"Just calm down for a minute Miss Donner. You've managed to survive your ordeal and we'll need to do some more tests to see if there are any other injuries that weren't apparent to us as you were brought in. We should also do a sexual assault examination now that you're conscious." My head was spinning.

"What in God's name for?" I felt my anger rise along with my voice, but I also felt myself fading again and I closed my eyes. Where was Riley? I needed him so badly. I could barely hear them anymore but I did manage to hear one more comment from the doctor.

"It's perfectly normal to block out traumatic experiences. We'll call for a psych consult."

When I woke again, I didn't have to open my eyes to know where I was. I could tell from the civilized smell where I was. I wanted to cry and keep my eyes shut. I didn't want to open them for fear that I would still be alone.

Slowly I did open my eyes and this time I noticed I wasn't alone. I had a roommate. I could turn my head now and saw she was in much better condition. She was sitting up in her hospital bed and eating her supper. But it wasn't whom I wanted to see and I shut my eyes, afraid of conversation.

I could hear the TV blaring from her side of the room and the topic made my eyes snap open.

"The search for Jady Donner is over. We don't have all the details yet, but we do know her kidnapper is in custody and Jady is in hospital, in stable condition. There have been no comments from her father Mr. Greg Donner, but his secretary has confided that he is relieved she is safe and alive." Then a picture of me flashed on the screen and I could feel my roommate's eyes. I closed my eyes again in disbelief. They took Riley in? Why? How did anyone know? Then the bile of anger rose in my throat. How dare my father pretend to be concerned? I couldn't believe all of this was happening. I opened my eyes and ignored my roommate's stares. I looked around for the button to summon my nurse. I needed to talk to someone. I needed to set the record straight. Riley shouldn't be in custody. I needed him here. Every cell in my body screamed for him to be here.

The nurse came pretty quickly.

"What's wrong honey?" I pointed towards the TV.

"It's all wrong. Everything they're saying is wrong. I need to talk to the police. I need to talk to someone." I was getting excited and my head pounded with every word I spoke.

"Okay, okay, calm down. Let's get the doctor in first to go over your condition and then we'll go from there." I took a deep breath, impatient but thinking if I did what they wanted, then maybe they would cooperate too.

The nurse left the room and I lay back down. I had barely rested for a minute when I felt a presence by the bedside. It was not the same nurse or the doctor. It was a different nurse but she was pushing a cart with pitchers of water.

"Can I get you something to drink?"

"Ummm...that would be good thanks." She poured me a glass and then placed the pitcher on my bedside table, taking the old pitcher away. She hesitated for a minute and then surprised me by sitting on the edge of the bed.

"I'm sorry. I heard your story and I just feel for you. You must have been through so much and if you need to talk to someone, please feel free. I see no one is here for you." My tears escaped before I could stop them, but I didn't feel comfortable talking to this stranger. I wanted to set the record straight though to anyone who would listen.

"It's not what everyone seems to be thinking."

"What is everyone thinking?" I stopped again, not wanting to say the words out loud.

"He didn't do anything to hurt me. He...He is a good man"

"Are you talking about your kidnapper?"

"He's...He's not a kidnapper." I felt defensive and unable to explain. "He's a good man."

"You mean he didn't kidnap you?" I didn't know how to answer. His face flashed before me and I wanted to sob. Oh,

Riley, I want to see you. How can I put into words what happened? I was tired, so tired.

"We love each other." I said this more to myself than to this nurse.

"You love him?" The words sounded so harsh and judgmental that my anger woke me up. I was about to defend my statement when the other nurse walked in.

"Who the hell are you? How did you get in here?" The stranger shot up from the bed and her frantic eyes looked for an escape. She then withdrew a camera from her pocket and took a picture before I had a chance to react.

"Security!" The stranger tried to break for the door, but two men in uniform blocked her passage. She shrugged off their grip.

"Yeah, yeah, I'm going." She walked out with the two large men as her bookends.

I looked to my nurse, confused and feeling panicked. She instantly was by my side and put her hand on my arm.

"It's okay. You're okay."

"Who was that? What did she want?"

"Oh honey, you're a celebrity right now. There are journalists crawling all over the place just looking for a way in. This one obviously found a way. I'm so sorry. We won't let it happen again." I stopped listening. Exhaustion took over. I was overwhelmed. I wanted to be back on our island. I wanted to be in our little cabin lying in our cozy bed with Riley by my side. I let the tears fall and rolled over on my side. The nurse gave me a pat on the back.

"You've been through a lot. Just rest honey, you'll be back home soon and things will return to normal." My tears turned to sobs. That was what I was afraid of. Unless someone could return me to the island and bring Riley back to me, nothing would be normal again.

The doctor came in after awhile and because I had cried myself out, I felt completely defeated and helpless. He checked my charts and pulled up a chair beside my bed.

"I'm sorry for what happened earlier. We've stepped up security and we'll make sure that doesn't happen again." I just nodded.

"How are you feeling?"

"I have a headache and I'm just tired."

"That's from the concussion. You also have the broken arm and we never came to a consensus about the sexual assault examination."

"I don't need one."

"Well, we can leave that for now, you're still in shock. But we do need to do it soon in order to use evidence in court if you wish to press charges."

"He didn't hurt me."

"You're pregnant.The dizzy spell was probably due to that and then you must have fallen." The words hit me hard. I felt like the wind was knocked out of me.

"What?"

"Sometimes when women are pregnant they get fainting spells. Sometimes it's low iron. We're running tests on your blood work now to see if that's the case."

"No. No, not that. I'm pregnant?"

"Yes, and I'm sorry, but if you don't want to confront the facts, I need to tell you that I know you obviously had sex since you've been kidnapped and considering the circumstances, I assumed it was a sexual assault." His words were still sinking in. I wanted to be happy. I was carrying Riley's baby and I suddenly didn't feel alone anymore. I rubbed my stomach and smiled for the first time.Then the look in the doctor's face took away my happiness and replaced it with anger. He was looking at me with pity and as one would look at a crazy person. Through clenched teeth I spoke,

"I wasn't raped. I can't expect you to understand, but you need to do what is necessary so that I can get out of here. If that means a psych consult, then get it done." The doctor had enough moral fiber to look ashamed and I suddenly felt bad for the guy. Looking at this whole situation through his eyes, who wouldn't have thought the same thing. He was just doing his job. He was showing concern and compassion.

"I'm sorry. I'm just overwhelmed with all this. I know you're just trying to help. I really need to speak to the police. Whoever I need to talk to in order to make that happen please try to get it done."

"Okay. I'll get someone here to talk to you. Once they give the green light and let us know you're in any shape to talk to anyone else, I'll bring in the constable that's been chomping at the bit to talk to you since you've come in." I bit my lip to keep from yelling. I wanted nothing more than to talk to the constable but I needed to jump through these darn hoops in order to do so.

"Please, just do it quickly."

***

It was a long night and my sleep was interrupted with unfamiliar noises and nonsense dreams. I could hear the steps of the nurses up and down the halls, beeps from machines and snores coming from my roommate. I wondered what Riley was thinking. I was so worried about him and was so angry with myself for the turn of events. How could I have been so stupid? If I hadn't gone so close to the edge with my ski boots then we wouldn't be in this mess. If I had had a dizzy spell anywhere else, it wouldn't have mattered so much. It was like Riley to sacrifice himself for me. Then I would think about the baby, our baby, and smile. I had a part of him with me and hoped I could fix things so that we could all be together.

I felt better today and I could sit up and even eat my breakfast when they brought it to me. I had broken my left arm so I was still able to have full use of my right. I was thankful that I didn't need to be dependent on the nurses to feed me.

Shortly after they cleared my tray of empty dishes another man came along with a cart full of books, magazines and today's paper. He wheeled it over beside my bed and when he looked up to see what I wanted, he stopped and stared for a brief second before catching himself.

"Sorry...what can I get you?" His reaction didn't register with me until I requested today's paper. It had been so long since I had looked at any news; it would be interesting to see what's going on in our world. Again he hesitated.

"Um, maybe you'd rather have a magazine or a book. We have a huge selection." I could see from his face that something was wrong and he was trying to keep me from the paper. The journalist posing as a nurse from yesterday flashed before me.

"I can handle it, just please, give me one."

"Okay. Just remember they like causing trouble. People don't believe half of what is written in these things." I appreciated his words, but they had already fallen on deaf ears as I looked at the front page. There I was; somewhat blurred as one hand was caught mid-way trying to shield my face. I looked pale, disheveled and panicked. In bold letters, the headline yelled,

KIDNAPPING VICTIM SUFFERS FROM STOCKHOLM SYNDROME.

It went on to say how many victims fall in love with the people that have hurt them due to the shock of the trauma and from being brainwashed over a period of time. Specifically it said,

"Jady Donner thinks she is in love with one of her kidnappers, Riley Williams. When asked about the man who tormented, kept her a prisoner for over four months, and allegedly raped her, she replied in a robotic yet defensive voice that "He was a good man" and that she loved him. Riley and his brother Byron Williams kidnapped Jady Donner on June 24th and kept her locked in a windowless room in a run down secluded cabin. According to Byron, Riley was the mastermind behind this horrible plan, hoping to bleed money from the multi-millionaire father Greg Donner, owner of the chain of Donner Drugstores. Mr. Donner was away on holidays when the kidnapping took place and when he returned, the Williams brother's plans went askew. Byron, having a change of heart didn't want to go through with the plans and after a hostile argument, Byron was left unconscious and Riley had fled with Miss Donner. Worried about the safety of Miss Donner, Byron turned himself into police, hoping the two would be found. The search that ensued included the police and Mr. Donner's own volunteers and was countrywide. Thinking Riley was holed up somewhere, Jady's face has been plastered on every TV and newspaper for the last four months. As it turns out, Riley Williams had her confined in a small cabin in a remote area. It is impossible to say how long it will take for Miss Donner to recover from her horrendous ordeal, but it is obvious from her hypnotic state and the conversation with her that there is a lot of damage to be undone.

I must have reread it at least four times, unable to believe what I was seeing. It wasn't until I looked over at my roommate, saw the pity in her eyes, the same paper open on her lap, that I knew it was really true.

"It's not true, none of it." The sympathy I saw in her eyes only increased and I hung my head feeling defeated. There was a lot of damage to be undone, but it was obvious from this woman's face that it was not me I needed to worry about.

I didn't have much time to mull over what to do. There was a commotion outside my room, which resonated down the hall.

"You can't go in there."

"I sure as hell can."

"She is in no condition to speak with anyone yet."

"I'll be the judge of that."

"She really needs to speak to a psychologist first."

"Look, the sooner I can talk to her the better."

The bickering went on for a few more minutes with the continued back and forth argument, neither side letting up. A third, calmer voice interjected.

"Both of you calm down. Eric I know you want to get to the bottom of this, but we need to respect both the hospital and the patient. Dr. Ryan, can I question the patient while her memory is still fresh if I promise to leave at any sign of anxiety or if she becomes upset?" A more subdued voice replied.

"Yes. I guess that would be fine."

"Thank you Dr. Ryan."

Two uniformed officers then entered my room and before they even had a chance to introduce themselves, a nurse came and helped my roommate into a wheelchair and moved her from the room. As they went by, the woman gave me a long look that I couldn't interpret.

"Where are we going?" I heard her ask the nurse.

"You're scheduled for a few tests Mrs. Adams." The officers then closed the door and pulled up chairs on either side of my bed. As anxious as I was to see them to clear things up, the sight of them now, made me nervous. How could I explain to them what had happened without them assuming I was under some spell? I could only try. I could tell immediately from looking at them that the younger one was the one that had been arguing with the doctor and the other older officer promptly made me feel at ease. He began to talk while the other one took out a small recorder.

"My name is Nate Dennill and I'm a Corporal here at the local detachment. This is my colleague Constable Evans." He nodded towards me, but he seemed new at his job, almost as nervous as I was.

"I know you've been through a lot, but we'd just like to ask you a few questions if you feel up to it. We would also like to record your answers if that's okay?"

"Yes, that would be fine. I..." I stopped unsure of where to begin.

"That's okay. Let's start with simple stuff. What's your name?" We smiled at each other and I liked him already.

"Jady Donner."

"Can you tell me a bit about yourself before all this took place?"

"I was away at University studying to become a teacher. My mom passed away when I was eighteen and...I'm not close with my father. For graduation he sent me a gift. A Cadillac." Constable Evans looked up from his notebook for a brief moment with an eyebrow raised.

"I didn't want it and was driving it back to him when...when it happened."

"Okay, now's the tough part. Can you remember in detail how it all started?"

"Yes. But it's not like the paper said. Byron's lying. He's the bad guy in all this. It was his idea and he is the one who almost killed me. Riley never hurt me, he saved me..." Corporal Dennill stopped me.

"Slow down. It's okay. Here." He handed me a glass of water from my side table and I took a long drink. I so just wanted to pour it all out at once and make them understand, but I could see I needed to start from the beginning.

I took a deep breath and did just that. I explained the whole story from beginning to end.

"I know it sounds bad and I'm not trying to justify what Riley did, but he didn't do it because he's a bad guy. He saved me in the end and it was me who had the change of heart. I stayed with him on the island because I *wanted* to not because he forced me to. *I* was the one who convinced Riley to stay there. He wanted to turn himself in. I wanted him to stay with me. I was being selfish and wanted more time...and now I've ruined everything." I buried my face in my hands and exhausted tears fell between my fingers.

I felt a compassionate, warm hand on my arm and a Kleenex was placed before me.

"I'm sorry. It's just all so much. I'm the reason he's in custody. I'm the reason he's in trouble. If I hadn't fallen, we would still be there. We would have been safe. How can I expect you to believe this incredible story? How can I expect you to believe I fell in love with someone who kidnapped me, but I don't suffer from some weird syndrome. I love him today and I would love him 20 years from now even if we were separated all that time."

"I believe you."

Both Constable Evans and myself looked at Corporal Dennill in disbelief.

***

"So what happens now? What's Riley saying?"

"He's refusing to give a statement. But now that I have heard the whole story it makes a bit more sense."

"I don't understand."

"Wouldn't you be a bit upset if you knew your only brother not only ratted you out, but lied about the whole thing." I hadn't thought about that. I couldn't imagine how awful he must be feeling.

"I need to talk to him."

"You need to get out of here first. Please don't rush yourself. Make sure you're in good condition. It sounds like you're going to have a lot of work ahead of you."

"What's going to happen to Riley?"

"Well, if you don't want to press charges, there's really nothing to hold him on. We'll start the paper work and he should be a free man by the time you get out of here. Maybe he'll be here to see you first." It was the best thing I had heard in a while and my smile must have revealed my relief. Corporal Dennill and Constable Evans got up to go.

"Thank you so much."

"It's not very often we come to question a victim and we leave with everyone happy. Here's my card if you think of anything else or need help."

"Thanks again." I reached for the card and looked at it absently as I thought about what he had said. Riley would be free? I would see him soon. I was so happy. So far the information about my pregnancy hadn't leaked out, so I had the excitement of telling him the great news. I just knew he was going to be as happy as I was.

Later that afternoon the psychologist came to also ask a few questions. I repeated my story and reassured the doctor that I was okay. This man, whose name escaped me didn't look as believing as Nate did.

"Have you heard of Stockholm Syndrome?"

"I had never heard of it until it was plastered on the front page of the paper."

"Oh yes, that was unfortunate. Well, it's where a victim who has been kidnapped comes to empathize with their kidnappers and in some cases even thinks they love them."

"I don't think, I *know*. I am not suffering from some syndrome. I am completely aware of what I'm doing and how I am feeling."

"I see." He was scribbling irritably in his notebook and I just wanted him to leave.

"I'll make sure to come back and see you again before you're discharged, to see how you are doing."

"I can guarantee you I will be *doing* the same."

He ignored my comment and left the room.

I could see him through the glass window in deep conversation with my doctor and when they both looked my way with serious expressions I could tell they were both convinced I was crazy. I really didn't care as long as they let me out of here. I was so worried about Riley and how he was feeling. He was alone and feeling betrayed by his only remaining family. I needed to let him know I was here and that he had a little baby to live for. He had a new family to love, one who would never betray or hurt him.

The next morning I felt good enough to get out of bed and take a shower without feeling faint. I would have to get better at doing everything one handed, but that would come with practice.

When the doctor came by to check on me I was sitting in a chair and reading the paper. I was now on page three and it was more about my father than about me. This time the headline read,

Drugstore Dad Wants Justice

Greg Donner, owner of Donner Drugstores, is elated his daughter is safe and getting better every day. When asked about the kidnapper, the otherwise professional and calm businessman became overcome with emotion. He admitted he was filled with anger towards this man that hurt his daughter and wants to make sure everything is done to put this menace behind bars for life.

I stopped reading then. I was the one overcome with emotion right now and it was definitely anger. What is he talking about? He doesn't even know how I'm doing; he hasn't come around to see. Not that I wanted him to. If he showed up here, I would ask the staff to escort him away. His other comments scared me. Could he do something to hurt Riley? Why would he want to put someone in jail that allegedly hurt someone he didn't even love or care about? Why did they only ever mention one kidnapper?

I swallowed my hate and smiled at the doctor when he entered my room.

"You're looking good today Jady."

"I'm feeling good." I was about to say I want to go home, but I didn't know where home was and it suddenly dawned on me I didn't have any place to go. I realized as much as I wanted to get out of there I needed a little more time to formulate a plan. I didn't just have me to think about any more I had this little one growing inside me to take care of now.

"Physically, I think you only need another day or two to restore your energy and to make sure you're completely recovered from your concussion." Inwardly I breathed a sigh of relief. That should give me enough time. But I sensed a "but" in his tone.

"But?"

"Well, after talking to Doctor Chard I have to say I share his concern." So that was what that shrink's name was.

"What concerns?"

"We both strongly agree that you are suffering from Stockholm Syndrome and need more intensive therapy..." I must have looked panicked because he followed it up quickly with, "It can be on an outpatient basis."

"Is this a condition on my release of this hospital?"

"No, no, it's just a strong recommendation."

"I appreciate your concern Doctor and I will give it a lot of thought." He looked appeased. He stood up then.

"Make sure you get a lot of rest. Today and tomorrow take some walks around the halls to see how your head feels. I'll check back in with you tomorrow and see how you're doing."

"Thanks."

As soon as he walked away I picked the paper back up. I went to the classified section and started looking for an apartment. I had enough money put away for the damage deposit and the first few months rent. I should be able to find a job as soon as my cast was off and then I could go from there.

I found a pen and began circling. I would follow them up with phone calls and make appointments to go check them out in a couple of days. I could stay in a hotel for a little bit until I found one. I rubbed my belly and felt happier than I had since I woke up here.

***

I was getting out. The only thing nagging at me was the fact that I had yet to even hear from Riley. I thought he would've been released by now. Every time footsteps echoed down the hall that sounded like the owner was a man with a heavier step, my heart skipped a beat. But nothing.

The doctor was still preaching the therapy thing and I kept him at bay and quiet by saying I would seriously look into it.

I had made about a dozen phone calls regarding apartments and had narrowed it down to six. The other half were either gone already or I didn't get a good first impression over the phone with the landlord. I had a night booked at a local hotel and as I was getting ready to go, I looked around me to see that I had nothing to pack. I only had the clothes I had come here with which weren't even mine. They belonged to the Cabin Couple. It made me sad to think about them and it made my clothes seem like souvenirs. I had no suitcase or any belongings of any kind.

When I left school I had packed one suitcase with all the clothes I owned and who knows where that had ended up. I would need to hit a thrift store too and get myself a few things to wear and see about a few furnishings also. I was just looking down at my ski boots wondering how ridiculous it was going to be walking around in those clown shoes when Corporal Nate rushed into the room out of breath. He was not in uniform and he was carrying boots.

"I'm so glad I caught you. I was worried I would have to search the city for you if you were already gone. I thought you might need these." He handed me the boots and although they were a bit big they were better than ski shoes. I was hoping the sight of him meant good news, but his tone seemed serious. He beckoned for me to sit down and he did as well trying to catch his breath.

"I'm afraid things didn't go as planned." When I didn't respond, he continued.

"Your father has thrown a wrench into things."

"What does my father have to do with any of this."

"Well he seems to be hell-bent on revenge and wants us to do something about Riley."

"How is it that he has any say in this?"

"Well the psychiatrist that came to see you here at the hospital was hired by your father."

"What? Why?"

"He's determined to prove that you're not in your right mind and can't be expected to make any sensible decisions. He's going with the whole Stockholm Syndrome thing and is adamant that you should not be able to make the decision to set Riley free. He's trying to say you're incapable and that he needs to take over. He wants Riley charged, a trial, with a heavy sentence being his goal."

"Why the hell would he be doing this?" I realized I was speaking more to myself than to him. The Corporal didn't know our whole history. I decided I needed to fill him in if I was going to get him to on my side and help me fight this whole thing. He seemed to be the only one who didn't think I was crazy.

"Wow, I can see why you wouldn't want to keep his gift. I think you controlled yourself better than I would have." This was Nate's answer once I had poured out everything regarding my father and my mom's death.

"Okay, so now why would he all of a sudden play the loving father role and try to act like he cared?" That question came from me. I was stumped. We both sat for a bit contemplating the question.

Instead of giving a theory, Corporal Dennill asked,

"So what are you doing now? Where are you going?" I told him my plans and he started to shake his head before I was even done.

"No, no no. I know where each of those apartments are and I wouldn't let my worst enemies live in those neighbourhoods."

"It's all I can afford right now until I get a job and by the sounds of it I'm going to need money to help fight my father in court."

"Let me think on this for a bit. I'll drive you to the hotel, but don't do anything about the apartments just yet. I'll see what I can do."

"You really don't need to do all this. I'll be okay."

"I know I don't and I know you're a tough one and will be okay. But you remind me so much of my daughter and I would hope if she needed help and I wasn't there, someone would do the same for her. Besides, I'm making no promises, you might end up in one of those dives yet, but I'll do my darndest to make sure that doesn't happen."

"What can I do in the meantime about Riley? How do I prove I'm not crazy? How do I help get Riley out?"

"I'm already looking into that too. I've got nothing solid yet, but leave it to me and I promise I will keep you in the loop the whole way. Right now you need to get out of here. You are also going to need to keep a low profile. Reporters are just dying to get more of a story out of you, and then, of course, twist it to suit them. C'mon let's go. You can sign all the final paper work and then we'll sneak out the back."

"Thanks again Corporal Dennill, I really appreciate everything you're doing for me."

"Call me Nate." He shot me a caring smile. It felt good to have someone in my corner.

As Nate was driving me to the hotel he explained that Riley was being held in custody over the weekend, but they would be shipping him off on Monday to the larger city nearby. The detachment had to give a press release and update the public on the chain of events.

He stopped talking as he looked over at me. I was overwhelmed.

"I'm sorry. This is a lot for you to deal with." I nodded, but I don't think we were talking about the same thing. I *was* overwhelmed by what was happening with Riley, but at that moment it was what I was taking in outside that was suffocating me. The never-ending train of cars, trucks and buses. The grey smoke coming from their tailpipes that didn't smell anything like the wonderful wood smoke I had grown to love. The large buildings all around that made me feel more claustrophobic than had I been surrounded by the tallest of mountains. It was hard to believe that I once lived in all of this and it had never effected me. I had lived and breathed it without even a moment's thought. Now compared to the pristine beauty of the island, it was as appealing as a garbage dump. Nate's voice brought me back around.

"I hate to tell you, but that means there will be a lot of press there for his court appearance tomorrow."

"He'll be in court tomorrow?"

"Yes."

"Can I go to court?"

"Yes, but that might be hard on you given all the publicity." I wasn't listening anymore. I would get to see Riley even if it was just briefly and even if I wouldn't be able to talk to him.

"Can you bring me to the bus depot instead?"

"If that's what you want."

"It's what I want."

Nate did a U-turn and started to drive in the opposite direction.

"The bus might not be scheduled for a run into the city until late tonight."

"That's fine." Nate then pulled over to the side and pulled out his cell phone.

"Hey Cindy, what time does the bus run out of here today? Uh-huh, okay thanks." He pulled out on the road again and I watched the bus depot as we went past it. I didn't say a word. I had no idea what Nate was up to.

We pulled up in front of a store.

"C'mon, the bus doesn't leave for a few hours. It's a long boring wait and an even longer boring ride. You need something to pass the time."

It turned out we were in a bookstore. I loved bookstores and libraries. Being such a recluse I had read many a book in my time. I immediately became immersed in the shelves. It was nice to see a new selection after reading and rereading the books at the cabin. I had to stop myself from looking for the same books. I wanted anything to help me remember every second. I knew they wouldn't smell or feel the same and I would only be disappointed.

"Pick anything you like. My daughter keeps trying to make a reader out of me so she keeps buying me gift cards. I don't have the heart to tell her I haven't cashed a single one. Now I can say I did without lying." Nate grinned, handed me a few cards and walked away. I saw him go stand in line to get a coffee.

I didn't even know where to begin. Then it dawned on me what I needed. I went to the law section and found a few I wanted. Then I found the area that housed the hobby books and felt fortunate to find the one I wanted there too. I paid for the books with the cards. I felt guilty using his gifts, but when I thought of what was ahead of me I knew I would need to hang on to every dime.

I joined him at a little table and he had a coffee waiting for me too.

"Thanks again Nate."

"Seriously, I should be thanking you. Now what can I tell my daughter I bought?" I showed him my purchases and he raised an eyebrow.

"Wow, that's some light reading there. I don't know what's worse, your choices or your future bus ride." I laughed and felt grateful again.

"I want to know what I'm up against. What *am* I up against anyway? What will happen tomorrow at court?"

"Well, they'll ask for a plea and then set a trial date. He will be kept in custody there until then."

"How long will that take?"

"It could take months Jady." When he saw my face fall, he added "I'm sorry. I know this must be hard." To change the subject he pointed to the other book in the pile.

"And what's that one, another yawner?"

"No, I'm hoping this one will help me keep sane." It was a book on painting watercolours."

"And that one will keep you sane?" I couldn't help but smile. He stood up to go.

"C'mon let's get you a bite to eat before you get on that bus."

"I really can't let you do another thing for me Nate. You've done enough, really." His face turned serious.

"Look Jady, you've got a long rough road ahead of you and I'm not talking about the bus. You need all the help you can get and you'll have to learn to take it when you can. Beside there isn't one good restaurant in this town so you won't be so thankful once you've eaten." He always managed to get a smile out of me, which was good, because I knew there were not a lot of smiles coming my way in the next few months.

***

Nate didn't give the food the credit it deserved. It was greasy, sloppy and I loved it. Halfway through the meal I had a thought that hit me hard and I put down my burger.

"I told you it was bad. You don't have to worry about hurting my feelings if you don't want to eat it."

"No, it's not that. Now I need to find a place close to where they're holding him so that I can see him regularly. He needs to know I'm there for him. I need to be near him any way I can."

"Well, I think I might be able to help you out there too, but let me get back to you on that one. Make sure when you get there you get the cab to take you to this hotel." He had written down the name on a piece of paper. It's not expensive and it's clean and quiet."

I finished my meal, unable to say anymore. Words weren't enough to tell Nate how grateful I was.

I watched the scenery fly by, holding my new unread book on my lap. I found it so hard to concentrate. I was thinking about seeing Riley in court tomorrow. I wished I would be able to talk to him. I wanted to talk to him before he went to court. I wanted to know what was going on in his mind. Nate told me that once he was finished in court and put in prison awaiting his trial, he could have visitors.

I tried to bring my attention back to the book on law. I had wanted a few that described the system and the ins and outs of trials, hearings and the rights of both the prosecuted and the one doing the prosecuting. Even though I wasn't the one pressing charges, I needed to know things my father might try to throw in there. I still didn't understand why he was doing what he was doing. For me it was just one more thing in my life that he was messing up. It was almost like he was determined to take everyone I've ever loved away from me.

I looked around me for the first time at the other people on the bus. What were their stories? Were they visiting loved ones or was this the way they always traveled? Some were sleeping and others reading or listening to music on their iPods. Whatever their story, I knew no one else was on the bus for the same reason I was.

When we pulled up to our destination, the smell of the local pulp mill was the first thing to hit me. Then the noise of the traffic and all the people made me want to get back on the bus. The greasy burger wasn't the best choice after the bland hospital food and I was regretting it now, scared it might come back up. I took a few deep breaths through my mouth until the feeling passed. I wondered how many times I was going to think about the cabin and miss it's peace and solitude.

I waded through the throngs of people and found a phone on the wall designated for phoning taxis. Within minutes, I had one pulling up in front and the driver didn't seem to question the fact that I had no luggage. I handed him the piece of paper with the hotel name written on it. Although it was only dinnertime, it was already dark and the street lights everywhere were no comparison to candle light.

I checked myself in and found the room exactly as Nate described it. Clean and quiet. There was no bar downstairs so I wouldn't have to worry about drunks staggering around the halls or loud music vibrating off the walls.

I had made it to my room just in time. The burger caught up with me and it wasn't pleasant. I lay down after, exhausted and sweaty.

Tomorrow I would find out where the grocery store was and get some stuff for sandwiches and some fresh fruit and vegetables. The room had a small fridge and that would do for now. I would also pick up a local paper to try and find apartments for rent here while I waited to see what Nate had in mind.

I must have dozed off because the knock on the door startled me. Disorientated and disappointed yet again with my surroundings I opened my door only to realize it was someone else's door that had a visitor.

I turned on the TV and lay back down. There were so many channels to choose from and yet I wasn't interested. I just wanted to look at my painting book and pretend I was back on the island. I closed my eyes and wished I could smell pine and water rather than the faint smell of smoke in a hotel room that had probably been a smoking room in days long past.

I ordered pizza and I ate two pieces, putting the rest in the fridge although I knew I wouldn't be eating those leftovers. Two greasy meals in one day were enough to last me awhile. I longed for the bear jerky and fresh canned vegetables made with my own hands. My stomach twisted in agreement and I stretched out on the bed. In the hospital bed, I had missed Riley but the bed was so foreign that it didn't seem he belonged there. But now here in a normal bed again, I missed him terribly. I put my hand on my stomach; at least I wasn't completely alone. This bed was way too big and instead of the cries of the loons echoing in the nights, only my own cries could be heard.

***

I was awake early, listening to the hissing of the small coffee maker in the room. The wonderful smell that usually brought me comfort did nothing to change my anxious thoughts this morning. I was so excited to see Riley, but wished it had been under different circumstances.

I called a cab much earlier than needed, and I got out about a block before the courthouse where there was a coffee house. Initially I thought of getting something to eat, but when I walked in the smell of fresh baking overwhelmed me with nausea rather than the usual reaction of overindulgence.

I stopped myself from ordering another coffee and got an herbal tea instead. I grabbed a seat looking out onto the street. I used to like people watching, but now I wished I was looking out over a lake observing a beaver dam being built. I hated this. I hated feeling like a sulky kid mourning over a lost toy. I needed to snap out of it. I had a little one to care for and I needed to have a clear head to do battle against my father.

I wasted as much time as I could and then walked down to the courthouse. I remembered what Nate had said about the publicity and cursed myself for forgetting as shouts announced my arrival. Paparazzi were swarming around me like bees and I pulled my ski jacket protectively around my body thinking more about my unborn baby than myself.

"Miss Donner, how can you say you're in love with a man that has kidnapped you and hurt you?"

"Jady, are you here hoping to stop the trial or have you come to your senses and are here to help put Riley Williams behind bars where he belongs?"

"How do you feel about the people who are saying you should be doing time too for loving a criminal?"

"How do you explain the fact that this is the first we've heard of the multi-millionaire Mr. Donner's daughter?" This last question made my head snap up and look directly into the eyes of the voice that spewed it. It was a female reporter and her cold eyes met mine. I wished I had it in me to be mean and spiteful. This would be the time to make a mark on my father's perfect name, but as much as I hated the man, this was not the way I wanted to bring him down. I pushed my way through, not uttering a word to anyone. It became overwhelming and a hand grabbed mine and pulled me through. When I came face to face with the owner of the hand I let go. Something looked familiar about her, but she was a stranger. As she escorted me away forcefully I wondered if she was just another journalist trying to get me all to herself for an exclusive. Once we were inside the doors of the courthouse she finally spoke.

"Wow, that was intense." I looked at her, still wondering where I knew her.

"Oh, I'm sorry I'm Susan, My father sent me, said you could probably use some moral support, that you were alone. He told me a bit about your situation, that really bites." I was still puzzled and we were no longer walking towards the courtroom but down the hall. I stopped and looked at her.

"I have no idea what you're talking about. Who is your father?" Susan laughed, took off her woven grey hat with one lone sunflower, ran her fingers through her brown hair and stuffed it all back under the hat.

"Nate Dennill is my dad." I smiled as I pieced it all together. It explained why she looked familiar, she really resembled her father. We stopped outside the women's washroom.

"Here. My dad said you would probably need these and he was actually right, we're about the same size." I stared down at the bag she was holding out to me and finally took it from her hands. I looked inside to see some clothes and it was then I looked down at myself. I was wearing the same clothes from the cabin. Although they weren't really dirty, they were a bit beat up from the fall and they didn't fit me properly. I was thankful for something else.

I went into the restroom and changed into the black jeans and a comfy red sweater. I was getting to be a pro at doing everything with one hand. I was glad because I would've been quite embarrassed to ask this girl I had just met to help me get dressed. The clothes fit me perfectly, the sweater was even baggy enough to fit over my cast. and I shook my head at the coincidence. I came out and Susan smiled.

"I think that looks better on you than me."

"Thanks. You're a lot like your father."

"So people tell me." We started walking back towards the courtroom.

"Are you ready for this?"

"Not even close."

We walked through the doors and found ourselves in a packed room. It seemed we weren't the only ones interested in the cases being presented today.

Unfortunately, Riley's wasn't the first on the list today. As we sat through case after case, Susan and I had time to get to know each other.

"I didn't know you lived here."

"Oh yeah. I left town after high school and came here to find work. I'm not a big studier so college or university didn't appeal to me. I started out as a waitress barely making ends meet and then I took an interest in what was going on in the kitchen. I always loved cooking with my mom when I was younger and I found myself hanging around in the kitchen at the restaurant more and more. I asked a lot of questions and finally one of the cooks said I should get some training since I was so interested. I looked into it, and found myself sitting in cooking school a month later. I loved it so much and now I cook at that same restaurant I started waitressing in. I would love to have my own place some day and do my own thing."

"It's amazing how things come to be isn't it? I was talking, but my eyes kept flicking to the door to see if Riley was walking through them.

"You're really looking forward to seeing him aren't you?

"Yes and no." Susan didn't say anything she just waited to see if I was going to elaborate.

"I want to see him. I just wish it wasn't here or under these circumstances." She nodded in understanding.

"My dad told me a bit of your story and it all sounds so surreal. It's hard to believe something like that really happened. What was it like staying at the cabin?" She picked the right topic to pass the time. I could talk openly about something that I loved and hadn't been able to share with anyone else. I had just started to tell her about Grace when I saw him. His beard was gone, making him look younger and more vulnerable. He was pale and he looked like he hadn't slept this whole time, but there were those eyes, those beautiful, mesmerizing black eyes. I only saw them briefly as he looked up for a moment. The rest of the time his eyes stayed riveted on the floor. He looked defeated and like someone who had lost everything. I really wanted him to look my way. I wanted him to see that I was there, for him. I wanted to send him a message with my eyes. I wanted to convey how much I loved him. But he wasn't looking up. I never took my eyes off the back of his head. The hair I had once shampooed was quite a bit shorter.

We all stood as the judge re-entered the room.

"What have we got here?" The judge's commanding voice demonstrated who was in charge.

"Your honour, Mr. Riley Williams has been charged with kidnapping, forcible confinement and assault causing bodily harm." The crown attorney's words were causing me bodily harm and it took everything I had not to yell out and tell them they were all wrong.

"We need some time to put everything together your honour. We would like to request a court date four months from today." The crown attorney was a beautiful woman who looked like she lived and breathed her job. She also looked like a woman who was on a mission and didn't take kindly to losing. The judge focused his attention on the defense attorney.

"Mr. Daniels, what do you have to say?"

"Four months is fine your honour."

"Do you wish to enter a plea at this time?"

"No, your..."

"I'm guilty." This came from Riley and instantly his lawyer turned to him and began murmuring in his ear. Crown took this opportunity to jump all over this admission.

"Your honour, as much as we would like the time to gather evidence, we also do not wish to waste any of the court's or your time. We would be more than willing to settle sentencing right now."

"I'm sure you would Miss Taylor. Mr. Daniels?"

"Sorry, your honour, my client is very distraught and needs to be assessed. We would not like to enter a plea at this time your honour."

"All right then, we'll see you in four months." The gavel striking down made me jump in my seat. *Please look this way Riley, Please look this way.* I was hoping as he was escorted out he would glance around or somehow pick up my vibe.

"Hey, watch where you're going!" Susan was yelling at someone in her way and security was there instantly to walk her out. She gave me a wink as she looked my way.

I turned to see Riley staring at me. He didn't smile. I smiled at him and mouthed *I love you,* but the only emotion that seemed to register on his face was guilt and then he was gone. I buried my face in my hands and tried not to cry. I gathered all the remaining strength I had and went outside to find Susan.

"Thanks." I managed weakly when I found her waiting for me outside.

"Hey, I do what I can for love." It didn't take long for the journalists to find us and we quickly ran to escape but their questions trailed behind me.

"What was decided?"

"Was it difficult to see someone who has tormented you?"

"C'mon, my car is just over here."

"Oh, even if you just have a cell phone and can call me a cab that would be great."

"And go where?"

"Back to the hotel I guess. I'm going to start looking for places and a job tomorrow." Some journalists were still following us, maybe hoping to overhear some juicy conversation.

"Let's get in the car, go for a drive. We need to get away from here and then we can talk and figure this all out." I was quiet while she drove. I was so disappointed in how everything turned out. Four months. Four months he would have to sit in there. What has been said to him to make him look so crushed? Why did he want to plead guilty? Why was he so willing to give up on everything we had planned? I was going to see if I could start visiting him tomorrow.

We pulled into a restaurant parking lot.

"I'm really not hungry."

"Look, I saw the look on your boyfriend's face and it spelled defeat. If you want to help him, you can't do the same. You will have to fight for the both of you. In order to do that you need to take care of yourself and that includes eating. They make the best milkshakes and fries here." Despite myself that sounded good.

"Okay, now you were just beginning to tell me about Grace. You had a pet raccoon? I want to hear the rest."

I filled her in on how Grace slept under the table and how she had begun to make a nest and I found myself smiling as I told Susan about her and the way Riley and I lived. Our food arrived and we both polished off every last fry as we shared stories about our lives. Mostly it was her listening, and me talking but she didn't make me feel like I was hogging the conversation at all, she seemed genuinely interested.

"And then Riley left for a hunting trip and stupid me, I went skiing. I walked too close to a rock ledge with my ski boots and fell off to the bottom. I woke up in the hospital." I left out the dizzy spell for now not wanting to explain the cause of that just yet. I stared at the bottom of my drink as I stirred it around. It wasn't the first time I wished I could reverse time and do over that morning.

"And he brought you to the hospital?"

"I…I think so. I assume so. It makes sense now, but at the time I didn't know what was happening. I still don't know exactly how he got me there."

"He went all that way, risking everything because he was scared about you?"

"I don't think he realized or thought about what was going to happen. I think, we both thought we were safe."

"Right, you didn't realize that his brother had already given him up. Holy, what a jerk to do that to anyone, never mind your own brother." The lovely trip down memory lane was slipping away and I was forced again to deal with the reality of today and my future.

"Okay, enough about that. Let's talk about where you're going to stay."

"I already told you..."

"Yeah, yeah yeah. I heard you. Look, my place has lots of room and you can stay with me as long as you like. You'll waste away all your funds staying in a hotel while you look for something decent around here. I'll keep my ears to the ground and see what I can find for a job." I was already shaking my head.

"Your father has already done more than enough for me I can't ask any more from your family."

"You'll be doing me a favour. My roommate moved out last month and I could use the extra income."

"You are such a bad liar."

"I'm not bringing you back to the hotel. Come and stay at least one night, see if it's a good fit and we'll talk about it again tomorrow. Okay?"

"Fine. You're just as stubborn as your father."

"That I am." With that she grabbed the bill and ran to pay.

***

Susan's house was welcoming the moment I entered. Her dog, Sookie greeted me with enthusiasm before Susan let her outside.

"Sorry, I forgot to mention I have a dog. And a cat, somewhere."

"No problem, I never had a pet, but I always wanted one."

The colours of her walls were earthy and warm and although none of her furniture matched, it all looked inviting and like it belonged exactly where she placed it. There wasn't an inch of wall space that was bare. You could probably walk into her house over a dozen times and each time find something you hadn't noticed before. She had alluring art, wooden and porcelain sculptures, hand made rugs and blankets thrown over the backs of chairs. Where there was room, there were bookshelves and even those had books overflowing onto the floor in front of them. I remembered her dad and the gift certificates and smiled as I ran my hands over the books.

She was rattling around in the kitchen, while I did my tour, not needing a guide. I noticed pictures of her, one black and white of a much younger looking Susan with a woman, and many of her father, Sookie and her cat, a tiny black and brown marbled one.

"What's the name of your cat?" I yelled into the kitchen.

"Kool Kitty!" Susan yelled back. I smiled. As if summoned, the cat strolled into the room and rubbed up against my leg, purring. I sat on the floor and she made herself comfortable on my lap.

Susan came in with a tray with two steaming mugs of tea and a big bowl of popcorn. She placed it on the table and plunked down to join me on the floor. Kool Kitty abandoned me for a more familiar lap.

"Who's with you in the black and white picture?"

"That's my mom." I sensed sadness and was afraid to question any further. I didn't need to.

"She died when I was six. It was tough on me, but even tougher on my father. It made us very close. I was an only kid." Her eyes scanned the photos on the shelf and she was quiet.

"I really like your place." She smiled, her reverie broken.

"C'mon, I'll give you a full tour and show you where you'll be sleeping." She had such a nice house and I was beginning to think she did very well as a chef. When we got to the room I would be calling my own for a while, exhaustion came over me and I yawned openly before I could catch myself. It dawned on her then that I had no belongings.

"I don't have to work tomorrow. You need to go shopping and we'll do some job hunting."

She sensed my hesitation and read it correctly.

"I know where all the best thrift stores are. I can find you a lot of new clothes for next to nothing. Right now you need to crash. There's a bathroom attached to the room and there are fresh towels too."

"Thanks Susan. I honestly don't know how I'm ever going to repay you and your father for all your kindness."

"I believe in karma. I believe what comes around, goes around. I don't do things for others in order to be repaid. I do it because I want to and I always get rewarded in abundance through all the wonderful things that come my way. Have a good sleep Jady, and I'll see you in the morning. Do you need anything else?"

"No, I think I'm good. Thanks and goodnight."

"Goodnight."

I woke to the smell of fresh coffee and the sun streaming in through a strange window. As I took in my surroundings, I felt more relaxed than I had in days. I was not in a hospital or in a hotel room, this felt comfortable. I felt a pang of guilt as I thought about Riley sitting in a cold jail cell, alone. Then the thought that I might get a chance to see him today brightened my spirits and I got out of bed and took a hot shower, making sure to cover my cast with a plastic bag. I couldn't wait to have this cumbersome thing off.

Wrapped in a towel I walked back into the room to find a pair of jeans and a sweater laying on the bed. She really was amazing. I got dressed and finger combed my long hair. It sure needed a trim too, but that would have to wait.

I walked downstairs into Susan's kitchen to find her drinking coffee and reading the newspaper.

"Do you want the good news or the bad news?" She smiled.

"Give me the bad."

"Make yourself a cup of coffee first. You might need it." The coffee smelled so good and I made it with two big scoops of sugar and lots of milk. I took a large gulp and closed my eyes, savouring the taste. As much as I missed the island, it was wonderful to be back in the land of dairy products.

"Okay, hit me with it."

"Well you're page one again." I sat down beside her and saw my face surrounded by a crowd of journalists on the front page of the paper. This time the headlines questioned, *Sorrowful Lover or Victim Looking For Justice? Was Jady Donner there to see her long lost love Riley Williams or has she awoken from her spell and wants to see that justice is carried out?*

It went on to allude to the fact that Riley had pleaded guilty, but was harassed by his lawyer to hold off on entering a plea. It said that the Crown Attorney was looking for blood and tried to take advantage of this and skip to a speedy sentence. Then it listed the trial date.

"So, what's the good news?" She flipped to the back of the paper. Here she had a bunch of ads circled.

"What's your fancy? Daycare, pre-school teacher or mechanic?"

"Really?" She handed the paper to me and went to make herself another cup of coffee. She brought the pot around to me.

"Do you need a refill yet?" I covered my cup with my hand. I felt a bit queasy and realized I really needed to eat something before I drank coffee. I also didn't want to have too much caffeine. I would need to find a doctor here and make an appointment.

"Actually, do you mind if I make myself some toast?"

"Oh my goodness, go ahead. Help yourself to whatever you want. There's lots of fruit and I'm a cerealoholic so take a look in the cupboard and pick whatever you want. I think I even have Fruit Loops in there."

"I think I'll start with the toast, but I might just have to have a Fruit Loop chaser." When I had my toast ready, I sat back down with the paper. Susan went to take a shower.

The pre-school job sounded inviting. I had all the training necessary and I wouldn't have all the work that a classroom involved. I wouldn't need to worry about report cards or all the extra-curricular stuff that came with having a regular classroom. The thought of working with young children appealed to me and it would give me the time I needed to figure out what to do about Riley's case. I wrote down the information and still hungry, fixed myself the bowl of Fruit Loops, washing it down with a large glass of orange juice.

In order to find a doctor I was going to need to trust Susan 100% and tell her about the baby. I was going to hold out a little longer. I really wanted to be able to tell Riley first.

I looked for a piece of paper and a pen.

Phone about the job.

Find out about visiting Riley.

Go shopping for clothes.

Find a doctor.

See about getting a new bankcard and ID.

I folded the note and put it in my front pocket just as Susan walked back into the kitchen.

"Well, what do we need to do first?" Susan and I were going to get along just fine.

***

I made the phone call about the job before we headed out and had just to put it back on the receiver when it rang. I handed it to Susan.

"Hello?"

"Oh, hey dad. Yup, looking right at her. Yeah, we were there. Have to wait awhile for a trial date." I was waving my hands in front of her indicating I wanted to talk to him as well.

"Yeah, we're heading out the door shortly. We're going to do some running around. Jady wants to talk to you before you hang up." She handed the phone back to me.

"Hi Nate. Thanks once again for sending Susan to help me out. She's been awesome." Susan winked in my direction.

"What I wanted to talk to you about was visiting Riley at the prison today. Do I need to make an appointment or can I just go down there?"

"Actually, I don't know. You can either just go down or I can make a few phone calls," he replied. I thought how badly I wanted to see Riley face to face, but I couldn't stand the thought of being that close and then be turned away.

"Can you make the phone calls for me?"

"Sure. Gotta run, say bye to my darling daughter for me."

"Will do." I hung up and as we got ready to head out Susan asked,

"Well, what did they say about the job?"

"Oh, the woman sounded really nice and she said to come by tomorrow at two for an interview."

"That's great."

"So shopping it is."

"Actually, I guess I need to go to the bank first and get a new bank card."

"Sure."

"Look, Susan, I really appreciate you taking the time to do all this running around with me."

"Hey any excuse to go shopping." I laughed and we walked to her car.

We had been shopping for over an hour now and had gone to a few different stores. Everything seemed like so much money and I needed almost a whole new wardrobe on a small amount of money.

"I'm sorry. This must be so frustrating for you. I just need to be careful since I don't know when my first pay check will be and I need to make what I do have last."

Susan was quiet for a minute.

"I have just the solution. C'mon, let's go."

We pulled up outside a thrift store and I smiled.

We left over an hour later with four bags of "new" clothes and less than $100 spent. I was so happy I offered to take Susan for lunch.

"Okay, I won't argue with that one, but I get to pick the restaurant."

"Well, considering I don't know my way around, that would probably be a wise decision."

Minutes later we were walking into a pretty fancy restaurant.

"Okay, I know I said I would pay for lunch, but I might end up doing dishes in this place."

Susan just smiled my way and walked up to the hostess.

"Hi Wayne. Can I have the spot by the window?"

"Sure, it's not that busy yet, go ahead grab any spot."

"Thanks."

I followed Susan through this gorgeous setting and we plunked into a booth by the window.

"This is the restaurant you work at isn't it?"

"Yup. They have the best food in town, even when I'm not cooking." I laughed.

The waitress came over and Susan talked to her while I browsed the menu, which had no prices on it. The choices sounded amazing though.

The waitress left and Susan eased my anxiety.

"Don't worry, order whatever you want, we eat for free here."

Seriously?"

"Yup, they're really good about it as long as we don't take advantage of it."

"That's a cool perk."

"Wait until you taste the food. It's a better perk than you can imagine."

"Anything you recommend"

"Honestly, it's all good, but if you like sweet, the lemon pancakes with the ricotta topping are incredible."

"Mmmmmm. That sounds great. It sounds like having dessert for lunch. My idea of heaven."

Within the next hour, after devouring the pancakes, I could vouch that I'd definitely had a taste of heaven.

"Oh my goodness, you were not kidding. Those were amazing." I took a long sip of my water, wishing it were a coffee instead which reminded me to find a doctor here. I was putting it off so that I could first tell Riley and then Susan. I'd rather see a doctor that had been recommended by someone.

"So, what's next?"

"Well, I've got clothes, my interview isn't until tomorrow and I have to wait on your father to see about visiting Riley. So I really don't know what to do now. To be perfectly honest, I feel exhausted and would love a nap."

"Done, I'll drop you back off at my place. I've got my own running around to do anyways."

"Thanks."

It felt good to stretch out on the couch. I realized pretty quickly that anytime I sat or laid down, Kool Kitty saw it as an opportunity to perch herself on me. Literally, she perched. I liked to lie down on my side and she would balance her body on my hip. She was so tiny you could barely feel her presence.

I had some talk show providing white noise in the background, more to block out the background city noises that I still had trouble getting used to. I curled up with one hand under the pillow and the other hand on my belly. They had performed an ultrasound at the hospital to make sure everything was okay after the fall. They thought I had been about 6 weeks along, but they had recommended I follow up with another doctor. I had been counting the weeks in my head and if the hospital's calculations were correct, that would make the baby's due date around the beginning of July. A summer baby.

I had never even contemplated having children. Besides the fact that I had never had a steady partner in my life. Combine that with my not too happy childhood, I really had no ticking clock or desire to bring a child into this world. Until now. Even now, considering the situation, I was ecstatic about having a baby. I was positive that once Riley learned about the baby he would fight to get free. The Riley I knew from our little island would have been happy too. But I was afraid that the man I saw in court was not the same Riley. The Riley I saw in court didn't see me, he saw past me. I didn't see love in his eyes, I saw fear and guilt.

I was still confident that everything was going to be okay. Maybe my vision of the future was skewed because of this new love I felt for my unborn child. I wanted a good start for our child and I needed both of us to be present for that. I didn't want our child to grow up without a father like I did. I wanted this child to have more than enough love to make up for my lack of it. I wanted this child to be sociable, kind and trusting like Riley.

These thoughts followed me into my dreams.

I woke up when I heard the door shut and Susan walked in with a few bags of groceries in her hands. I got up quickly to help her, too quickly. I instantly felt dizzy and sat down with a thump on the floor, the room spinning.

"Hey, are you okay?" Susan was by my side, groceries dropped and forgotten.

"Yes, I'm good. I just got up too fast." Susan helped me to my feet.

"You should get your iron checked. That might be the problem." I smiled,

"That's a good idea." I helped her put the groceries away and just as we were finishing the phone rang.

"Hello? Hey dad." I could see that were going to have a father-daughter conversation first so I went into the other room to give Susan some space. I curled up on the bed with one of the law books. About fifteen minutes later, Susan knocked lightly on the bedroom door.

"My dad wants to talk to you."

"Hi."

"I phoned the prison today and they said that technically you could come anytime you want, but they do like when people make an appointment ahead of time. Visiting hours are 2-6." He proceeded to give me the phone number and I wrote it down. I thanked him and hung up. I would phone first thing in the morning.

I walked back into Susan's living room and found her watching TV and folding laundry.

"Do you want to wash your new stuff today?"

"That would be great."

I went and gathered up my bags and sorted them into three piles. I threw in the first load and joined Susan on the couch.

"How about spaghetti for supper."

"That sounds good. When I do get a job you're going to have to let me cook too. I'm not as good as you by far, but I can make a fine loaf of bread. It will taste even better now that I can make it with eggs and milk."

"How did you manage to live without some of those things? I would die without milk in my coffee."

"It's amazing what you can get used to and actually prefer, especially when you're happy." The tears rolled down my cheeks before I could stop them. Every little glimmer back into that life made me feel so sad. Never before in my life had I wished for anything more than to be back there with Riley right now. I wanted to curl up in bed with him by my side. I wanted to taste our canned tomatoes and freshly caught fish. I wanted to smell him again.

"I'm so sorry Jady. You must miss him very much."

"More than I ever thought was possible." We changed the subject and watched TV until the buzzer went off on the washing machine, reminding me to change over the loads. I leaned my head against the doorframe before returning to the living room. I shed a few more tears and wished again that I were washing these clothes by the lake with Riley by my side.

***

"What do you mean he doesn't want to see me?"

"I'm sorry miss, he's refusing to come out. He says he doesn't want any visitors."

"And you told him who I was?"

"Yes ma'am and he still wouldn't budge." I sat down hard on the bench behind me, speechless. The guy in uniform stood in front of me for a few minutes, looking distressed, but eventually he walked away.

I had been on such a high this morning. I had woke up hopeful and looking forward to the day. I had the job interview and I was anticipating seeing Riley today and telling him the great news. Now what? I had done what Nate had suggested I do and I had made an appointment. I never thought this would be the outcome of my visit.

My interview had gone great and it looked very promising. The Preschool supervisor would be giving me a call by the end of the day. Then I came straight here, so excited about seeing him, finally.

Determined, I stood up and strode up to the front counter.

"Excuse me? Would you be able to pass on a message to an inmate here?"

"Sure."

"Could you please tell Riley Williams that his fiancée is waiting for him and refuses to leave until he sees her even if this requires days." The man's eyebrows rose and he looked up from writing his message to see that I was very serious.

"I'll get this right to him..."

"Jady...Jady Donner."

"Okay, Miss Donner."

"Thank you." It wasn't until I sat down and placed my hands in my lap that I saw that they were shaking. I don't know what had happened to him and maybe he had a change of heart but regardless I was telling him my news and then he could decide if he wanted to continue running from me.

About ten minutes later, the man was back.

"Sorry miss, he's still not coming."

"Fine, I'll wait."

I did just that. I sat on the hard bench for as long as my tailbone would allow and then I paced. I raided the vending machine with what change I had. I crunched my Smarties angrily as I waited.

As six o'clock approached the man behind the counter approached me nervously.

"Sorry, Miss Donner, visiting hours are over."

"That's fine, I'll be back tomorrow." The man locked the doors behind me and I wanted to park myself on the front steps, but I didn't know whether to scream or cry. What the hell was going on?

I waited for a bus and went back to Susan's. I phoned Nate.

"Is there any way you can find out for me the name of Riley's lawyer? I know they mentioned it briefly in court, but I was a bit distracted and now I can't remember it."

"Things didn't go well up on The Hill I presume?"

"Up on the what?"

"Sorry that's cop talk for the Correctional facility that is holding Riley. It's up on the hill so that's what we all call it, The Hill."

"He is refusing to see me."

"I was afraid of that."

"Why, what made you think that would happen?"

"Just because he wouldn't talk to us. He didn't defend himself or tell us his side of the story. It's like he's already bought into what the other side is saying."

"What do I do?"

"Well, you're on the right track. Talk to his lawyer. Maybe this bullshit is coming from him. If that's the case I suggest you find a new one for Riley."

"Any suggestions?"

"I might have a few. I'll check my directory and I'll find a name and number for Riley's current lawyer for you. How did the interview go?"

"I think I did pretty well"

"That's good, you're going to need some money. These lawyers I have in mind don't come cheap." I ignored the dread creeping through my body, feeling myself tense up. I knew this was going to be hard, but it made it a lot harder when the person you wanted to help didn't want it.

Susan walked in as I was hanging up. My heavy sigh gave me away. She had worked that day and she looked tired as well.

She unzipped her tall boots and walked into the kitchen. She poured herself a tall glass of wine before she said her first words.

"You look like your day was not much better."

"Riley refuses to see me."

"That sucks." She plunked herself on the couch and started to sort through her pile of mail.

"How are you feeling?"

"Down and angry. How about you?"

"The other chef was sick and it was a busy day. I'm beat. I'm sorry about Riley. What do you think is going on?"

"I don't know. I think someone is feeding him bad information. He's not the kind of guy who is suddenly out of love. He's pretty damn loyal."

"Was that my dad?

"Yeah, he's going to get me the number of Riley's lawyer so I can figure out what's going on."

Her face brightened for a second.

"Hey, what about the job?" The phone rang just as she finished her sentence.

"Yes, just a second."

"Hello?"

"That's great. Really great. Thank you." I sat down with a small smile.

"Well I take it, it went very well."

"Well, that's at least one bit of good news."

"When do you start?"

"Next week."

"Let's celebrate, I'll make pizza."

"I'm glad we celebrate the same way."

The next morning, I went back to the school that housed the pre-school. I was going to be the pre-school teacher for a group of about 20 children. I would have two other teachers to help me. Today, I was getting a more thorough tour and would meet the other staff. I could bring home the school's manual and the previous teacher was there as well to give me her day plan. She was going on maternity leave. This was not a permanent position, which fit with my own plans.

"You can change whatever you like. But because you are coming in mid-year I suggest you stick with it as much as possible at first. It's hard on the kids if you introduce too much change all at once." I nodded in complete understanding.

When I went back to Susan's the message light was blinking on her phone. It was from Nate with the name and number of Riley's lawyer.

I called him immediately.

"May I tell him who's calling." His receptionist coolly asked.

"Jady Donner. He's representing my fiancé, Riley Williams."

"I'm aware of who you are, Miss Donner. One moment." The cool breeze suddenly formed ice over the lines.

"Yes Miss Donner. This is Mr. Moneta. How can I help you?"

"I was wondering if I could set up an appointment to come and meet with you?"

"For what reason?"

"Well, to discuss Riley's case." I already did not like this guy.

"We can set up a meeting, but I don't know how much I will be able to help you. It is conflict of interest Miss Donner. You *are* the victim in this case." The dislike turned to hatred.

"I'm not the victim Mr. Moneta. I am the fiancé."

"Not according to Mr. Williams." I chose to ignore his comment. I was not going to let him get to me. I had already made up my mind anyways.

"Actually, on second thought Mr. Moneta you're right. A meeting is not going to be necessary." There was a pause and I could tell that this was something that rarely happened to this man. He was surprised.

"Well, if you change your mind I'd be more than accommodating."

"I have no doubt Mr. Moneta. Thank you for your time."

I phoned Nate back and left him a message.

"I need that list."

I went back to the Hill for visiting hours, not really expecting a different outcome, but determined anyways. This time I came prepared. I packed a bag full of healthy snacks and brought a book to read.

I greeted the guy at the counter and told him to repeat my message to Riley. He looked at me with an ounce of pity.

I took up my spot, started crunching on my carrots and opened my book.

I managed to finish all my snacks and half the book by the time, Keith, whose name I now knew after he took pity on me and brought me a hot chocolate from the staff room, locked the doors behind me at 6:01 pm.

I wasn't sad or mad this time, I was only getting more determined.

I spent that weekend going over the manual and the day plans. I read over all the songs, finger plays and poems. I went to the library, got a card and rediscovered my excitement for teaching as I browsed the shelves looking for children's books and art ideas.

As Monday approached, I met with the lawyers on Nate's list one by one. I was getting discouraged. All of them had been following the story closely in the media and I could see by the look in their eyes and their tone that they all thought Riley was a sicko and had a hard time believing I could actually love this guy.

I then spent every afternoon that week sitting in the waiting room up on the Hill. Keith and I became good buddies and he even ordered in a pizza once for us to share. I didn't have the heart to tell him that it had no taste whatsoever in comparison to Susan's homemade one.

On Friday, everything changed. I knew I was running out of time. My new job started on Monday and I wouldn't have the time to shop for lawyers nor could I spend time leisurely reading and eating pizza with Keith.

My luck began to change when I met Meaghan Birch. She was a newer lawyer who had just passed her bar. Her office was in a state of chaos which she kept apologizing as she scrambled to look for a pen or a piece of paper. There was no icy receptionist to greet me, there was none at all.

"Sorry about the office and lack of a Wal-Mart greeter, but I just fired my old one and I've got interviews lined up for a new one this afternoon. I'd like to tell you that my office is like this because I just moved here, which I did, but it tends to look like this even a year after I have moved."

I was questioning this pick as well and was beginning to wonder what kind of list Nate gave me. But when she sat down to listen, she gave me her full attention.

"I need a new lawyer for my fiancé Riley Williams."

"And what has this Mr. Williams been accused of?" I was beginning to like her. I filled her in on the case and there was no rising of the eyebrows, judgmental, or worse yet, pitiful glances my way.

"You don't strike me as someone who has been victimized." Change that, I loved this woman.

"No, that's what I'm trying to get everyone to understand."

"Leave this with me and I'll see what I can do."

"You'll take the case?"

"Look Miss Donner. My biggest fear in life is being bored. This case sounds anything but. I will go talk to Mr. Williams. He's got to want to work with me as well."

"Thanks Miss Birch." I shook her hand and left feeling like my luck might be changing.

I went to the Hill and chatted with Keith. Initially, I told him just to tell Riley I was there as usual, but then I stopped him before he walked away.

"Wait, let me add something to my message today." I scrawled a note to give to Riley.

"I talked to your lawyer. I think he's an asshole and whatever bullshit he's feeding you is wrong. You know how stubborn I am. I will keep coming back until you see me."

I was only somewhat surprised this time when Keith came back within ten minutes and he was grinning.

"You can go into the visiting area now Miss Donner, he'll be there shortly."

"Thanks." I barely could get the word out of my mouth. It was happening. I was going to see him and be able to talk to him face to face. My previous bravado was fading fast. What if he really didn't want me in his life anymore? I had worked so hard never to be in a relationship so that I could keep my heart intact. Would I return to my bitter, angry self or would the baby be enough to keep my new, softer, self alive?

I found a seat at a long table with chairs all around. There was only one other man with visitors. It looked like his mom and dad and they all looked so forlorn. They were doing more staring at each other than talking.

When Riley walked in, I held my breath at the sight of him. Gaunt and pale, he was still my man and the love I felt for him came rushing from me in waves that I thought would drown everyone in the room. Everyone but Riley. The waves didn't seem to reach him. He was on an island, but not our island. It looked like one he had created for himself.

He sat down across from me with blank eyes, circled in black. I reached across the table to grab his hands.

"No touching ma'am." It didn't matter anyways, Riley didn't extend his hands to meet mine.

"Riley, what's going on?" He continued to stare at me blankly.

"Please talk to me, you're freaking me out."

"I have nothing to say to you."

"How can you say that. I love you. I miss you so much I can barely breathe." His eyes flickered briefly to meet mine. It was enough to give me hope that he was in there somewhere.

"Riley, what's wrong? Why are you so angry with me? I'm so sorry I fell and ruined everything. I'm sorry you felt you had no choice but to bring me in and in return it cost you your freedom. I'm sorry your brother betrayed you." Again the flicker. "But Riley, what's done is done. We can't change the past, but we can fight for our future."

"There is no future for us."

"How can you say that? We can fight this. I will meet with your lawyer and we'll get you out. You don't deserve to be here."

"I do deserve to be here. I took advantage of you when you were weak and vulnerable. You don't love me, you just think you do. You're sick and when enough time passes you'll come around and hate me for what I did to you." I felt like I fell all over again. I had a hard time breathing and the pain I felt in my old wounds reverberated throughout my body.

"Who's feeding you this bullshit?"

"I don't know what you mean. It's all-true. I'm a horrible person and I deserve to be here after all I've done."

"You've done nothing but save me and make me feel alive again. You've created a person who can love and trust again. You make me want to live and share a life with someone. That someone can only be you. I'm not sick. Do I look sick? Do I sound delusional? Was there ever a moment on the island that you thought I was there only out of fear and manipulation? If you think that's the case then you must think you have way more power than any superhero I've ever heard of. I could have left any time. I could have gone in that canoe and found my way back. It was me that begged you to stay longer. It was me who never wanted to come back to this real life. It is me that is sitting here looking at you and loving you the same as I loved you in our cabin. And it is me that wants you to fight for us, for our family."

This time his eyes not only flickered, but their watery surface looked into the mirror image of my own.

"That's right Riley, I'm pregnant. You are going to be a father and I need you to be present in your child's life. Now, tell me what the hell is going on and who's feeding you these lies." His whole body crumpled onto the table. He lifted his head from his folded arms, but now he was smiling through the tears.

"You're really pregnant?"

"Yes, that's why they think I fell. I get dizzy spells now from time to time."

"Have you been to the doctor yet?" There was my old, concerned, loving Riley back.

"No, I wanted to tell you first."

"Oh my God, Jady, I can't believe it." His face clouded over again.

"Just tell me everything Riley."

"It's my lawyer. He says that the media is making it out to look like you have this Stockholm Syndrome and chances are the jury will see it this way too. Obviously he believes the same. Initially I tried telling him this wasn't the case. Our love was for real. But he said given the situation I had no way of knowing this for sure. I've done some research on this syndrome and you wouldn't even know you had it. Victims just fall for their kidnappers because they are in a vulnerable state. I started to believe him myself. Until I saw you and then everything came back to me. All those feelings we had on the island, our time together was very real wasn't it?" I just wanted to hold him close.

"It's all very real. I think I've found you a new lawyer. I think she will be more helpful."

" I'm so glad you're stubborn enough to force me to see you. I want to reach across the table and pull you close right now. Now, tell me what's been going on from your side."

I filled him in on the stay at the hospital and how Corporal Dennill and his daughter had been my life preservers. I told him about the job and how I could make some doctor appointments since now I could confide in Susan.

"Oh Riley, you would really like her. She's down to earth, funny and so sweet like you."

"I'm so glad you have someone to help you. I just wish I could be there, but I feel so much better that you have someone you can count on." I knew this was an unintentional referral to his brother, but I didn't want to bring him up again.

"How about you? How are you doing in there?"

""I'm getting lots of "me" time." He smiled, but it was surrounded by sadness. "Look, it was pretty rough. I was devastated by the thought that I had hurt you and scarred you even more than your family did. I really didn't want to live anymore, but now everything has changed, hasn't it? I have a baby and a beautiful woman whom I want to marry. I need to kick this into high gear and get my ass out of here."

""I will do everything I can from my end to help you."

"I know you will."

For the remainder of the visiting time, we reminisced about the cabin and everything we missed about it.

"I wonder if the Cabin Couple watch the news and have figured out that our hideaway is their place. I hope that if they do, they seek us out so we can explain our story and apologize for everything."

"I know, that's what I was thinking about. I want them to know we didn't trash the place, that we probably loved it as much as they have over the years."

"Okay Miss, visiting time is over."

I couldn't believe that much time had passed already, but when I went to move and felt stiff all over I realized my back said it had been a few hours.

"I'll come back tomorrow and maybe Meaghan will have had a chance to talk to you by then and we can see where we can go from here."

"Jady, I love you. No matter what happens remember that. Please do everything to take care of yourself and our baby. That's your priority right now."

"I love you too Riley. I won't give up until you're on this side and I can hold you close again." I walked away before he could see my tears.

***

"Congratulations! That's great." Susan went to hug me when I told her the news and then she pulled back to look at me. "It *is* good, isn't it?"

"Yes, it's very good."

"And you finally got to see Riley?"

"Yes." I felt like I was glowing when I said it. I felt so much better now that I had seen him and had a chance to talk with him.

"He was happy with the news and will work with his new lawyer to try and clear this all up."

"New lawyer? So you found one?" So much had happened that day and I had a lot to catch her up on. We were eating supper in her living room. My meal was barely touched since I was the one doing most of the talking.

"Yes, the last one on the list. She seems really great. I guess time will tell. She's going to look into the case and talk to Riley and get back to me."

"Wow! It sounds like you've had a really eventful day."

"Mmmm..." I scooped in a mouth full of food. "Before I forget, now that it's out there, do you know of a good doctor. I need to make an appointment."

"Let me talk to my friends with kids and see whom they recommend."

"Thanks."

"Oh hey, another friend of mine is having a showing tonight at the art gallery. Do you want to get out?"

"Man, that sounds like fun. I could use a night out. Is it dressy? Will my thrift store clothes get me in the door?" Susan laughed and almost spit back out her last mouthful. She washed it down with a swig of wine and then beckoned for me to follow her into her room.

She had a fabulous walk-in closet and waved her hand over the line-up of clothes.

"Have your pick. It's not going to be too dressy, but definitely more than jeans and a t-shirt."

We spent the next hour playing fashion show. I wondered if this was what it would've been like in high school if I had had a best friend. I realized again what I had missed out on. It was fun and it felt so easy and comfortable with Susan. I could be myself, like I was when I was with Riley.

I put on a few outfits just to get a laugh. It was obvious right away, that they were not me. We narrowed it down to two. A colourful wrap around dress with a pair of her borrowed black boots, or a patchwork-hippy looking skirt with a warm colored sweater and a pair of high brown boots this time.

"Man, you have nice clothes. Which outfit matches my cast?" She laughed before answering,

"I get bored so easily and then I get myself some new things. Usually thrift store stuff too, just even for the uniqueness of it. But then I'll see a piece, and no matter what the price I'll have to have it. It's my one vice. It could be worse. Which one is it going to be?"

"I think I'm going to go with the brown sweater and hippy skirt."

"Good choice. Okay, now get out of my closet so I can get dressed too."

I went the bathroom and played with my hair. By the time Susan walked out in a gorgeous wine colored dress that accented her burgundy highlighted dark hair, I had failed miserably at some some sort of up do with my mane. Getting dressed was one thing with a cast, styling my hair was another.

"Here, let me in there." Susan finished off my hair with a few clips strategically placed.

"I think I need a haircut."

"I have just the girl. I'll phone tomorrow."

We headed out the door and shivered in her car as we waited for it to start up. This last week of November had been stuck in a cold snap and I missed the warmth of wood heat.

After we could no longer see our breath, we drove to the art gallery. It was hard to find a parking spot so we knew there would be a lot of people.

We found the coat check and as we walked in, I watched heads turn in Susan's direction. She was quite a sight and I wondered why she was still single.

She found her friend who was hosting the show at the center of a crowd of people. When the crowd thinned, Susan walked up and they hugged.

"Payton, this is my friend Jady." She shook my hand.

"The two of you together put my show to shame. You are Art itself." I blushed despite myself.

" Great show Payton."

"Thanks." Just then, another crowd swarmed her with compliments and Susan gave a wave and we took a tour.

Payton's work consisted of photographs and they were incredible. She had an eye for making the mundane, fascinating and beautiful. A frosty branch with a lone berry hanging on it. A close up of a single dew drop in a fern-like leaf. I was amazed and inspired.

"You know, so many times at the cabin the views were so incredible I wished I had a camera. I still regret it. I wanted to hang onto all those beautiful shots."

"You still can."

"How?"

"Paint what you have up here." She tapped her head.

"I can't paint."

"How do you know if you've never tried? You said you picked up a book, so you have at least the creative inspiration in your body. Try it out."

My mind was spinning and excited at the thought of it. I was no longer seeing Payton's pictures. I was visualizing all the scenes from the cabin like a slideshow in my brain.

We stayed until the media that was there to cover the show spotted me and started to herd over to us. We ducked out the back as quickly as we could, not wanting to steal the limelight.

Grabbing a decaf coffee and a piece of pie at a local coffee shop, we talked about future plans.

"What are you going to do once the baby arrives?"

"Well, I'm hoping by then Riley will be out and he can work while I stay at home with the baby."

"And if he's not." I would've been lying to myself if I thought her comment didn't sting, but I would've been kidding myself even more if I had denied this thought had not passed through my own mind.

"Well, by working from now until then, I should have enough hours to collect unemployment insurance and that will be better than nothing." The next part I said to Susan took some courage and my pride was faltering as I spoke.

"I'm hoping I can stay at your place until then. I can't give you a lot, but I thought I could pay for groceries and give you some money for rent." She was waving her hand before I had finished my sentence.

"You don't worry about that. My house is already paid for. My dad helped me with that. I only had a roommate for the company and I like cooking for more than one. It was getting a bit boring. You feed my ego. And if worse comes to worse and Riley is not out by the time the baby comes, you can stay for as long as you like." This time it was me shaking my head.

"Oh no, I couldn't do that. That's all you need is a crying baby keeping you up at night when you have to work. I can't ask you to rearrange your life any more than you already have."

"C'mon I have no siblings. You're going to deny me being a special aunt that can spoil a baby. Besides I'm a sound sleeper, I can sleep through a hurricane."

"So what do I need to start painting?" I changed the subject then, not wanting to think anymore of the possibilities of Riley not being there when the baby was born. As much as I loved Susan, I wanted him there, for the baby and for me.

The next morning, Susan wasted no time and phoned one of her friends who had just had a baby.

"That's great, thanks." She said at the end of the conversation.

"Dr. Griffen's your man. My friend Tara said he's the best. She said he's friendly, never rushes you and knows his stuff. Tara said when she stayed at the hospital after having Jacob, he seemed to be there, 'round the clock, attending to both her and other patients. Even when he wasn't the doctor on call. She gave me his number."

"Thanks, that solves at least one problem. I'll give him a call on Monday for an appointment." I had been browsing through the newspaper while she had been on the phone, enjoying the one-cup of caffeinated coffee I allowed myself for the day. There was an ad for prenatal classes being offered at the clinic.

"So how badly do you want to be a special aunt?

Her eyebrows rose inquisitively.

"What are you up to?"

"I need someone to play daddy during my prenatals. Are you up for it?" Susan smiled.

"You betcha. I always wanted to be a father."

"What do you have planned for the day?" Susan would be going to work for the lunch and dinner crowd.

"I was going to get you to drop me off at the library on your way to work. I want to browse their baby section for the how to books and some baby name ones too."

"Sounds so exciting."

"Hey, don't knock the library. I've spent the better part of my life in the library."

"That explains a lot." I threw a pillow at her from the couch as she ducked out of the way to go take a shower.

I had always loved libraries. They had been my sanctuary when I was younger and the books were my friends when I had none. I loved the way books from the library smelled and the whisperings that went on between people just added to the world I built around myself. I could escape into whatever book I was reading. When I was younger it was Nancy Drew and Trixie Beldon and then as I got a little older I devoured anything by Steven King. It wasn't until a few years ago that I was watching Oprah and she had her book club going. She was recommending East of Eden by Steinbach and I went to the library and browsed the back cover. It sounded interesting and after reading this classic, it opened up a whole new door in reading. I read whatever Oprah or the librarians recommended. They had their own shelf of books they thought deserved to be borrowed. I ate it all up and couldn't get enough. I had to pull myself away to read my boring textbooks for my classes. Whatever spare time I had, was spent reading.

That's another thing I loved about the cabin. It was like they had a little library of their own and new books for me to discover and read over and over.

Now I was in aisles I had never ventured down before. The parenting and pregnancy books. I was excited once again at the prospect of new territory.

I scanned the shelves looking at something to jump out at me. There were so many options it was overwhelming.

"This one is the best of the lot." A woman was holding out the "What To Expect When You're Expecting."

"That is if you're looking for that or if not, just tell me to mind my own business."

"No, actually, that's exactly what I'm looking for. Thanks."

"How far along are you?"

"Only about six weeks."

"I'm guessing this is your first, otherwise you would know already what to expect." She smiled and I really noticed her then. She was pretty and athletic looking. She had her blond hair pulled back in a ponytail.

"How about you? Are you expecting too?"

"Yes but this is my second so this is the book I'm looking for." I glanced at the book she was holding. It had something to do with adjusting your first child to a new baby.

"I don't think it's going to be easy. My little guy is two and he loves having his mom and dad all to himself." I winced when she said dad and dreaded any question that might come my way in regards to the father in my situation.

"Thanks for the heads up on this book. How about a good baby name book."

She eyed the lines of books and pulled two from the shelf.

"These two should cover it. One has more traditional names in it and the other has newer, funkier names. Whatever your fancy." She glanced at her watch. "Well, gotta run, my husband took our little guy to the pool so I could do some running around and my time is up. Nice chatting with you, best of luck."

"Same to you and thanks again."

Her wave was more dismissive than a farewell as she walked towards the sign out counter.

I took the bus to the hospital. I was finally getting this darn cast off and I couldn't wait. Sitting in the waiting room I pulled out the baby name books and started browsing.

Aaron, Abigail, Aiden, Alicia... I skipped ahead a few pages, *David, Desiree, Devon...* I had just begun and I was already overwhelmed by the possibilities.

I went up to the counter and asked for paper and a pencil. I started making a list of the names I liked. Not just the name itself but also the meaning attached to it. Andrew meant manly and brave, Dillon, faithful, Evan, strong fighter, Makena, handsome, fiery, Nayeli, love, Nya, tenacity. The lists were endless. I ended up filling up the whole page. One side for boy's names and one side for the girl's. I could see it was going to be a tough choice. I went through the list again and crossed off any name that I didn't like the shortened version. Anthony might become a Tony, Elijah, an Eli, Cassandra-Cassie, Christina-Chrissy. You could call them by the name you wanted, and then they entered school and the kids decided what mutation it would become. Then there were names that rhymed with words that could become problem creators. Of course then there were the names that brought up images of the certain bully at school or the boy you had a crush on and broke your heart, although I couldn't recall any of those.

Finally, I had a list I could bring to Riley and then he could go through it and rule out the ones he didn't like. My name was called and before I knew it I was back on the bus cast-less and feeling a few pounds lighter. My hand was still weak and the doctor had recommended a few exercises to strengthen it that I could do at home.

I went back to Susan's and grabbed a quick bite to eat before I headed to the Hill. I was starving and went to make myself a chicken sandwich, but as I stood there making it, the very smell of it was making me feel ill. I needed to sit down. I had a horrible sour taste in my mouth. I brushed my teeth instead and had a tall glass of water. I was still hungry, but as I browsed the cupboards, nothing appealed to me. I wanted something salty. I ate a whole sleeve of crackers followed with another glass of water and that was all I could stomach. I looked longingly at the couch, wanting to curl up with a blanket instead of going anywhere. I looked at my list of baby names and got excited again at the thought of Riley seeing the list. I grabbed it and a bag of mints and went to catch the bus.

I showed up ten minutes late, since the bus I was on broke down and they had to bring in another one to shuttle us onto. It was so cold you couldn't see more than a few feet in front of you through the fog. I drew my coat closer to my body and quickly climbed the stairs to the entrance. I was surprised to see quite a few people still waiting. We all sat there for an additional half hour before they finally came out to tell us that visiting hours were cancelled due to a lock down. There was moaning and groaning and one little girl broke into tears. I felt like joining her. I was so tired. I wanted to curl up on the bench and use my coat as a blanket rather than venture back out into the cold to catch yet another bus.

I filed out with everyone else and waited for another fifteen minutes for the next bus to come. I got off at a local grocery store rather than go home. I needed to find some food I could stomach. Susan had a great selection of food but it was all healthy. I wanted junk. I loaded up my basket with potato chips, Ichiban noodle soup, more soda crackers, and popcorn. Salt, salt, and more salt. I rubbed my belly, sorry kid.

I wasn't that far from the house, but when I arrived at Susan's after walking that short way, I had frosty eyelashes and stiff frozen fingers and legs. I ran a bath and ate potato chips while soaking in the warm water. It was great that I didn't have to put a plastic bag around my arm. I felt sad at not getting to see Riley, but I felt worse for him. I knew that my visit was what he would be looking forward to. I hoped he would call later. I couldn't call him, but he told me he could call out, only at certain times and there was always a wait.

The phone was ringing as I dried off and I ran to answer, thinking it might be Riley. I tried not to be disappointed when I heard Susan's voice.

"Hey, how are you doing?"

I described my day and asked if hers was any better.

"It's crazy busy. I thought the cold would keep them at home but it turns out people actually want to eat a warm cooked meal, out. Oh well, I've only got a minute, I keep forgetting to tell you. I picked up a couple of chick flicks for you the other day. We have them for a week. I won't be home until late, so I thought I'd let you know so you wouldn't be bored. They're beside the DVD player."

"Thanks. That's exactly what I needed." I thought of the popcorn I could eat while I was watching them.

I looked through the pile and found only one I had seen before. I popped in a different one and as the previews played, I made some popcorn for supper.

Halfway through the movie, as I was drowning my second bowl of popcorn with my tears, the phone rang again. I tried not to get my hopes up this time.

"Hi Jady, it's Meaghan. Meaghan Birch." It took me a few seconds to register the name.

"Oh yeah. Hi."

"I hope I'm not calling too late, but I just finished reading all the paper work on Riley's case. It sounds too interesting to pass up. I'd love to represent him. I'm going to try to set up a meeting with him on Monday."

"That's great news. Thanks Meaghan."

"I won't keep you. I'll be in touch. You should have some chicken noodle soup."

"Pardon?"

"You sound like you have a cold."

"Oh, uh...thanks, I will."

I laughed as I hung up. I grabbed some more Kleenex and finished watching the movie.

***

I was eating crackers for breakfast and Susan strolled into the kitchen with wicked bed head and looking like she hadn't slept at all.

"Are you okay?"

"It was crazy all night and when I got home I was so wound up I couldn't sleep at all."

"Man, I didn't even hear you come in. I was out."

"I'm happy for you. Now move out of my way so I can make some coffee."

"Are you working again today?" She brightened for a moment.

"Nope, and I hope you have no plans because I have something in mind for you." "Really? Any hints?"

"Nope, it's a surprise." As the coffee brewed I had to go into the living room. The smell of the coffee that I had craved so badly now turned my stomach. I grabbed my bag of crackers and headed to the shower.

A couple of hours later, after a hearty breakfast for Susan and Fruit Loops for me, we were in a studio with a few other people. It turned out, Susan had found out about a beginner's watercolour painting workshop. She had picked up all the materials we needed and I was not just excited, but touched she had gone to all the trouble.

I was so pumped afterwards that I had Susan take me to the dollar store and I bought whatever I could to start, cheaply. I picked out a few canvases of different sizes, some brushes and the hard part was buying only a few paints to start with. I already had a picture in my mind and knew some of the colours that would be needed.

Some people write or read to carry themselves to another world I was looking forward to bringing back a part of the cabin into my life through my painting. My biggest concern was that I wouldn't be able to bring alive on canvas what I had in my mind. When I voiced my concerns to Susan she only said,

"You'll never know unless you try."

Try I did. It took a couple of canvases and I was thankful I had only spent a few dollars on them but finally, by the fourth one; I was getting the knack of mixing colours and applying shading. I was trying to capture loons on the lake with a sunset lighting up the background. I wanted to give it to Riley as a gift. Maybe it would help brighten his day and make him think of happier times.

"Hey, that's pretty good."

"Thanks, I think I like it too."

"What do you want for supper?"

"I'm eating it." I pointed to the cup of noodles that I had beside me.

"That can't be good for you or the baby."

"I know. I can't help it; it's all I can stomach. Everything else just makes me sick to even smell it."

"Are you going to phone on Monday for an appointment with that doctor?"

"Yes, mom." Susan laughed.

"Alright alright, I'll back off. I think my dad's coming by tonight to play some cards. Are you up for it?"

"Sounds good to me."

"Are you nervous or excited about starting your job tomorrow?"

"A bit of column A and a bit of column B."

"You'll be great. Well if you're not hungry, I'm going to scrounge up something for myself before my dad gets here."

I returned to my painting, adding some finishing touches. I didn't want to mess with it too much. I liked the way it had turned out.

We spent a fun evening with Nate playing crib. They were still playing when I called it quits at ten. I wanted to get a good night's sleep for my big day tomorrow. My shadow, Kool Kitty, followed me to bed.

I woke up long before I needed to and was out of the house and at the bus stop before Susan had even stirred. She had offered to drive me but I felt she was doing more than enough. The school was not that far from the house and when the weather was warmer I would be able to walk down there.

On my earlier tour of the school I had noticed it's welcoming entrance. There was a mural painted in the front hallway of animals and trees, butterflies and many colourful, bright flowers. It could cheer anyone up, even on this cold winter day. I greeted the lady at the front counter, I recalled her name was

Kim and then found my way down to the classroom that would be mine for the next seven and a half months. The environment was a bit more subdued in this room. We had to keep in mind the special needs children that were enrolled who could not take too much stimulation.

I set up everything I needed for the day and as I was doing so, the two other teachers who would be my helpers came in. I had met them briefly when I had come for my interview and when I had visited for my tour. Brandi was very quiet. She briefly said good morning and went about her morning routine. She set up the craft for the day and made sure the snacks were cut up and ready to go. Carla was more talkative and energetic. She went around the room, tidying up and rearranging the books, giving us a commentary the whole time.

The children began arriving shortly and the moms lingered long enough to meet me and then they went off to run their errands or grab a coffee, childfree for a couple of hours. We let the children play for a while and then slowly started gathering them for circle time. This was my thing and I loved it. Stories, games, poems, songs and a "show and tell" here and there. I loved watching the children's faces as they learned new things and shared their stories. It reminded me of why I went into education in the first place.

The morning went by fast and I was tired, but happy, with the way the day was going. Carla and Brandi sat with me in the staff room and we ate our lunch, going over the morning's events. Even though Brandi was quiet with us, I had seen a different side of her with the children. With them she glowed and came out of shell. She laughed and read stories to them. She held them close when they were hurt or crying, and she had endless amounts of patience for their unlimited questions and requests for help.

Carla was the boisterous entertainer. She joked with the children and got down on the floor and played cars, farm animals or had pretend tea parties and picnics. They were an amazing pair who complimented each other beautifully.

The afternoon went just as quickly and before I knew it, I was sitting in front of Riley recapping my day and feeling better than I had in a long time. Riley smiled as I told him my stories about the children and was happy for me that I had good people to work with.

After I had gushed about my day for a good hour I stopped.

"I'm so sorry Riley. I'm so ignorant. Here I am, going on about my life and how happy I am and you're stuck in here."

"Oh baby, don't you dare worry about me. It would kill me even more to know you were out there and not happy. It would make everything we created on the island feel like it was for nothing. We carved out new people there and I will get my turn to live my new life."

"Did Meaghan get a hold of you?"

"Yes, actually I met with her this morning and you were right, she's great. I think she will really be able to help me out. The main thing she said is to prove that you're not suffering from Stockholm and that I didn't do anything to you against your will or that you were under any influence. She's going to get a physiatrist to ask you a few questions, do an interview for our side. She didn't get into too much detail today, she just wanted to talk and get to know me better. I hope she got a good feeling."

"There's no way after meeting you she could have anything but." Riley smiled and gave my hand a quick squeeze as the guard turned his back to walk the other way.

"How are you feeling? Y'know, baby wise?"

"I could live on salt and Fruit Loops right now, but I was reading in the baby book that this maybe only temporary. Some poor women have it their entire nine months. I sure hope I'm not one of them."

"You won't be, it will be over before you know it." He stopped and stared at his hands.

"What is it? What's wrong?"

"The time will go by fast and I just wish..."

"What Riley?"

"I just wish I could be there. I want to be there for the visits to the doctor and to feel our baby kick for the first time. I wish I could take care of you now and that you didn't have to work while you're not feeling good." I swallowed my tears not wanting him to see them.

"You will be. You will be out of here before you know it and then you'll be wishing you were back in. I'm probably going to get pretty crabby as I get bigger." He smiled at my attempt to cheer him. We both knew no matter how crabby I would get, he would never rather be where he was right now. I wanted the same things he wanted, but I didn't need to make him feel worse by telling him how much I wished he could be there too.

Saturday and Sunday I tried to relax as much as possible. I felt so tired and couldn't believe I could nap as much as I did and still sleep at night. I chewed mints endlessly to try to get rid of the horrible sour taste in my mouth, but everything only worked for a short time. I planned my lessons for the week.

I visited Riley and we talked about the baby and we went through the list of names. He crossed off a few more he didn't like and we had it narrowed it down to five.

"I don't know what it is, but none of them really jump out at me." I confessed after we had looked at the list for a while.

"I was thinking the same thing but I can't seem to think of one that does."

"Well, we still have lots of time, maybe something will come to us."

I finished watching the movies Susan had picked up since she had to work all weekend. She would have Monday and Tuesday night off so we would be able to catch up then. I think she felt bad that I was spending so much time alone, but I tried to console her telling her I was so tired I wasn't much company right now anyway.

When Monday rolled around again, I felt well rested and, although the nausea was still there, I found if I ate crackers before I even got out of bed, it made it easier to greet the day. I was excited to go to work and I was looking forward to my doctor's appointment. Luckily, Susan's recommendation had been a good one. Hopefully, Meaghan would call and there would be some good news for a change.

As I was waiting for the bus that morning, an ad on the side caught my eye and reminded me that Christmas was fast approaching. I thought of how nice it would have been to have Christmas at the cabin. We would have had handmade decorations and gifts. A wonderful home cooked meal with our canned goods and smoked meat. I was so lost in my fantasy that I almost missed my stop.

Christmas was going to be hard if Riley couldn't be with me to enjoy it. I rubbed my belly, as I did so often now, and wished that by the following Christmas we would be a family all together again. It might not be a cabin Christmas, but it would be special all the same if we could be together.

***

"Please fill out these forms and then take this cup to the washroom down the hall." The woman with pulled-back grey hair handed me a small plastic cup I assumed I needed to pee in.

I walked back down the hall holding my cup of pee, feeling a bit embarrassed, but then I noticed everyone who walked by me didn't even give me a second glance. I guess this was a hospital and a person walking around with a small plastic pink cup holding yellow liquid was a common sight.

I placed the cup in the tray the secretary motioned to and began to fill out the forms. It was pretty straightforward. They wanted to know my medical history, allergies, past surgeries and if I was on any meds, if I drank or smoked or ever did drugs. I never did. I was so angry so much of the time and had wanted to get my parents attention so I was a perfect candidate for all addictions, but I couldn't be bothered. I guess I didn't have the peer pressure everyone else had, seeing as I had no peers.

When it came to checking off the box for marital status I teared up looking at the empty seat beside me that should be filled by him. I checked off single with regret and loneliness.

The secretary marked down my height and then weighed me. I was already up five pounds. They sent me for blood work and, as I stared at the five vials of blood they collected, it amazed me we actually had that much blood in our bodies to spare.

After all of that, I waited an additional half an hour before I met my doctor. Her name was Dr. Ngozi and she was from South Africa. I was told you either loved her or you didn't. At first I didn't know what to make of her. She was gorgeous and dressed to the nines with high heels and beautiful jewelry.

She went through my forms and asked me to change into a gown and hop up on the table. She checked me over both inside and out and then we sat down to talk.

"What kind of symptoms are you experiencing?"

"I'm feeling pretty nauseous most of the time. I thought because it was called morning sickness you would only have it in the morning."

"It was most likely a man who came up with that name, probably because most men only see you in the morning and then don't really pay attention the rest of the day." She smiled then and I realized I would be in the category that loved her.

"You are about eleven weeks along, your ultrasound next week will give us a better determination. If you find you are still feeling rough at the next visit, we can look into some meds to help with that. Are you taking a prenatal?"

"Yes."

"Good. Any other questions at this point?"

"I've been reading some pregnancy magazines and there's always a list of things I should and shouldn't be eating. Do you have any suggestions or foods I absolutely should avoid?"

"Jady, I have one word for you. Moderation. I think everything is fine in moderation. If you go overboard on anything, pregnant or not, it is not good for you."

"I just feel so bad right now since I'm eating such junk. I just can't seem to stomach anything else."

"Don't worry about that. You will find enough to feel guilty about for the rest of motherhood. It will pass trust me. Make an appointment with Dianne for a month from today. They will phone you when they have an ultrasound appointment for you."

"Thanks."

I walked back to the bus stop with mixed emotions. I was happy with the doctor's visit. It made everything feel more real, but I felt very alone. I wished I had family to share in the news and updates. Susan wanted to be there, but she had to work. I caught a bus going to the Hill, looking forward to debriefing Riley.

He was adorable, asking more questions than the forms I had to fill out. He wanted to know what my blood pressure was and if they had any concerns. He wanted to know if I really should be working right now especially with kids who might be giving me all their cold and flu viruses. I smiled at his paternal concerns and assured him everything was just fine.

"Did she ask why you were there alone?"

"Come to think of it, she didn't even mention it. I noticed a lot of women in the waiting room were alone. Not all husbands want to be there for all that stuff you know." My answer was meant to lighten things and make him feel better, but my comment fell short.

"This husband wished he could be there for every little thing. I think husbands nowadays take many things for granted. I would give anything to be there for the things other men might consider ordinary and mundane."

"I know. I don't doubt that for a second. I will keep you posted on every little detail, I promise. Any word from Meaghan?"

"She told me that she would spend this week nosing around to see what the Crown was up to and why they were pushing this case so ferociously." I knew deep down who was responsible for that, but I didn't know the reasons. I knew there was a confrontation in my near future that I could only avoid for so long if I wanted to be of any help to Riley at all.

Our farewell routine now consisted of a quick kiss and hug and a loving touch to my belly. As I got on the bus, I touched the spot where his hand had recently been hoping to retain the warmth he placed there.

I carved out a routine for myself that week. I would go to work, then visit Riley, have dinner with Susan if she was off, or if she were working, it would be on my own in front of the TV. I usually had some prep to do for the next morning, either a craft project or some learning game I wanted to try with my group of children. Whenever I left work I had piles of stuff to take with me in order to do my prep at home. Colored paper, scissors, glue and whatever else I needed to complete the task. Finally by mid-week Carla asked me,

"Why do you cart all that stuff home? Why not just stay an extra hour and get it done here? We'd stay and help you if you wanted."

"Thanks, but it's really no big deal. I do it while I'm watching TV and it's done in no time." Carla shrugged her shoulders and let it go. I wasn't about to tell her that I needed to rush out the door to visit my fiancée on the Hill. I think everyone at work knew my story, but no one talked about it, not even Carla and that surprised me. I figured it was only a matter of time before someone brought it up. Until then, I didn't feel the need to advertise my situation.

By the end of the week it felt like some normalcy had returned to my life. I still wasn't feeling good; stomach wise, but I stopped feeling guilty about it. I tried to sneak in vegetables and fruits in other ways beside Fruit Loops or the specks of carrots in my Ichiban soup.

Thursday night when I came home from visiting Riley, the message light was blinking on the machine. I listened to it even though I was sure it was for Susan. It wasn't. It was Meaghan asking if I could come by her office on Friday when I got off work. Even though her voice sounded serious I still held on to the hope that it was good news she had for me.

All that Friday, I had a hard time concentrating. Many times Carla and Brandi had to repeat things to me.

"Where are you today?" Carla asked during lunch.

"I'm just really tired today. I couldn't sleep very well last night."

The rest of the afternoon they both seemed to make an extra effort to help me out with the children. I appreciated their efforts and continuously looked at the clock eager to be on my way to see Meaghan.

When the end of the day came, I barely said good-bye and was out the door to catch my bus.

This time a secretary greeted me and thankfully I didn't have to wait long before I was told I could go in.

"Thanks for coming on short notice." Although I was thinking, short of visiting Riley, I didn't have much going on. Out loud I told Meaghan,

"No problem. It sounded important."

"It is, but you're not going to like it." My heart fell at her words and I braced myself for the worst, not knowing the conversation that was about to take place was going to make the next four months of my life hell.

"Well, I've talked to the Crown and she's unwilling to budge."

"Meaning?"

"She's a new upstart that has been given the opportunity to take on a high profile case. She has something to prove. Right now, what she wants to prove is that you are suffering from Stockholm and that Riley is an evil individual that took advantage of his victim and she's out to make him pay." I let her words sink in.

"There's nothing we can do to change her mind? To convince her that I'm not crazy and that I really am in love?"

"Well, that brings us to the next part and the part you are really not going to like." I felt scared, I thought what she had just told me *was* the worst part.

"Now, what I'm about to tell you remains in this office. I'm not supposed to advise you either way when it comes to this case. You are the supposed victim here and you are the witness for the crown. This is the only advice I'm going to give you and this is going to be very hard for both you and Riley. But I think if you are really serious about this and want to help him then you need to break off all contact until the trial."

"What? What will that achieve?" The bile and sour taste was rising in my throat.

"In order to convince the Crown and the future jury that you are not suffering from Stockholm it would be better if you two didn't see each other. That way when we reconvene for the trail I can say, look she's been away from him for four months and she still feels the same way. I need to prove it's not Stockholm. There's no way to prove it beyond reasonable doubt, but I think the separation will greatly help."

"Do you have a washroom I can use?" My question surprised her and she gave me directions.

I just made it to the washroom before I threw up whatever I had managed to keep down that day. I slumped down on the floor and let the tears fall. Four months without being able to see him? Four months without being able to let him know about my day and how things were going with the pregnancy. By the time I saw him I would be more than halfway done. What about Riley? I knew, without him having to say it, that my visits were keeping him from going insane in there. He didn't say anything about how bad it was, he didn't have to. I could see by fresh bruises on his face that there was fights' taking place. I could see by the bags under his eyes that he was not getting much sleep. I could see by his gaunt body that he was not eating well either. I dragged myself off the floor and wet a paper towel with cold water. I ran it over my face and slurped some water from the tap. Taking a deep breath I went back to Meaghan's office.

"Are you okay?"

"Yes sorry. I understand what you're saying and I will do anything I can to help Riley. Have you told him about this?"

"Yes. He's refusing." I nodded not surprised that he would sacrifice his freedom in order to continue to see me.

"I'll talk to him."

"Look Jady, I'm not giving up. I will continue to work hard on trying to get a small sentence and focus on accessory to the crime rather than be the mastermind of it like his brother portrayed. I will keep you posted as much as I can."

"Thanks Meaghan, I really appreciate all your help and hard work." I turned to walk out and she called my name once more.

"If you need anything, please don't hesitate to call me." I nodded but as I left I thought,

The one thing I need right now, you told me I can't have. It was going to be a long four months.

***

There was enough time after seeing Meaghan that I still had an hour left of visiting time with Riley. I wanted to visit him, but dreaded the conversation that needed to take place.

Riley was still loyally waiting for me at one of the long tables and I was happy to see that he was. He looked up from studying his hands as I walked in.

"I'm sorry, I was..." He held up his hand to stop me.

"I know where you were. And it's a no."

"Hear me out Riley. We're not about shutting each other down."

"You're right. I just can't imagine living my life in here for the next four months without you. You're my buoy; you keep me afloat when I just want to let myself drown. I'm so scared of drowning in here."

"You're stronger than you give yourself credit. If living without you for four months means a lifetime with you, I'll take it. I'd do anything to give you a better chance of winning this trial. I'm scared of what the next four months are going to bring for both of us, but it's not just about us anymore, we have someone else to think about. You have to be strong, you have to keep afloat to be part of your baby's life." Riley was quiet as he reached across the table and quickly and discreetly wiped my tears.

"I'm sorry for being selfish. You're right."

"You're not selfish. You don't know how to be selfish. You're a wonderful man who's going to make an amazing father. You just need to dig deep and every time you feel like letting go, think of our baby and our future together. It will happen for us. And I'm not giving up on trying to see if I can get things moving faster."

"Please just make sure you take care of yourself. Let it ride Jady. I don't want you to take on any stress, please do that for me. I promise on my end to hang in there."

"I can do that."

Our time was up before we were ready to say good-bye. Our hug, which was supposed to be brief, transferred our sorrow, love and hope and when I went to pull back after our allowed time had passed, Riley lingered and hung on.

"Riley, they'll give you a hard time on the other side." I whispered into his ear as I saw the guard walk towards us.

Riley gave me one more tight squeeze and whispered back,

"I love you." He let go and walked away without saying another word.

I sat in the waiting room, not crying, not doing anything. I just didn't trust my legs to walk.

"C'mon honey you need to eat something." I pushed away the food Susan was trying to give me. I had come home and shut all my curtains. I crawled into bed with my clothes on and had been there ever since. It was Saturday afternoon and I knew I needed to eat, for the baby's sake. I had told Riley to swim, to stay afloat and yet here I was, wanting to let go.

"It's Corn Pops. I bought a fresh box. I have Honeycombs too." I smiled despite myself and sat up. She put the tray on my lap and went to open my curtains.

"Please don't."

"How about your lamp then? It's way too dark in here to even see what you're eating. Maybe I'm tricking you into eating something healthy."

"Okay." The light illuminated her pretty, but worried face.

"I have the weekend off and I rented a whole bunch of tear jerkers and comedies. Your pick. I loaded up on the junk food and cream soda. You can bring a comfy blanket to the couch and park there instead. What do you say?"

"You don't need to worry Susan. I know I'm going to need to be strong not just for myself, but for Riley and our baby. I need to get us all through this. I do not get the luxury of falling apart and being depressed for the next four months as much as I would like to, so I'm allowing myself this weekend to feel it all at once".

"Hmmm, good plan. Might as well do it right." I started to gather up my blanket.

"Honeycombs huh? Did you get Doritos too?" Susan laughed and gave me a hug.

"Everything's going to be fine, you'll see."

The pit in my stomach wanted to argue, but the hope in my heart wanted very badly for her words to be true.

I followed through on my plan all weekend. I stayed in my PJ's, ate junk food and switched back and forth from laughing so hard my sides hurt, to sobbing myself into a flu-like state. Both Sookie and Kool Kitty didn't know what to make of me.

As Sunday night approached, I knew I would have to get it together to go to work the next day, but every time I thought of the end of my work day not including a visit to see Riley, I wanted to return to bed and stay there.

Susan came and sat on the edge of my depression.

"I don't want to say anything to down play or insult what you're going through. I'm not going to pretend to understand because I don't. I do want to be here for you and I'm just going to say what I'm about to say once and then it's up to you. I'm not a nag and I'm definitely not your mom. I have always found that the best artists and writers are those that have lived with some sort of tragedy. They use their art as their therapy and produce the best work. You've only begun your painting and I think you have a talent there. Use this next four months to immerse yourself in your painting and let it be your therapy." She left without me answering. I think she already knew she had planted the seed and I felt a small part of the sadness fall away.

***

I got up the following morning in a better mood than I expected to. As I brushed my teeth, I debated where to start. I thought I would pick up the Parks and Rec leisure guide and see what kinds of classes were being offered. I finished brushing, satisfied I had a starting point. I picked out my clothes, and for the first time, could stomach something other than Fruit Loops.

As I boarded the bus, I felt like it was going to be a good day.

The clouds started to roll in on my sunshine around lunchtime. I had a plan after work to go to the library, but it was still hard to deal with the reality of not seeing Riley. So many times during the day when the kids said something cute or Carla made me laugh I thought of telling Riley and caught myself. It also dawned on me I had to add two things to my list that were not pleasant, but I felt they needed to be done. One, I had to talk to Crown to see if I could persuade her that no crime had actually been committed and two, I had to have that conversation with my father. I knew he was behind all of this and was pushing this case for some reason I needed to know. I knew him well enough to know I couldn't make him change his mind, but maybe I could at least find out what was going on inside that twisted mind of his.

As it turned out, every day was different. I kept myself as busy as I possibly could, painting up a storm, but those two things on my list weighed on me more than even my ache of not seeing Riley.

I needed to get them over and done with before it disturbed my sleep any more than it already had.

I phoned the Crown's office and made an appointment to see her. The other, more dreaded meeting, I knew I couldn't phone ahead. I was afraid if I did, he would make excuses to get out of seeing me.

I walked into his office after work on trembling legs and a rapid beating heart. I thought of the baby inside me and the promise I had made to Riley to avoid stress. I took a few deep breaths and slowed my heart rate.

"I'm here to see Mr. Donner." I said to the not surprisingly beautiful woman who sat at the front desk.

"Do you have an appointment?"

"No, just tell him his daughter is here." She looked at me with unabashed shock and it took her a minute to find her voice again.

"Don't bother telling me he's not in, I know he is. Is anyone else in there with him?"

She just shook her head no and didn't even bother to stop me when I walked towards his door and opened it. It wasn't until I was already in that she ran behind me, yelling.

"Sir, I'm sorry. She kind of took me off guard." He looked up then and, as much as he always had a reign on the emotions he allowed to show on his face, I was sure I saw a bit of surprise there. He waved his hand at her, as if irritated by a fly. She backed out of the room closing the door behind her. I'm sure at this point she wished she were a fly, on the wall.

"I wondered when you were going to stroll in here." He leaned back nonchalantly in his chair, all traces of surprise gone from his face.

I sat down in a chair across from him; scared my shaking legs would give me away.

"Why are you pursuing this?"

"No beating around the bush eh? How about 'Hi father, thanks for the car."

"You mean the target on wheels which is the reason I was scooped up to begin with?"

"You were always good at turning the blame back to me."

"Answer the question."

"Well, how can I let anyone who hurt my darling daughter get away with it?"

"You mean how would it look to the public? Let's be honest here, you never gave a crap about your darling daughter before."

"Well now, that's why I sent the car, as a peace offering." I was seething inside and I needed to remain calm so as not to lose my cool before I had a chance to find out what I needed to know.

"I was bringing the car back to you. I didn't and don't want peace. I only want you to let it go. I don't feel a crime has been committed, not by Riley."

"You mean the man you supposedly love? The same man who kidnapped you and almost killed you?"

Through clenched teeth I managed, "He never hurt me. You have the wrong man. It was his brother who grabbed me and it was his brother who almost killed me. Not that you care about that. All you care about is your precious reputation and your business. That's all you ever cared about. When the news came out that I had been kidnapped and that I was your daughter, you had to quickly look like the caring father. You could still have your stupid reputation if you went after the man who actually committed the crime. You could blame the blunder on the police and we would all be happy. But for some strange reason you don't want me to be happy. Why?"

He wheeled his chair around and gazed out his big glass window. It looked down on the city and it must have made him feel powerful. With his back to me, he spoke quietly,

"Your mother made me happy once. I did love her you might not believe that. She was beautiful and smart. I pictured our lives together. Me, building the business and her the dutiful wife, hosting dinner parties and raising our strong sons to inherit what I built." He turned the chair around then to face me. His voice was filled with contempt and anger.

"Then you came along and ruined all my plans. I didn't want you and she did. It created a wall between us and nothing was ever the same. Giving birth to you made her weak and it was because of this that she became ill. You, my darling daughter killed her, not me. And that is why I hate the sight of you. You took away my happiness and I will do everything in my power to make sure you never taste it either."

Initially I was taken aback by his frankness. I didn't think he would be so brutally honest and actually answer my question. His words hurt me more than I would ever let on or admit.

I stood up then.

"You know you didn't have to go to all this trouble and pretend to be this dutiful father. I am just as repulsed at the thought that I am your relation as you are. I would have denied profusely to the press that I was your daughter. I would have claimed mistaken identity. I have my reputation to worry about too."

This time I used the momentum of my trembling legs to move me out the door before he could say anything else.

***

As soon as I came home after the meeting I took a long shower and then did an hour of yoga. Still I felt tense and angry. So I did the only other thing that seemed to make me feel better. I ate a whole container of chocolate ice cream. Afterwards I felt bloated and full, but my brain finally seemed at rest.

I got all heated up again when Susan got home and relayed the story, wishing I didn't need to vent on her after a long day of work. Without Riley I had no one else to talk to.

"Holy crap, he's some piece of work eh?"

"Yup."

"Tell me you don't believe the stuff he's spewing, about your mom."

"No, but it doesn't make it hurt any less."

"What are you going to do now?"

"There's nothing I can do about him. I need to convince Crown that they have no case."

"Do you really think you'll be able to do that?"

"I won't know unless I try."

"I'll make you dinner and we'll celebrate."

"Celebrate what"

"Standing up to your father. That took a lot of guts. I'm proud of you."

"Let's not call him that anymore."

"Father?"

"He's never been a father to me and he sure as hell won't be in the future."

"On that note, are you okay with my dad coming to dinner. I had invited him earlier, but if you're not up to company, I can call and cancel."

"Nope, don't. There's a real dad for you. It will be great to see him."

We ate a fabulous dinner of chicken Parmesan, fettuccini, garlic bread and a never-ending bowl of Caesar salad.

Everything Susan made was always from scratch and you would never find a jar of sauce or a box in her pantry (except for her cereal addiction that is.) It felt good to want to eat again and not be repulsed by the smell of food cooking.

As we sat eating more ice cream (Susan didn't bring up the fact that one whole carton was missing) Nate spoke with a twinkle in his eye.

"I have some good news for you."

"Man, that would be nice for a change."

"Riley said to say hi and that he misses you more than the sky misses the stars on a cloudy night."

"What?" Nate's sparkle turned into a huge grin.

"Nobody ever said I couldn't visit. He needs someone coming around to make sure he's okay." I stood up so fast I knocked over the chair. I hugged Nate so hard that when I let go my arms ached and he was blushing.

"Hey, it's what any decent person would do."

"I've never known so many decent people in my life. Thank you so much Nate. That makes me feel so much better. Tell me every detail of your visit. How did he look? Is he getting enough to eat? Is he sleeping? Is he getting any trouble?"

"Slow down. He's fine. He asked the same questions about you. He's happy knowing you're okay."

Nate went on then to talk about their conversation, which was nothing other than idle chitchat. I hung on every word, imagining Riley's voice instead of Nate's.

When he was done, I told him over and over how much I appreciated him doing that for me, for us. I felt so much better and what Nate had done almost washed away the bad feelings that were lingering like unwanted cat hair.

When I went to bed that night, I wondered, like I had many times when I was growing up, how different my life would have turned out if I had had a good father like Nate in my life. The twisted thing about fate was that then I might not have ever met Riley.

Nate's update was just what I needed to continue doing what I needed to do to get through the days.

I went to work, poured myself into the tasks at hand and then went home and painted for a few hours. Christmas was fast approaching and I wanted to make a painting for both Susan and Nate as a way of saying thank you. I devoured prenatal books at the library. I loved reading about what the baby was doing right at that moment. I kept a journal of my thoughts and how I was feeling daily so that later I could read it back to Riley and make him feel like he hadn't missed a thing.

Life continued on this way for the next month, which brought me to Christmas. I was dreading it. I at least had Susan and Nate, but I thought of Riley sitting in that place all alone surrounded by grey walls and only the smells of the desperate around him.

I had come up with an idea at my last prenatal. I was at Meaghan's office to ask for her help.

"Are you able to show documents to your client during your meetings?"

"Yes, of course."

"I need a favour."

"I'm listening."

I slipped her a piece of paper with four grey rectangle pictures on it.

"Is this what I think it is?"

"Yes, can you do it?"

"I would love to play Santa. Just this once." Susan winked at me and I walked out of her office leaving her holding the ultrasound pictures of our beautiful baby.

***

Nate and Susan kept their Christmas quiet, which helped. They didn't have a big family and were used to just relying on each other. They had some fun traditions that I felt privileged to be a part of. We piled into Nate's truck on Christmas Eve, armed with eggnog, straws and popcorn and drove around looking at the Christmas lights in town. They would give out their own ratings for the tackiest, most religious, most amount of electricity used, and the prettiest. It was great to drive around and see the surroundings from a different perspective.

When we came back to the house, I left them alone and retired to my room. Their other tradition was to open one gift that night and I wanted to give them some space to do their own family thing.

I wrote in my journal and described the evening to Riley. The drive had given me some ideas of how I wanted to decorate our house some day and I wanted to incorporate the Dennill's tradition of the drive-by ratings into our future Christmases. I loved the colored icicle lights and the glowing white deer on the front lawns. Susan had an artificial tree, but I had a vision of making it into a day where we would take a drive into the woods and pick one out. We would cut it down and then decorate it while drinking hot chocolate and listening to Christmas music. In the spring, I wanted us to plant a tree somewhere to make up for the one we cut down. We would wake up on Christmas morning and open stockings and then have a special breakfast of waffles, whipped cream and tons of yummy toppings to choose from. Then, of course, opening presents and a fabulous huge dinner. It always made me feel better to think about our future rather than dwell on the present.

Growing up, Christmases were quiet as well, but not sweet and comfortable like it was with Susan and Nate. Mom tried to make up for the fact that my father was not home and bought me a lot of things, but something always felt wrong. Mom never cooked a Christmas dinner and we would be one of those families that either ordered in or had a pre-made dinner that the staff had made for us. The kids at school would bring homemade cookies and gingerbread to school in their lunches and I was always so envious. The only cookies we had in our house came in a box or a bag. Even the gifts mom got me were not very personal. At first, she got me a bunch of things that were as if she had asked someone at the store, 'what do you buy an eight/ten/twelve year old girl? So it would be all the stuff the more popular girls got but I was never interested in. I didn't follow any set styles and my hobbies revolved around reading and not much else. But there was my mom buying me everything but books. When I became a teenager she switched to gift cards, but for clothing stores not bookstores. Most years I took the stuff she had given me and donated it to the Salvation Army. It wasn't that I was a spoiled, unappreciative brat; I just thought someone else could use the stuff more than I could. My mom would never notice. By the time I was a teenager, I think she hardly saw me at all.

A knock on the door brought me out of the past.

"Hey, can you come out here for a second?" Susan's head was peeking around my door.

"Sure."

I walked out into Susan's living room and was greeted by an easel that was large and glorious.

"No, you guys!"

"Hey just don't forget about us when you're rich and famous." Nate grinned and handed me a wrapped box that was heavy. Inside it was filled with many paints, paper and canvases.

"Thanks. Both of you."

"No problem. We can't wait to see what you've been working on lately." I had kept my paintings under wraps for the last month and I knew it was killing Susan. She was going to have to wait a little longer. I was holding out until Christmas morning.

"We're just about to have some appies and watch the Grinch Who Stole Christmas-the original, if you want to join us." I knew the invitation was not just to make me feel better, I knew she really wanted to make me feel included, but I begged off saying I was so tired.

"All right, but if you change your mind, we're here." I gave them both a big hug and crawled into bed hugging my pillow wishing I had something that belonged to Riley. Something that had his smell on it.

The smell of bacon frying and coffee percolating woke me up the next morning and my stomach grumbled like an alarm clock. I got up and took a quick shower. I joined Susan and Nate at the kitchen table and we had a big breakfast of eggs, bacon, hash browns and toast. I hadn't had a big breakfast like that since I had lived in the dorms. There was a tiny restaurant around the corner from my dorm that served the best breakfasts. I would go on Sundays, book in hand, and eat a huge plate full for less than five dollars. They would always refill my coffee until I left making swishy sounds as I walked and jumpy from caffeine. But Susan and Nate's version was by far the best.

After breakfast, I finally let Susan see what I had been working on. I had two paintings both individually wrapped, one for her and one for Nate. The one for Susan was of the island in the winter. The trees were all laden with glimmering frost. The air was thick with fog that hung around the base of the island. All you could see were the treetops and then right in the middle was a bright red canoe parked on the shore, taking a rest for the season.

Nate's was of the beaver dam lit by the full moon and stars. A beaver was swimming its way over with a large tree in its mouth. The moon was a ripple reflection in the lake and the trees were just shadows in the background.

“Jady, these are amazing. They make me want to live at the cabin myself and we all know I’m a city girl through and through. They’re like looking at pictures.”

“That’s what I hoped for. There was so many times on the island that I wished I had a camera to capture these beautiful moments and now I have a way to get my memories out, on canvas.”

“Well you’ve done an incredible job. Thanks Jady.” It was Nate this time singing praises. I waved my hand, becoming embarrassed. I was about to get dressed to go out for a walk as the weather had turned a bit warmer, and I didn’t want to invade their space while they were opening gifts.

“Where are you going?”

“I thought I’d take Sookie for a walk.”

“C,mon and join us. I see some presents with your name on them.”

“You’ve already done so much for me already. Really you guys, it wasn’t necessary.”

“There’re not from us. Santa brought them last night.” Susan grabbed my hand and plunked me down on the couch and handed me a cup of hot chocolate.

“I’m playing Santa.” Susan was more giddy than a three year old.

“One for dad, one for me and one for Jady.”

Nate got a book on fly-fishing. Susan opened a package that had a wonderful teal sweater in it. My gift was a piece of paper with my name on it saying my registration was confirmed and I could begin my pottery class in January. I was thrilled.

Susan continued to hand out gifts and my pile got larger. They got me some baby books including a pregnancy journal to keep track of everything going on. A generous gift certificate to a local maternity store, a little indoor herb garden growing kit and a beautiful puzzle of a grizzly bear with mountains and a waterfall in the background.

"To get a little bit of your garden back."

There was also plenty of chocolate and a beautiful bracelet beaded in aqua and silver.

When it seemed everything had been opened and we were surrounded by crumpled glitter, green and red, there was still a glint of mischief in Nate and Susan's eyes.

"What are you two up to?"

"We have one more gift for you." They handed me an envelope with my name on it.

"What's this?"

They just shrugged, "I guess you have to open it to find out." They shared a glance as I tore the paper. Inside was a map. It was the area of the cabin taken from an aerial view. Shas mountain was circled in red and beside the circle the words "How about Shas for a boy or girl?" My eyes filled with tears and I held the paper to my chest and closed my eyes.

"Well what is it?"

"How did you get this?" I handed over the map to show them.

"Riley mailed it to dad. What does it mean? Who are Lucy and Rudy Kroll?" I looked up to see their puzzled faces.

"What?"

"Here in the corner of the map. Lucy and Rudy Kroll and their phone number and address."

They handed the map back and I saw what they were talking about. I knew immediately who they were.

"The Cabin Couple." Nate and Susan were still looking puzzled so I explained. They are the people that own the cabin that Riley and I stayed in. Shas. I love it."

"Shas?"

"It's Riley's idea to name our baby. It's the mountain we climbed."

"It's a very cool name."

"Thanks. Thanks for this. For everything. I feel spoiled and blessed. I've never had a Christmas like this before."

"We know it's not the one you wish you were having, but we tried our best. Next year it will be everything you've ever wished for."

I sure hoped so. I went to bed that night holding the map close to me. That small piece of paper just made my Christmas absolutely perfect.

***

I was itching to phone the number Riley had given me, but I didn't want to contact them until after Boxing Day at least. I was nervous as to how they were going to react, but I also wanted to clear the air and let them know their place was safe and cared for.

Susan dragged me shopping on Boxing Day, which turned out to be a good thing. The sales at the maternity shop she had given me a certificate to allowed me to get way more than I would have on any other day. I didn't need any bigger clothes yet so I bought clothes for when I would need them. It was hard looking at these shirts I considered to be so big and imagine myself fitting into them at some point in the next seven months.

Susan did her share of shopping and came home with a lot of great deals. We stopped for lunch at her restaurant and then we made one more stop on the way home.

"I'm so sorry it took me so long to bring you here. I told you I would get you an appointment ages ago." We were at a hair salon. I had been wearing my hair up in a ponytail for so long I had stopped thinking about a haircut. It seemed to have lost its shine at the same time I landed in the city.

"What would you like?" A petite redhead asked me.

"I'm in your capable hands. Do whatever you like. I'm open to suggestions."

"Oh, I like her already. I rarely get that in here." She took me to the back and washed my hair with some heavenly smelling shampoo. I tried very hard not to think about Riley's fingers massaging my scalp.

She gave my jet-black hair a shoulder length cut with long layers that felt light and healthy. I left the salon shining again.

That night, when I went to bed I felt content. I had a new haircut, new clothes and a name for my baby. Besides the fact that the baby's father was in jail, what more could a girl ask for?

I lay in bed the following morning staring at the clock. It was still too early to call. I would take a shower and have breakfast and then I would call.

I ate my bowl of oatmeal in silence. No TV or radio and Susan was at work today. What was I going to say? Had they been out there since we left and now knew someone was there? Did they figure it out from all the media hype? Would they be angry? I was nervous and yet I couldn't wait to meet the couple that had created and lived in the haven we had called home for four months. Would they agree to meet with me?

I glanced at the clock. 9:30. Still too early? It dawned on me then that they could be like many others out there and were back at work. Our preschool was shut down until after New Years, but besides the school system, and myself almost everybody else was back at work. I picked up the phone with trembling hands and took a deep breath.

On the third ring an elderly lady with a thick accent answered. I almost hung up. Everything I had rehearsed in my head dried up on my tongue.

"Um...Hi, my name is Jady Donner. I'm...um..I was staying in your cabin..."

"I know who you are. The police called us and told us what you did. You're just lucky we didn't press charges. We don't want to speak to you." There was a click and then the dial tone. I finally hung up the phone, disappointed and ashamed. Why did I think it was going to be okay with them? We had broken into their little sanctuary and lived in their space. They didn't know anything about us except what they had read in the papers. I wished she had given me a chance to explain. I wanted to call back or even to visit, but I didn't want to harass these people. I just had to let it go. She was right, I was lucky that they didn't want to press charges and I had to leave it at that.

***

Before I knew it, my holidays were over and I was back to the routines that came with work. I had convinced Susan to go out with some friends for New Year's Eve instead of just hanging out at the house with me. I was in no mood to go out and I was more than happy to stay home with movies and a bag of chips.

Back at work everyone talked about their holidays and how much they ate, drank or the things they got as gifts. Both Brandi and Carla looked well rested and ready to be there with the kids. I was happy to be back too. It made the time fly by faster than sitting at home. I had completed a few more paintings and hoped to give them to the girls when it was time for me to leave here. They still didn't know I was pregnant and I was going to put it off until I was showing, which wasn't yet. I had a little bulge now at fourteen weeks, but it could easily be covered with bulkier shirts. I was looking forward to being at the point where I could talk about it openly, and could hardly wait to feel the baby move inside me. I had to stop myself all the time at work from rubbing my belly, which would be a dead give away.

I waited until the second week of January before I phoned the Crown attorney assigned to Riley's case. It was pretty high profile and they had given it to a newer lawyer who had worked her way up the ladder and was trying to make a name for herself. She was a young woman named Olivia Andrews. I had received all this information from Meaghan.

I had called ahead and I had an appointment with her after work. I wasn't as nervous as I had been when I went to Greg's office, but I wasn't feeling super confidant either.

"I'm so glad you came in to see me. I needed to go over some things, seeing as you're one of our main witnesses. I was hoping I wouldn't have to subpoena you, or is that why you're here? To tell me you're not going to take the stand?"

"Oh, I'm taking the stand, but I'm afraid it won't do anything to help your side." Her eyebrows raised in amusement. She was a very well dressed, tall woman with her dark hair pulled back in a long ponytail.

"Well, I'm afraid you're wrong there."

"You don't even know what I'm going to say on the stand so how can you already know I'm wrong?"

"You're going to tell your story am I correct?"

"Yes."

"Well then, that's all I need from you." I was confused and my face must have registered this thought.

"There isn't a jury or judge in this world who would think you honestly fall in love with someone who kidnapped you and held you in a remote cabin for four months." I knew she was probably right and I had to change tactics.

"Listen, I'm sure you've spoken to both brothers and I'm also sure you have strong enough instincts to know when some red flags are flapping you in the face. You know deep down who is the criminal here and you know you have the wrong one sitting behind bars. You need to make something right here. You need to let this go. A crime is usually committed on a victim. You don't have one in this case. I am not a victim of any crime committed by Riley. You are going after the wrong man and only you can stop this."

Her face turned to stone and her voice matched her expression.

"Listen to me very clearly. You may very well be in love with Riley. But you fell in love with him *after* the crime was already committed. You were kidnapped first and *that* is the crime. There is no question in my mind that someone broke the law here and I will make sure they pay for that. What happened after the fact is not my concern. I am doing my job and I know what I'm doing. I will be in touch if I have any further questions." This was obviously my cue to leave and I really didn't know what else to say. I left her office wondering if I had just made everything worse.

I was two for two, and not in a good way. The Cabin Couple and now Mrs. Evil Crown. The only good thing coming from my list was my painting. I guess Susan was right, drama and tragedy made for good art.

I was feeling pretty discouraged when I walked into Susan's place. I wanted to be able to talk to Riley. I wanted him to tell me everything was going to be okay. I needed to feel his arms around me and rest my head on his big shoulders.

"Hey are you okay?" Susan was in the kitchen cooking dinner. I pulled up a seat on one of her tall stools. She poured me a wine glass full of sparkling apple juice and placed a plate of cheese and crackers in front of me. I ate and drank mindlessly and vented. Susan listened as she prepared our meal, being a good friend as usual.

After I had droned on for a while I stopped myself mid-sentence.

"I'm sorry. You don't always have to listen to all my drama and woe."

"Are you kidding me? Your life is better than any soap opera. I haven't had to pick up a single book since you've moved in." We laughed and clinked glasses.

"Okay, but seriously now. Don't let some power hungry witch get you down. When you take the stand she's thinking you will help her side, but she doesn't know you. You are pretty solid and you will come across like the honest, good and very sane person you are. When you tell your story they will be wooed by your romantic tale and they will be wondering what crime really has been committed. They will see and get to know Riley through your eyes and they won't have the heart to convict him on any crime."

"Have I told you recently how great you are?"

"Nope."

"Well you are. Thanks."

"That's what friends are for. C'mon let's eat. You're looking mighty thin."

I patted my growing belly.

"Shas thinks you're pretty great too, well your cooking anyways."

"Mmmmm...I like this baby already."

"That's the baby's heartbeat? That's amazing!" Susan was just as excited as I was. Tears were flowing down the side of my face and making the white paper sheet that covered the examining table wet.

Susan was there with me for my prenatal visit at fourteen weeks. I had gained twelve pounds already and I was feeling pretty good now that the nausea had passed.

When Dr. Ngozi passed the wand back over my baby and we could hear the heartbeat again we were all silent, listening to that miraculous sound. I so wished Riley could be beside me to hear it as well. Susan squeezed my hand as if sensing my loneliness. To hear that heartbeat again made everything seem worth it. I had a living being inside me. Something that Riley and I had created. So many times when I woke up in the morning I wondered if everything that happened was real. Did I live in the cabin? Had I met and fallen in love with Riley? There had been only one thing up to now that had kept it real for me, the wooden ring that I wore upon my hand, but now I also had the sound of our baby's heartbeat.

Susan took me for a drive that night out of the city limits. We drove out to where people usually had their summer cabins. Away from all the city lights and traffic you could see all the stars in the night sky. We both had hot chocolate and shared a bag of caramel corn. She had brought lawn chairs and because the night was cold we had dressed warmly and brought blankets that we tucked around us.

"How are you feeling, really? About all of this?"

"Do you mean Riley or the baby?"

"Both."

"I miss him desperately, but to be honest, I have wondered about all this Stockholm Syndrome stuff. I have been doing a lot of research lately at the library about it and it fits my profile. In the articles and books I have read, they say captives start to sympathize with their captors when they're isolated from other people and when the captor shows acts of kindness. Of course both of those factors were present in my circumstance. From what I've read, it says it brings you back to the infant/ bonding stage. You are relying on your captor for food and safety just as you did as a baby, relying on your mom. That scared me and made me think of how vulnerable I was going into the whole situation. Having my background, between my mom's death and feeling invisible to my father, it left me in a position to be at the mercy of someone like Riley and his brother. But when I came into the situation, I was determined to hate both of them. I was a bitter, angry woman whose wall was so thick the big bad wolf could not have blown it down. But not only did Riley break those walls down he fell in love and unearthed a woman I never even knew existed. I am a new person, thanks to him. He didn't turn on the charm in order to manipulate me or change the situation, he was just himself and has been consistently so. The longer I am away from him, the more I realize how much I love him. He helped me rediscover life and actually love it again. How can any of that be a bad thing? It's so frustrating that I can't give someone a shake and have him released. This whole thing is crazy and he shouldn't be there. He's a good man and he should be sitting beside me right now. No offence. I love your company..."

"Hey, say no more. I've always believed everything happens for a reason, but in this instance I can't wrap my head around it. What purpose is being served with Riley sitting in jail? Is it meant to prove to both of you, that what you have is real; so that there is never a time in your future lives that you will question it? If you hadn't had this time apart would he wonder if you had only loved him because of the way things had begun for you two? Would you have questioned it down the road? It's hard to say. This way you will know for sure. There will be no doubt." I thought about what she had said. It made sense, but it was a brutal way to learn you really loved someone.

The sky lit up then with the northern lights, as if it had been waiting all along for us to be quiet in order to start the show. It wasn't as spectacular as it had been on the island, but it was breathtaking nonetheless. There were more blues and yellows and they were spread out across the sky like someone had used a wide paintbrush in broad strokes.

"There's another painting for you."

"You read my mind."

"Here, I have something for you." Susan handed me a small wrapped rectangle. I opened it to find a small Dr. Seuss book. It was a revision and meant to be read to the baby in utero. I loved it and read it aloud on the spot. We both laughed when I finished, more because we didn't want to cry.

"That's so cool. Thanks Auntie Susan."

"Hey, now I like the sound of that."

"It does have a nice ring to it doesn't it?"

The lights gave one more last hurrah and then they were gone like someone had blown out a candle. We finished up our hot chocolates and as if the lights had provided warmth, we suddenly felt the chill of the cool night and packed up our chairs.

"I needed that, thanks Susan."

"Hey we all need a heartbeat party. It's a pretty special time and I know I'm not Riley, but I'm here whenever you need me."

***

One minute we had been celebrating, and the next we were clinging to each other hoping my worst nightmare hadn't just come true.

That night after we had celebrated, I woke up bleeding. I was still half asleep and confused. I almost forgot that I was pregnant and that this was not a natural thing to be happening to me. When I came around and realized what might be happening, I started to yell for Susan.

She helped to calm me down and did not fall apart. She drove me to the hospital and they brought us in right away, Susan having had the sense to phone ahead.

The familiar wand passed over my belly, in the hand of an unfamiliar doctor who did nothing to calm my nerves. He looked stern and serious and after what seemed like forever, couldn't find my baby's heartbeat. My tears were being shed along with his sweat and I was gripping the sides of the hospital bed in sheer panic.

He walked out to get someone else and I turned to Susan with a trembling voice,

"Something feels wrong Susan. I just can't place it, but something is just very wrong."

"You stop. I'm sure everything is just fine." Her words didn't match the lines on her brow or her tight grip on my hand.

The doctor came back with a nurse in tow. She once again squirted that cold jelly on my stomach and listened to no avail. My tears rolled down, no longer restrained or hidden. I was scared and they were doing nothing to put my fears to rest.

"Go get Dr. Brown and bring the portable ultrasound." The nurse nodded and was almost out of the room before he had finished giving his orders.

Susan and I didn't speak. We had nothing to say. I didn't even know this baby yet and it was amazing the attachment that had already formed. The thought of losing someone whom you hadn't even met yet was a bizarre thought in any other circumstance other than an unborn child and their mother. *Please, let me meet my baby.*

Another doctor came in with the nurse on her heels rolling in the ultrasound machine. She picked up my chart briefly and then placed it down on the end of the bed.

"So Miss Jady, let's see what that baby is up too." With all the confidence in the world, she reapplied the jelly; completely carrying on like there was no problem and oblivious to my tears and the smell of panic about us. I was so absorbed in bracing myself for bad news that initially I didn't hear the doctor's words.

"Sorry. What did you say?"

"I said, you have quite an acrobat here. Look at that baby go."

Susan and I stared intently at the screen trying to see what she saw, still not believing her words. There was rapid grey movement and then that sound, that beautiful beating sound that made the tears fall yet again.

"Your baby is fine, very fine in fact." She gave me a smile and her words were the only indication that gave even the slightest hint that something had been wrong in the first place.

"Thank you." The words came from Susan's mouth and I seconded the motion. Dr. Brown left as fast as she came. In her wake she left one very happy mom.

When we got back home, we both stayed up, Susan with a tall glass of wine and myself a cup of milk.

"I'm so sorry you had to go through that. It was pretty scary. I'm so glad everything turned out all right."

"I'll toast to that. That Dr. Brown was amazing wasn't she? As soon as she walked in the room it was like she chased away all terrible thoughts. She just acted like it was a normal ultrasound. No panicked mom or that it was in the middle of the night. I admire people like that." I rubbed my belly lovingly.

"I think that baby is a fighter like her mom." We shared a smile and polished off our drinks.

"Well then thank goodness for that."

"Listen, I don't know about you but I'm exhausted. Are you okay?"

"I've never been better or should I say more grateful than I am right at this moment."

Susan gave me a long hug and headed off to bed.

When I went shortly after, I lay awake trying to slow down my own heart beat, but so thankful for the one beating alongside mine.

***

Valentine's Day, twenty weeks along and popping out. I had no choice, but to sit down with Joyce, the lady who hired me and let her know.

"So are you planning to work until the end of June when preschool ends?"

"That's the plan."

"Well, then we have nothing to worry about. Congratulations Jady. Just make sure to let Carla and Brandi know so that they can take over any heavy lifting or if children need carrying."

"For sure."

I left relieved that she hadn't made a big deal about it. When I told the girls they were happy as well.

"Why didn't you let us know? We could have helped out more when you were feeling rotten." They both knew first hand how I felt and what would be coming. Both of them had two children already.

"Thanks you guys. Right now, I feel great. Lots of energy. It's only my hips at night time that are aching."

The advice began with everything from special body pillows to life saving sleep positions. I smiled as I prepped the crafts for the week, happy to have such good people around me.

Later I tried not to think about Riley sitting in his prison cell as I heard the girls discuss their valentine plans. Carla was having dinner cooked for her and Brandi was going out to dinner with her husband.

"What about you...Oh jeez Louise, sorry Jady. Me and my big mouth."

"Hey don't worry about it. Susan has to work tonight, but she probably made me a beautiful dinner to reheat." I winked to let her know I was fine and there was no hard feelings.

As usual, Susan did what she did best and went out of her way to make sure I wasn't forgotten. When I got home from work there was a fresh bouquet of multi-colored flowers waiting for me and a huge box of chocolates. I hadn't forgotten her either and had phoned the florist earlier and had a small bouquet of flowers sent to her at work. I knew she would get a kick out of that.

Susan had also left an envelope with a note. It said that her father dropped it off earlier. I opened it, excited, knowing that it could only be from one person and that wasn't Nate.

Inside the box was one paper rose. I held it up to my nose, not in the hopes that it would smell like a real flower, but that it would carry even just a hint of him. His hands had held this and he had thought about me as he created it.

Of course there was no note. That would make it too obvious. They checked the ingoing and outgoing mail and it wouldn't take much for the word to get back to Crown that we had been in contact and wouldn't bode well for Riley's case.

Less than two months now until Riley's trial. I knew Meaghan was working hard at putting everything she could into it. She kept me posted as much as possible. She was really focusing all her energy on two things. One, there really is no victim in this case and two, Riley is just an accessory and not the main man in this scheme. She was going after Byron and pushing the fact that I was not suffering from Stockholm Syndrome.

Meaghan was hoping the whole thing would be thrown out based on doubt. It came down to Riley's word against Byron's and Meaghan was counting on Riley's character speaking for itself on the stand. She was trying to dig up anyone she could from Byron's past he had rubbed the wrong way or had had disagreements with. It wasn't too hard to do. Almost every boss Byron had ever had did not have good things to say about him. Along with being unreliable, stealing, and just mouthing off to the boss, the list was endless.

Riley on the other hand, everyone who came in contact with him liked him and always said the nicest things about him. When Riley did work, he was always on time, gave one hundred percent of himself and most people that Meaghan talked to, said that his biggest down fall was his brother. He had to call in sick or quit all together due to Byron and what Riley told people were his "health issues."

The ironic thing was that even the dirt that Meaghan kicked up when uncovering Byron's past managed to throw a bit of sun Riley's way. The store owners that the brothers held up and robbed, would say that they were afraid of the older, bigger one, but the younger, smaller one always hung back and apologized and made sure no one was ever hurt. It was said time and time again, that the younger one kept the older one calm and under control. I just hoped this would mean something in court.

***

I stepped on the scale again, not believing in the numbers I was seeing.

"30 pounds! I gained 30 pounds! But I'm only 23 weeks along! I have a long way to go. How big am I going to get?" The nurse just smiled as she wrote down the numbers in my file and directed me into my doctor's office.

"Is it normal to gain that much weight?" She laughed.

"There is no such thing as normal when you're pregnant." Dr. Ngozi winked and took my blood pressure.

"You're looking good. Everything is coming along nicely." She always had a way of putting me at ease.

When I got home and told Susan, she laughed too.

"I'll take it as a compliment that my cooking is doing its job."

"I'm going to be a whale by the time I'm ready to have this baby." Susan put another tasty dish in front of me.

"So be a happy whale."

Week 27 and 42 pounds gained. I was reading in my pregnancy book to keep your weight gain to 25-30 pounds. I was beyond that and still about 12 weeks away. But the doctor was still happy with me. My blood pressure was low and there was no indication of diabetes.

The ultimate best part was I could feel our baby now. Every time I lay in bed at night and felt Shas's movement, I wished I had another hand there to share in the moment. Our baby loved music and mornings. Norah Jones seems to be the favourite right now. I read aloud and I gave a play-by-play while I painted.

There was only a week left to the trial. I was looking forward to seeing Riley, but anxious as to how the whole thing was going to go. I needed to think positively and just hope Riley would be out when Shas was born.

That was how I was marking my time now. By how many weeks pregnant I was and how much time was left until the trial.

Meaghan was encouraging when I visited her, but I could tell by her body language that she was anxious too and not as confident as when I saw her initially. I had to be prepared for a negative outcome and Susan and I had been devising a plan B.

I had agreed to stay with her for a while if Riley was given the sentence, which Meaghan was preparing me for. The worse case scenario was that the jury believed Olivia's case, which would be that Riley was the mastermind behind the entire plan and orchestrated the whole thing. That came with a maximum seven-year sentence, something I couldn't even fathom. The next best outcome would be that the jury didn't believe Olivia and thought Riley was only an accessory. Finally, the verdict Meaghan was hoping for was that there really had been no crime committed. There was no victim and although abduction occurred, initially Byron did it and it was Riley who rescued me and brought me to safety. Of course this was the one we were all hoping for.

Regardless I needed to plan for whatever the outcome. The problem was I couldn't think past the next few months. I needed to believe that Riley would be out and that we could continue on with our lives preparing for an addition to our family. I couldn't even think what I would do if he got the maximum sentence. I couldn't go there. Not now. Susan had tried to bring it up a few times, but I had changed the subject and being the good friend that she is, she let it go. I could see by the look on her face that she was concerned.

Susan came home one day with a bit of promising news that took my mind off of the hamster wheel for a while. Payton, whose art we had seen that one night, had seen the painting I had given Susan for Christmas. She had really liked it and wanted to see the rest of my work thinking there was potential for a show. I was delighted with the turn of events and rustled together the paintings I had been working on the last few months. I saw them now with a critical eye and wondered if they were good enough. When I looked at them, I saw the cabin and all the memories that came with them. It was just like I had developed pictures taken from my time there. I woke up every day and went to bed every night with the visions imprinted on my mind. Looking at my paintings was, for me, more calming than a day at the spa was for some. I just hoped Payton thought the same.

When Payton did come for a peek she brought yet another surprise. The owner of the gallery was with her.

"This is good work. I have an opening on May 3rd. You will be sharing it with a few other artists. Are you interested and can you do a few more?"

"Yes, yes…to both questions."

"Great, I'll be in touch." She turned around and began to leave. Payton was her shadow and I followed both of them to the door. It had all happened so fast I began to wonder if I had imagined it all. Payton turned to me and gave me a silent thumbs up to verify that it was all very real.

When the door shut, I did a little happy dance and picked up the phone. As I had on so many occasions I wished I could call Riley with the news, but dialed Susan's work instead.

***

I was happy to have Nate with me. I was terrified about testifying. I was so scared of making things worse. We were at Susan's restaurant eating breakfast.

The media had been waiting for me outside of Susan's place and Nate had to bully his way through the crowd to get me to his car. They had many questions. I hadn't seen much of them the last few months. With no drama going on, I had become boring, but now that the trial was beginning I was big news again.

"We've been told you haven't seen Riley in four months. What will it be like to see him again?"

"Do you still love him?"

"Are you still engaged?"

"How does it feel to be manipulated and betrayed by someone whom you have been quoted to love?"

The biggest question on all their minds was,

"Is this Riley's baby?" I felt like saying, "You do the math", but I kept my mouth shut.

"Are you keeping the baby? Won't it be hard keeping a rapist and an abductor's baby?"

"How are you going to explain to this baby that its daddy is sitting in jail for hurting its mommy?"

The words were so cruel and it took everything I had not to yell back and cry. Nate tried to get me out of there as fast as he could. He worked very hard to make sure we hadn't been followed.

Susan saw the look on my face when we got to her restaurant and I crumpled into her arms.

"Oh, hon. I'm sorry. C'mon, have a seat over here. I have a decaf coffee loaded with sugar and cream waiting for you and a big plate of blueberry pancakes hot off the grill."

She led me over to a quiet, secluded table and joined Nate and I for a bit until she was sure I had calmed. I told her about the nasty comments the journalists had fired at me.

"Just remember they sometimes eat here too." She winked at me and apologized, but she needed to get back to work. She said she would come back and check on us when she got a minute.

Nate and I tried initially to just tip toe around small talk. I knew he was waiting for me to open the door.

"I'm really nervous about testifying."

"Y'know the first time I had to testify as a witness in a case I puked up my lunch. I was so scared and felt like everything was riding on me."

"It *is* riding on me."

"No, it's not. It really isn't. The jury and judge are taking everything in. One thing about a trial with a jury is the human element. You just tell your story and they will see and hear you as a person and will try to put themselves in your shoes. You don't act like a victim. You're a strong-willed woman and that will come through loud and clear. No one can make you do anything you don't want to do. They will see that and it won't matter how much Olivia tries to twist your words, you will just look human."

The anxiety that ate away at me made it very difficult to swallow the lovely breakfast Susan had prepared for us.

My palms were sweaty and I felt the beating in my chest so hard I thought it would look like a cartoon character's heart beating out and leave an impression on my bulging sweater. Any minute now Riley would come walking out and I was regretting eating a big breakfast. I was scared that I was going to have to run out of the courtroom, my stomach was churning so badly.

A ghost in a poorly fitted suit walked out. Could that really be him? He looked like a very thin shadow of the Riley I once knew. I saw his eyes skim over the people around me, but when they met mine it was with misted eyes. He went from meeting my gaze to smiling at my expanded form. I was so shocked by his appearance I didn't mouth the words I love you, like I had planned. He gave me a weak smile before he sat down with his back to me. As I studied his side profile I could see faded yellow marks that could be nothing but the former lives of bruises. I was aware of being watched and as I peeled my eyes away from Riley. I could feel everyone else's on me, studying my reaction. I was quick to blink back my tears.

I could hear whispered murmurings and it seems I had caused quite a stir with my obvious new bump.

The media had swarmed me when I had arrived and I had to act like a linebacker to make my way through without having to comment. I had nothing to say and I was afraid anything I did say would be distorted anyways.

The courtroom was silent and standing as the judge entered the room. I was so focused on Riley's face I didn't even hear the words uttered in the beginning. It was like the volume was slowly turned up and I tuned back in to hear Olivia call me up as her first witness.

"Miss Jady Donner, can you tell us in your own words what happened the night of June 23rd?"

"I had been driving the Cadillac and stopped to get gas."

"The Cadillac your father bought you?"

"Yes. When I stopped, Riley and Byron were there fuelling up as well."

"Can you indicate to the court where Riley and Byron are seated today?"

I pointed to Riley, but didn't let my eyes rest on him for long. His eyes began to tear and I was afraid of falling apart before I even began. Then I pointed to Byron and let my eyes burn into his. His eyes only filled me with anger and gave me motivation to continue.

"Were any words exchanged at the gas station?"

"No. I wasn't there long. I filled up and continued on my way."

"On your way where?"

"To...to Greg Donner's. To return his gift." The last two words were filled with sarcasm.

"Greg Donner, your father.

"Like I said, Greg Donner."

"What happened after you got gas?"

"I drove for about half an hour and then noticed red lights blinking by the side of the road. I saw Riley waving something to get my attention and also saw that one motorcycle was lying on its side with the wheel off. I pulled over to help."

"How can you be sure it was Riley waving you down?"

"I recognized him from the gas station."

"You recognized someone who, you said yourself, you saw briefly and..." Olivia consulted her notes, "it was raining and dark. Again, I ask you how can you be sure?"

"I know who I saw and it was Riley." I still kept myself from looking his way; from looking into those beautiful black eyes that mesmerized me right from the moment I saw them.

"He tried to warn me, but I didn't get what he was trying to tell me."

"What was Riley doing?"

"He had mouthed the word "run", but when I turned around I was knocked down to the ground by Byron."

I noticed Byron scowl at this piece of information that he was hearing for the first time.

"Again, Miss Donner how can you be sure it was Byron? Did you see his face?"

"Once we were back in the Cadillac, he told me to drive with a gun pointed in my face." I saw all eyes of the jury shifted from me to Byron.

"After you were struck down, did you lose consciousness?"

"I...I don't know. I remember things spinning a bit and then things started to focus once I was forced into the car."

"So you were confused for a bit?"

"Wouldn't you be after being hit in the head with the butt of a gun?"

The judge reminded me to stay focused and answer the questions only.

"I might have been confused, but I can say with 100% confidence that it was Byron who sat beside me in the car and forced me to drive to the cabin."

"How can you be so sure?"

I realized then what she was getting at. Taking a deep breath in order not to let my anger get the best of me I regrettably answered,

"It happened much too fast. I didn't see who hit me and struck me down. I do know it was Byron who held the gun to my head and told me to drive."

Olivia let me continue until I came to the part where Byron told me to pull over and put a bandana over my eyes.

"Why do you think he did that?"

"So that I couldn't see where we were going, I assumed."

"And then?"

"Then he got back in, but on the driver's side and he drove the rest of the way until we got to the cabin."

"Byron drove?"

"Yes."

"Again how do you know? Your eyes were covered by a bandana, how could you see who it was?"

"I couldn't. I just assumed..."

"When you arrived at the cabin did you see then who had been driving?" Again she had me.

"No, I fell asleep and when I woke up they both came out of the cabin."

"Did you still have your bandana on?"

"Yes but I could see out a gap at the bottom of it and it was dawn when I woke up."

"So they both came out of the cabin?"

"Yes, but it was *Byron* who dragged me into the cabin, slapped me in the face to stop me from screaming and it was *Byron* who pushed me into the tiny windowless room which was to become my home for the next two weeks." The initial fear I had felt on that day resurfaced and I felt my throat closing off. My heart was fluttering and my palms sweaty. I pictured that tiny room with the stained mattress and remembered thinking I was going to die in there.

I looked up then into Riley's eyes to see shame and guilt. But the tears told me of the love he felt for me, the love that rescued me from the fate awaiting me in that dark room.

"Miss Donner, are you all right?"

I looked to my right and saw it was the judge talking to me. By the look on his face, it was not the first time he had asked me. He was looking concerned.

"Do you need a break?"

I nodded, unable to speak; afraid it would come out in a sob.

***

"What happened during that first week?"

"Byron went and did small jobs and Riley was left in charge of me."

"This was according to Riley?"

"Yes."

"And you were completely isolated and no one else was around besides Riley and Byron?"

"Yes."

"So Riley was responsible for making sure you ate, allowing you to wash up or use the bathroom and for your general well being."

"Yes. He was kind and he seemed to be genuinely concerned, as well as, apologetic for the situation I was in."

"Wasn't he the reason or even part of the reason for the situation you were in?"

"Yes, but I don't agree with your theory that he was the mastermind. Riley was just going along with what his brother had planned, not the other way around." Olivia didn't pay any attention to my last comment; she was looking in her notes.

"Jady, do you have a best friend?"

"No, not really."

"It's a yes or no question."

"No."

"Have you ever had a boyfriend or a close relationship with anyone?"

"No."

"Why is that?"

"I…I have never been one for making friends."

"So here you are in the middle of nowhere, being held against your will and you end up not only becoming close with one of your kidnappers, but becoming engaged to him. How does that happen to someone who has never let anyone come close to her?"

I looked at Riley before I answered.

"It wasn't easy at first. It's not in my nature to be sociable with people. But I thought…"I looked again over at Riley.

"I thought if I could get close to Riley I might be able to get him to help me escape." I noticed it wasn't just me looking over at Riley to note his reaction; the jury had their eyes on him as well. He shocked me by just smiling at me as if to say, I knew that all along and it's okay. I didn't know if he was doing that for me or so that the media had nothing to make comments on.

"Now, obviously things didn't go as planned. What happened?"

"I ended up developing real feelings for Riley."

"How did you end up at the other cabin?"

"Riley took me there to take care of me."

"What happened?"

"Byron was holding me at gunpoint near the edge of a cliff. I…I was scared, and forgetting where I was, I took one too many steps backwards and fell." I thought about what Byron had said to make me take that painful step, but that was not about to be spoken aloud, not by me or by Byron. That would mean admitting I had been the one with the gun pointed at me. Without blinking an eye Olivia continued,

"And Riley found you?"

"He knows that area inside and out."

"Once you were healed at the cabin from your wounds, why did you not return?"

"I didn't want to. Riley did. He thought we should and I convinced him not too."

"Why?"

"I didn't want to lose what we had. I didn't want to go back to the real world. At the cabin, life was simple and I was happy for the first time in my life." My eyes welled up again at the thought of our life and what it had become. I looked at Riley and realized just how much I missed him and our whole life on that island. Again I was filled with regret for the day I chose to go for a ski.

"And Riley agreed to stay?"

"He wanted me to be happy too."

"So Riley had also developed feelings for you?"

"Yes."

"And he told you this."

"Yes."

"How did the relationship evolve?"

"Riley proposed to me."

"And you accepted?"

"Yes."

"Did Riley share your feelings for people?"

"I don't understand your question."

"Was he also an introvert, like you who didn't like to be around other people?"

"I don't know if he's an introvert but he didn't have a huge circle of friends either."

"Did you both agree and not want to return because of having to be around other people again?"

"We had created a wonderful world for the two of us there. I guess we didn't want to have to go back and to be apart from each other. I convinced him to stay for the winter."

"You convinced him? And he agreed?"

"Yes."

"So what happened to change things?"

"He went hunting to get us meat to tide us over for the winter and I went for a ski and fell. He came back and took me to the hospital where he was taken in, thanks to the lies told by his brother Byron."

"Just answer the question asked, Miss Donner."

"Was it at the hospital that you discovered you were pregnant?"

"Yes."

"And you're going to tell me that you were not coerced into having intercourse? It was consensual by both parties?"

"Yes." It was hard to keep the anger out of my voice.

"No more questions for now your honour." Olivia turned her back to me. I appealed to the jury.

"Listen. Riley Williams is a kind exceptional man whose only fault was that he loved his brother and wanted him to have a better life. I wasn't brainwashed nor am I suffering form any delusions." I spoke the next words directly to Riley. "I fell in love with Riley not because of our circumstances or because he manipulated me, but because he is who he is." The judge spoke to me,

"Please just stick to the questions asked, Miss Donner."

We had a small recess and then it was Meaghan's turn to ask a few questions.

"During the time on the island, who was responsible for your food and well being?"

"We both were."

"Did you have to rely on him solely for your food or did you have to ask his permission to go to the bathroom or to clean yourself up?" I almost laughed at the absurdity of the question.

"No. I went to the washroom whenever I wanted to and I took care of myself. I did a lot of the cooking and baking and definitely didn't need to rely on him for everything."

"So for the last five months you were on the island you did not feel like his captive?"

"No."

"So you were only held captive for two weeks out of the whole time you were gone?"

"Yes. Once we were on the island I could have taken the canoe and left any time I wanted. I never felt threatened or held against my will."

Having Meaghan asking me questions should have been easier, but I was still just as nervous.

"Do you feel all the choices made were your own to make during your time of confinement?"

"No. I obviously would not have chosen to be confined in the first place. I would not have chosen the room I was confined in and I would have chosen to walk."

"What about after you fell and Riley brought you to the other cabin?"

"I chose to stay there. I chose to develop a relationship with Riley. I never felt coerced or brainwashed into making any decision. I fell in love with Riley on my own accord."

"Now you have refrained from any contact with him during the last four months. Did it make any difference for you or change the way you felt about Riley?"

"It only made me miss him and love him all the more."

"What was happening right before you fell, the first time?"

"Byron was walking me by gun point out to the cliffs. He was angry that Riley and I were getting close. He was accusing Riley of things I knew not to be true."

"Such as." I paused; I had decided already I was not bringing Becka into this so I answered leaving her out of it, but still remaining honest.

"He said that once they got the money for me Riley would have killed me just as quickly as he would."

"So you assumed he was going to kill you at this point?"

"Yes."

"Where was Riley?"

"Byron had sent him on an errand to get him out of the way."

Olivia objected to my comment and the judge sustained it and asked me to rephrase my answer without assuming what Byron's plans were.

"You were scared for your life around Byron, but not with Riley?"

"Never with Riley, always with Byron. I never trusted him." I didn't look over at Byron to see his reaction.

"Can you describe a bit of your day to day life on the island?"

Olivia objected again, questioning the relevance.

Meaghan argued that it showed the normalcy of our lives and how it was two people going through the daily routines just as everyone else would. The judge allowed me to answer.

I eagerly described our life there. Our daily walks, harvesting of the garden, learning to can and prepare meals with little resources. Our wonderful hikes, fishing trips and our maintenance and upkeep of the cabin itself.

"So even though you were living in a place that did not belong to you, you were respecting your space and even leaving it in better condition than when you found it?"

"Yes, of course. We loved that place and loved our time there. We would still be there if it was up to me."

"You believe Riley came back for you on his own accord?"

"Yes. He came back after his hunting trip just as he said he would. I don't believe for a second he was planning on leaving me there to die.`

"Thank you Jady. No further questions at this time your honour."

Olivia said she just had a few more questions for me.

"How did you learn that Byron sent Riley on an errand the last day of your captivity?"

"Riley told me Byron sent him."

How did you find out who knocked out Byron after you fell?"

"Riley." I was beginning to seethe as I followed her line of questioning.

"How did you learn Riley rescued you?"

"Riley."

How did you learn it was Riley that took you to the cabin?" I looked to the judge, exasperated.

"Just answer the questions Miss Donner."

"Riley."

"You can step down now Miss Donner. Thank you. That will be enough for today."

I got off the stand feeling beat up and exhausted.

The next day a psychiatrist for the Crown took the stand and all the questions that Olivia had asked me that seemed harmless at the time were now like heavy rocks thrown into quicksand.

"Can you tell us a little about Stockholm Syndrome and how it works?"

"It's where a captive starts to develop empathy and in some cases even feelings for their captors. The circumstances help to create an environment for these feelings to flourish. The captive is isolated and at the mercy of their captor, relying on them for food, comfort and survival. They are dependent on them for personal hygiene such as going to the washroom or washing up. It has been said that it reverts the captive back to an infant stage where they are completely reliant on their captors for their well being and survival just as they were on their own mothers at birth. It recreates the bonding process that takes place and therefore it is no coincidence that strong feelings develop."

I couldn't believe my own stupidity. I had known all that. It was exactly the words I had read when I had researched Stockholm. How could I not have seen the connections to the questions she had asked me?

"So, in Jady's own words, she had said she had to rely on Riley to bring her food, allow her to use the washroom and clean herself up. These are just the circumstances you refer to, aren't they?"

"Yes. There was a memorandum written by Dr. Ochberg in which he states three things need to occur in order to apply the label Stockholm Syndrome. The first being the captive develops positive feelings for their captor, secondly the captor makes it known the feelings are reciprocated. Finally the two feel joined together in their distrust or their hatred for people on the outside."

"In your opinion, does this fit this case?"

"Definitely. Miss Donner testified that she had feelings for Riley, which were also felt by him for her. Then she also testified that they didn't want to leave the island because they didn't want to be around other people again. There's that sharing of mutual distrust or dislike for the real world as Miss Donner put it." I was angry at how my words had been twisted.

"So in your opinion, do you think Jady Donner fits the criteria for someone suffering from Stockholm Syndrome?"

"Yes."

"And if that is the case, then that means she would defend her captor and would make it difficult for her to have a testimony that was without bias?"

"Yes, she could easily answer the questions to shed a more positive light on the incident without even being aware that she was doing so."

"Thank you."

Meaghan approached the doctor.

"Have you heard of any cases where the supposed victim and the captor had no contact for four months and still maintained they had feelings for one another?"

"No, I haven't"

"Thank you."

Unfortunately, I couldn't afford to take any more time off work to watch all the court proceedings. I had to take one day off for my own testimony, but since I was only temporary I didn't have any vacation time. Joyce had a heart though and would usually let me duck out a little early. Court usually went until four and if I caught just the right bus I could watch the last hour. At times I would get really lucky and either Nate or Susan would be available to give me a ride. I really only wanted to go to be able to see Riley. Sometimes they quit early and I had a hard time containing my disappointment. I had to duck quickly into the bathroom to cry so as not to let the media catch their opportunity for a front-page picture.

The media were becoming a serious problem. They hung around before, during and after court hounding me with questions and taking many pictures. Then the day came when they showed up at work. They surrounded parents dropping off their children, taking pictures and asking them questions that were both humiliating and insulting.

"Did you know that Miss Jady Donner, the woman who looks after and teaches your child is a victim of a kidnapping?"

" Do you think the trial has affected her ability to work?"

"Does she appear unstable or do your children talk about her?"

It only took two days of this when Joyce called me into her office.

"I'm sorry Jady. We can't have this here. It is making the parents very uncomfortable and I can't say as I blame them. The cameras and crowds are scaring their children so badly; they don't want to come to school. The phone calls of parents complaining are pouring in."

I hung my head.

"I know and I understand. It's okay Joyce."

"If it's any consolation, the parents do feel terrible for you and defend you saying you've been a wonderful teacher. I have to say I agree. It's not a good situation and I don't know how we can do anything but let you go. We can't just hire someone for an indefinite time. You have no idea how long this trial is going to continue. We need to hire someone for the duration of the maternity leave. Again, I'm sorry Jady."

I took her hand and told her how much I appreciated the kind words and the opportunity to work there.

Carla and Brandi were not as forgiving.

"What? That's crazy! Let me talk to her." I had to stop Carla from stomping into Joyce's office.

"It's okay you guys really."

"No, it's really not Jady. She could sit down and have a meeting with the parents and find a way to get the children in the building safely. She's just not even willing to try." Brandi, always the calm thinking and rational one came up with the logical solution. As good as the idea was, I consoled them,

"It's okay. The media are just not going to let up until this is all over and I don't want to subject any of the families to it." I laughed, "Besides I had wanted to be able to see the whole trial and now I will get the chance to."

They laughed with me, but they both knew this was a blow. They knew how badly I needed the money. I tried not to let them see how worried I was.

***

Now I could stare at the back of Riley's head all day. I tried to follow the trial itself, but there were a lot more intricate details that filled the days than I had thought. So many witnesses. So much to prove without a shadow of a doubt. They needed to make sure the date that the abduction took place was written in stone. Even my father took the stand to correctly identify the car that he had bought me. They had the car on video at the gas station and my father testified that it was indeed his generous graduation gift to his daughter.

Not once did he look my way. Nor did he utter a word to me. He didn't dare try and fake any affection in front of the media. He was smart enough to know it would be scorned and the media would snatch that up like hungry wolves.

The car itself was long gone, sold to a guy whom they had dredged up to testify. He had bought the car from Byron and had taken it apart and sold the parts. I stole a glance over at Mr. Donner himself during this testimony to see how he felt about his precious car being taken apart like Lego. I wasn't surprised to see a face of stone.

While I avoided the media, he saw it as an opportunity to see himself on the news.

"Mr. Donner, we've noticed you and your daughter don't sit beside each other. Are there hard feelings between you two?" I slowed my step to hear his answer.

"I'm afraid Riley Williams has turned my one and only daughter against me. She doesn't believe he has manipulated this whole situation and has conned her into believing she loves him. It's like those cults you hear about. They separate them from their family and brainwash them. They feed their minds with nonsense and that is what Riley has done to my daughter."

"Why is it only recently we have learned you have a daughter?"

"My daughter has a lot of pride, she's like her father that way, and she wanted to make her own way in the world and not rely on our family name or business. She wanted to remain in the background and..."

And I walked away disgusted with his lies.

That first week was all about the crown and her building up her case against Riley and making me look like the victim. Byron was up tomorrow and my anxiety was resurfacing.

Like a camouflaged snake, Byron arose from the bench ahead of me and walked up to the stand. I lost all fluid in my mouth.

He was sworn in and Olivia began her questions.

"Can you tell us Byron, to the best of your recollection, what happened the night in question?"

"My brother Riley and I were stopped for gas when this fancy Cadillac pulled up. My brother pointed out the license place with the name Donner on it."

"Just to clarify, what did that name mean to you?"

"I actually had no idea. It was Riley that pointed out it was the name of the chain of drugstores all across the country. Then he saw her get out of the car."

"Objection, your honour. Mr. Williams cannot testify to something he did not see directly."

"Let me rephrase the question. Did Riley tell you that he saw Miss Donner get out of the car?" Byron's eyes raked over me before he answered.

"Yes. I remember because when she got out of the car, Riley said che-ching."

"Meaning?"

"She came from money. It was while she was in paying, that Riley let me in on his plan. He was always scheming and planning, trying to come up with a bit of pay off. He saw this as his chance. He figured she must have a daddy out there who would pay big money for his little girl and if we nabbed her, we could get a pretty penny for her."

I saw Riley hang his head and other people might read into his body language and think it meant guilt, but I knew him. It was disbelief and betrayal that wilted him. I wanted to reach out and hold him close.

Byron went on to describe how it all went down with the fake motorcycle accident and the actual abduction, ending with bringing me to their remote cabin. The difference was that it was Byron who faked the accident and Riley who grabbed me. It was Riley that took me by gunpoint and led me into the cabin. He did go on to say that Riley did look after me during my capture, but he twisted this as well. He said that Riley told him of his idea to stay so that he could get close with me and gain my trust.

" He was going to get her to fall for him so that he could get her to make the phone call to daddy. He figured he could get way more money that way than if we made the call. He was leading her to believe they would run off together. But her fall wrecked all his plans. He didn't get a chance to make the call."

"What caused her fall?"

"She was running away from him."

"From Riley, your brother?" She motioned towards his slumped, prone body.

I was angered to the point I finally understood the saying my blood was boiling. If you were to pour me into a glass right then, it would be blistering hot. I couldn't believe what he was saying.

"She was trying to get away from him and ended up stepping right off the cliff. Initially Riley was ticked and thought his plans were ruined. But turned out she was still alive and he came up with another plan."

"Which was?"

"To take her to the god forsaken island and heal her. He thought he would look like a hero who saved her life. He was determined to not let that money go."

"Jady healed within a week or so, why stay there for four months?"

"She was a tough cookie with a huge chip on her shoulder. She was a princess and liked money herself. Riley was not in her league and was not falling for his charms as easily as he had hoped. Like I said, he was not about to give up on the money."

I looked over at Riley and he was no longer slumped and defeated. He was sitting rigid and his jaw was clenched. I had never seen Riley angry, but I guessed he was now.

"Then why did he come back for her and bring her to the hospital?"

"He had finally got her on his side and had her believing she loved him and that he felt the same. He decided he was just going to make the call to her father himself. He was going to leave her to die. I convinced him to go back for her."

"Objection."

"Ms. Olivia," the judge was beginning to sound irritated, "This witness cannot testify as to what is in someone else's mind. Please keep your questions to what your witness saw or heard directly himself."

"Sorry your honour. Mr. Williams, did Riley tell you of his intentions?"

"Yes, he told me he didn't care what happened to her. He said he was not going to go back and like I said, I convinced him to go back."

"Why didn't you go back for her yourself?"

"When he had originally brought her there I had gone to the police and told them everything, but Riley had never told me where that cabin was. It was his secret. So when he finally came to the surface, I told the police and had them ready and waiting for him at the hospital when they came in."

I got up then and walked out on legs barely strong enough to make it to the door. A few journalists followed me out, but I quickly went to the women's washroom. I was trembling uncontrollably as I locked the stall behind me. Tears of anger flowed. Would the judge and jury believe his lies? If I didn't know Riley the way I did would I?

"Hey are you okay in there?"

A female voice called from the other side of the door.

I choked back a sob,

"I'm okay, thanks."

"That was quite a story. I'm sorry that must have been rough." I wiped away the tears and came out to wash my face with cold water.

I was just about to tell her what a liar he was when I saw a flash of plastic under her jacket. It was a media tag.

I washed my face with extremely cold water, dried off with a paper towel and walked past her without saying a word.

I walked back into the courtroom with Meaghan questioning Byron. Riley gave me a concerned glance and I mouthed,

"I'm okay."

"If Riley had gone to all that trouble to get close to Jady so that she would make the phone call to her father, did he tell you why he would suddenly give up to make the call himself? Especially since as you had said, he had finally won her over?"

"It was all a game to him. He told me he saw it as a challenge to get her to like him and once he succeeded he joked to me that he couldn't remember why he was doing it in the first place. He said he didn't need her to make the phone call anymore, he said he just wanted to be rid of her."

Even though I knew the words were all lies, they hurt all the same. I could see it was having the same effect on Riley.

"You say you convinced Riley to go back for her. If you had that kind of influence over him why didn't you convince him not to go through with the whole plan to begin with?"

Byron looked uncomfortable and struggled to come up with an answer.

Like a fighter going in for the kill, Meaghan continued,

"Is it possible that you went to the police station right after Jady and Riley disappeared because you had no idea as to their whereabouts and you thought they might turn you in, so you wanted to beat them to the punch?"

Olivia objected but the objection was without basis, the judge allowed Byron to answer.

"No, like I said, I was worried about her safety." It was hard not to notice that Byron's voice had taken on a tone of irritation.

Meaghan lifted her hand.

" No further questions your honour."

Olivia called up a few more witnesses including the men in charge of the search and rescue. It turns out they had been looking for us for over a month before calling off the search. I wondered why we had never heard the helicopters.

An officer also took the stand. He was the one that took the information from Byron when he first came in, shortly after we had disappeared. He testified that Byron's story on the stand was identical to the one Byron gave him.

"So, when Byron Williams came in, what was his emotional state?"

"He seemed to be genuinely distraught. He expressed concern for her safety. He said he hadn't been so worried about her when he had been around to keep his brother in line, but after taking off with her to the other location he thought it best he come forward for her sake."

After the officer answered Olivia's questions, the judge called for a recess and it was then I noticed Nate slip in the door.

"Sorry, I meant to be here sooner, but something came up at work. How is everything going?" He was escorting me through another door in the hall. The media were swarming around like horseflies to a swimmer, but Nate whisked me into a room that resembled a boardroom. It was nice and quiet and he handed me a cup of take out coffee and a fresh cinnamon bun.

"It's decaf"

"Thanks Nate." I took a long sip before I answered his previous question.

"Besides a whole bunch of lying, I really don't know how it's going. If the judge and jury believe all the bullshit he's doling out, then Riley's hooped. All I can hope is that between Riley and I, we can convince them otherwise."

"I've seen Olivia before. She could make a nun look bad. She has a knack for twisting people's words around to her benefit. Are you second guessing your testimony?"

"Always. I wondered initially if I should have taken the stand at all. Do you really think if I had decided not to testify she wouldn't have subpoenaed me anyways?"

"Mmmm, good point. I guess you're right."

" I'm hoping that two people's words again Byron's will help."

"I sure hope you're right. I think Riley needs all the help he can get right now." I thought of his thin, pale face and thought *He needs more help than he will ever admit.*

***

The rest of the day was taken up with other witnesses the Crown called up. There was the gas station attendant that worked the night we came through and got gas. He testified remembering us, especially me since I was a woman driving a fancy Cadillac. He only remembered Riley and Byron because they were there at the same time as myself.

Meaghan then asked a question of the attendant.

“Is there anything else you remember about the two brothers? Anything about their character?”

“The big one,” the attendant motioned towards Byron sitting in the second row now.

“The court recognizes that the witness is indicating Byron Williams. Continue please.”

“The big one was mad that he had to come in and pay before he could pump his gas. He was yelling at me about how stupid it was. Then it was Riley that came in after. He apologized for his brother and took the time to chat before he left. He asked me how long I had worked there and if I liked my job. It was like Dr. Jekyll and Mr. Hyde.”

The last comment was stricken from the record after Olivia objected it to.

Forensic Identification Services was next, testifying that the tire tracks found at the side of the road where Riley faked his accident matched the motorcycle police had found at the cabin.

Again Meaghan cross-examined,

“Was the motorcycle registered?”

“No, both motorcycles were stolen.”

“Both motorcycles?”

“Yes, there were two found on the scene.”

“So you have no way of knowing if the tracks that were found at the side of the road matched the bike ridden by Riley or Byron.”

"No ma'am."

At Susan's that night, I was quiet during dinner.

"Are you okay?"

I wanted to tell her how stressed out I was about my present money situation. How was I going to be able to pay Meaghan's fees now that I didn't have a job? But I didn't want to tell Susan what I was thinking. I was afraid she would want to help even more and I already felt guilty about how much she was doing for me.

"I'm just worried about how things are going."

"It will be just fine. Whatever is meant to be will be, right?"

I had no choice but to agree, what else could I do?

When I went to bed I lay there for a while thinking of what else I could do for money. Who would hire an obvious pregnant woman with the media shadowing them? All I had right now was my painting and I hoped that the showing on the third of May would be successful enough to bring me a little bit of money.

***

The next night we all discussed how the case was going over dinner. The orange chicken dish with cashew and rice noodles looked and smelled so delicious. I could tell from the sighs around the table that it tasted as good as it looked, but I couldn't taste a thing. Nate and Meaghan had joined us, and although I was feeling discouraged, Meaghan seemed hopeful.

"I know it seems as though Byron and the doctor's testimony were damaging, but you did very well Jady. I think you came across as believable and not at all suffering from any Syndrome, no matter how much Olivia tries to twist it to look that way."

“I don’t know. She did a very good job at making sure I answered all the questions so that they fit into each criteria that she was looking for.”

“You still come across as a normal intelligent woman who is genuinely in love of her own choosing not because she felt threatened or brain washed. Honestly I‘m feeling really good about the whole thing so far. It is going very well and I‘m feeling confident that the jury will side with us.” I don’t know if Meaghan really believed what she was saying or was just saying it to cheer me up, but it did make me feel a bit better. Riley would be taking the stand soon and I was looking forward to hearing his voice again. I knew once everyone heard his version it would only verify what I had said and his gentle and kind demeanor would speak for itself.

***

The following week more witnesses took the stand, this time for Meaghan. She questioned all the people whom she had found in her digging.

She questioned a nurse who had been on duty the night Riley brought me in. She testified to the fact that Riley had been very overwrought and concerned as they examined me. When the police came to take him in he did not fight them or appear angry, all he was concerned with was that I was going to be okay.

“That doesn’t sound like the behaviour of someone who had to be convinced to come back for Jady instead of leaving her to die.” Meaghan spoke this last statement to the jury.

Olivia objected and Meaghan conceded, knowing full well the jury heard the point she was trying to make.

It was midweek and we were working towards Riley’s testimony on Thursday. I had a prenatal right after court and as I stepped on the scale I was bracing myself for the big number that I knew would be presented. Sure enough, week 29 and weight gain of 45 pounds! No wonder I felt cumbersome and lethargic.

I couldn't believe how fast this time had gone. It felt like I had just landed in the hospital and found out I was pregnant and alone, and now here I was with about 10 more weeks to go. Unfortunately, still alone.

I was not alone at my prenatal classes. Susan was there for the first one like she said she would be. There was also another familiar face. The woman that was so friendly at the library was also in this class. It turned out her name was Sonja and, although she had a husband, he was away on business and she was there alone. After the class Susan and I went out for dessert.

"I hope you were paying attention."

"Why you weren't?"

"I just couldn't focus. I kept thinking about Riley's testimony tomorrow. I feel so guilty. It's so difficult to be so happy about this baby when all of this is going on. I sat there tonight looking around the room at the other pregnant women who have their men by their side and as great as it is to have you there with me..."

"Say no more. I get it. I'm sorry he's not there with you now, but he will be...soon."

"I keep thinking about home and the dysfunctional family I grew up in. I think of Riley's upbringing and I just want it to be different for our baby and yet we're not off to a good start."

"You're already ahead of the game. Shas has both a mom and dad full of love to share. Everything will work out, you'll see. Until then, I'm loving the looks I'm getting as your "significant other" in class." We shared a laugh and finished our deep-dish brownies.

I knew something was wrong before Riley even spoke. Every day, the last two weeks, Riley and I would share glances every chance we got. As he took the stand after being in the courtroom for over half an hour, he had yet to look my way once. Now, sitting right in front of me, he stared at the floor and avoided my eyes. My hands began to sweat and cool beads were forming on my forehead.

Meaghan pulled no punches and got straight to the point,

"Riley, who originally got the idea to kidnap Jady for money?" The long pause made me wish I had skipped breakfast.

"Byron was telling the truth. I had planned everything. I've always been the stronger brother and able to manipulate and con people. Byron's too hot headed and tends to get people mad and that's dangerous. I've always used to my charm to get what we need to survive. I saw this as my big pay off to keep us going for quite some time."

"Your honour, can I please have a moment to confer with my client? He's obviously upset and not thinking clearly."

"He seems to be thinking very clearly. Let him continue." Meaghan shook her head and gave me a defeated look.

"I came up with the whole plan and convinced Byron to go along. I played her like I play everyone else and convinced her I loved her in the hopes she would phone her daddy for me and maybe get some more money out of the deal, but it got to the point where I couldn't take it anymore and had to get away from her. I figured I'd take my chances and would cut my losses and try to get what I could out of dear old dad on my own."

I couldn't breathe. It felt like my throat was closing and I tried very hard to take a deep breath, but I couldn't. My heart was pounding in my head and I was trying not to panic. The last thing I heard was Susan's voice, which sounded like she was a continent away.

"Jady! Jady are you alright? Please someone, help her. Something's wrong!"

"He's lying." I barely had my eyes open again and I was talking.

"Sshhhhh, hon. It's okay." I opened my eyes then completely, not recognizing the voice.

"It's okay. I'm a nurse. I think you just had a panic attack. Understandably so. If I were you, I would go to your doctor and just make sure that's what it was to be safe. How are feeling now?"

"He's lying. I don't know why, but he's lying." I felt confused and angry. The nurse smiled and turned to Susan, who I just noticed was by my side. I turned to her.

"Why is he doing this? Why does he want to give up the next seven years of his life to be in prison? Life he could be sharing with me, with his baby." I felt like crying, but more out of frustration than sadness. I just kept shaking my head.

"Are you okay to stand up?" I nodded and slowly stood up. I felt a bit light headed at first but it passed.

"Do you want me to find out when you can see him? I think Meaghan is still here, I can ask her."

"I don't want to see him. I'm not ready to talk to him yet." She nodded, understanding.

"I still love him and I have not even a tiny inkling of doubt that he doesn't feel the same, but I'm too angry right now. Besides he'll refuse to see me anyways. He won't be able to face me right now either. Let's just go home." I thanked the nurse and promised to make an appointment with my doctor.

I was scared to face the media, but there was no avoiding them. Susan tried her hardest to shield me, but this time they were adamant and even a pit-bull couldn't defend me in their midst. I tried not to absorb their words, but like a leaky roof, a few comments made their way through.

"How does it feel to know you've been conned and all Riley's words were a lie?"

"How are you going to explain to your child where and why their father is not around?"

"Now that you know the truth, do you regret keeping his baby?"

I wanted to yell at them all and tell them all they were blood-suckers looking for anything negative and hurtful to print. They lived for this kind of crap and I wanted to take out my anger on them. I managed to keep my cool by reminding myself I didn't want my future baby watching their mother explode on national television or captured in print for the archives.

I got Susan to pick up fast food on the way home and I ate it angrily. I didn't want anything healthy in my unhealthy state of mind. I rubbed my belly and apologized as I consumed my fat laden fries.

"Do you want to get out tonight to get your mind off of everything?"

"What do you have in mind?"

"We could go and see a movie?"

I thought of the alternative, which would be to paint, and I couldn't stand the thought of painting pictures of our life at the cabin right now.

"Sure. That would be great."

That weekend my birthday came and went and I didn't say a word. Susan didn't know when my birthday was and I had hoped she wouldn't ask until it was long over. I really didn't feel like celebrating.

On Sunday, Nate came over and asked if I wanted him to talk to Riley to find out what was happening.

"No. Meaghan has been phoning and leaving messages too. She's trying to get to the bottom of this and it sounds like she's none too happy with him either. I haven't returned her phone calls. I'm just not ready to deal with any of this. I know whatever happened to make him change his story is probably justified in his mind, but I'm afraid it won't be in mine. I just need time. Right now I'm focusing on this baby, my prenatal and my upcoming art show. I need to think about my future and how to take care of myself for the next while. I've been focusing so much of my energy on this trial and I need a break."

"I understand." Nate stopped, but I could tell he wanted to say more.

"Spit it out. What's on your mind?"

"Well like you already said. You know something must have happened to make him change his mind and it's just killing me to know what that is."

"I do want to know, just not yet. I had been working on a three year or less plan in my head and that's all been thrown out the window. I need to focus my energy on a career plan that allows me to make enough money to support me and my baby."

"Okay. I'll leave it alone. You let me know when you want me to do some digging. Now who wants to play some cards?"

"Now you're talking. I hope you brought some money." Susan and her father both laughed, but I could tell from the look they shared that they both doubted my quick recovery. If only they knew how hard I was trying not to cry.

We sat around watching some mindless reality TV, making fun of the lives of others. It took away from the horrible reality of my own.

I excused myself when it was still early. I had a sudden urge to paint and I thought I'd better take advantage of it.

I was still working on my vision well into the early morning. By the time I finally laid down my brush, the sun was just barely opening one eye and I had an entire painting outlined. In the background was the scenery of an early winter in the forest. The orange and yellow fall leaves were still hanging onto the trees for dear life, but there was a light covering of snow on the ground. In the foreground was a woman with her back to the viewer and in the distance was a raccoon giving a glance back, seemingly about to disappear in the thick forest ahead of it.

That raccoon was my Grace and she was about to move forward, taking the risk to venture out, but at the same time wondering why this woman whom she knows loves her is sending her out into this scary wilderness.

I was terrified. I touched my belly.

"For you Shas, I will be brave."

***

My next prenatal, Susan couldn't make it, but I didn't mind. Sonja was there by herself again and we gravitated towards each other.

After class we went for coffee.

We ordered a decaf for me and a mint tea for Sonja and two pieces of apple pie. I joked,

"Man, I miss my caffeine. I swear that's half the reason pregnant woman are so tired, because they have to give up their coffee."

Sonja laughed. We sat there the next two hours; our conversation flowed so easily from one topic to another. We shared many interests. She was a teacher as well and an avid reader. She discussed her different experiences in the classroom. We compared books mutually read and loved and exchanged lists of must-reads. Yet not once did she bring up the missing father of my baby. And for that, I liked her even more.

Sonja inspired me. If she could be my friend and not pass judgment or question the reason I was there alone, I could pass on the same courtesy to the one I loved. I did what I had been dying to do that last four months. I shared good news with the one I always thought of first. I wrote a letter to Riley. There was no reason to refrain from contact now.

I started by filling him in on all the great news I had to share. The upcoming art show and all the pregnancy stuff. The heavenly feeling of the baby's heartbeat and how I thought we would have an active baby on our hands. The more I wrote the more I felt connected again. I ended the letter with a paragraph more for my own therapy than to appeal to Riley.

I know you well enough that you would not have done what you did, if it wasn't for some darn good reason. I also know in your head you think it's the only possible solution. I just want you to know how much I miss you and that as of July you will be a father. We need you in our lives. I want to trust you and want to believe that you have weighed the consequences of your choices. I love you and I want to see you even if it means seeing you in a visiting room.

I went to bed knowing that tomorrow would be a better day. I had some phone calls to return.

I called Meaghan first. Her receptionist put me right through. Instead of being angry with me for not returning calls, she was apologetic.

"I'm so sorry Jady, I had no idea he was going to do that."

"I know Meaghan. It's not your fault. I don't think its Riley's either."

"Yes, I agree. He won't see me yet, but I won't give up. I'll get him to talk and tell me the truth yet. The problem is that even if he gives me a damn good reason as to why he lied on the stand, there's not much I can do with it."

"What do you mean?"

"What judge and jury is going to believe him if he takes the stand again? Who's to say which time he was lying, the first or the second time? It's not good. We need to find concrete evidence pointing the finger at Byron and only Byron as the mastermind." I knew what she was saying was true, but it was still hard to hear. What evidence are we going to find that didn't surface up to this point?

"I wrote him a letter and I'm hoping he'll let me visit him. Maybe I can talk some sense into him and get some information he hasn't thought of yet."

"If anyone can, it will be you. He can't shut himself away in there he will fade fast Jady. You need to remind him he has a family now to live for."

I hung up the phone trying not to let Meaghan's words deflate my rising spirit.

I took a walk to the mailbox to send the letter to Riley. My art show was only four days away and I needed to contact Payton to see what needed to be done before the show. I had completed thirty-five paintings and had no idea how to price them out. I was pretty proud that I was able to finish as many as I did. I hoped I would make enough selling my paintings to at least make ends meet for a little while. But I was far from having enough to pay Meaghan for all her hours. This weighed on my mind frequently.

Spring was around me everywhere. It should have made me feel renewed, but the positive energy that had filled me last night and this morning was draining fast. I was like a canoe filled with many holes that was trying to get across the lake. I had so many odds stacked against me.

I popped the letter into the slot and began the walk back. My idea was to head back home and drown my sorrows in a container of frozen black cherry yogurt. I saw a bus approaching and looked up to see I was near the bus stop. It would be the bus that would take me right by the stores I needed to get more paint materials.

I got on the bus deciding to tackle my projects rather than add a few more pounds to perfect my penguin waddle.

***

"This is unbelievable Jady!" Susan was looking at all my paintings that were now adorning the walls of the art gallery.

"You've seen them all already."

"Yes, crowded in my house, not all up to see at once. It's amazing. It's hard to believe you did all this."

"It still seems too surreal for me." We were walking around, taking it all in, Susan drinking wine and myself a sparkling cider. We were dawned in fancy outfits. I smiled to myself since our choice of clothing was as different as our choice of beverages. Susan was in a shorter, tighter skirt that showed off her tiny build and lovely long legs. Myself in a long dress that was tight to my body, but for different reasons. My dress accentuated my growing belly and I was more than okay with that. It was like I was sharing this incredible night with someone special.

Looking at the other artist's work on the walls made it even more incredible that I was sharing this space with these talented people. One man had a collection of breathtaking abstract oil paintings. The other artist was a woman who also used watercolours but all of hers were portraits in black and white. You had to look very closely in order to see they were paintings and not photographs.

People stopped us continuously to share comments about my work and it only helped to raise my spirits. As we took it in, surrounded by all the visuals of my cabin life, I felt like someone caught in a vivid dream.

I hadn't received word yet from Riley and I didn't know if I was going to. I wasn't giving up hope. I decided I would continue to send him letters, keeping him up to date on everything that was going on in our lives.

"Jady! Fabulous! I'm getting such positive feedback and I think we will have many buyers by the end of the evening." Payton came over to us gushing. She had done such an incredible job with this show and had made every effort to increase security to keep out the journalists who were only interested in gossip rather than my art. My paintings would be displayed for a week and I only hoped a few of them would sell.

Nate approached us then, in uniform. He had been working a traffic shift up here and came during a break.

"Well done Jady. I can see why you loved the place so much. It makes me want to move there as well."

"Thanks Nate." I had sent an invitation to the Cabin Couple in the hopes they would see the paintings and feel the mutual love we had for the place, but as the evening grew longer I knew they were not going to come.

Linda, Rose, Sonja, Brandi and Carla were there though, and they were all very much in awe of my talents. I was becoming a bit embarrassed by all the attention and excused myself to go to the bathroom.

I ended up selling ten paintings that night and fifteen more by the end of the week when my show closed. I was finally feeling more secure financially and it was time to talk to Susan about the plans that had been brewing in my mind.

"Why don't you want to stay here? I was thinking about how to set up the spare room as the baby's room." The disappointment on her face made me feel guilty and a shadow of doubt tried to find a home on my ideas.

"I really appreciate everything Susan and trust me the thought of leaving your place and finding my own is both daunting and scary. But I really want a place for us to call home. I need to face reality. Riley won't be a part of our life for at least seven years and we need to make a life of our own. I would really like your help to find a place." Her eyes brightened with the last sentence and her shoulders seemed to relax. "There are a lot of nice places right around here so that we can stay close and hang out on your days off. I'm not moving far away

Susan. You mean too much to me and I want Shas to be close to his special Auntie Susan." Her face broke into a full-fledged smile and I could see it was all good again.

"I'm going to go pick up a paper."

"I'll make breakfast. I'm getting pretty good at French toast." She gave me a big hug and she was out the door just as the phone was ringing.

"Well Miss famous painter. How does it feel to have made so much money doing something you love?"

"It feels like a dream come true. Thanks for organizing it all Payton."

"Hey it's great to support our local artists. I have the list of all the buyers. I'll drop it off later, for your own personal records." I thanked her again and hung up.

I was just finishing our toast and looking for the syrup when Susan came back in paper in hand. We sat down with our breakfast and pens in hand and we began to circle.

I was still home when Payton dropped off the list. Susan was in the shower. We were planning on going for a drive and looking at a few of the places we had picked.

I quickly glanced over the list seeing some familiar names, my friends showing their own support. One was marked anonymous and my thoughts instantly went to Riley.

"What's this one." I pointed to the suspicious one.

"Oh, some guy phoned and said he was from out of town and couldn't make it in for the show so he actually asked if I could walk around and describe each painting. I thought maybe he was whacky but he did end up buying one."

I looked at the address given and fully suspected to see the address of the jail, but it wasn't. Maybe I was wrong.

I plunked the list down by the phone. Susan was ready to go and excited again at finding a home, I didn't give the anonymous person another thought.

We came home just before it got dark after looking at about ten houses. Just by doing the drive by alone we had narrowed our list down to half. We could tell by cruising around our individual selections that they would either need a lot of work, had a little or a non-existent yard or they were not in the best of neighbourhoods.

We were just getting our shoes off when the phone rang. Susan answered it while I ran for the bathroom, this darn pregnant bladder of mine.

I heard her on the phone and it sounded like a work phone call, figuring out schedules for the week. She hung up as I was walking into the kitchen to make a cup of tea.

"Hey, how come you have anonymous beside my dad's address?"

I instantly turned off the water.

"What?"

"You have anonymous written beside my father's address." She was standing beside me now showing me the list.

"I knew it." I needed to sit down and just made it to the chair before I felt like my legs couldn't hold me anymore. I didn't know how to feel. I was elated that Riley had bought a painting it meant I was right. He did love me and hadn't given up on me, but it also meant Nate was seeing him behind my back. I shared aloud what was in my head and Susan looked just as perplexed so I knew she wasn't in on it.

"You know my dad, Jady. You know he wouldn't do anything to intentionally hurt you. He would have a very good reason to be doing this without telling you."

"I know. I'm hurting, but for different reasons. It stings to know that Riley refuses to see me or return my correspondence, but will see your father. "

"It probably doesn't hurt Riley as much to see my dad as it would to see you."

"But he could be seeing me! He could be out and free in three years and seeing me even closer if he had just done what he should have!" I was upset and my voice was rising.

"I know hon. But we both know there's more to this whole story. I'll phone dad and get him to come by in the morning. Now that we know, he might as well tell us what he's up to. Maybe he has some answers for you." I stood up suddenly and snatched the list from the table.

"What?"

"It just dawned on me I never looked to see which painting Riley had bought"

"Well?"

It was the one with my back to the onlooker and Grace in the background giving her one last glance. I didn't know whether to feel touched because this is the one painting that had me in it or to be sad because this painting was also saying good-bye.

***

"I'm sorry I didn't tell you that I was visiting him. He told me not to tell you. But honestly Jady, I have no idea why he did what he did, but I do intend to find out. He's scared of something; I can see it in his eyes. All he ever wants to do is talk about you, Jady." I blinked back the tears forming.

"How is he doing in there Nate?"

"I won't lie. He looks like hell. The good thing is, that prison hasn't done for him what it does to many. It hasn't created a jaded human being. He's still humble and passive, but he looks pretty fragile. I hope I can find out some information soon. Meaghan is on board and we're doing all we can. I promise you Jady, I will get to the bottom of this. It might not help shorten his sentence, but if we find out what he's hiding, then maybe he can let all this go and at least let you visit again."

I left Nate at the coffee table talking to his daughter and went back to my room to paint. I was happy to have something to pour my energy into. My prenatal classes were done although Sonja and I still got together once a week for a chat. I was seeing the doctor every week as well since my due date was only a month away. I couldn't believe so much time had passed already. Riley's trial had already been over for six weeks and even though I kept myself busy he was never far from my thoughts. When I was eating lunch I wondered if he was eating at a massive table with many other guys. Had he made friends or were they just strangers who sat together? No matter how much time went by, I still couldn't get used to him not being beside me when I went to sleep. I wondered every night if he was thinking the same thing.

June brought sunny weather with blue brilliant skies. Susan and I got out walking whenever we could and if she couldn't, I could usually round up Sonja to come with. With the warm weather came an unexpected call.

"Jady? I had to call to say how sorry and wrong we were about you and your guy."

"Ummm...okay." I was frantically trying to place the voice.

"It's Lucy Kroll. From the cabin."

"Oh my goodness hello. I really don't think you owe us any apologies."

"Oh yes we do. We just figured you two were like the rest of the new generation out there. You know, all those that seem to have no respect for anything or anyone these days. I swear it's that darn TV they're watching and have you seen those horrible video games they're playing? No wonder the world is falling apart." I hear a man's voice murmur in the background.

"Yes, yes. I'm getting around to asking her. Jady we went to the cabin for the first time this past weekend and we couldn't have been happier. Y'know we bought all that paint and then

Rudy got sick and we never got to finish. I'm still pretty healthy, but my arms hurt when I do too much. I keep going to the doctors, but they don't know what they're talking about." The murmur again in the background.

"Yes, yes. Anyways we are so impressed with everything you guys did there. You left it in better shape than when you broke in." I couldn't help but grin at her unintentional barbed compliments.

"We'd really like it if you could join us for dinner one night, to make up for being so rude to you, before."

"That really isn't necessary. You had every right to be rude."

"Well that may be, but we still want you to come for dinner. I make a pretty fabulous pizza."

"Well I can't turn down pizza now can I?"

We made plans for an evening later on in the week and I hung up feeling so much better now that one guilt in my life was alleviated.

Lucy and Rudy very quickly became part of my weekly list of people that I got together with and because of that they were renamed Auntie Lucy and Uncle Rudy. I had initially called them Mr. and Mrs. Kroll, out of respect, but Lucy would have none of that, so we compromised. At first I thought I was doing it all for me, to alleviate my guilt and to fill the large void of missing extended family. But as I arrived at their door for my weekly supper date and I saw the looks of eagerness in their eyes, I felt better knowing this was just as fulfilling for them as it was for me. After the second visit we had already fallen into a routine of eating dinner and dessert and then moving into their rec room to play cards and eat popcorn for a few more hours. I always left with a few less quarters; Lucy as it turns out, was a pretty good card player.

The week of my due date, I came to supper with a gift to give. I handed them one of my paintings. It was one of the few that actually featured the cabin as its centerpiece. They were speechless and thrilled. Lucy commanded Rudy take down one of their framed pictures from their living room wall. It was obvious it had been there for a while by the yellow rectangle it left in its shadow. I felt honoured when they hung up my picture instead.

"Thank you Jady."

"No, thank you guys. The last few weeks have been just what I needed. I might be busy and tired over the next few weeks, but I will make a point to bring baby by as soon as I can. Plus I'm moving into my new place this weekend so you'll have to come by so I can treat you to supper for a change."

"We would absolutely love that." I got a hug from both of them as I headed out the door, elated at how full my life was becoming.

***

The next night Susan and I were watching a movie and had just finished off a huge plate of homemade nachos. I figured I had already gained a whopping 57 pounds this pregnancy, what did it really matter anymore?

At three o'clock in the morning I started to have stomach pains. Initially I blamed the nachos and then the pains were waking me up every ten minutes and then every five like clockwork.

I got out of bed and got dressed in comfortable clothes. I wasn't scared I was excited. There just seemed to be a slight grey cloud lingering as I thought of the most important person who was missing. I reminded myself that I was about to meet an even more important person and that got me moving again. I phoned the hospital to see when they wanted me in and they said I could come in now and they could get the doctor to check me over to see how things were going.

I woke up Susan and, surprisingly, both of us arrived calm and laughing at the hospital.

The doctor was there and after she did an initial check she gave me a choice to get comfortable there or go back home until I was no longer comfortable there.

Susan and I went back to her place where I could pace and talk through the contractions. It was hilarious at first because I would be walking along and then the ripple of pain would come and I would stop talking, as Susan would continue the conversation as if nothing was happening.

Finally, it got to the point I couldn't even talk through the pain and the contractions were spaced about two minutes apart.

Back at the hospital, they checked me over again, but I had a ways to go. It was so slow in the maternity ward they said I might as well stay and claim my room. The nurses suggested I walk as much as possible and that's what Susan and I did.

Twelve hours later I was still walking and the pain had intensified. Every time it came on, I thought of those pumps you used for air mattresses. The plastic accordion looking things that compressed when you stepped on it and then inflated back up. That's what it felt like my insides were doing. I put off the epidural for as long as I could, but after another six hours and nothing, I gave in.

Another whole day went by and we all gave up deciding to go for the C-section. By 10 am over 40 hours after I had thought I was having nacho induced gas attacks, Shas Williams was born. A beautiful, healthy boy, the spitting image of Riley. I couldn't be happier.

The nurse bundled the two of us in the hospital bed and we were wheeled back to the room where we both slept solidly for another twelve hours.

When we woke up, we were hungry, but I was only allowed clear liquids. At this point they did some more tests, weigh ins and moved us around to clean and change my bed. The main nurse told me she had instructed everyone just to leave us to sleep, and I told her how much this had been appreciated.

The nurses kept telling me I could move Shas to the bassinet if I wanted to sleep more, but I didn't want him to leave my side. I liked having him there, his warmth and his wonderful face to look down on whenever I wanted.

Soon, visitors came streaming in. Susan had been in the surgery room with me so she got the honours of seeing him first. Nate and Meaghan came together and then, soon after, Lucy and Rudy joined the crowd.

I rested for a bit and then came Sonja, still waiting for her bundle of joy to arrive. While she was there, Carla and Brandi came and brought flowers and a fruit basket. I couldn't wait to dig into it.

Susan and Sonja stayed the longest and were finally kicked out by the nurses a good hour after visiting hours had ended. I joked with Sonja that she was hoping if she stayed long enough, then maybe her baby would come while she was already there.

Finally, it was just the two of us again. I cuddled Shas in close and we both nodded off, exhausted and content.

***

It was hard to believe I had been in our new home with Shas for a month already. The house was pretty sparse, but it was ours. Shas's room was the most furnished room and it was my favourite space to be in. Rose had informed me that Shas meant Grizzly Bear in the Carrier language. This was the language of the local First Nations people. After I learned that, Susan and I decorated Shas's room with bears. He had a bear border, curtains and gorgeous bedding to match. All his furniture was a dark wood that was surrounded with green and brown walls. The entire space had a calming effect on both of us. Susan's friends who were moms told me that beyond anything else I should not skimp on the rocking chair. They said I would be living in it while I was nursing so to make sure I was comfortable in it. I followed their advice and was glad that I did. They were right; I did spend many hours in that chair the first month. I was more than okay with that. I didn't feel lonely; I had the best company I could ask for.

Shas was a good baby, but then again I had no other baby to compare him to. According to the baby books, sleeping and eating were the things that helped set the bar on which you decided if you had a good baby. Shas did both well. He ate as often as he could and then he crashed for a bit in between. I was actually thankful I didn't have much in my new house because I couldn't seem to find the time to clean what I did have. I called Brandi in tears once when it seemed like Shas was never going to stop eating and was only taking catnaps.

"How do you find time to get things done?"

"You don't. Your house cleaning is not going anywhere. Just do the basic things you absolutely need to do and forget the rest. This time will go so fast that before you know it, they will be going to school and you will wonder what happened. Enjoy this time."

That was what I was trying to do. Susan came over when she could and helped out by cooking meals for me, which was a huge blessing.

Sonja had a baby girl a week later and they were also doing well settling into their own routines. I knew it would only be a matter of time and we would pick up our weekly coffee sessions, this time with our babies in tow.

I was trying to remember all the things to take with me as I went out for the first time with Shas. It was tough for Lucy and

Rudy to make it out to my place, so I promised them I would come by that afternoon and visit them.

Even after following Lucy into her living room, and people shouted "Surprise!", it still took me a few minutes to realize it was a baby shower meant for me. All my newfound friends were there. Sonja, Carla, Brandi, Meaghan, Rose, Susan and of course the wonderful host, lovely Auntie Lucy. We ate, oohed and aahed over Shas and opened beautiful and generous baby gifts. Adorable clothes, books, blankets and stimulating toys.

I looked around the room at all these wonderful ladies, the room filled with laughter, love and a few different conversations going on at the same time full of joy. I had more friends in this room than I had had in my entire life. I couldn't believe I had closed myself off from this for so long. It was still hard for me to believe what should have been a horrendous kidnapping could have led to not only allowing love in for the first time, but opening the door for lifelong friendships to form.

I grabbed a plate, filled it full and went back to immerse myself in my new world of motherhood and womanly companionship.

***

I had just returned from a late walk with Shas in the stroller to find the light was blinking on the answering machine. As usual, I wondered if Riley had finally decided to call and I had missed it. When I pressed play it was Meaghan's voice that echoed in my empty house.

"Jady, when you get this message please call me." Her voice sounded urgent. Still holding Shas in my arms, I called her back.

"Can you come in and see me?"

"When?"

"Now."

“Yeah, I can do that.“

“Good, Nate will come pick you up.“ I hung up wondering just what was up. She didn’t sound happy so I wasn’t about to get my hopes up that it was good news about Riley. Nate was involved, so I assumed they had uncovered something.

I tried to pry it out of Nate on the ride to Meaghan’s office, but he was quiet.

“Let’s wait until we get to the office.” My anxiety was building as we pulled into the parking lot.

Waiting in her office was Meaghan, but also a woman I hadn’t seen before. The two of them stopped talking as I walked in. The woman briefly looked down at Shas and gave a smile that contained a hint of sadness. Meaghan asked her to step outside to the waiting room for a bit. She nodded and closed the door behind her, leaving Shas and me in the room with just Meaghan and Nate.

“Okay you guys you’re freaking me out. Spit it out. What’s up?”

“To begin with, we think we’ve discovered why Riley lied on the stand.”

“Okay…”

“Nate and I figured, just like you probably did, that someone must have got to him and said something to make him change his mind. We scoured the list of visitors before the trial and there was no one but you, Nate and myself so we had to rule Byron out. There seemed to be no direct contact and he couldn’t have reached him through correspondence because all the mail is pre-read, plus the only phone calls between prisoners are the ones they make themselves. We then tackled all the witnesses and other inmates to see if any names jumped out. This was a long process, but it was Nate that found the connection. Riley’s cellmate and the man who fenced the stolen cars for Riley and Byron shared the same last name. We figured this was Byron's source and was how he got a message through to Riley. We just found this today so we won't have a chance to talk to Riley about it until tomorrow. We still don't know exactly what message Byron passed along to make Riley do a 180, but we'll hopefully find out soon enough."

"Well, we all knew there was something that wasn't right. I appreciate all that you guys have done and all the time you've put into this, but it really doesn't change anything does it? Whatever Byron said scared Riley enough to lie and decide he'd rather be apart from us and in jail, so I really can't see that changing now. Even if he does decide to change his mind again, like Meaghan said, there is not a judge or jury in the world that will believe him now."

Shas started to stir in the car seat and I took him out and sat him on my lap. Holding him close not only helped my nerves, but covered up my shaking hands. We were close to finding out at least why Riley did what he did. For me, this meant I might actually get to see him now that we were learning the truth. He would get to meet his son. I wished we could go see him right this minute.

Meaghan gave Nate a nervous glance and it was then I realized they were not done talking yet.

"There's more." She picked up her phone. "Send her back in please."

The woman, who was a stranger to me walked back in through the door and Meaghan motioned for her to take a seat.

"Jady, I'd like you to meet Kelly Emmitt. She is your father's accountant."

***

As if picking up on my nervous tension, Shas started to fuss. I was thankful to have an excuse to stand up and pace with him.

"I don't understand." Why was this woman here and what did she have to do with me?

"I've worked for your father for a long time..." Kelly looked as nervous as I felt and her voice cracked a bit as she spoke.

"Please don't call him that," I interrupted her. She looked flustered and confused for a moment and then corrected herself.

"I've been working for Mr. Donner since he first began his business. I've been doing his books right from the beginning when his business was nothing more than one drugstore and now he has many accountants overseeing his various locations across the country, but I'm still his personal accountant overseeing everything. There have been a few things I have done for your...for Mr. Donner that I'm not proud of. But I was compensated very nicely each time and foolishly I let it slide. But now..."She glanced over at Shas, "I needed to come forward and it may not erase what's been done, but hopefully it can do some good."

It was my turn to look confused. I looked to Meaghan and Nate for some clue as to what this woman was about to say, but they looked away from me. I could tell from their avoidance that Kelly had already told them what she was about to tell me and it wasn't going to be good.

"Mr. Donner has had me write up many cheques over the years for names I didn't recognize and didn't question. It was his business and I left it at that. That's why I've kept my job for as long as I have. It wasn't until the trial that I realized what I had done. I recognized the names immediately. I remembered because it had been big amounts. Now I'm afraid of what it meant." She looked around as if waiting for someone else to tell me, to rescue her from the task.

"One cheque was for $100 000 and it was made out to Byron Williams. The second cheque was for $50 000 and it was for Judge Wayne." Nate stood up quickly and took Shas from me. I sat down quickly feeling the blood drain from my face. I reminded myself to take deep breaths.

"What...what does it mean? When did this happen?"

"I wrote the cheque to the Judge when Riley's trail began and the cheque for Byron on the day you were taken. I think...I think Mr. Donner paid Judge Wayne to throw the trial and paid Byron to kidnap you."

"But Riley admitted to everything. Why would he need to pay the judge?"

I detected a satisfied smile, before she answered,

"Well Mr. Donner wasn't counting on that. He actually paid the judge for nothing."

"Why would he pay Byron to kidnap me? Why now after all these years would I be a concern to him?"

"To be perfectly honest, I was wondering that myself. I did some digging and found something interesting. As soon as you turned 21 you became a threat."

"A threat? How could I be a threat? What could I possibly do to him?"

"Maybe nothing to him, but you were a threat to his business, to his money. Even if you don't want to be, you are his daughter. Your mom was a smart cookie and she somehow managed to get Greg to set up a trust fund that you could cash in when you turned 21."

"I didn't want nor do I want anything to do with his money. Even if I did, that man has plenty of money, why would he care about a few dollars in a trust fund. He didn't have half as much money when my mom was alive as he does now."

"This is the amazing part. Your mom didn't set it up with a certain amount of money, she set it up as a percentage."

"A percentage of what?"

"A percentage of his business. 15% to be exact."

"How did she manage that?" I asked this not really expecting Kelly to know the answer.

"All I can assume is that Greg agreed, not knowing at the time how big his business was going to get. Today that is a huge amount of money."

"Like I said, I don't want…"

"It's up to you of course, but it's not just about you anymore is it." Kelly looked towards Shas and instead of feeling anger towards this woman, I softened. She was right.

"But I still don't understand. Why Byron? How would he have known Byron?"

"Like I said, I've been with Mr. Donner from the beginning so I know a lot about the man. He's had many…relationships."

"You can call them what they are. They were affairs. I knew when I was young, I always knew. I didn't think he would stop having them, even now."

"Well, he had…an affair with Byron's mom." I stood up again.

"Whoa!! Are you trying to tell me Byron's his son? What about Riley?" The panic rose in my throat and my startled voice made Shas stir in Nate's arms. He shushed and rocked him back to sleep.

"No, no. Riley and Byron are not actually brothers. Riley's father learned of the affair soon after Becka was born and turned to the drink." I sat back down and put my head down on my knees to rest and take more deep breaths. This was going to kill Riley. All this time dedicating his loyalty to a man whom he thought was his brother.

"Did Byron know this? Wait, did Riley know this?"

"I don't know. I don't think so. I've been doing nothing but thinking about this lately and I think Mr. Donner just recently told Byron. It was probably how he got him to do his dirty work." Kelly's tone was bitter.

"Why now? Why are you telling me all of this? Why come forward now?"

"Like I said. I didn't realize the connection until your trial was all over the papers. Then you had your baby. I've always seen you through his eyes. As the daughter who was trouble. He said you were rebellious and had always caused him grief." I swallowed the anger that was building and tried to focus on what she was saying. "Then, suddenly, I saw you as a mom."

"Look, I'm trying very hard right now not to be rude, but how is it you know all this?"

Kelly looked like she wanted to run from the room right then. She looked again at Shas, sleeping soundly.

"Like I said, it was when you became a mom that it hit home for me. You see I'm a mom, of two boys. They're grown now. I've made many mistakes, but I refuse to make any more. They deserve better." Her eyes began to tear and she waved her hand in front of her face. Meaghan came to her rescue.

"Look Jady. Kelly was not just your father's accountant all these years. She had a...relationship with him and is now his wife. Her sons are his sons as well. Her sons help run the business."

"When I saw what Mr. Donner...my husband had done to his own flesh and blood, it made me think he would do the same to my sons in a heartbeat should they threaten his business. I don't want them to be like him. I want them to care about people, about their family. I want to show them what he has done is wrong." Kelly took a deep breath, but looked calmer as if she had suddenly lost about 20 pounds of guilt. I believed her and softened. She had been intimidated and bullied like everyone else who got drawn into Mr. Donner's web.

"It's not your fault. Thank you for coming forward with all this information." Kelly looked over to Meaghan and she nodded. Kelly stood to leave, but before she walked out the door she turned back,

"I really want the best for you and your baby, and I've always felt very sorry about what happened to your mom. I truly am sorry." I nodded my head. It was all I could do to keep it together. I was afraid of what else would come out of my mouth if I should open it.

***

Nate handed Shas back to me after Kelly left, as if he knew he would keep me calm. He did the right thing, I just had to look down at my sleeping baby and nothing else seemed to matter as long as I could hold him close. I looked up at Meaghan.

"What does this all mean? For Riley?"

"Well, it 's good news. He will be granted a second trial based on the new evidence of a paid judge and in light of Byron getting paid to do the job right from the beginning. The focus will be on Byron and Mr. Donner right now."

"Will they be arrested?"

"We will need to talk to a judge, obviously a different one, and get a search warrant in the morning. We will want to see both Mr. Donner and Byron's bank records to collect concrete evidence and if we can search both of their homes, we might be able to find more to support our new case."

"And Riley?"

"We should be able to get him released as early as tomorrow morning." I felt the butterflies flutter from my stomach all the way up my throat and flush my face. I couldn't believe it.

"Really?" Nate smiled at me and came up to hug me.

"It's really happening kiddo. It was only a matter of time before things turned around for you."

I left them to arrange all the paper work needed to approach the judge.

That night as I rocked with Shas in my rocking chair, I whispered to him,

"Just think Shas, by this time tomorrow it might be your daddy rocking you to sleep."

I woke up startled, my heart beating rapidly. Initially, I thought it was Shas crying that had brought me out of my deep sleep. Then, as the phone rang out again, I realized what had woken me. I glanced at the clock as I picked up the phone. It was 6am.

"Hello?" I was too tired to think about who would be calling me at this time of the morning.

"Oh thank God you're all right!" Meaghan's voice was filled with relief.

"Why wouldn't I be?"

"Nate and I worked hard on everything after you left and we decided the sooner we get a search warrant the better. We were afraid Kelly might change her mind and confess to Mr. Donner about what she did and he would disappear. We went and sought out a justice of the peace last night. We just finished looking into his bank statements and we made a frightening discovery. He just transferred another large sum of money into Byron's account late last night. We were terrified Byron had been paid to finish the job he started."

"Well, that's not what he got paid for, unless he was going to nab me today."

"Nate's on his way over to keep you company and to make sure that doesn't happen."

"It just doesn't make any sense. Last time, my father didn't pay him for the job until he had already taken me. Why would he pay him now?" It then dawned on me that I had slept through the night. Shas had not cried to be fed. I dropped the phone and I could hear Meaghan repeating my name as I ran to my room and Shas's bassinet. Then as I get closer I slowed right down. I was so scared at what I would find.

It was empty. I ran back to my front door and saw that it had been broken into and was standing ajar. I opened it and ran out into the street, half expecting to see the back of Byron as he walked away with my baby. If I had seen him right then, I think I would have killed him. There was not a single sign of anyone on the street. The birds went right on chirping as if everything was right in the world and my baby hadn't been stolen right out from under my nose. I crumpled where I stood and sobbed.

My arms ached with their emptiness. The thought of Byron holding my baby in his arms repulsed me. I was sobbing so loudly I didn't even hear the police sirens until Nate's arms were around my body and helping me to stand.

"He's got him Nate. He's got my baby."

"C'mon honey let's get you inside. I've got everyone out looking for them. We'll find them." He must have called Susan because she showed up minutes later and let me fall apart all over her.

"This can't be happening. Tell me I'm sleeping. Tell me this is a bad dream and I'll wake up any minute." Then the entire nightmare enfolded in my delayed brain.

"He didn't take Shas for a ransom. He already got paid. He took Shas to kill him. Greg is afraid I will fight for a piece of his pie for my son. He wants him dead and out of the way."

"Oh Jady, I'm sure that's not it." But I caught the quick look of panic that she shot her father as if to say, "It's not, is it?" Nate turned away and that was my answer.

"We need to go and talk to my father. We have to stop this. I need to convince him once and for all I don't want his money, not for me and not for my son."

"Listen Jady. We have Mr. Donner in custody. I have the best guys questioning him. If he has some answers they will get them out of him. Meanwhile I've put out a description of Byron. We have roadblocks everywhere already. We will get him."

I walked away from both of them and went into Shas' room. I picked up the onesie he had worn the previous day and was thankful I had not thrown it into the wash yet. I inhaled it and closed my eyes. I was trying to stay calm and not feel so utterly helpless. I felt so out of control. I wanted to be out there looking for my baby. Then I thought of Riley. If anyone would know where Byron was going it would be him. I ran back into the living room to talk to Nate, still holding the onesie like a protective talisman.

***

My head ached from crying and my feet were sore from pacing. Hours later, my patience worn out, I asked Susan to phone her father. He had left soon after Susan arrived to help organize the efforts to find Shas. I had tried to phone Meaghan, but kept getting her voice mail.

"I need to know if Riley is going to be released. I need to talk to him before I go crazy." The phone rang in Susan's hands.

"It's Meaghan." Susan handed me the phone.

"My God Jady, I just heard. I'm so sorry. I was busy all morning arranging Riley's new trial. I do have good news for you. Riley will be released at noon today." I didn't hear if she said anything else. I hung up the phone.

"Susan, can you stay here, just in case anyone phones?"

"Sure. Where are you going?"

"Riley's getting released and I'm going to go and pick him up. Do you think your father would mind if I took his truck?" He had left it and gone to the station in another member's police car.

"I'm sure he wouldn't mind. Go ahead."

I grabbed Nate's keys that were on the front table and almost ran out the front door. It wasn't until I was behind the wheel that I realized I still had Shas's onesie in my hand. I put it beside me on the seat and hoped Riley would have some answers. I went to leave and stopped again. Hopeful, I went and grabbed Shas's car seat from Susan's car and placed it in the back of Nate's truck.

I put on some more miles pacing in the front lobby of the jail. My friend Keith was not there and I was glad. I was not in any mood to be social. I hadn't eaten a thing and every time I even got a whiff of something, I felt like throwing up. My stomach was in knots and I could barely breathe. Every time the door would open, my heart would thump. I was exhausted and my sides ached. I finally grabbed a bottle of water from the vending machine. I felt dehydrated and was hoping to dull the ache thudding in my head.

Shortly after twelve, the door opened and there was my Riley, skinny and pale, but he was standing before me, in the flesh. I ran to him and his arms went around me. I felt his shoulders shake and I knew he was crying too.

"I have so much I need to tell you, but we can talk on the way. Meaghan told me about Shas and I think I know where to go. Do you have a car?"

"I have Nate's truck."

"Even better. We will need it for where we're going." I didn't ask any questions. I let him lead me out of the building by his strong hand, which felt so good to hold again.

Riley immediately went behind the wheel and wasted no time on getting us to where he had in mind. He was deep in concentration until we hit the highway and then I could see his muscles relax a slight bit. I was sitting right beside him, needing to feel his warmth, needing his security. I was terrified, but feeling more hopeful than I did when I had first discovered Shas was missing.

"Where are we going?"

"The guy that buys and chops up our stolen cars has a piece of property with a cabin on it not too far from ours. That's where I think he is."

"Why Riley? What happened that made you choose to spend even more time away from me, from us?"

Riley's pained expression made me want to rephrase my question.

"I'm sorry Riley. I know that you will have a very good reason, but it still hurts."

"No, I'm the one that should be sorry. I brought all of this on us. I should never have trusted him. I should have told you and Nate in the very beginning and then none of this would be happening." I waited for him to finish. I could see he was struggling with an immense amount of guilt.

"They switched my cell mate the day I was to testify. I was suspicious, but he was quiet. Then right as I was to be brought to the courthouse he began to talk. He told me that Byron had a message for me. He told me that if I testified that Byron was the brains behind this idea, he would finish the job he started with you." I could see Riley choke up and he had to stop talking. I leaned in to feel him closer and squeezed his right hand that was resting on my leg.

"I was so terrified he would hurt you or Shas that I changed my testimony. I didn't want to see you because I was afraid he would think I was still scheming, plus it just hurt too much to think I would have to look at you across a table for another seven years. But then Nate came to see me; he actually tricked me because he came with Meaghan. Initially, I didn't want to see him either, but he told me he didn't come for an explanation, he just wanted to visit. I saw it as a way of knowing what was going on with you and Shas." He looked over at me briefly, his eyes misted.

"I need to make one stop. I'll only be a minute." He turned right at the next street and then pulled up to a blue house. He jumped out of the truck and was back as fast as he said he would be.

"What was that all about? Or do I want to know?"

"Probably not." We were both quiet for a while, and then Riley broke the silence first.

"I wished I could have been there when he was born. That will be the biggest regret in my life, that and believing Byron. I blew it by allowing Nate to visit. I think Byron thought I had changed my plans and is punishing me by taking Shas."

"Oh, Riley, no. That's not it at all. My father is behind all of this. He was behind this right from the beginning. Didn't Meaghan tell you any of this?"

"She told me I was being released because of the crooked judge and then she told me about Shas. I really didn't give her a chance to tell me anything more. I just wanted out of there to see you and go find Shas. What does your father have to do with any of this?"

"He had this set up from the beginning. I don't know all the details yet, but I do know that he had it set up with Byron to nab me and the plan was to kill me right from the beginning. Byron and my father had no intention of letting me go alive. Did Byron ever say anything to you about any of this?" I could tell by the clenching of Riley's jaw that he hadn't."

"Why would he do that? Did he get paid for it?"

"Yes." I hesitated.

"There's more. I can tell by your voice. Tell me."

"I think you should pull over for this."

"I'm not wasting a single second. I've already wasted enough time. Please Jady, just tell me."

"My father took advantage of him. He had an affair with your mom. He is actually Byron's father." Riley removed his hand from my leg and gripped both hands on the steering wheel as if we were driving through gale force winds. I pushed on. "I think he used this information with Byron and probably promised him even more money in the future if he did this for him."

"How do you know all this?" I explained Kelly's role in all of it and Riley nodded silently. I let him be for a while; to let it all sink in. It was only beginning to sink in for me. I couldn't believe my father would go to this extent to make sure I never laid a finger on his money. My mind had been so preoccupied with Shas I hadn't given much more thought to his role in this whole thing. Was that why he bought me the Cadillac? Did he know I would never accept it and drive it back to him? Did he purposely place Byron at that gas station that day to be on the look out for me?

"I'm sorry my father messed up your life as badly as he messed up mine."

"Don't ever be sorry for what your father has done. You are nothing like him and he doesn't deserve to have a daughter like you or a grandson like Shas." As if I had been refueled, my tears began again. Riley put his hand back on my leg.

"Tell me everything about him. Tell me about the day he was born." That I could do. I shared every little thing, trying to make it a part of Riley's memory. I wanted to etch every detail in his brain to the point that he would forget he had missed a single minute of it.

***

We pulled off the highway two hours later and went down a gravel road barely wide enough for Nate's truck.

"Riley, what if he's not here?"

"He's here I can feel it. He may not be my real brother, but we've grown up like brothers and I can sense him here. Call Nate, tell him where we are." I shot him a puzzled look as I phoned Nate on my cell phone.

"I wanted to give us a head start. I need some alone time with Byron."

"Please be careful. Now that I have you back, I never want to lose you again."

"You won't." I called Nate and only got his voice mail. I left him directions and then shut off my phone as we pulled up to a garage.

"There's a cabin out back. That's where they will be. We'll walk from here." We got out and walked down a narrow path, trying to step quietly. This cabin was well used and looked like it had all the amenities. There was smoke coming from the chimney, but there was a large propane tank outside that looked like the main source of heat. There was a cistern lid on the front lawn so that meant the cabin had water that got trucked in. It made me feel a little better that Shas was in a place that at least had water and heat. What troubled me was the silence. I expected to hear a hungry crying baby and the lack of sound terrified me. Please, please, don't let us be too late. As we approached the door, Riley told me to wait there.

"Riley, I'm so scared." I whispered.

"Everything is going to be okay." He held me close and it felt so good to breathe him in again. When his arms left me I wrapped my own around me. I was aching to hold and feed my baby boy.

"Please be careful." He opened the door slowly and disappeared behind it.

I heard Shas crying and if Riley hadn't appeared before me holding him a moment later, I would have gone in after him.

Despite the circumstances, Riley looked like a proud papa. I took Shas from him and held him close, the crying ceased.

"We need to go." Riley whispered and I didn't hesitate to ask any questions. I turned to leave, Riley close behind me. The gunshot rang out amidst the tall, silent witnesses. Riley was lying on the ground, half out the door.

"Run." This time I listened. In shock, I held Shas close to me and didn't stop until I was at Nate's truck. Trying to catch my breath, I looked around but didn't see any movement. Quickly, I buckled Shas into the car seat. The second gunshot echoed around me and I winced as I caught my finger in the latch. With Shas safe, I looked at him through my tears.

"I'm glad he got to see you, my little boy. You have a brave wonderful father."

I got behind the wheel, gripping the steering wheel, hoping to still my shaking hands. Briefly, I thought about going back in, but the small cry from the back seat reminded me why I was here. He needed at least one parent in this world. I put the truck in reverse and just about crashed into Nate's police car.

I rolled down the window as he approached.

"Please be careful. He has a gun." Nate didn't say a word, only nodded and dropped a can of pepper spray in my lap.

Waiting for what seemed like an eternity, I pulled my shirt up to my nose trying to catch the last smell of Riley before it disappeared. I was scared my tears would wash away his scent. Movement caught my eye and I could see many bodies in grey spill past the truck I was sitting in. The dark blue pants with yellow stripes were everywhere. Nate came up to them before they had a chance to go any further.

"Call the bus. Tell them we have two..." Shas's cry from the back seat drowned out the last of his words.

***

I should have gone to the funeral but I couldn't bring myself to go. It wasn't his fault that he didn't get a fair shake at life. Yet at the same time, the blood that ran through my veins was also in his, but I would never think to kill someone to gain my father's love or money.

Shas gave a little cry in my arms and Riley opened his eyes.

"How are you feeling?"

"As long as I can wake up to see you two sitting there, life is fabulous."

"Are you hurting anywhere? Do you want me to call the nurse?" I reached over to his bedside table and handed him a cup with a straw. He took a long drink and then lay back in the hospital bed.

"Nope, I'm good." But I could see him wince a bit as he tried to reposition himself. The doctor said he was lucky. The bullet had lodged itself in Riley's side but had missed all major organs. In surgery they had removed it and Riley was recovering nicely. Byron didn't fair so well. He had died from the bullet wound inflicted on him by Riley.

Nate told everyone that arrived on the scene that it had been self-defense and there was an officer placed outside Riley's hospital room. Another officer had been in already to question Riley about the entire incident. Riley had told the truth to a point. When asked why he didn't let Nate know where he was going right from the beginning, Riley said we were in such a panic to get to Shas that he didn't think about it until we were on our way. The officer took his notes and left. They would be busy investigating the scene to put together a case for trial. Another trial. Nate said not to worry about it, the evidence would support Riley's story.

There was a knock on the open door and Lucy peeked her head in. Rudy was right behind her.

"Are you up for visitors?" My face brightened at the sight of them. I had filled Riley in about the Cabin Couple and I couldn't wait for them all to meet.

"For you guys anytime." I made the introductions and the room filled with conversation and laughter. Riley's face regained some colour and he even found the strength to sit up and hold Shas for a little while. When I saw him wincing again I took Shas from him, knowing he wouldn't hand him over on his own accord.

After an hour of visiting, Lucy started rifling through her large handbag.

"Rudy and I thought we'd come by to give you these. You might need them to finalize the paperwork." Riley was surprised when Lucy handed them to him.

"What's this?"

"Ask that lovely fiancé of yours." Riley turned to me as he scanned the papers, still not understanding.

"What's all this?"

"It's the deed for the cabin and the land we own surrounding it"

"The land *we* own?"

"Yup. We are now the proud owners of the cabin and the miles and miles of land that you love so much." Rudy and Lucy's grins were as wide as my own. Riley looked overwhelmed.

"Seriously? You did this? For me? For us?"

"For us. For our future."

***

"Happy birthday dear Shas, Happy birthday to you." We finished singing and helped Shas blow out his one little candle in the middle of his grizzly bear shaped cake. I looked around the cabin now filled with our own personal things amidst Lucy and Rudy's décor. Susan, Meaghan, Sonja and her family of four, Lucy, Rudy, Rose, Nate and our new friend Sean were all there to help us celebrate Shas's first birthday.

It had taken us awhile, but we had made our dreams a reality. We waited until Riley was fully recovered and then we held a small wedding ceremony at the cabin with our same little group, plus a justice of the peace. To see Lucy and Rudy's face beaming while we said our simple vows made the day complete.

We had built up a guide outfitter camp at the cabin and hunters came from all over the world to hunt with Riley. We twisted Susan's rubber arm to come and cook for our clients for the few months they stayed with us and we had recently hired Sean who had a small plane. He would fly Riley and the hunters into the smaller lakes that were too difficult to hike into. As Susan helped hand out pieces of cake, I saw her hesitate in front of Sean and watched as his eyes followed her around the room as she handed out the rest of the pieces. I smiled to myself and looked across the room to see Riley's eyes on me as well. The love and happiness I saw there warmed my soul. I had my own hands full with Shas, taking care of the books, and continuing with my painting. In the next month I would be busy canning all the vegetables currently growing in our bountiful garden.

Riley and I had visited the spot where he had buried Becka. We put up a gravestone and Riley had carved a special angel to watch over her. Riley could now visit her anytime and was finally at peace with her death. I think it made him feel better that we could talk about her openly and we were going to make a point of making sure Shas knew he had a special Aunt Becka watching over him.

After Shas's party, I brought everyone back to the main road with the bigger boat we had purchased for just such a purpose.

Riley and Shas had stayed back on the island since I was going in for our large grocery load.

After I had taxied everyone to his or her respective homes and had spent over a thousand dollars on two carts full of groceries, I sat parked back at the Hill. There was one more thing I needed to do. I had put it off, but it was time to complete the journey I had started so long ago.

He sat in front of me a different man. In an orange jumpsuit, looking as thin as Riley had, sat the man who by blood was my father.

"When you sent me that Cadillac, I honestly toyed with the idea that it was a peace offering. It was for only a brief moment. I was driving across the country, not just to return your *gift*, but to get some things out in the open. I've spent my life hating you. I've hated you since you let my mother die." I was waiting for him to interrupt, but the broken man sitting in front of me was not the same man who would have had a sharp reply. "But I don't hate you anymore. I came here today to thank you." The broken man looked up from his very interesting hands.

"If you hadn't sent me that car, I would never have met Riley. I would never have had my beautiful boy, Shas. I would have never opened myself up to trust and friendships. I would have remained bitter and alone for the rest of my life and then I would have been just like you. Now, my life is full and my soul is happy and content." I stood up to leave. "I never thought I'd be saying this, but thank you. Thank you for giving me that stupid car."

When I walked away, I didn't have to look back to know Greg Donner's face held no smile.

ACKNOWLEDGMENTS

First and foremost I would like to thank my ever supporting husband. He planted the seed for this novel on a hiking trip we took. Bill was my first reader and my biggest inspiration next to nature and our boys.

A big thanks to the Dawson Creek Page Turners. My lovely book-club helped give me wonderful and useful feedback.

Thanks goes to Tamera Golinsky for sharing her Crown wisdom and helping to shape the trial accurately.

Finally to my mom, Lucy, one of my biggest fans and to my dad Rudy, a fellow writer who I know is smiling from up above and proud to know his daughter shares some of his talent.